Kagan's Superfecta

AND OTHER STORIES

# Kagan's
# Superfecta

## and other stories

*by Allen Hoffman*

ABBEVILLE PRESS / NEW YORK

FRONTISPIECE BY FRITZ EICHENBERG

DESIGNED BY ANDOR BRAUN

ISBN   0-89659-234-0
ISBN   0-89659-271-5 (Special Limited Edition)

Library of Congress Cataloging in Publication Data
Hoffman, Allen.
Kagan's superfecta and other stories.
Contents: Kagan's superfecta—Hymie the torch—
Building blocks—[etc.]
I. Title.
PS3558.034474K3          813'.54          81–69912
ISBN   0-89659-234-0                       AACR2

*To my parents*

 Contents

 Kagan's Superfecta

Most days Kagan was relaxed as he circled endlessly around Ninety-fourth Street searching for a parking space. Yes, he might eat pistachio nuts, or he might fiddle with the radio to pick up the race results, or he might even engage in an absurd, repetitive debate with Ozzie, his angel; still, compared to everyone else, who developed ulcers, suffered heart attacks, or committed homicide while seeking a parking space, Kagan was perfectly relaxed. And why not? It didn't cost him any money. Not that Kagan was cheap. On the contrary, Kagan was very generous, but, as usual, Kagan was also very broke, and while driving up and down West End Avenue, he couldn't place a bet. While crossing Broadway, he couldn't borrow from a shylock. ("No parking on Broadway except Sundays and holidays so why drive up and down Broadway when there's no percentage?")

No, Kagan wasn't like other people. Other people went crazy trying to park cars on the Upper West Side of Manhattan. At first they circled nervously and finally they circled frantically as they came to the terrifying conclusion that they had become one more mechanical appendage of the steering system. Parking on the Upper West Side was positive, irrefutable proof that man was nothing and fate everything. A proposition most people dedicated their lives to denying. No wonder people went mad. In a world reverberating with howling falsehoods, parking on the Upper West Side was a terminal whisper of reality: dandruff cannot be cured, parents disown children, and Sanforized jeans shrink. Most days Kagan did not find such a proposition disturbing. ("Who needs success? I want a few laughs.") But today was not most days. Today was Erev Yom Kippur — and not just the day before Yom Kippur, but the day before *Shabbes,* too. A little before sunset both would begin

3

simultaneously, so Kagan wanted to get home, wash, dress, eat, and hurry off to the *shtibl*.

And Yom Kippur is more than a whisper of reality; it is a hundred-piece symphony that runs twenty-five hours without skipping a beat. On Yom Kippur everyone must atone because his fate is at stake. Everyone is like everyone else, a plain simple human being before a Compassionate Master. On Erev Yom Kippur even Kagan was like everyone else, which might not be such a bad thing except that Kagan was trying to park on Ninety-fourth Street — so Kagan was going crazy. And what does a man of integrity ("I'm not saying I'm righteous — I'm saying I'm just as good as all those people who think they are") do when he goes crazy? He blames his wife.

"What the hell does she know about Yom Kippur anyway?" he muttered, his eyes darting from one side of the street to the other. "A lot she knows! Fran from Connecticut. Yom Kippur in boring-land. A comic strip. Everyone's alike and everyone gets into his car and everyone arrives at the temple on time and everyone parks his clean car on the parking lot with the yellow stripes and everyone smiles. What the hell does that have to do with life?" In anger, Kagan gripped the steering wheel so tightly that his knuckles turned white. Parking lots with yellow stripes!

Things weren't that way when Kagan was a kid. That's for sure. Not on your life, thought Kagan. Kagan grew up with life. Surrounded by life. Almost drowned in life!

The quick twinge of memory calmed him. Kagan decided to savor it. He surrendered, slouching down behind the wheel, loosening his grip, and welcoming the return of distant streets and ancient corners, fire escapes and candy stores.

WHEN Kagan was young, really young, Rosh Hashanah was a treat and Yom Kippur was a bore, a dread.
Nothing to do, nothing to eat, and all the grownups
droning on and on, endlessly pounding their breasts in
short, choppy, tedious strokes. And all that sighing!
With all that carbon dioxide (and Kagan didn't even
believe in science — why should he? it never made
sense), it's a miracle no one died. No one even fainted,
not even Mrs. Rubinstein, and she used to faint at the
drop of a hat. The Duke of Windsor abdicated — Mrs.
Rubinstein fainted. The seder night of Passover, Hir-
shorn the plumber's wife went into labor. The ambulance
attendants rushed up the steps and Mrs. Rubinstein, a
spineless heap, plunged into their arms. They opened
their stretcher and rushed her to the hospital, siren
roaring and lights flashing as ferocious screams began
in the plumber's apartment. And Rubinstein? Rubinstein stood on the sidewalk, a corner of his white linen
seder-night napkin tucked under his belt, a high *yarmulke* on his head, uttering plaintively after the ambulance, "Rivka, what's for dessert?" All the while the
flashing lights were growing smaller, the siren's howl
more distant, and upstairs the cries more insistent and
more urgent.

That was a neighborhood! Oh, how Kagan loved that
neighborhood, but he didn't kid himself. He had run
away as fast as the others, but he had loved it, too, as
much as he had hated it. What's for dessert? Forty-five
years, starting in Poland, she makes one thing. Where-
fore is this night different from all other nights? What's
for dessert? Compote!

"WHAT did Fran know about that?" Kagan cried.
Fran said that he romanticized it all. It wasn't that way,
she claimed. "Even so," he asked slyly, "do you think

I'll talk that way about you someday?" She called him
a shit. (Fran was a modern woman; she shit with the
door open. "It is honest.") What did she know? She
was from Connecticut. Kagan, a shit? A bastard, maybe, but not a shit. (Kagan was not a modern man.) Leave
it to a modern woman to get everything wrong — even
when she's right.

And all the time she complains about the same stories.
When they got married, did he promise her a new
routine every night? Year in and year out he's not
supposed to complain about the same wife, but the
material is supposed to change from show to show.
That's not the way it works. (Kagan had been in show
business! Oh, it would have been nice to have had a
stage career; he had the talent all right.) Everybody
knows the first thing you do is change the audience.
You take the show on the road. That's what you do. But
that takes money. Everything takes money. And if there
was one thing Kagan didn't have, it was money. He and
Fran agreed on that. That's about the only thing he and
Fran agreed on.

Kagan snorted. What did Fran know about that? She
had no idea just how much money he didn't have. And
Kagan wasn't about to tell her either. Some things are
sacred: a man's shylocks, for instance. If she ever found
out about them, that would be it. Kagan often wondered
why he didn't tell her.

He hadn't signed his life over to her. He had only
married her — in Connecticut, yet. The marriage might
not even be good in Manhattan. A thought which Kagan
found appealing: married in Hartford, engaged in
Bridgeport, reconciled in Westchester, separated in
the Bronx, footloose and fancy-free in Manhattan. All
at the same time!

And Kagan wasn't a legalist. He hated legalists. This

separated him from most of his Orthodox brethren. Kagan was a man of the spirit. (That didn't exclude the flesh.) He prided himself, no, he exalted himself on being a man of the spirit, but he was also a man of the people. The rich make all the laws so why shouldn't the poor have a few? It's true that as a high-school teacher he earned more than most of the poor but he spent more and was just as broke as any one of them. Forget the credit union, forget the loan companies, he had the shylocks to prove it! Yes, Kagan was a man of the people; in this he remained constant — more or less. Kagan smiled. He wasn't a liar. And, anyway, the thought of all those idiotic forms where it always asks "Marital Status" amused him. "See accompanying map," he would reply. Theirs was an affair of the latitude and longitude, all right. She didn't give him enough latitude and he had gone on for too longitude. Fifty-four forty or fight! How could he fight? He couldn't even find a parking space. And Yom Kippur was coming!

Kagan stared out at the unrelenting wall of parked cars. You'd think they'd give a guy a break Erev Yom Kippur. Where is Ozzie anyway? Erev Yom Kippur a guy needs his angel, so naturally, no angel. What a world. And people think I'm crazy? Kagan shook his head and decided to drive slowly around one more time.

Latitude and longitude — there must be a joke there someplace, but it's not there now. The rhythm isn't right, Kagan reflected. Still, it's better than the stuff you hear on TV. Kagan once had an act — well, really, a routine. It wasn't so bad and one year, his best year, he played a lot of places with it: the mountains, Atlantic City, even a Communist camp. (Kagan, man of the people!) As Kagan himself admitted, he took that act everywhere except to the top. Anything for a joke. Okay, here goes. Good evening, ladies and gentlemen, let me give you a little piece of advice. Never marry a foreigner. Let me tell you about my wife. She's a foreigner. My wife's from Connecticut, maybe you've heard of it. I thought she'd massage my back, wash my feet, and serve a lot of low-cholesterol dishes. But, folks, never marry a foreigner whose eyes don't slant. And don't let the contact lenses fool you. Sometimes they slip around and create some pretty weird effects.

All foreigners are not alike. In Connecticut their eyes don't slant. . . . Hartford! . . . Ah. . . . It sounded romantic. For that matter, everything north of Fourteenth Street sounded romantic: Central Park, Rockefeller Center — even Fifteenth Street sounded romantic. But Hartford sounded like the twin city to Xanadu. It wasn't just a dream. I was there. It's another country. The kids ride bikes — that belong to them.

Believe me, just because you don't have concrete under your feet doesn't mean life is a picnic. For a picnic you need a hamper. God forbid you should use a brown paper bag like a *mensch*! No, you need a hamper so you'll look like a faggot trying out for the role of Little Red Riding Hood.

I know all about foreign places because of my wife. Basically, my marriage was a geographical relationship. You see, if you get married in a foreign place like Hartford, it isn't recognized south of Fourteenth Street. All the places in between are neither here nor there. Legally, in Hartford I'm a married man; in Bridgeport I'm engaged; in the Bronx I'm legally separated; in Manhattan, north of Fourteenth Street, I'm going steady; and south of Fourteenth Street I'm footloose and fancy free.

You know, on those forms where it asks "Marital

Status," I have to put down "see accompanying map."
It's not so surprising when you think of it, since ours is
strictly an affair of the latitude and longitude. When
she puts it down on the lattitude and I get it up on the
longitude, everything is Rand-McNally. The rest of the
time it's fifty-four forty or fight.

Kagan laughed. Not bad. A routine like that and still
no parking space. Where is justice? He looked at his
watch, a garish iridescent green contraption that he
had received as a consolation prize on a quiz show. A
dummy prize, really. The other contestant, some boring broad from Yonkers, won eight hundred dollars
and a boat. And what did he win? One shiny pickle-
green watch and fifty dollars' worth of *trayf* Colonel
Sanders Kentucky Fried Chicken — and I keep kosher
yet! Some luck! That's like Mao Tse-tung winning fifty
shares of AT&T. Not bad, a routine there somewhere. A
routine but no money; that's the story of my life. Could
I have used the money! Could I have used my life!
Kagan sighed. And not just the money, the boat, too.

She certainly didn't know what to do with the boat.
Hell, I had her, but "your host" managed to melt his
smile long enough to speak. "It is finger-lickin' good,
Mr. Kagan, but our policy is no trading of prizes on the
program."

"Who's trading prizes? We're sharing a little."

"I'm sorry, Mr. Kagan." I'm sorry Mr. Kagan, my ass.
They can't trade prizes but they can give me lousy
questions. How many astronauts have walked on the
moon? What a dumb question! Who asked them to go?
They had no business up there in the first place.

Kagan stoically glanced at his green watch. Winning
is better than losing but losing is action and action is
better than no action. Kagan could wear the ugly,
pickle-green bastard, all right, but still — why didn't

he get the easy questions? Who knows, Kagan mourned philosophically, maybe there's a reason I get the hard ones.

Kagan looked about more carefully. Cars aligned with curbs for blocks as if God had created them that way. Still no spot. I'll go; it won't hurt.

Kagan ceased his slow prowl for a parking spot and was heading downtown at a steady speed when a voice broke in on his thoughts.

"*Mikveh! Mikveh! Mikveh!* Kagan, leave it to you. You're too much."

It was Ozzie, Kagan's angel.

"Yeah, Ozzie, what's wrong with the *mikveh*? A Jew goes to the *mikveh* for a ritual bath before the Day of Atonement."

"Kagan, you think it will help you on next year's quiz show? You'll have pickle-green watches up and down your arms until you look like a Timex frog."

"Look Ozzie, what do you care why I'm going? I'm going to the *mikveh*. It's the right thing to do, isn't it?"

"Suddenly you are governed by the right thing to do?!"

"Listen, this is Erev Yom Kippur, the eve of the holiest day of the year. A man and his angel should get along. What do you say?"

"Kagan, if you can't park on Ninety-fourth Street, how are you going to park on Seventy-eighth?"

"I don't have to," Kagan answered smugly.

"No? What are you going to do? Drive your Sixty-four Falcon right into the *mikveh*? It won't work, Kagan. For this junk heap you need more than a mere dip for the Day of Atonement, you need resurrection of the dead. You need the automotive Messiah. And, Kagan, even a man of faith like you wouldn't buy a car like this from the Messiah."

Kagan smiled. "You forget. I haven't paid for this one yet. Ozzie, how long does it take for a quick dip? I'll leave it double-parked."

"All right, Kagan, but get your little pagan head together. Is the power of this divine dip to be applied towards a boat and eight hundred dollars or towards avoiding a ticket for double-parking?"

"You lack faith, Ozzie. You're too analytic. You should have been a scientist instead of a divine."

Right in front of the *mikveh*, Kagan pulled his old Ford alongside another car and hopped out.

## 2

KAGAN blanched, closing his eyes, as he met the hot, moist air of the *mikveh*. He felt the puddles underfoot and opened his eyes. That's all I have to do — break my back in a *mikveh*. Fran would never believe it. I could muster witnesses, too. Half the Upper West Side must be here. Maybe Ozzie knew what he was doing when he stayed outside. That's some crazy angel!

"Hey, fella!" a voice called through the mists. "You pay over heah."

Kagan stepped toward the voice and found the *mikveh* attendant standing next to a table with an open corrugated cardboard box on it. The little refugee, sweat rolling down the tautly drawn skin of his forehead and temples, pointed to the box.

"I didn't want to pay until I was sure you were going to fix the air conditioning," Kagan said.

"Say, dat's a good one."

"You got a student discount?"

"Here, we charge 'em more."

Kagan relaxed. The heat eased. He had a naturally curious bent of mind.

"You charge 'em more? Everybody else charges 'em less."

"Students take too long in the *mikveh*. They don't have nothing better to do."

"Yeah," Kagan said, satisfied. "That sounds right. How much is the businessman's special? A real commercial quickie?"

"Five dollars."

"Five dollars! What's in the *mikveh*, champagne?"

"It's tax deductible. You want a receipt?"

"Receipt," Kagan said in earnest amazement, "I want a loan."

As Kagan dropped his five-dollar bill into the box, he felt a thrill of astonishment. In that *farshtunkener* soggy cardboard box on that moist table enveloped by clouds of steam and attended by a sweat-covered, bony-skulled little man lay the coolest, crispest five-dollar bills in town. Who would have guessed? Kagan was proud to be a Jew. No wonder the *mikveh* man didn't let the heat bother him; he was standing next to the cool stuff.

"Listen," Kagan proposed in earnest confidence, "do you need a partner to run this steambath?"

"I need a son-in-law," the *mikveh* man answered.

"I've got one of those, unfortunately," Kagan said ruefully. "Not a son-in-law, a wife — believe you me! I wish I could help you out. I know what it is to have a problem."

"I'll solve it, the Lord willing."

"Yeah," Kagan agreed, "I'm sure you will, but you can still help me with mine. It's Erev Yom Kippur. I need a few bucks for a few months. You may not need a partner, but I do."

"You don't got a job? I need someone to clean up."

"Oh, no, I got a job."

"What do you do?"

"I teach. City high school."

"What's the problem?"

"I got a lot of heavy expenses lately. My wife had an operation."

"Too bad."

"Yeah, she is in terrible pain. I got to keep a nurse for her. Double pay for Yom Kippur."

"The nurse is Jewish?"

"Sure, this is America."

"You're telling me?"

While they were talking, the stock of green grew larger and cooler. Kagan felt himself sweating profusely.

"Listen," Kagan suggested in the most confident and confidential of tones, "a thousand could see me through."

The *mikveh* man didn't respond.

"I said a thousand would get me through."

"I need a son-in-law, not a partner."

"Yeah, but you do me a favor and maybe I'll do you a favor."

"You're a matchmaker now?"

"You never know."

"I know," the *mikveh* man said pleasantly. "Partners I don't need."

"Thanks a lot," Kagan said in a sarcastic, hurt voice as he walked away.

"Say, come back here," the *mikveh* man called passionately after him.

Kagan expectantly leaped through the billowing vapors toward the voice of return. "Yes?"

"You forgot a towel."

"I need a towel? For me it's the bottom of the *mikveh*."

"You shouldn't talk that way Erev Yom Kippur."

"I have no choice."

"You always have a choice. Take the towel now. With a crowd like this, I might run out."

"Yeah, of everything but money."

"I've got expenses, too."

"Bottom of the *mikveh*," Kagan threatened darkly.

"You'll change your mind. You'll be glad you have a towel."

"If I don't, it'll be bad for business." Kagan took the towel and continued into the hot, wet, jostling mob. Some greeted him, but Kagan ignored them and worked his way over to the wall where he located an empty hook and commandeered a stool. He sullenly began to undress. Why are some people like that? he wondered. A son-in-law he wants. Grandchildren. *Naches. Mazel Tov?*

"Hey, Moe," a voice interrupted. "What are you doing here?"

Kagan, half undressed, looked up to see Bienstock the furrier.

"What do you think I'm doing here, Bienstock, trapping otter? You think only you holy men come here? Even the poor have a few sins."

Another voice called in greeting, "Hey, Moe, you know how the *mikveh* works? You shower first."

Everybody's a *maven.* Young Goffstein, the *shmuck.* "Do I know how a *mikveh* works? I used to be a lifeguard in a *mikveh*," Kagan began the routine.

"Yeah, we heard. You told us that last year," young Goffstein smirked.

"Yeah, Goffstein, and you heard *Kol Nidre* last year too, wise guy. Tonight when the *chazan* begins *Kol Nidre*, are you going to call out, 'Hey, we heard that last year!'?"

"There is a difference," Goffstein protested.

"Yeah, you don't understand *Kol Nidre*. I got to get out of here," Kagan said with a conviction he himself didn't understand.

"What's wrong?" Bienstock inquired.

"My God!" Kagan remembered, "I'm double-parked!" Kagan leaped up, grabbed his towel, and headed for the divinely ordained pool. The place was packed. He couldn't take this naked, flabby, self-conscious crowd. Nobody had been in the army or spent any time in a male locker room. Everybody moved with tight-assed modesty. Kagan thought these must be the kind of people that you were always reading about, people who fuck with their socks on. But Kagan remembered that he was double-parked.

"Gangway, gangway!" Kagan called as he bulled his way through the crowd.

"Don't push. Someone will get hurt."

"Yeah. I could get hurt; I'm double-parked. You're all dreaming about cooked chicken in soup that the missus made and I'm having nightmares that my goose is being cooked by some *momzer* in the Twentieth Precinct."

"Kagan, don't tell lies Erev Yom Kippur!"

Noticing Schwartz behind him, Kagan bristled. Before he could respond, Schwartz continued didactically, "Falcon, Kagan, you drive a Falcon, not a goose."

Kagan's face twisted into a smile. "Yeah, that's right. That's not a bad line."

"Ladies and gentlemen, may I have your attention please!" Schwartz continued. Kagan laughed along with everyone else. "I know you're all in a hurry, but we have in our midst a *cohen* who is double-parked."

"*Oy*," an old man said, "a *cohen* double-parked! Why didn't he say?"

"Years ago a *cohen* stood for something. As a matter of fact, he stood for plenty," Kagan muttered. For a judgmental guy, Schwartz has a sense of humor. So if he's such a great guy why doesn't he write me a routine? With a good routine. . . .

Kagan headed down the steps into the pool. Why in blazes are these things always as hot as . . . ? For some reason, Kagan couldn't say it. Kagan was respectful. In a strange way, it was true, but when it came to holy stuff, he had a lot of respect. The steamy water was uncomfortable, and he looked around querulously, half expecting to see rotting vegetation — maybe hay with a little cabbage, floating ripe and redolent past some half-submerged hippopotamus. But the water was surprisingly clean, and the pale, white hulks totally submerged themselves seriously and carefully, even devoutly.

Kagan descended until the warm, receptive water was up to his waist. As he waded into the pool, he felt the softly oscillating clutches of the heat receive him. In his naked return to thermal oneness, the perfect ninety-eight point six, that sheltered return to consanguineous fluids, he felt the warm waters reproach even as they welcomed — why, Kagan, did you resist us? How could you hesitate? Find us repulsive? But before Kagan could answer, they whispered "sh" and, nodding in gentle waves of reunion, held him fast in the warmth and perfect unity of the pool.

Kagan, the waters a fraction of an inch below his nostrils, peacefully watched the bodies resolutely submerging and surfacing. His watching turned into meditation as the unifying procedure became a natural process to calm the universe; the edgeless, cornerless bobbing seemed to occur within his mind, inside his brain, simultaneously with its occurrence in the pool.

Kagan sensed deep within himself that the harmony of this purifying pool could become his vision and the *mikveh*'s oneness could silence the loansharks who hunted him as their natural prey. Kagan wished to elude them through the fluid currents of repose. He felt impelled to submerge like an amphibian until the waters half-covered his eyes and the serene fluid of the *mikveh* would enter his searching, troubled hazel eyes. Then, when forced to leave the pool, Kagan could carry with him his true vision — the universal harmony hidden behind the hard edges and sharp corners of a frantic world.

"Hold that pose any longer, Kagan, and when they remake *Run Silent, Run Deep*, you can play the submarine."

Kagan stood up.

"Kagan," Schwartz continued, "the idea is to go all the way under the water."

Judgmental son of a bitch, Kagan thought as he gulped a breath of air, collapsed his legs under him, and crashed underwater. As his head submerged totally into the water, he felt the tug of his hair floating upward, trying to escape. But it was dragged down with everything else, hovering over him like a dark, tremulous, inescapable hand.

Kagan felt his heels bump against his rump and then shot his feet downward in a ferocious thrust, ejecting himself bolt upright from the pool. Blowing air and tossing his head like a creature from the deep, he opened his eyes and watched Shapiro's prissy-assed movement as he climbed up from the pool. What's wrong with these people? he thought. Why aren't they normal?

"Hey, Shapiro!" Kagan's voice boomed out, amplified by the waters. Everyone, including Shapiro, turned. "You sure this is how Mark Spitz got his start?"

Desperately wishing that he could explain to all present that Kagan was *meshugge* and a mere acquaintance of his (which he wasn't), Shapiro departed the scene in embarrassment.

Kagan watched him leave more prissy-assed than before, but visions of the entire Twentieth Precinct scribbling tickets all over his car arose in place of Shapiro's disappearing buttocks.

Kagan scrambled out of the pool and, drying himself off, scampered back toward his clothing. On the way, he met an old Jew with long gray beard and earlocks gingerly picking his way toward the waters. Kagan stepped in front of him and, flashing the V-for-victory peace sign, proclaimed, "Flipper lives!" Before the old man could begin to comprehend what had happened, Kagan had disappeared.

Kagan dressed hurriedly, too hurriedly. He felt the damp squish of his socks in his shoes. He shuddered, for Kagan knew with certainty that that was how you got athlete's foot. His shirt grabbed his damp back and wouldn't let go. And he didn't even have a comb. How did he know this morning that he would wind up at the *mikveh*? He smoothed his hair with one hand and flung his towel toward the hamper with the other as he headed toward the door. A voice caught him before he could exit.

"Hey, fella, c'mere!"

"I'm double-parked," Kagan called, still heading for the exit.

"C'mere," the voice coaxed.

"I'm double-parked."

"It's the first of the month. The coppers don't ticket until the tenth; I know."

Kagan turned back to the *mikveh* man.

"I didn't know that."

"Vell, they don't even get the kvoda until then."

"Hey, that's good to know."

"You gotta know the kvoda or they'll run you to death."

"You're telling me!" Kagan agreed.

"How much you need?"

Kagan could imagine how much was in that box! And people, five-dollar bills popping out of their pockets, were still pouring in.

"Two thousand," Kagan said struggling to hold his voice even, "could save my life."

The *mikveh* man registered no surprise. His expression didn't change at all. The sweat rolled off the tightly drawn skin. It dawned on Kagan that maybe all the hot moisture had shrunk his skin to such a snug fit. Kagan had found a lifesaver. Where else but the *mikveh*?

"Two thousand," Kagan explained, "would let me turn my life around. I couldn't pay you right away, but you'll get it back."

The *mikveh* man stood there silently. Still expressionless, he said, "How would twenty do?"

"Twenty thousand?" Kagan whispered. His mind did cartwheels in the corrugated box.

"No, twenty dollars."

Kagan felt crushed, tricked, humiliated. How could he do that to Kagan? Kagan hadn't done anything to him.

"I'll tell you what," the little man said, "let's make it thirty."

"Listen," Kagan said, more in curiosity than in anger, "I'm talking two thousands and you're talking two tens. What makes you think so little will help?"

"*Nu*," the man said, "after Yom Kippur comes Succos. A man needs a *lulav* and an *esrog*, doesn't he?"

"Yes, that's true," cordially answered Kagan, who

had never purchased his own set in his life, but had used the synagogue's. "And they cost more than ever," Kagan complained.

"We'll make it forty."

"Listen, it's Erev Yom Kippur. We're both excited, it's only natural. You said twenty. You mentioned thirty. Now forty. Who'll get it right? Let's make it fifty, an even half a hundred, then there won't be any problem."

The *mikveh* man, with no change of expression, nodded and reached into the box. He calmly counted out ten five-dollar bills onto the damp table.

"You couldn't spare another fifty, could you? An even hundred?"

"No," he said evenly.

"Fifty, that's the quota, huh?" Kagan laughed self-consciously.

The man picked up the bills and began to hand them to Kagan.

"You gotta know the kvo-da," Kagan mimicked as he reached out to receive them.

As the *mikveh* man turned his hand over to deliver the money, Kagan saw the toneless, tattooed numbers on the *mikveh* man's forearm. The numbers, sitting there worn and ugly like dead bugs, grabbed Kagan's eyes. Kagan was confused; why the surprise? The man was a refugee; Kagan had known that at once. He knew that the *mikveh* man knew that he, Kagan, was surprised and staring. When Kagan looked up fearfully, he found the *mikveh* man's eyes gazing from his taut-skinned, expressionless face.

"Dat's right," the *mikveh* man nodded.

Kagan drew his hand away and in shame ran out the door. Fearful, he jumped into his car.

"I can't believe you didn't get a ticket," Ozzie said in

a voice exasperated with waiting.

Kagan did not hear him. His mind was on the *mikveh* man's arm.

"Kagan," the angel said, "don't tell me you rifled the Chosen People's pockets?"

Kagan looked down to find the bills still in his hand. My God, he thought, he doesn't even know who I am.

"Where are you going?" the angel called.

But Kagan had already leaped out of the car and was running back into the building. Inside, several customers were paying. Kagan shouted over them to the *mikveh* man.

"You don't even know who I am!"

Without looking up, the *mikveh* man called, "I know who you are. You're double-parked. Go!"

Kagan took another step toward him and said in appreciation, respect, and triumph, "But you know the quota!"

The *mikveh* man looked up and nodded slowly. "And yet — you are double-parked. Go."

Subdued, Kagan returned to his car. As he settled behind the wheel a patrol car slithered past his double-parked vehicle. Kagan shivered in amazement. As the police passed him, Kagan saw the numbers on the trunk of the car. Five — seven — three — four. Kagan felt a tremor of recognition race through him. Five — seven — three — four, Kagan chanted. I must not forget. I must not forget. For Kagan knew in the seat of his pants that that was a superfecta. Eight . . . ten . . . twelve thousand dollars!

"Ozzie!" he screamed, "I've got the numbers!"

"Don't you always," the angel said sarcastically.

"No, no. This time they're the real ones," Kagan yelled in elation. "You'll see! You'll see!"

"Oh," the angel said, changing his tone.

Kagan became attentive.

"When are they for?" the angel continued very calmly and very politely.

Kagan knew that tone and began to squirm. He kneaded the steering wheel with his fingers and changed his position on the seat. He realized why the angel was suddenly so polite: Kagan wouldn't bet on any race that was run on *Shabbes* or a holiday. And tonight! Tonight was both *Shabbes* and Yom Kippur! And Kagan had the numbers today. Damn! Damn! Damn! screamed Kagan to himself, pounding the wheel in frustration. A sure thing and it might not do him any good.

"Listen, Kagan, you go right by an Off-Track Betting shop on the way home. Just three dollars at OTB: bing, bing, bing and it's yours."

"Ozzie," Kagan mourned, "I've got a few principles."

"Yes, and they're wrong, Kagan. I've told you that a bet placed before the Sabbath on an event to be run on the Sabbath is not a transgression of the Sabbath. Of course, betting itself is not such a meritorious act, but there is no problem with the Sabbath."

"Ozzie, that's not the way I work."

"Kagan, that's the way the law, the *Halachah*, works. Don't you think it's time you quit relying on your own judgment and started trusting the law? If a man were to shoot an arrow before *Shabbes* and it killed a man on *Shabbes*, the man who shot the arrow did not transgress the Sabbath because his act, his act of shooting, was done before the Sabbath."

"But what about the man?" Kagan wanted to know.

"He didn't violate the Sabbath."

"No, Ozzie, the man who got killed."

"What about him? He's dead!"

"That's the point. A man gets shot out of the blue and

nobody cares. A man, a human being, died, what about him?"

"He's dead," Ozzie screamed. "What about him?! They bury him. They sit *shivah*. They wail. If he was rich, they name a yeshiva after him."

"But what about the other man?" Kagan wanted to know. "He gets off scot-free just because he fired the arrow before sundown?"

"No, Kagan, he's a murderer, all right! But he's not a transgressor of the Sabbath. The case illustrates a principle!"

"Well, I don't know about principles, Ozzie. All I know about is *Shabbes* and Yom Kippur fall on the same day this year. They're one and the same. I don't bet *Shabbes* and I don't bet Yom Kippur."

"But you're not. That's the point."

"And if I do bet: God won't mind my thinking about a superfecta during *Kol Nidre*?"

"And, Kagan, if you don't bet it, you're not going to think about it?"

Kagan was silent. Of course he was going to think about it. And yet — where had he heard that before? — there was a difference, wasn't there? A difference between thinking and betting. I can't.

"And anyway," Kagan said, "I don't have time. By the time I get a parking space, I'll hardly have time to eat."

Before they knew it, they were back at Ninety-fourth Street.

"Look, Kagan, a spot right in front of your building."

Kagan beamed. Yes, this is my lucky day. And tomorrow, because of Yom Kippur, alternate-side-of-the-street parking regulations are suspended. Who said God doesn't love the Jews?

"Kagan, no excuses now. Go win a bundle and say

goodbye to penury and woe."

"Penury and woe?" Kagan said backing the balky Falcon into the spot. "You make it sound like a law firm." But would I ever like to say goodbye to penury and woe, Kagan added to himself.

"That's right, penury and woe. If you want to make your life a joke, all right, but I don't want to hear you crying about it the rest of your days."

Kagan had parked, but he remained inside the car to finish the conversation. To think some people found him a poor listener.

"Yeah, yeah," Kagan agreed. "I'm awful about that, I really am. A real crier, disgusting. I can't help it; that's me. But let me ask you something. You've got hot pants, nothing personal, mine aren't so cool themselves, but a gambler you never were. You've always discouraged me from any action. You're always quoting the odds. So why all of a sudden you're so desperate that I should play?"

"Kagan, listen, I don't bet, but I know that if you bet that number today, it will win tonight. And, Kagan, I know you. I'm your angel, remember me? You think in the back of your scheming sanctimonious mind that God will reward you for not betting tonight by turning that number into the winning number for tomorrow night. Quit gambling with God, Kagan. You almost got a ticket today."

"But I didn't!" Kagan announced triumphantly, springing from the car.

"And yet — " the angel called after him.

The words instantly collapsed the buoyant joy in Kagan. He stumbled on the curb and with a confused heart barely dragged himself onto the sidewalk. He didn't know whether to turn into his building or race over to the OTB parlor. He stood expressionless on the sidewalk. Confused and fatigued, he felt as it he were carrying an unbearable burden that would crush him even more quickly if he were either to take another step or attempt to put it down. The numbers, five — seven — three — four, raced through his head faster and faster until he was standing inside his own head watching them rush around the inside of his skull like the incandescent traveling letters of the headlines running around the Allied Chemical Tower in Times Square: 5734, 5734, 5734.

He might have stood there all day and night had Mrs. Goldshmidt not held the door open for him.

"I know where you've been. I can tell from the hair," she said.

"Yes," Kagan answered, watching the dancing, dazzling points of light circumnavigate his cranium. Yes, yes! Five — seven — three — four! Yes!

"You've been to the *mikveh!*"

"*Mikveh.*" Five — seven — three — four. "*Mikveh.*" Five — seven — three — four.

"My Ernie used to go."

"Used to go." Five — seven — three — four.

Kagan entered the elevator. Every floor lit up 5734. He ran out when the elevator man opened the door for him.

### 3

KAGAN stood in amazement in front of his own door with a lost feeling and a sense of terror; it didn't say "5734." It said "8C." Not knowing what to do, he rang the bell. Nothing happened He rang the bell again.

"Just a minute!" Fran's distant voice called.

Fran! Fran! What the hell does Fran know about five — seven — three — four?

The numbers disappeared and Kagan's point of view returned to his eyeballs. How could Fran know anything about five — seven — three — four? Kagan had sworn to her that he had quit gambling. And it was true. He had. Hundreds of times.

He took out his key and opened the door. Their small cat rubbed against his leg in greeting. Kagan let the creature indulge herself for a moment, then carefully stepped around her.

"Who is it? Moe?" Fran called.

Kagan crossed through the small, jumbled living room. Fran was on the john — with the door open.

"God damn it!" Kagan howled in pain. "Do you have to shit with the door open Erev Yom Kippur?"

"Moe, when I came into the bathroom, you weren't here."

"Would it have killed you to close the door?"

"C'mon, Moe, how was I supposed to know you were going to walk in?"

"How was I supposed to know you were going to walk in?" he mimicked. "Because I live here. Because it's Erev Yom Kippur and I want to eat so I won't starve to death tomorrow."

She sat there. "You're right, I apologize. It was stupid of me."

"You're damn right it was stupid of you!" he yelled. "Come out of there this minute. You have no business in there Erev Yom Kippur or any other day."

"I'm not finished," she laughed.

"Then why can't you shit with the door closed like a normal human being?" he screamed, slamming the door, not knowing why she had laughed, and wondering why that guy shot the other guy with the arrow, much less on *Shabbes* of all days. What did Fran know about that?

He stomped into the bedroom. What's wrong with her? he fumed. Is this what I live for? To come home and find the bathroom door open? In the old neighborhood, you had to close the door. You'd better; the toilet was in the hall. You had to be quick, too. But that was long ago. Kagan barely remembered that.

Then they had moved to the "new building." They still called it the "new building." It was old when they had moved in; it was older when they had moved out. And now? Ancient, a tired clump of old, dirty brick on Avenue A with a tired, old, sat-on, lived-on, slept-on fire escape. It sagged so much, it looked more like wood than iron. But it remained the "new building." Hey, Pop, you want to drive by? Sure, let's see how the "new building" is doing. What did Fran know about that?

Still, maybe it wasn't her fault. Very few, practically no one, knew about that stuff. In high-school French, Mlle. Fleischman told them about the Pont Neuf, the New Bridge, of Paris, and do you know how old the new bridge is, class? One year, they guessed. Two, three, four years. Kagan wanted to guess a thousand years, but he couldn't. It was a setup. Her routine called for a brand-new bridge. Kagan played straight man. What a nitwit she was! What a dumb question.

A dumb question. Kagan looked at his pickle-green watch. It was late! They'd better eat fast. He looked up to tell Fran to hurry when something on the bed caught his eye. He stepped over to see a small gift-wrapped package.

Oh, my God, cringed Kagan, it's our anniversary! No, that's in June, Kagan recalled with some certainty. A shudder of horror captured Kagan — her birthday. Some affected friend at the office gave her a precious gift and I forgot. Shit, does she have to have such stupid friends? They'd love to break us up. Wait a minute, wait a minute, Kagan cautioned himself. Fran had a birthday this year and I remembered it. No, not a birthday; that's out. Hmmm? Perplexed, Kagan picked up the package, hoping that by touching it, he would be able to divine its purpose. Kagan couldn't stand people who shook gifts. It seemed barbaric and unfeeling, as if, somehow, the gift could get dizzy. Kagan touched it carefully. Hanukkah? That's pretty good! How could Hanukkah be the night of Yom Kippur?

Fran appeared in the doorway. "Open it. It's for you," she said.

Kagan looked at the gift in surprise. For him? That he had not divined. "For me? Is it my birthday?"

"No, it's just a gift. It's for you. Open it. It won't bite you."

Kagan tore off the paper to find a small paperback, *Tree Trails in Central Park.*

"Won't bite me?" Kagan raised his voice. "Why don't you give me a bicycle to run into them? *Tree Trails in Central Park*, my God!" My God, Kagan thought, this kid is too much. If it were a joke, it would be a great routine, but she really believes I'm going to go out and learn the names of trees, when the dogs who piss on them don't bother to look. Kagan heard a choking sound. Fran was crying — Connecticut.

"I just wanted to give you a gift," she said. "I'm sorry."

"It's all right. I can't say I wanted it, but it's very educational."

He stood there like an idiot. He felt like a fool. Erev Yom Kippur and she had given him a gift and he's yelling at her. Who knows, in Hartford they might fast

Hanukkah. And it beats a gift certificate to Colonel
Sanders Kentucky Fried Chicken. Speaking of which,
they'd better eat their chicken.

"Listen," he tried again, "it's lovely. Thank you." He
sounded unconvincing. "I had a hard day. . . ." I must
have, I haven't had any easy ones lately. Something
must have been hard about this one. Why should it be
any different? "Yes," he said quickly, "I had a hard day
at the *mikveh*."

"At the *mikveh*?" she asked, tears still flowing.

"Yes, at the *mikveh*. They ran out of towels. How do
you like that? They charge five dollars and they run out
of towels." He was truly indignant.

"What did you use?" she asked.

But Kagan's mind had leaped back into that soggy
cardboard box to dip among the five-dollar bills.

"What do you mean?" he asked, thinking about those
five-dollar bills. Why, that guy must be a millionaire.
Okay, good for him, but why did he think Kagan had to
be one, too? Five dollars!

"How did you dry off?"

"With a towel, why?" he answered, wondering how
the *mikveh* man knew that the patrol car was coming.
Maybe there was something to that ESP stuff.

"I thought you said they ran out of towels."

What towels is she talking about? "Oh," he impro-
vised enthusiastically, "*those* towels! I used Shapiro's
towel."

"A dirty towel?"

"Well, yeah, but Shapiro's so uptight he didn't touch
his ass or his balls with it."

Fran smiled at that. He looked at his petite, graceful
Connecticut wife, thirty-one and after six years of marriage to a character like himself still a good-looking
girl. Hair like Little Orphan Annie; Kagan was twelve

years older but she didn't get any Daddy Warbucks! He
had liked the curly hair and the lithe body, but it was
the kind, gracious charm that had misled him into
thinking that he should stand under a wedding cano-
py. And the shy, twinkling, girlish smile (sweet but
hoping for passion) that he had never seen before. He
was always a sucker for that, wasn't he?

Kagan leaned over to embrace her. She cried as he
kissed her on the cheek. What a crazy time for a gift.
Wanting to comfort her, he awkwardly fiddled with
the button on her blouse. He unfastened it and cupped
her breast. There are some advantages to the modern
woman, Kagan thought. All that unhooking of bras in
his youth. The old neighborhood. He kissed her again.

"C'mon," he said gently. "I got the tree, if you got
the trail."

She turned away. "You don't have to fuck me because
of my tears."

"Oh, no, your tears have nothing to do with it. I hate
to fuck sad women in the afternoon. I want to fuck you
because I hate to write thank-you letters. If you don't
give me my chance to respond, you'll never get a
thank-you note."

She was undecided.

"It could ruin our marriage!" he warned.

"There's no time," she said surrendering.

"We'll hurry."

"How was the *mikveh*?" she asked, undressing.

"What do you mean how was the *mikveh*? It was the
*mikveh*." What a dumb question! Wait a minute —
they were making up. He already had his pants off and
it was Erev Yom Kippur! "There were a lot of nice
asses, but none like yours."

He pinched hers.

"It's late. Leave your socks on," she said.

They hurried, but not fast enough. Kagan was caught and passed by five — seven — three — four. When he heard them behind him, he closed his eyes, but their hoofbeats became deafening. He thrust and raced them for the wire, but it was five — seven — three — four, then Kagan and Kagan. (The last nose to nose.) Fran jumped up. Kagan lay there, his eyes closed and his body ravaged; five — seven — three — four, penury and woe win; Kagan and Kagan lose.

"Let's eat!" she said, scrambling toward the kitchen.

The phone rang. Kagan sat up and called, "I'll be there in a second."

He pulled on some shorts and ran into the living room.

"Is it for me? Is it Stein?"

"Just a moment please," Fran spoke into the phone. Putting her hand over the mouthpiece, she said to Kagan, "Moe, it's for me. It's the office, do you mind?"

"Hurry up! I have to call Stein."

Kagan returned to the bedroom and took his suit, his only suit, out of the closet. He had even had it cleaned. The hell with the suit. He had to call the Steins! They were in the "new building." Upstairs, near the plumber. Mr. Stein — that's what a Jew should be — honest, sweet, charitable. And Louie! Kagan had started going to *shul* with Louie. Without Louie, he wouldn't even know how to pray. Every *Shabbes* with the Steins, Louie and his dad.

At first, Kagan's old man couldn't make heads or tails out of it. "All day he sits in *shul* praying like a *tzaddik* and all night he sits in the candy store playing cards like a bum! A kid like this I never had! Either you go to *shul* or you go to the candy store. Moey wants to do both!"

It was true. And it stayed that way, but his pop

started going to *shul* with him. "I'm sure as hell not going to go to the candy store like a bum!" The four of them used to set off together from the "new building" to the little *shul*. The Steins moved before they did, but they always remained close. Louie and his wife and kids still went to the old folks for Yom Kippur.

Kagan ran out of the room to make his call. Good, she was off the phone.

"Moe, the soup and chicken are ready. Let's eat."

Kagan was dialing.

"Moe, it's late!"

"Shhh! I hope the Steins haven't left for *shul* yet!"

"Allo!" Old Mr. Stein answered the phone.

"Mr. Jacob Stein?" Kagan asked stentorially.

"That's right. Who's this?"

"I'm calling from Restaurant Associates to announce that you have won a gourmet meal for twenty-five tomorrow at the Four Seasons Restaurant. Would you like to begin with the shrimp cocktail or the smoked eel?"

"Oh, Moey, it's you! We were worried. We thought maybe something happened."

"Mr. Stein, I've been rushing around all day. You didn't think I wouldn't call?"

"Moey, without your call it wouldn't seem like Yom Kippur. Thank you."

Kagan heard the sweet voice coming over the tensile wire strung under the frantic world of Manhattan, and Kagan felt good. He was happy, even excited, to know that among the serpentine loops, tangles, convolutions of subterranean madness upon which the whole *me-shugginer* island stands such a voice could successfully make its way through. Happy, not just for himself, but for everyone. Kagan felt the moist warmth of tears in his eyes.

"Mr. Stein, there's nothing to thank. If it weren't for you and Louie, I wouldn't be going to hear *Kol Nidre* tonight."

"No, Moey, it would have been someone else. You always had it in you."

"I want to wish you that you should be sealed in the Book of Life — and an easy fast."

"A *cohen's* blessing. Thank you. May you and the missus be sealed in the Book of Life. A good year. . . . Louie wants to talk so I'm gonna go now. Be well."

"You too, Mr. Stein."

Louie's younger, less accented voice came on. He and Kagan exchanged wishes to be sealed in the Book of Life.

"How are the kids, Louie?"

"Okay, everybody's fine. How about you?"

"All right. Hey listen. I have a question for the man who got *smicha* from Reb Moshe Feinstein."

"No eating tomorrow, Moe," Louie teased.

"Gee, that's a shame! What'll I do with the cheeseburgers? No, listen, Louie. Is it true that if you shoot somebody with a bow and arrow on *Shabbes*, no, I mean before *Shabbes*, the shooting, not the hitting-him part, is before, but the guy gets killed afterwards. Right away, of course, but after *Shabbes*. Louie, do you know what I'm talking about?" Kagan appealed.

"You mean the case where the arrow is shot before *Shabbes*, but the arrow kills on *Shabbes*?"

"Yeah, yeah, right! Reb Moshe Feinstein knew what he was doing when he ordained you. Yeah, in that case, he didn't violate *Shabbes*?"

"No, he didn't violate *Shabbes*."

"Not at all, Louie?"

"Not all all, Moe."

"Oh," Kagan said.

"Why do you want to know, Moe?"

"So a guy could bet before *Shabbes* on a *Shabbes* race and it wouldn't be violating *Shabbes*?"

"Yes, that's right. You're becoming a scholar, I see."

"Not me, Louie. Don't worry about me."

"You got something good, Moe?"

"Terrific, terrific," Kagan mourned. "Louie, what should I do?"

"Moe, I'm not worried about you. Not with your soul. Don't worry. It's Yom Kippur."

There was a pause. Louie continued, "You really want to know what I think? I would do it, but you're a *cohen*, a priest. I always said that you were more religious than I am. You won't do it."

"You're right," Kagan said with no great enthusiasm.

"Moe, it's late. We better get off the phone."

"Yeah."

They wished each other a good fast. After he had hung up, tears began to flow. Fran, concerned and solicitous, put her hand on his shoulder.

"Kagan?" she inquired gently. She always called him "Kagan" when she was worried about him. "Kagan, what's wrong?"

"Nothing, Fran, nothing," Kagan said as he dabbed at his eyes.

"Why are you crying then?"

"They're good people, Fran. They're good people. They would never hurt you," he explained.

"Then why cry, darling?"

"You don't understand," Kagan said softly. "They just wouldn't hurt you. They're good people."

Fran didn't understand. Perplexed, she returned to the kitchen and served the chicken soup. Kagan came in and sat down.

"Lieberman," Fran said purposefully changing the

topic as Kagan continued to wipe his eyes with a napkin, "said the chicken was so sweet it would be like eating licorice."

"Like eating licorice?" Kagan repeated in nauseated amazement. "And he wonders why he doesn't have more customers. Like eating licorice. That sounds awful."

After a pause, Kagan shook his head despairingly. "Like licorice. . . . I guess it doesn't always pay to advertise." What a crazy guy that Lieberman was. He was always trying to get Kagan to go to Gamblers Anonymous. What did Kagan need that for? Those people have no backbone so they have to lean on each other. My God, would I be embarrassed. What do I have in common with them? I gamble. They gamble. So what? If I wanted to quit, I would quit. And I could quit. It's that simple.

Of course, I'm broke. It's true, but so is the government and nobody seems very upset about that. And as long as I can afford your prices for kosher licorice, I mean chicken, and for meat, Lieberman, I can't be too broke. What a salesman! Chicken as sweet as licorice! What a thing to say about a bird before Yom Kippur.

"What are you thinking about, Moe?"

"About Lieberman. My spot is good for Monday. If we don't use the car this weekend, I'll give him the spot on Monday. Of course, we'll use the car, if it's running, but if we don't. . . ."

Kagan was amazed and delighted at the spontaneous responses that always bailed him out. Very often he opened his mouth and started a sentence with no idea what he was about to say, but something was always there. Often very good things indeed. Sometimes, it seemed to Kagan, his best things.

Occasionally, he thought that if Ozzie were cooperative and asked all the appropriate, quick little questions one after the other, Kagan might turn out to be a great thinker, or at least a powerfully sensitive social philosopher. Unfortunately, Ozzie wasn't cut out for that role and Kagan had to ask his own questions and wait around interminably for his own muddled answers.

Why was such a terrific quick thinker such a lousy medium thinker? Sensing that this was a medium-speed inquiry, Kagan didn't bother to wait for a medium muddled reply. Instead, Kagan looked at his pickle-green watch, a definitive act that dealt with the present — he'd better eat; suggested the future — Yom Kippur, *Kol Nidre*; and bespoke a difficult and unfair (even unsupportable) past — why should he, Kagan, get the hard questions? Immediately, Kagan felt better. Why shouldn't he? He could take Fate's best punches.

"Did the cleaner get the spot out?" Fran inquired.

Kagan had forgotten about that spot. He had backed into the shrimp dip at a party. Leave it to me; all my life I avoid shrimp, only to have it goose me in the *tuchis* at the Shelsingers.

Kagan got up and took off his jacket.

"No spot, hallelujah!"

But there was a cleaning ticket stapled onto the back, at the bottom of the seam. Kagan hungered to know the number on that ticket. He thirsted to unfasten it but in his present state he was afraid of giving himself away. Fran was no fool. It takes a hardy and wary breed to survive in Connecticut, miles from a dairy restaurant.

"Moe, may I ask you something?"

Fran carefully avoided looking at Moe. Her eyes remained fixed on the chicken she was about to cut.

"No, no!" Kagan interrupted, "don't use the knife with the serrated edge. You'll never get it off."

"Get what off?"

"The chicken," Kagan explained. "It's like licorice."

They both laughed. Fran stopped but Kagan continued, shaking his head in disbelief. He put his jacket
over a chair. The cleaner's ticket faced him.

"Moe, are you gambling?"

"Why do you ask?" he answered. "Because of what I
asked Louie?"

Fran nodded.

"If I were, do you think I would ask that in front of
you?"

Fran didn't answer. Kagan continued, "I heard the
rabbi talking in the *shtibl* and I didn't think I heard it
right, but I did. They have some pretty weird laws."

"I'm sorry. Forgive me for asking."

"That's all right. It's a natural question. May I ask
you something?"

"Sure," Fran answered, curious.

"Would you mind if I asked for a little ketchup on
my licorice?"

"No," she laughed, "but, Moe, that's pretty spicy
stuff before a fast. Are you sure?"

"Just a little to take the edge off the sweet stuff."

As soon as Fran left the table and turned to enter the
kitchen, Kagan fumbled for his jacket and unfastened
the cleaner's ticket. It fell, numbered side down, into
his hand. His heart pounding, he pawed at the ticket
lying in his palm, finally managing to turn it over.
Thank heavens, he sighed. It was not five — seven —
three — four. Kagan quickly crumpled it up and flipped
it into the waste can. Thank God.

"Why are you smiling, Moe?"

"I think we are about to invent strawberry licorice,"
he said.

Terrific, it wasn't the number! Nobody bets cleaning

numbers. Laundry, maybe. Katzi's, certainly. My God,
I should have called Katzi. He would have appreciated
it. Laundry, maybe; cleaners, never! Who wants to be
taken to the cleaners? Oh my God, the number! Should
I have bet the number?

The arrival of the ketchup dispelled his confusion
over the number. Kagan looked at the dull-red sedentary sauce. It seemed so distant from its origins, fresh
ripe tomatoes. Old tomatoes in new bottles. Kagan was
suddenly depressed. The tomato is poor and happy in
the country — and breaks its neck to make it to the city,
and what happens? It gets pickled, stewed, spiced,
preserved, pulverized, and stuffed into a glass bottle
where it sits like red sludge. Kagan wanted to lean over
and in whispered tones ask the tomatoes if they had
been the first in the family to go to college. Kagan
knew. Listen, I know. Everybody thinks you have it
made. You're under glass where the bugs can't get you.
You have a nice clear bottle; plenty of light, no dark
corners, a label to call your own. Oh, and every time
you call your family up, they want to know how the
ketchup is doing — so what's new in the bottle? Ten
pounds of preservatives; how could anything be new
in the bottle? No, Kagan thought sadly, you can't tell
them that. So you hardly call and everyone thinks you
never think of them and you're a snob.

"You changed your mind?"

"No, it's late," Kagan said aloud. He pounded a little
ketchup onto his boiled chicken, but it slid off the wet,
steaming flesh. With a fork Kagan speared a piece and
spun it in the ketchup as if he were eating spaghetti. As
he chewed it, he thought it tasted more like chicken-
tomato soup than ketchup. That thought cheered him.
There are a few possibilities in the old bottle yet.

"We better finish up."

"Yes."

They cleaned up and in preparation for the fast, brushed their teeth. It was one of the few times, perhaps the only time, Kagan brushed his teeth. Fran had to do it or she would be very uncomfortable. Kagan did it because he found it a pleasing modern ritual: Crest before *Kol Nidre.*

As they were about to wish each other an easy fast before leaving, Kagan shouted, "The shoes!"

They dashed back into the bedroom and rummaged about the closet for their rubber-soled shoes. Fran put on her white tennis shoes and Kagan laced on his old, black, high-cut basketball sneakers.

## 4

AS they left their building, Fran turned toward the Conservative synagogue where the *chazan* sang and the rabbi spoke. Kagan turned left, down West End Avenue, toward the *shtibl*, his small Orthodox synagogue, where the *chazan* chanted *Kol Nidre* and everybody prayed. Kagan felt smooth and loose as he loped toward *Kol Nidre* in his sneakers. Maybe those crazy black kids know what they are doing, after all. Kagan knew he was no kid; he fancied that he moved like an old Knick. Dick Barnett, perhaps, suiting up for a little pick-up game in practice. You boys are going to see that the old man can still make it happen. He looked at his pickle-green watch and hurried. It was late. Of course, because it was late and he was in a hurry, who had to show up and bother him?

"I thought you'd never get out of there," Ozzie said.

"You know women, Ozzie."

"Kagan, if you run like hell, you can make it," the angel rasped.

"Look who's talking about hell!"

"Kagan, I know who's running. It's worth fourteen thousand at least. Maybe more."

"No, Ozzie! I don't bet on *Shabbes* and I don't bet on Yom Kippur. It's not my thing. I'm sure you're right, but it's not my thing."

"It's the law!" the angel countered.

"I know it's the law and I do the best I can with the law, but. . . ."

"Kagan," Ozzie pleaded softly, "it's your last chance. Think of the charity you can give with it."

This last remark stabbed Kagan. The thought of charity made Kagan very uncomfortable. Not only did he not give because of his precarious financial state, but, worse, he had become a financial basket case, mercilessly soliciting funds from, well, from anyone. Kagan didn't discriminate. Oh, he thought, it would be nice to give charity. After all, didn't Prayer, Penitence, and Charity avert the Evil Decree? Five — seven — three — four to the Evil Decree!

"Ozzie, I'm sorry. I can't."

"Kagan," the angel mocked, "you still believe that God will print the winning ticket after Yom Kippur? Kagan, five — seven — three — four has to win tonight if you play it. And I'll give you five superfectas for every ticket you buy."

Kagan stopped dead in his tracks, but his heart started dancing like a beggar at a Rothschild wedding.

The angel continued, "Have I ever promised you anything I didn't deliver?"

"No," Kagan said softly. It was true. Ozzie was one devilishly stubborn, cheap angel, but once he gave his

word, that was it. Ozzie, Kagan suspected, was an angel
from the old school and Kagan respected him for it.
Whatever you might say about Ozzie (he was a lousy
advertisement for angels!), he kept his word. Five
superfectas! Five superfectas on only one ticket! *Gevalt!*
If I parlay the winnings, I'll wind up a millionaire! A
billionaire! So long, penury! Goodbye, woe! Hello, charitable gift-giving! The numbers were warming up in his
head. He could feel the fever throbbing. Deep in the
medulla oblongata (it was the only precise term he
knew above the spinal cord), he could feel his nerves
firing, like distant artillery in a Russian novel. Although
distant, the firing pattern was perfectly discernible:
five — seven — three — four.

"Run, Kagan! Run!"

"Ozzieeeeeee," Kagan mourned in heartfelt sorrow
for both himself and the angel, "I can't!"

Kagan hurried toward the *shtibl* but the magic had
disappeared from his step. The old black, Bob Cousy
sneakers didn't help at all. He felt the hard, torturous
pavement against his feet. The jarring cascaded up his
legs into his suddenly aching joints where it was stoically absorbed with all the other bruising crashes Kagan
had sustained in a lifetime of running this way and that
at the last minute, always the last minute and for what?
For this and that! His soon-to-be arthritic hips (thank
God, Kagan sighed, it shouldn't be cancer) absorbed it
all with a shrug of the pelvis. The curb is high; the
sidewalk is hard. So what else is new?

In his head and mind, though, Kagan wasn't terribly
despondent. Usually, *klop!* it all hit Kagan in the head,
but now, with a curious gaze, Kagan looked about from
the crow's nest as beneath him the shabby, creaky,
degenerating ship of his body labored toward some
unknown landfall. Kagan was curious, like a child who

releases the safety brake on his father's car and enjoys the sudden change of state from rest to motion without considering that the car must stop somewhere and he does not know how to drive. Thus Kagan moved toward *Kol Nidre*. He turned onto Ninety-first Street.

With his slowly accelerating gait, Kagan swung his head to the left and saw the chimpanzee in the window. It was a very famous monkey. Larger-than-life pictures adorned the apartment walls: the chimp wearing a funny chef's hat with Johnny Carson, the chimp in a sailor suit with Fred Astaire. Now, however, the chimp's glory was past, relegated to the great, fuzzy black-and-white blow-ups on the wall behind him in his trainer's office. The chimp sat in the window watching the Jews run to *shul* Erev Yom Kippur. His long, hairy, tired arms dangled below his motionless feet. Kagan was struck by the ape's soft, tender non-complaining eyes. This chimp knew what *tsouris* was. He had all his fingers and toes, thank God. He could see and hear. Sometimes sirens frightened him. No, it must be something else, something deeper.

With that old face, Kagan thought, I bet this monkey would like to hear *Kol Nidre*. Who in the *shtibl* would believe that a monkey would enjoy *Kol Nidre*? Kagan smiled at the thought of a new photograph on the wall: the chimp in a prayer shawl standing next to the rabbi. (Today you are a Bic Banana!) It might do the *shtibl* some good.

"Ozzie, are you still there?"

"Kagan," Ozzie burst out, "straight to the corner and take a left to the OTB. It's not Yom Kippur yet. Don't worry if they're saying *Kol Nidre* without you. The law demands that *Kol Nidre* start before Yom Kippur proper."

"Ozzie, I had something else in mind. You know

how it is in the *shtibl*. People talk a little Torah, discuss wise commentaries, say heavy things about Yom Kippur."

Ozzie did not respond. Kagan continued, "Well, I never have anything to say, and since you're an angel and know the entire Torah, I thought you might give me a few things to say. Kind of make me look good."

"You want some Torah to say?"

Kagan didn't like the angel's tone. "Yes, that's right. You do know the whole thing."

"Kagan!" the angel bellowed, "I thought man had *chutzpah*, but you're too much."

"What did I do?" asked Kagan.

"You don't accept my Torah. You spit in the face of my Torah! And you ask to hear Torah from me?"

"What does one thing have to do with the other? Maybe if you teach me other parts of the Torah, then I'll come to accept yours. Doesn't it say somewhere you can study for the wrong reasons because in the end the Torah will bring you the right reasons? And anyway, didn't you tell me the world was created for the Torah?"

"Deceitful Son of Adam!" the angel hissed.

"Torah's Torah, isn't it?" Kagan replied.

"You want to hear Torah, Priest of Israel? I'll tell you my Torah. The Law, the Ten Commandments, was given to Israel on Yom Kippur."

"Oh, really, I didn't know that. Yeah, that's the kind of stuff I want to hear."

"Yes, Israel was given the Ten Commandments on Yom Kippur" — the angel's voice was rising in a crescendo — "because the first time they were given, Israel turned its back on them. The world was created for the Torah, Son of Man, and all the nations of the world save Israel refused it. And Israel, holy Israel, went to Sinai and in preparation for the Torah, what did the

Chosen People do? You built a golden calf! An idol! You denied Creation! You rejected God! And Moses himself destroyed the tablets. And we angels wept, we begged God to destroy Israel. 'What is man?' we cried, 'that he is worthy of Thy Torah?' Kagan, do you hear? Elsie the Cow is a childish way to sell ice cream! But for a god?! Even Howard Johnson and the Dairy Queen chased Elsie out of this idolatrous town. And the Holy Nation didn't even choose Elsie. They chose Daisy the calf. Shame! Shame! And yet. . . ."

"And yet?" Kagan beseeched.

In hurt and bitterness, the angel screamed, "And yet God thundered, 'Mercy! The show must go on!'"

"Yes," said Kagan, "the show must go on," and moving quickly now, he took the steps two at a time and entered the *shtibl*.

Kagan squeezed through the tightly packed room as the rabbi finished his talk. "We hope and pray and feel confident that our prayers will be accepted for us and for the entire nation of Israel." I must be the last one to arrive, Kagan thought. Last to *Kol Nidre*, last to *Shabbes*, first to *kiddush*. Not bad, there must be a routine there somewhere. First in *shul*, first in *kiddush*, first in the pockets of his coreligionists. First to pray, last to pay, in the *mikveh*, all the way.

Kagan reached for a *tallis*. As he was about to don the prayer shawl, he stopped. He had just remembered that he had forgotten. Every year he forgot.

"Bienstock, do you make a blessing putting on the *tallis*?"

"Yes, make the blessing."

Kagan nodded his head in appreciation, quietly murmured the blessing, and draped the prayer shawl about him.

"It's a funny thing. Every year I forget. It's almost a

custom or something the way I forget. I forget religiously," Kagan joked, but Bienstock, his eyes closed,
was opening his old, worn prayer book to *Kol Nidre.*

Kagan felt warmly toward the gently swaying furrier.
And he felt warmly toward the old *machzor,* the ancient,
large prayer book for the Day of Atonement. Kagan had
always liked the old-style prayer books with their sol-
emn, mottled covers and their frayed, yellowing pages.
His grandfather had had a *machzor* like that. It was his
father's, "your great-grandfather's — a wedding gift."
After the old man's death, Kagan had asked about it but
no one seemed to know what had happened to it. It was
a shame. A *machzor* like that could give you a jump on
the service. Kagan sensed that by now it could almost
pray by itself and he would have only to turn the pages
and chant "Amen." Maybe, Kagan thought, it will turn
up yet. Aunt Yetta might have come across it. I'll call
her after the holiday.

The *shtibl* was very still. Kagan hurried into the
small chamber between the synagogue's main room
and the women's section. This adjunct to the men's
section wasn't really even a room. Architecturally, it
was part of the same long narrow room that housed the
women's section. Functionally, however, it was separated from the women's room by a waist-high wooden
railing with a curtain above it. Usually eight or ten
men, including Kagan, sat around a table, but tonight
was not a usual night. The table had been moved out
and in its place stood several additional chairs. When
Kagan entered, only one final chair was available. He
climbed through the small group of familiar and not so
familiar people to the unoccupied seat. "We didn't
think you were going to make it," Benny said.

"Who didn't?" Kagan asked with conviction.

Someone *klopped* the reading table with his open

hand. Everyone became quiet with anticipation. A moment later the *chazan* began to chant quietly.

"In the heavenly assembly. . . ."

The decorum was shattered by half the congregation calling out, "the earthly assembly." The *chazan* himself was *klopping* the reading table in righteous, even surly, indignation. The rabbi emerged from under his *tallis*, raising his arms in smooth patting gestures to quiet the congregation, as if all of Israel were stuck together like dough and a little pat here or there was all that was needed to prepare the loaf of Israel for its natural ferment, *Kol Nidre*.

Kagan laughed. He had a sense of tradition that embraced such catastrophes. The same thing happened every year — like clockwork, like Yom Kippur itself — since in some books this introductory formula to *Kol Nidre* read, "In the heavenly assembly and in the earthly assembly," and in others it was the reverse. Every year the same tumult occurred as the holiest day of the year began. Kagan wondered if the heavenly assembly had similar problems. He made a mental note to ask Ozzie.

"Listen, Benny," Kagan heard himself saying, "you know that chimp down the street? I think he's Jewish."

Before Kagan could explain or even before Benny could react, the earthly assembly had quieted down and the *chazan* had begun *Kol Nidre*.

Kagan listened to the sounds with a quiet heart. Although the "ay" wasn't a particularly soothing sound in itself, all together, "*Kol nidray, veassaray, vacharamay, vechinuyay, vekinusay*" had a soothing effect like the rabbi's patting gesture. Kagan heard the fearful necessity: life is perilous but it must go on. *Kol Nidre* makes it go with all those "ays" as in "*Oy vay!*" You can make it in such a difficult and crazy world.

Kagan put his *tallis* hoodlike over his head. He rarely did so, but the warmth of the *chazan*'s hushed tones seemed to welcome the intimacy of the prayer shawl about his head. Kagan felt that they all were one congregation. All standing together before God on the eve of the holiest day of the year, Yom Kippur, the Day of Atonement. All equal.

You can't tell the players without a scorecard, Kagan had joked, but he knew that you didn't need a scorecard to tell the name of this game — life or death. It was obvious from the uniforms. Some were wearing shrouds, but not Kagan. (Theatrical or not, there's a limit!) When Kagan asked why, he was told, "We wear white to be like the angels. The angels wear white and they don't eat; they sing God's praises all day."

Kagan couldn't buy that after hanging around with Ozzie. It's true Ozzie didn't eat, and for all Kagan knew, Ozzie wore white, but it certainly wasn't any shroud. More likely a turtleneck. As for praying all day, there wasn't much chance of that unless you counted his praying to get laid. If we're like the angels, Kagan thought, a pity on us.

In the old days people didn't run around like the angels on Yom Kippur; they were just afraid of death. They wore shrouds to get their heads together, not for some heavenly costume ball. Kagan remained a traditionalist: he was afraid of death and he admitted it. As for being an angel, well, Ozzie could have it. Where was Ozzie? Strangely enough, Kagan had never seen him (heard him really) on any Yom Kippur. Maybe everybody playing angel by praying all day embarrassed him. Who knows, he never comes into *shul* anyway.

Kagan's reflections ceased as his eye caught the white woolen *tallis* hanging near his face. Up close he could see the rough woolen weave, somewhat uneven but regular. He found it very reassuring that all those coarse, rough fibers could come together to form a sacred garment, a *tallis*. He wanted to reach out and touch his fellow Jews, but his hands cradled his *machzor*. Instead he looked down at the page, and as he did so he heard the *chazan* begin the repetition of *Kol Nidre* in a more forceful voice.

Kagan surrendered himself to the prayer. He no longer felt the need to reach out and touch his brethren for they were already in contact through the "ays" of *Kol Nidre*, those unlikely sounds of comfort and sustenance that connected each Jew to his fellow. Kagan began to sway with the congregation as if they all were physically attached. His mind relaxed, experiencing directly and understanding indirectly. At the same time that he was hearing, indeed saying *Kol Nidre* with all his heart, in some mysterious way that did not contradict his full participation he was also intellectually aware of the paradox that this most sacred prayer, expressed through the softest and the most fragile utterances of the communal heart, was also a complex legal formulation — oaths, vows, pledges, null, void! He could hardly understand the English translation, but he knew what it meant: although people are human and God is divine, man is made in God's image, and on Yom Kippur man's aspirations are divine. Don't we dress like angels? Aren't we afraid of death? People try their best, but they are people and their performance is human. Oh, so human! Kagan could write the book on that routine; what man couldn't?

Kagan prayed and in his praying he intuited the message of *Kol Nidre*: life is a sacred paradox. We are created in the image of God, but we are cast in the mold of dust and are subject to the rules of both. The only way to realize our image is to understand our mold.

Our mold is a year with hundreds of days filled with a myriad particles of dust that we might mistake for ourselves or what we should be. It is a mold of vows and oaths and nulls and voids. A mold that demands atonement and demands life so that our image can be liberated.

As Kagan swayed and chanted the ancient formulation, he felt fulfilled as a man of the people; for tonight they were all men of the people. Kagan swelled with the magic of community. They were all attached by the reality of *Kol Nidre*, the weave of the *tallis*, the furs of Bienstock, the wool remnants of Mr. Isaacson, the calming pats of the rabbi — and, yes, even the remedial-reading tests of Mr. Maurice Kagan, Room 204. Each person is unique and yet a necessary part of the whole. Again the paradox: humanity is only common when it is uncommon for we are all in God's image unique. Kagan prayed — with humility and with hope — as the *chazan* burst into full voice for the final repetition of *Kol Nidre*.

The *chazan* and congregation, still concentrating intently, then asked communally and responsively that the people of Israel be forgiven for their sins. The *chazan* intoned the prayer recited at the beginning of every festival: "Blessed art Thou who has given us life . . . and permitted us to arrive at this season." People began talking in a wave of relief that swept through the *shtibl*. Relief that Yom Kippur had begun and an intense emotional and spiritual high, *Kol Nidre*, had been reached. Some sat down only to stand up again as their neighbors reminded them of the need to recite a certain Sabbath psalm. Again someone in the main room *klopped* the reading table. Although the more boisterous quieted down and the service continued, a low murmuring persisted.

Kagan remained standing after the Sabbath psalm, his *tallis* over his head. He did not remove it even though it wasn't his thing. The hooded-figure look conjured up for him more the medieval Christians persecuting Jews than it did the Semitic men of the desert. But tonight he wanted to remain under the *tallis*'s influence. Only reluctantly did he even turn the page.

Benny leaned over and took his ten-year-old son's *machzor*. Turning to the right page, he said, "Look inside a little bit. This is Yom Kippur."

"How many times did we say that?" his son asked.

"What?"

"*Kol Nidre*," the child said.

"You were here. How many times did you hear it?" Benny asked the boy.

The boy sat with an embarrassed smile.

"Do you think we said it once? Five times? Fifty times? You must have heard something."

"Three or four, I guess," answered the boy.

"Three. Look. See here in the *machzor* it says 'three times,'" Benny said, showing him the place. The father sat back and continued, "This isn't the bakery where you pick a number, any number. This is a *shul*. Look in the *machzor* instead of daydreaming and you'll learn. You think you're at the track with Kagan where you can pick any number? You're not. We read *Kol Nidre* three times. It's a triple. Not a single, not a double, not a. . . . What do they call it when you pick the first four horses in order? Kagan, what do they call that?"

But Kagan couldn't answer. The question had unleashed it all. He blinked his eyes but he still saw the four horses pounding towards him. They had just started the race at the rear of the ladies' section and they were already running 5 — 7 — 3 — 4. He could see the horses straining at the hard metal bits in their long, tender mouths. Behind the pounding hooves, he could see the wheels of the sulkies. They were roaring through the women's section. Kagan wanted to scream, "Duck!" but the horses didn't touch the women. Kagan thanked God for sparing Mrs. Bienstock, the furrier's mother, as the lead horse (what a bright clear five on his side!) dashed through her. Such fury certainly would have trampled such an old woman, who as a child had lived through the Kishiniv pogroms. But Kagan's mind did not remain for long on the old praying woman. His attention quickly returned to the phantom of Yonkers Raceway. The entire race was before him: the horses were trotting the entire race almost in place. Kagan saw the grandstands and the infield swirl by. The six-branched electric candelabra in memory of the six million became the tote board as the trotters pounded into the backstretch still 5 — 7 — 3 — 4. Kagan saw the apparition sliding slowly forward in its pantomimed frenzy.

The *mechitzah*, the gauzelike curtain (in the theater they had called it a scrim) separating the men's section from the women's, was the finish line! In his astonishment and fear, Kagan couldn't speak. He didn't even know for whom he should root! How could he feel anything but terrible if 5 — 7 — 3 — 4 won? He could have won a fortune, really cleaned up — plus Ozzie's payoff for him. And yet — wouldn't it be something if that number won?

Kagan sat in great amazement and near terror as if he were witnessing some fundamental defining of the universe. He had no idea what it meant, but he sensed that it was terribly important to him, to all sorts of people and places and creatures and things that he could but dimly imagine. Many things would be irrevocably determined by this event. He sat there as if he were witnessing the formulation of the laws of nature: gravity goes either up or down, gentlemen, there can be no other solution.

The lead horse, a large gray creature, charged through the finish line, the unruffled, unmoved curtain of separation. Five, Kagan muttered to himself. A medium-sized brown horse elegantly crossed the finish line a length behind. Seven, said Kagan, registering its arrival. Three and four, running neck and neck, were a little further back. Kagan couldn't believe how close they were. First one horse would edge ahead temporarily as it leaned into its stride — only to be nosed by the other. Three was on Kagan's left, and as they came within a foot of the curtain three seemed to have a slight but definite lead. Five — seven — three — four was going to win the superfecta! It was really going to happen! Kagan's heart beat fiercely, his mouth was dry, his knees were weak. Thank God he was sitting down.

Just then, in the back row of the men's section, to Kagan's right, where number four was driving toward the finish, a not so familiar face stood up, pushed back his half of the curtain, and asked, "Do any of the ladies need a *machzor*?" He pushed the finish line into the nose of number four! Three had been winning! Three had been ahead, but four hit the finish line first! Or had been hit by it?! Kagan couldn't believe his eyes. How could it be? He stood up and looked over to the memorial tote board. It was flashing the results: 5 — 7 — 4 — 3! Kagan collapsed back into his seat in stupefaction. He turned to see if anyone had claimed a foul, but he couldn't tell. Benny's oldest son was in the way. Kagan sat motionless as if he were returning to earth in some kind of a time capsule. He heard a voice calling his name and turned around.

"Moe," Benny was asking, "what's the name of the crazy bet?"

"It was close, Benny. It was close," Kagan shuddered.

"Yeah, it's close as anything in here. It's those women back there. If you open a window, they go crazy. They sit there in eighty-degree weather with their coats on. Every year I try to open the window and they ask me if I want to kill them."

"What do you answer them?" Schwartz asked.

"I tell them the truth. I think they're crazy, but I don't want to kill anybody," Benny answered.

"Benny, you're a natural diplomat," Schwartz commented.

"Say, Kagan, what do you call that bet?" Benny asked again.

"A superfecta," Kagan replied drily, but the word quickened his juices. Kagan turned to Schwartz. "Say, who is that guy?" he whispered.

"What guy?" Schwartz asked in a regular tone of voice.

"Sh!" Kagan hissed, not wanting to embarrass the man.

Just then the man squeezed by them. He was an older man, perhaps an old man. It was hard to tell for sure. The skin color was good, but the flesh was a little sunken. His features, too, looked as if they had known more precise days, but they still weren't bad. In the right kind of professional photograph they might still look strong. Once they must have been "chiseled," and now, rather than "weathering" gracefully under the temporal elements, they had caved in a little. Gravity pulls down; the whole face seemed to sag a little.

Kagan watched him work his way through the main room to the men's room. After he had disappeared, Kagan again asked his question.

"Who is that guy?"

"I don't know," Schwartz said, revealing a trace of aggravation, "but the next time he borrows a *machzor*, maybe he won't be in such a hurry to give it away."

"Yeah?" Kagan asked, amused at the idea of the not so familiar face giving away Schwartz's extra prayer book. "How many can you use at once?"

"Yeah, well, actually I asked if he wanted one. He didn't have any."

"Oh, a socialist after all," Kagan said, but then he remembered his question. "Who is he?"

"He's a Jew, a plain Jew. Who knows who he is? I don't think anybody here does. He comes every year for Rosh Hashanah and for Yom Kippur. He'll be here tomorrow and then we won't see him until next year."

"Just like that? He comes and no one knows who he is?"

"Maybe the rabbi knows. None of us does."

The older man was finding his way back to the small room. It took him some time to pick his way among the densely packed Jews. When he finally came up to the men, Kagan spoke to him.

"I saw what you did," Kagan said mysteriously.

"What's that?" the older man asked innocently.

"Moving the curtain there."

The older man smiled. "Those are the breaks," he chuckled. "Some days you can't get a *mitzvah*. No one needed a *machzor*."

"Yeah," Kagan said in true disappointment.

"As a matter of fact, it wouldn't have been my *mitzvah*. It's not my book. It's his," he said pointing to Schwartz. "You didn't mind my offering it to the ladies, did you? I should have asked."

"No, not at all," Schwartz lied.

Kagan stood and offered the old man his hand.

"My name is Moe Kagan."

"Good," the old man said, shaking Kagan's hand.

The older man returned to his seat and to Schwartz's *machzor*.

Schwartz smiled at Kagan.

"I guess he liked your name. It never sounded like much to me."

"Yeah," Kagan said, agreeing with the first part of Schwartz's remark. "I wonder who he is."

"You really think he can loan you money?" Schwartz needled.

"That's all you think I think about, isn't it? Well, you're wrong."

Kagan was truly offended. That's all they think I look for in people, the dollar sign. If these wise guys ever needed money the way I do, they would kill for it. I can't even greet a stranger on Yom Kippur without everybody making a joke out of it.

"Moe, I didn't think you wanted to ask him where he gets his suits."

Kagan smiled. That was some strange suit. An old, heavy, rumpled dark green wool job. When and where did he get that? That is some old suit! He must be able to afford one newer than that. Who is he anyway? Kagan wondered. Maybe he wears it because he wants to. Maybe he is an eccentric millionaire who comes to pray here where he is anonymous so that he can concentrate on his prayers. At his big synagogue they probably kiss his ass because of all the money. That figures. Boy, do they kiss ass for money! Everywhere. Don't they think God knows what is going on? That's probably why he is here posing as a poor man: he is embarrassed to stand before God on the high holidays with all those people pressing their lips to his *tuchis*. Still, it must feel pretty good the rest of the year.

Maybe he will give me eight or ten thousand to straighten myself out. What's it to him with his kind of money? If I had it, I would give it to him just to get a new suit, but what does he know about need? What a crazy idea, Kagan thought. How the hell is he going to straighten me out when all he can do is twist around the finish line?

As he thought about that finish line, the image of horse number four nosing out number three at the crooked finish line appeared before him in a freeze-frame instant replay. *Gevalt*, thought Kagan, this is better than NBC. The image faded and Kagan began to wonder who really would win the superfecta. He looked at his pickle-green watch. It was early, too early. The race wouldn't be run for at least another hour.

Kagan tried to return to his prayers, but it didn't work. The wiggly Hebrew print kept turning into horses before his eyes and the page numbers distracted him to the point of madness. How do they expect a person to pray with numbers on every page? he moaned. I'd better settle down and then maybe I'll be able to pray a little.

He sat back and listened to Danny, Benny's older son, and his friend talk about school. They were in college together. Freshmen? Sophomores? Time passed quickly, too quickly. Kagan was once in school. Apparently they were both taking biology. Becoming doctors, perhaps. Become doctors, Kagan thought, you make a fortune, you don't work too hard, and everyone calls you "doctor." They began discussing the dissection they had performed earlier in the day.

"Through all that stuff, I couldn't find the pancreas," Danny said.

"They sure felt funny, didn't they?" his friend said.

My God, Kagan thought, what's wrong with those

kids? That stuff is disgusting. And to discuss it in *shul* on Yom Kippur! Benny should tell his kid to stop. Boy, kids today — they really are different. And these are the nice ones yet. Imagine what the others talk about? When we were kids, we didn't talk like that in *shul*. We didn't talk; if we did, we'd get a bat in the head. Sometimes maybe we used to whisper about something important like a World Series. But a biology class, a dissection! We didn't even discuss that stuff in biology class. It's too disgusting.

Oh, the frog that Kagan had to dissect! He couldn't eat breakfast before school. Kagan's mother wanted to know, "Where does it hurt that you can't eat breakfast?" The smell stuck to our hands like glue. Every morning that half-cut frog lying there. No wonder surgeons wear gloves. That sticky, smelly, spongy stuff.

Kagan couldn't stand it and Hershkowitz, his lab partner, claimed that he couldn't either. Since Hershkowitz wanted to be a doctor, he was certain that he could get used to it but not right away. "These things take time," he said. Yeah, they only had until Friday so Kagan had to pay him, the *momzer*. Thank God, the baseball season had begun. Three batters — six hits; a quarter a shot. Lining up action, Kagan ran around the cafeteria with such frenzy that the class adviser thought he was running for the student senate. Some senator he would have made. He was lining up bets to pay Hershkowitz two dollars a period to dissect that frog.

What a con man. The *momzer* became a big surgeon and charges a thousand dollars an hour. If I ever need open heart surgery, Kagan thought, I'm going to deduct the ten bucks I already paid him. What a *momzer*! No shame.

Kagan had shame. Sometimes Kagan thought it was his specialty. Kagan wasn't much on guilt, but he was very big on shame. It made for a funny world. Those little guilts that hounded others didn't afflict Kagan. Without hesitation, he did things that others feared — the job had not been created on which Kagan wouldn't clock out early. But Kagan could never do the big shameful things that others did furtively even if he would never be suspected. Take right now, for example. Kagan kept wondering what the results of the race would be, and he was ashamed that that was what he was thinking about, but he couldn't get it out of his mind. Again he checked his watch. Would they finish at the track the way they had finished in the *shtibl*? A chill ran down his spine. It was so crazy that Kagan wouldn't bet against it. In his mind, of course. On Yom Kippur Kagan didn't bet. What was Kagan to do? He couldn't bet on Yom Kippur and that was it.

How could Ozzie have been wrong? That part didn't make much sense. Ozzie never lied, at least so far he hadn't. And if Ozzie were going to tell a lie, why would he tell one that Kagan was sure to discover? Then Kagan remembered that the race had not been run yet and, perhaps, Ozzie was right. Kagan's sentiments, however, lay with the *shtibl* finish. That way he would not have lost anything by not betting. More importantly, Kagan sensed that he had witnessed something of great importance that he wanted to have confirmed.

Kagan looked around in surprise to discover that everyone was standing for the silent devotion midway through the evening service. Had he been daydreaming for so long? Apparently. Everyone became quiet as the *chazan* concluded. And then, total quiet, which soon gave way to a hushed murmur of prayer. Kagan put his *tallis*, hoodlike, over the top of his head. Earlier, during *Kol Nidre*, it had helped him to concentrate. This time, however, as his eye examined the rough woolen weave, in contrast, his mind envisioned the smooth, colorful racing silks worn by a jockey or a driver.

Kagan removed the *tallis* from his head. It was a little cooler, but not much. Benny was right: it is close in here. How can those women keep their coats on? Couldn't they open the window a little bit?

Kagan tried to concentrate but could not. He attempted to vocalize the words since sometimes that helped. It forced him to read every syllable, but even that didn't help. His mind was a blank and he knew why — the race. Kagan tried again, but by the time he got to the bottom of a page, he had no idea whether he had read it or not. This, of course, disturbed Kagan, but it wasn't as if he were not trying to pray. He was trying very hard; he had even put his *tallis* over his head again although it was stifling hot under it. How much could he do? He was a prisoner of lousy concentration, a mental inmate of Yonkers Raceway, sentenced to the superfecta.

Kagan was wondering what he could do when he heard the hoofbeats. The dull echoing beats resounded at a slow, funereal pace. They drew closer and multiplied about him. Many dull, resonant poundings but all to the same slow, steady pace. What could they mean? In shame, Kagan removed the *tallis* from his head and looked about him.

Collectively immersed in private prayer, most had arrived at the Confessional and were pounding their hearts as they intoned, "We have sinned." He had mistaken this sound for hoofbeats. Kagan crawled back under his *tallis* and turned to the Confessional. He did not like to skip on Yom Kippur, but he couldn't pray anyway. At least he might try the Confessional.

"We have acted unfaithfully," Kagan cried with an urgency that he hoped would create a new reality of prayer. He pounded his breast. Without pausing, he continued, "We have betrayed you." He beat his heart again. "We have spoken slander." The beats, the pounding, still seemed like hoofbeats. Kagan raced through the first part of the Confessional but one horse kept pace with him. He arrived at the Confessional's summation and Kagan knew that he had plenty to confess. "Pardon our transgressions that we have committed before you unwillfully and willfully." The grievously heavy blow Kagan delivered to his heart on Yom Kippur sounded only like a larger horse pounding down the backstretch. Kagan tried to throw the horse off his trail. He pounded slowly. He beat quickly. He tapped softly. He thrashed harshly. His chest ached. His fist smarted but the horse remained with him, and whenever Kagan tapped softly or paused for a moment he heard all the other horses moving along at the sure, steady, penitent pace.

Kagan wanted to escape to someplace where he could thoughtfully consider all these strange events. Kagan knew that he was not the king of concentration, but this was ridiculous even by his standards. Maybe, he thought, these are the sounds of the race that I witnessed earlier. What good was that? Even if they were, such bizarre fragmentation was very unsettling. To think that such seemingly haphazard phenomena could occur any time to complete some earlier experience! He felt like sitting down, but he remained standing. If he couldn't pray with the congregation, at least he could stand with them. He stood with them and among them, encouraging them and attempting not to listen to the insistent sounds of contrition, which in his ears steadfastly remained equine.

Only after the majority of the congregation had finished the prayer and sat down did Kagan do so. As the congregants calmly sat waiting for the *chazan* to begin, conversation casually returned. Kagan felt better as the beats ceased, and when Danny and his friend returned to their dissection, he was immeasurably appreciative. Medicine saves lives, he thought, and that is commanded on Yom Kippur; a sick man must eat if a doctor tells him to do so. That is the *Halachah*. Kagan prepared to listen attentively to their uplifting discussion until Benny interrupted.

"First of all," Benny told them, "that's a little disgusting. It may be important, but you don't talk about it in *shul* where everyone else has to listen. And you certainly don't discuss it on the night of *Kol Nidre*. It is Yom Kippur. We have an entire book, the whole *machzor*, to discuss."

"Hey, Benny," Kagan said. "Isn't it a *mitzvah* to save lives on Yom Kippur?"

"Yeah. What does that have to do with anything?" Benny asked.

"Well, if they become doctors, they might save lives. You never know. They'll need to know about biology."

"Kagan, are you out of your mind? These kids had a basic dissection today. Half the kids in America do it."

"Yeah, I know," Kagan admitted, "but you never know where it can lead."

"They can win the Nobel Prize after Yom Kippur," Benny said.

"You're too hard on them, Benny. It's not always so easy to concentrate. At least they're discussing life."

"Kagan, they're discussing life, but the wrong life. Today they should be discussing their own lives."

"On Yom Kippur I wouldn't remind God that I was chopping up his little creatures in the morning. He might like frogs. Some people bet on them, Moe, in jumping contests. Don't be so judgmental. How would you feel if they had dissected Secretariat this morning?" Schwartz remarked.

"Right away, you start in with the horses," Kagan retorted.

"Moe, tell the truth, I started with the frogs, I *finished* with the horses. Like you, Kagan. I finished with the horses," Schwartz answered, referring to Kagan's constant claim that he had quit gambling.

"Schwartz, you will note that the frogs were one of the plagues. I don't remember horses being mentioned anywhere," said Kagan, feeling better.

"The horse and his rider He threw into the sea," Schwartz quoted in Hebrew. "No, Kagan. The horses and Egyptian jockeys were drowned in the Red Sea. I guess they don't quote that out at Belmont."

Screw you, you judgmental son of a bitch, Kagan thought. These kids are trying to make something of themselves and everybody puts them down. Then they wonder why there's a generation gap. These kids should be encouraged. Some day they might do some good. Anyway, it's better than talking about the stock market.

"Anyway, it's better than talking about the stock market," Kagan said.

"I'm sure it is," Benny said. "What does that have to do with anything? Who's discussing the stock market?"

"Business in this country is holy. I bet on a horse and it's a scandal, but you buy a stock and they give you *maftir.*"

"Kagan, you are crazy," Benny said seriously, but without giving offense. He had often told Kagan that he was crazy. Kagan did not argue, but he did say, "Crazy. Yeah, I'm crazy. We'll see."

In the past, Kagan had not reacted because he had believed in perfect judgment. Not in this world, but some other time. Kagan was confident that God couldn't find Belmont worse than AT&T. At least at Belmont they took care of some dumb animals. God certainly approved of such care for his creatures. Kagan was certain of that. Kindness to animals was a great Jewish virtue. The Torah said if you see a donkey crouching under a burden, you should help it. Of course, when they read this, Kagan could not refrain from stating the law slightly differently. "If you see a donkey crouching under a burden, don't bet him unless all the others are carrying the same weight." At least some horses get a good home. If you give your money to Ma Bell, does she eat any better? A million more homes will have Touch-Tone phones and dialing will become a lost art. Kagan enjoyed the dial spinning around. There was something very dramatic about it. Round and round she goes; where she stops nobody knows.

No, Kagan never reacted when Benny called him crazy because Benny was sincere and some day they would both see. Now, however, he felt like answering Benny, "Yeah, and you don't know the half of it." He wanted to tell Benny, look, if you had an angel who is supposed to be perfect but, instead, tried to get you to bet on Yom Kippur and get himself laid the rest of the year; and you had a kosher butcher who was supposed to bankrupt you but, instead, tried to get you to go to Gamblers Anonymous, you wouldn't be so sane yourself. But who knows, they would all see. Lieberman, the butcher, included.

Someone opened the ark and they all stood up. Someone else closed the ark and they all sat down. The *chazan* arrived at "for we have sinned" and everyone beat his breast. Kagan leaned over to Danny and his friend. "And the beat goes on," he joked in a serious voice. They laughed and he would have continued talking with them (he feared heavy hoofbeats), but it was terribly inappropriate.

Kagan tapped his own heart gingerly but heard nothing. He listened to the others but only heard Jews beating their hearts on Yom Kippur night. He was elated; he felt as if he had overcome some great existential trial — until he looked at his watch. By now, the race was over. It had been run. That's why he didn't see or hear any horses. It was all over!

Kagan immediately became preoccupied with how he was going to find out the results. He had to find out; there could be no doubt about that. He couldn't go by the Off-Track Betting office. That wouldn't help. They had closed long ago. The night results wouldn't be in the window until tomorrow morning and by then he would go crazy. Normally, Kagan would turn on the radio at home "for the news" and just happen to get the results. Or if he were too nervous like tonight and Fran was certain to catch on, he would climb into his car and without turning on any lights sit in the friendly, enshrouding darkness listening to the results. That was what he would like to do tonight. Unnoticed but noticing, he could sit there waiting to hear the results. That's what he wanted to do all right, but there was no chance of that. Tonight was Yom Kippur and he wasn't about to turn anything on, radio, TV, or light bulb.

Oh, my God! He had promised to meet Fran at her synagogue. Inevitably, she finished later. The rabbi had to speak, the *chazan* had to sing, the choir had to sing. Last year Kagan had to wait in the back for half an hour. It almost drove him nutty. Last year he had prayed well, so what did he need an instant replay for? But tonight he would have enough time to get the results before he met her. Afterwards, there would be no chance. Even if they went for a walk, Kagan couldn't get that information without her noticing.

It would have to be before, but where? Kagan looked at his watch. What could he do? He could slip into a bar and try to hear the results on TV. If he were lucky, they might not ask him what he wanted to drink before he found out. But that meant he had to get lucky; they had to have the right channel and these days all the news shows were very hip; they weren't afraid of experimenting with the format. They could put the sports anywhere. It was outrageous! Some of those smiling idiots would tell you what the temperature had been (as if you didn't know) before they would tell you that a President had been shot. Benny thinks I'm crazy! Doesn't he ever watch the news? Just the market, probably.

No, he couldn't go into a bar. That trick was only good for the Triple Crown, run on *Shabbes* afternoons. For the Kentucky Derby, every TV in every bar in America was turned up full blast, every joint was packed, and every bartender and waitress watched, too. All you had to do was slip in right before the horses went to the post. After the Derby everyone would shout at once. (Believe it or not — it was worse than the *shtibl*; the rabbi should drop in for a Derby. It would make him feel better about what goes on here Yom Kippur.) And, shouting to no one in particular, Kagan would slip out of the bar unnoticed. But tonight they were sure to notice him. Nothing is happening and Moe Kagan enters wearing a hat, suit, and old-fashioned, high-cut, doesn't-anybody-here-remember-Bob-Cousy basketball sneakers. Not notice him! They'd probably ask for his autograph or call the cops — maybe both. (I'm sorry, folks. No autographs *Shabbes* and Yom Kippur.) But worse than all that would be their knowing that he was wearing rubber-soled shoes because of Yom Kippur. A *shandah* for the *goyim*!

Imagine what they would think — and say — about Jews! Not that they didn't think or say those things anyway, but he couldn't justify their libels. Better he should go crazy.

Who would know the winner of a superfecta? Ask the man who owns one. Obviously, a winner would know, but aside from him, who? All the players milling around on Broadway would know who won the race. Some might even know who came in second. But third and fourth? Forget it, yesterday's news. All they know is that they didn't win. Who would know? Of course, who else? Big Abe. That little man knew everything. Kagan glanced at his watch. It was getting late. Big Abe went home about now. And what if Big Abe wasn't on Broadway with his cigar and the usual crew discussing tomorrow's races? Kagan would have to get him at home, but later for that. Maybe he was still on the street.

Big Abe knew everything that was on the news or posted in the OTB. He carried a small transistor and never missed a news broadcast. Some inner clock told him when it was the hour or half past. No matter what Big Abe was doing, listening to, or saying, he would reach into his pocket and his transistor would come up to his ear. Big Abe's timing was so remarkable, he rarely heard an ad. Bingo, straight into the news. When the news was over, he flipped the radio off and shoved it back into his pocket. And he never forgot anything he heard. Big Abe just stood there, blinking his eyes, not because he was intimidated but because he always blinked his eyes as if he thought that after the next blink they might start working again. If they ever had. There was something about Big Abe that suggested he had been born with his thick lenses, blinking eyes, and a lit cigar. (A *rachmones* on his mother! Some birth

it must have been! There must be a routine there someplace.) What did Big Abe do before the transistor?
Eyeglasses and cigars have been around a long time,
but transistor radios are a recent invention.

Kagan enjoyed thinking about Big Abe. Big Abe would
give him the results so thinking about Big Abe seemed
to be solving his problem and it kept the numbers from
going crazy. Kagan could feel them throbbing in the
back of his head under his *yarmulke* whenever he
stood up or sat down, which was impossibly frequent
on Yom Kippur. The ark opens — up; the ark closes —
down. Kagan tried to focus on the little man's cigar. It
always looked like the cigar was leading the shuffling
little man down the street. (If Big Abe had been a
vocabulary word, he could only be homunculus —
Kagan couldn't put that on a blackboard without thinking of him.) Those long-cigarette ads — where the
cigarette was always bumping into something — had it
all wrong. Abe's cigar's virtue lay in its early warning
ministrations.

Big Abe had once walked into a gas station and
everyone had started yelling at him. "No smoking! You
want to blow us all to Kingdom Come?" Blinking, Abe
withdrew the small bouquet he was preparing to place
at the base of the nonleaded Exxon pump in memory
of his sister and asked if anyone could help him across
the street to the cemetery. Kagan smiled. He could
picture it all. Once on his way to Belmont he had
pulled into the gas station with Big Abe. Before he
could tell the attendant how much gas he wanted, the
guy growled, "For Christ's sake, keep him in the car."
There was such fear in his voice, Kagan thought the
guy was talking about a dog. "What are you talking
about?" Kagan had asked. "Him!" he said pointing to
Big Abe. They had never forgotten Big Abe, nor Kagan.

He made it a habit to buy gas there whenever he went out to Belmont. In a minor way, Kagan was a celebrity. "Jesus, that guy thought we were a cemetery!" "Oh, he's fine. Just the same." "Brother!"

Kagan would find out from Big Abe: five — seven — three — four as Ozzie maintained or five — seven — four — three as he, Kagan, had seen and heard. Kagan became nervous. Something was at stake, but what was it? He had the chill and the tingling, all right, but that was kid stuff. You could get that by watching TV or at the movies. Kagan had the real thing. His flesh and the encapsulating air around him seemed sensitized — even magnetized — to some inscrutable force that was at the very root of Action. But what was the Action? Kagan became nervous. He looked about. Thank God, they were almost finished. Big Abe, Big Abe would know. Kagan held onto Big Abe. The little, nearly blind man was unflappable (in this crazy world, yet), and that reassured Kagan. Big Abe would know; he knew everything. Although Kagan did not know who had won (indeed, he didn't even know what was at stake), the fact that Big Abe knew the results calmed him. Such a ready, constant, and available source of information suggested, at the very least hinted, that Kagan was on the right track — plugged in — not altogether unsuccessful in his attempts to negotiate passage through this absurd world. If information was present (and it was — ready, constant, and available), might not knowledge be present, perhaps within Kagan's grasp? And if information and knowledge, why not understanding? Kagan might be close without knowing it, the way Big Abe was across the street from the cemetery. Yes, why not?

Kagan was exhilarated by such a thought, but as he considered it, he was not quite so sanguine. Someone had told Big Abe where the cemetery was. Who would do such a thing for Kagan? And Big Abe had almost blown himself to Kingdom Come. Deep down, Kagan felt a quivering of recognition — there was more than a little self-destruction in his frantic life. Still, Big Abe had made it and Big Abe definitely knew the results! How could the results not be on the news? And yet, who wanted to go to a cemetery?

Kagan was aware of excitement in the *shtibl*. The *chazan* was singing the last *kaddish* in the bold holiday tune. There was a tune! Everyone hollered "Amen" and "*Yosher koach* — Congratulations" — at the end. A little like the Derby at Mooney's, come to think of it. The rabbi was announcing when the morning services would begin. Seven o'clock, everyone should come on time so they could begin promptly. As the congregation sang the final prayer, a short, lively rhythmic one, everyone relaxed. Everyone except Kagan. He removed his *tallis* so quickly that he almost knocked Danny and his friend over.

"Kagan, what's the rush? You can't eat supper," Danny said.

"Kid, I gotta see a man about a horse. It should never happen to you guys," Kagan replied earnestly.

Danny respected Kagan's devastating vulnerability. He did not answer other than to wish Kagan that he might be sealed in the Book of Life. Kagan shook his hand and returned the wish. Everybody was shaking hands now and exchanging wishes. They milled about unhurriedly; tonight there was no supper. Kagan had to make a break for it. What's the fastest way out of here? Through the women's section. Murmuring "*gut yontiff, gut yontiff*" in all directions, he headed toward the women's section. He had opened the gate and was about to step through the curtain when he felt a hand

on his elbow. Kagan turned to find himself facing the
not so familiar face who had earlier moved the finish
line. Kagan was impatient.

"You can ask them if they need a *machzor* now, but
you know what the answer will be," the older man said
smiling.

Kagan assumed that this was a joke. "Yeah, we're
done now. Who needs a book?" he replied.

"Of course," the man agreed, "we're done until
tomorrow."

"If they had enough *machzors* tonight, they'll have
enough tomorrow," Kagan said.

"Sure, why not?"

The older man released Kagan's elbow. Kagan said,
*"Gut yontiff, gut Shabbes,"* stepping through the curtain. But it was not so easy. The older man had grasped
Kagan's hand and was wishing him that he be sealed in
the Book of Life. Kagan had to step back through the
curtain to return his good wishes.

"It's a funny thing. Everybody runs out of *shul* like
it's a race. What kind of race could you have in *shul*?"

Kagan touched the older man's sleeve. "Yes, what
kind of race?" Kagan implored.

"What kind of race?" the older man shrugged. "Believe me, take it easy. People race, they don't even
know why or what for. Keep your shoes on!"

The older man turned to exchange greetings with
another not so familiar face.

Kagan stood there. Keep your shoes on, he repeated
to himself in amazement. Keep your shoes on! What
these old guys won't do with the English language. He
rushed through the women's section, almost trampling
old Mrs. Bienstock as she was bending over to put
away her *machzor.* Mumbling an apology and wishing
her a good inscription, he grasped her elbows to keep

her from falling over. When she was steadied, he rushed
out as the old woman surfaced to find no one near her.


## 5


KAGAN raced down Ninety-first Street toward Broadway. Keep your shoes on! Keep your shoes on! What
does he think I am going to do, run barefoot? Keep your
shoes on, Kagan repeated almost maniacally. Aware of
the insane repetition, he continued to engage in it
anyway. Keep your shoes on. Keep your shoes on. This
continued until Broadway, when he looked up to see
his butcher shop in the shadows and switched his
mindless chant to chicken as sweet as licorice —
chicken licorice — chicken licorice.

Next to the OTB, in front of the bar, he saw a group of
waiters, as he called them — always waiting for something. Waiting for a race to begin, waiting for a race to
end, waiting for an office to open, waiting for the results.
God forbid they should be just standing around re-
laxing. No, always waiting.

"Have you seen Abe?"

"Yeah. He just went home. He decided not to wait for
the paper."

Kagan tore off down the street. My God, he thought,
if I don't catch him before he gets home, I'll have to talk
my way past the guard without having him ring me up.

Kagan ran up Broadway and turned onto Ninety-
third, crossed Amsterdam, and saw a dull glow shuffling
along in the shadows. Kagan raced after Big Abe and
caught up to him under a street light in front of the
junior high school.

"Abe, Abe, wait a minute," Kagan called as he raced up.

Big Abe followed his cigar around to face the direction of the call.

"It's me, Abe, Moe Kagan."

Big Abe just nodded his head.

"Abe, you shouldn't walk on this side of the street. Somebody can jump out and grab you. There's nowhere to go. They have you against the fence here."

Kagan stopped talking and for a moment they just stood there. Finally, Big Abe spoke.

"You need money? How much?"

My God, that's what they all think. Money, money, money. He's no better than those jokers in *shul*. Worse, at least they don't smoke on Yom Kippur.

"Abe," Kagan said, "let me ask you something. You're a Jew. Why are you smoking on Yom Kippur? It's Yom Kippur! Yom Kippur!"

This last Kagan delivered with a sense of outrage and recrimination.

"Oh, yes?" Big Abe said with mild surprise. "It wasn't on the news."

"It wasn't on the news? Don't you have a Jewish calendar? Everybody has a Jewish calendar!"

"We don't have one," Big Abe replied.

"Why do you think I'm wearing these? To look like Bob Cousy?"

Kagan pointed to his sneakers and lifted one foot off the ground for Abe to see. Unseeing, Abe blinked reflexively in the direction of Kagan's feet.

"It's Yom Kippur!" Kagan pleaded.

"It wasn't on the news," Big Abe said evenly. "Maybe it'll be on tomorrow."

"Tomorrow might be too late."

"Maybe," Big Abe conceded. "What can I do for you

today?''

Kagan drew a deep breath.

"Abe, listen, you know I never bet on *Shabbes* or Yom Kippur, but what was the superfecta tonight?''

Kagan saw the cigar glow bright red as Big Abe drew on it.

"The 'perfecta?''

"Yeah, the 'perfecta!''

"It paid over fifteen thousand dollars.''

"Who won?'' Kagan asked hoarsely. "What was it, Abe?''

"It was five — seven — four — three,'' he answered.

Kagan gasped for breath. Five — seven — four — three! Five — seven — four — three! He stepped over to steady himself against the base of the street light. Kagan blinked his eyes. He blinked them again. Five — seven — four — three! Kagan could see only the numbers and then he blinked again and saw the freeze-frame finish for fourth with the not so familiar face pushing back the *mechitzah*-finish line into the number-four horse's face. Kagan collapsed against the street light.

"Moe, maybe you shouldn't fast. Come on up. I'll give you a glass of water. My wife can't fast either.''

Kagan silently hung onto the post. Then, as suddenly as he had collapsed, he struggled to his feet and grabbed Big Abe by his lapels.

"What about the finish? Did they say anything about that?''

"Moe, how did you know? I guess you heard them talking in front of the shop. It was a photo finish, all right, but no one knew it at the time. At the track and over TV they announced it as five — seven — three — four but then they developed the photo to confirm it and the photo had it five — seven — four — three.

Everybody who saw it on TV said it looked like the finish line was crooked, but the photo itself was very clear. Five — seven — four — three. Seeing is believing. No doubt about it. Clear as day. . . . Say, Kagan, are you all right?"

Kagan, still holding Big Abe's lapels, was motionless. The air in his lungs, nose, mouth and in front of his face had become magnetic. He couldn't breathe. He tightened his grip on Big Abe's lapels as if his hands grasping through the asphyxiating field could keep him from being enveloped and consumed by the Action Forces. Like so many other drowning victims, Kagan discovered that it is impossible to breathe with one's hands. Still, he remained attached to Big Abe's lapels until the short, blinking man calmly drew on his cigar, causing the lit end under Kagan's nose to glow red with combustion, sending a sharp intense surge of heat into Kagan's face. By reflex Kagan released Big Abe and stepped back.

"Kagan," Big Abe said solicitously, "come on up. I'll give you a glass of water. No one will know."

Kagan didn't hear the offer. As if drunk, he backed into the street lamp, grabbing the pole at the last moment to keep himself from falling.

"Kagan, are you all right?"

Kagan was still clutching the metal pole. The purposeful electrons pulsating inside toward the bulb high overhead were all right. Kagan, however, could not see or hear. The Action Forces had invaded his eyes and his ears. Something had been decided and Kagan didn't know what. He had sensed Reality and lost his senses. Kagan felt neither the pole that supported him nor fright at the loss of his senses. His senses had always misled him. What good were they now? He had watched and listened to the world all his life and what had he seen? What had he heard that could compare with to-night's events?

Aware of the Forces in his ears and eyes, Kagan straightened up. He had known from the moment they had invaded his apertures of perception that the only way to remove them was to assimilate them. "Out" was in. There was no other way to get them out short of chopping his head off. Kagan realized the sad, horrible, irrevocable truth: these Forces would have to be pushed, shoved, and forced through into his head, perhaps rearranging his mind and reorienting his soul in the process. Faced with the fear of change, the recognition of truth, what could Kagan do but hope it was all a mistake?

"Are you sure?" Kagan croaked.

The short, blinking man pulled his transistor radio out of his pocket and by the time Kagan leaned forward for an answer all he heard was that the Office of Economic Opportunity wasn't what it used to be. Kagan turned away and stiffly, almost blindly, moved down the street. Although turned on now, he couldn't see through his eyes or hear what was beyond his ears. Looking out from his old mind, he could see the Forces invading his eyes and he could hear them in his ears.

Arriving at the broad expanse of Amsterdam Avenue, Kagan did not pause but plunged off the curb into a swift wave of traffic racing with the synchronized green lights uptown. A taxi, avoiding a collision, shot forward to clear Kagan's path. Behind it a huge Greyhound bus heading north blasted a maniacal hissing toward Kagan and braked with shocking fury. The sudden swerve of the rushing bus threw the passengers up against the windows to see Kagan marching mechanically toward the rear wheels. The alert driver accelerated and the swerving bus surged into the middle lane. The colorful tin wall of license plates above the blast of noxious fumes escaped before Kagan arrived, and the bus flew up the avenue unbloodied and bound for Boston.

KAGAN arrived in front of Fran's Conservative synagogue, where services had just ended and the sidewalk held the well-dressed throng. The men were putting their *yarmulkes* into their pockets and the women were improving their grip on their purses. Kagan would have charged relentlessly into them had Fran not been on the steps.

"Moe, Moe, over here!"

Moe kept walking straight ahead.

"Moe, Moe!" she repeated.

Moe turned. Fran made her way through the crowd to his side.

"Kagan, are you all right?"

"It's you!" Kagan said in amazement that he could see and hear.

"Who did you expect?" she asked suspiciously.

"No one. Nobody."

"Why did you come here then?" she asked, confused and hurt.

He looked up to see the synagogue, the institutional doors and stained-glass windows. Well, what do you know, he thought. Here I am, isn't that something!

"Are you all right, Kagan?"

Kagan found himself taking her hand.

"No, Fran, I'm not all right and you can help me."

"What's wrong, dear?"

"I have to find someone, Fran."

"Who?"

"I don't know," he answered. "Where could he be? I left before he did, so I don't even know which way he went."

"Moe, I don't understand."

"I don't either, Fran. Maybe someone saw him leave."

"Kagan," she said, taking both his hands, "what are you talking about? I don't understand a word you're saying."

"I'm not making sense, am I?" he agreed.

"No, you certainly aren't."

"Why does it bother you tonight?" he joked half-heartedly.

"Because it's Yom Kippur and you don't look very happy."

"You're right," he said softly. "Listen, in *shul* tonight, there was an old man who wanted to talk to me and I didn't have time for him. I didn't even wish him a *gut yontiff*."

"Why not?"

"Oh, Benny wanted to tell me something. You know how he is. By the time I turned around, he was gone."

"Who was he?"

"That's the thing. Nobody seemed to know. He comes every Yom Kippur. An old man in a green suit the color of a bright Ping-Pong table, just terrible."

"A Ping-Pong table?"

"Yeah, it's darker than a pool table. Just awful."

"Can't you wait until tomorrow morning?"

"It's Yom Kippur and I feel terrible. What if he doesn't come tomorrow because of me?"

"But where can you find him?"

"That's the problem," Kagan admitted sadly. "How do we know where to look?"

Kagan stood there trying to think of something, any-thing.

"Maybe someone else saw him leave," Fran sug-gested. "But they would have gone home, too. That won't help."

"Oh, it might!" Kagan called. "Let's go!"

Clutching her hand, Kagan took off toward Broadway.

"They study for a while at the *shtibl*. The laws of Yom Kippur, that kind of thing."

"You think he's still there?"

"I doubt it. He's not the type. Someone might have seen which way he went. Everybody's wife was there for *Kol Nidre* and most of them walk their wives home. Then they return to study. Maybe somebody saw which way he went."


"YOU mean the fellow in the rumpled green suit?" asked Bienstock looking up from the study table. A large book lay open in front of him.

"Yes," replied Kagan eagerly. "That's the guy."

"You know, it's a funny thing," Bienstock reminisced. "I haven't seen a suit like that in thirty years. Do you remember Sadie's brother, Herman? He had a suit like that. And you know where he got it?"

"Where is he now?" Kagan implored.

"Oh," Bienstock said gently, "he's been dead for twenty years. But if you ever ate down at the dairy restaurant on East Broadway you must have seen him."

"No, Bienstock, not him. Where did you see the old man tonight? The old man in the rumpled suit."

"In *shul* here."

"Did you see him later?"

"Yes, we walked down Broadway with him. A nice old fellow."

"Where did you see him last?"

"What's wrong, Kagan?"

"Plenty, Bienstock, plenty! Just tell me where you saw him last."

Bienstock heard the urgency of Kagan's plea.

"We turned left on Eighty-sixth Street and he kept going on Broadway. Downtown on the west side of the street."

"Thanks, Bienstock," Kagan said, running for the door.

"Kagan, can I help you?" Bienstock called.

"You have already."

Kagan ran down the steps to the sidewalk, took Fran's arm, and dashed toward Broadway. At the corner, Kagan turned right and rushed even faster. Fran began panting as Kagan dragged her down Broadway.

"Moe, do we have to run?" she gasped.

"We'll never catch him if we don't," Kagan explained without slowing up.

"I can't, Moe!"

Fran slowed to a walk.

"C'mon, Fran, c'mon! This is important," he pleaded.

"Moe, I can't."

"Fran, you're always saying we don't do enough together and when you get your chance, you won't come along."

"I can't, Moe. I can't."

"But you're good at spotting people in crowds, Fran. I need you."

Fran drew a deep breath.

"Moe, if this is so important, why don't you run on ahead and I'll follow as quickly as I can."

"Good! Good!" Kagan said racing down the street.

He stopped short, spun around, and raced back to her.

"You know what he looks like? Old guy, rumpled green suit."

"Between a Ping-Pong table and a pool table," she responded.

"Good, you got it. Keep an eye out!"

Kagan took off down Broadway. He raced the five blocks to Eighty-sixth Street without looking around. At Eighty-sixth Street, he was stopped by a red light. As he stood on the corner, he began frantically looking in all directions at once. He squinted into the greasy spoon on the opposite corner and peered down the street. The light changed, and as he ran across the street he glanced into the taxis stopped by the crosstown light. Kagan didn't believe that the old man would ride on Yom Kippur, or eat either; still, you never know, sometimes people wind up doing some pretty crazy things that they never planned to do. That's how I got married, didn't I?

Half running, half walking, and looking everywhere — hotel lobbies, all-night groceries, laundromats, darkened florists, the other side of the street, inside buses, down side streets, into faces on street corners, Kagan continued down the street in a frenzy. But he didn't see a rumpled green suit or anything that even faintly resembled one.

People began to notice Kagan. Rushing about in his high-topped sneakers, he rarely looked in the direction he was moving. One of the young whores called out.

"Hey, fella, you lookin' for somethin'?"

"Yes," Kagan replied eagerly. "Yes, I am!"

"Well, good," she said sliding her mouth open into a wide, receptive grin. "Maybe I got it, honey."

"How long have you been standing here?" Kagan asked suddenly.

At the unexpected query, the grin left her face and her jaw muscles tightened.

"What business of yours?" she asked sullenly.

Kagan paid no heed to her offended tone. "I'm looking for an old guy. A white guy, wearing an old-fashioned green suit, somewhere between a Ping-Pong table and a pool table."

"Sounds like a sharp dude," she said coyly.

"Did you see him?" Kagan asked hopefully.

"What if I did?" she continued.

"Well, where is he?" exploded Kagan.

"You want to go out or not, man?" she said defensively.

"Did you see him or not?" Kagan demanded. He stepped menacingly forward.

"Shit, man. I didn't see nobody. I only here a minute myself."

Kagan rushed on down the street. After he was a safe distance away, the whore called after him, "I ain't no missing-persons bureau. Try the police for your faggot friend."


AT Seventy-ninth Street under the pool hall, two young policemen stood motionless on the northeast corner. Kagan, in front of the church on the other side of the street, spotted them.

"Officer!" Kagan screamed. He waved his arms and started across the street against the traffic light. Horns blared as Kagan dashed toward the island separating the uptown and downtown lanes.

"Officer!" he called again.

Noticing his coat and tie, the policemen relaxed their grips on their nightsticks.

"Wait for the light," one of them called.

Unmindful of the advice, Kagan waded into the uptown lane, barely scrambling away from a taxi.

"You're gonna get killed like that," the cop said.

"Yeah," Kagan agreed. "Listen, did you guys see an old white guy in a crumpled green suit? He must have been around here in the last half hour."

The two policemen looked at each other to confirm

their ignorance.

"No, I didn't. Did you?" asked one.

"No, sorry," said the other.

"It's a crazy color green. You're probably too young to remember the style unless you watch the late show: Boston Blackie, nineteen-forties. In color, it's between a Ping-Pong table and a pool table. In the dark, it might look a little darker. The guy's about seventy, hunched over a little but pretty healthy-looking for his age. He would've been going downtown."

"No," said one.

"Uh-uh," said the other.

"Yeah, well, thanks anyway," said Kagan, racing back to his side of the street.

As Kagan dashed into the traffic, he heard one cop ask, "Isn't he a little old for perpetrator shoes?" He heard, but didn't care. Kagan was madly scanning the great canyon of Broadway and was almost overwhelmed by the torrent of traffic coursing through its asphalt center.

At Seventy-second Street he stopped and stared about the busy intersection. The light changed but he didn't cross the street. Kagan stood staring farther down Broadway, but he knew it was hopeless. Traffic, people, but no green suit. Kagan blinked at the strange frantic world that hid his . . . his what? Where is he? Kagan thought, my . . . what? My man, yeah, my man, all right. No, more than man. I need him. He's my — he predicted the results of the race. "My prophet?" Kagan wondered aloud in amazement.

It was a wild and disturbing thought. A prophet yet! An angel wasn't enough! Who knows, mused Kagan as he stared down Broadway with greater concentration. He looked past the subway kiosk, a strange menacing mask with its bright magazine-stand eyes. No rumpled green suit, just the downtown stream of traffic bucking the crosscurrent of Amsterdam Avenue, before veering left toward Lincoln Center and even past that to Times Square, and from there . . . even farther.

For a few moments Kagan let the swirl of lights mesmerize him. He found a moment's respite in the frantic but ordered pattern of the traffic: Broadway, up- and downtown to the left; Amsterdam just beyond; and the lighter refrain of the Seventy-second Street crosstown immediately before him. Kagan felt as if he were staring out to sea and sensed the finite limits of his search. A moment earlier he had been frantic in his chasing after fate, but now with the small vehicular waves of Seventy-second Street playing at his feet, and the powerful currents coursing toward the great depths of Manhattan beyond the horizon, he felt calm. The limitless expanse of waves and sky imposed a more accurate perspective than the one harried souls encounter in their relentless charge through the small, crowded corridors of life.

Kagan watched the individual lights in the streams flow together into great rivers of red and white, with dashes of yellow and orange. As Kagan turned to head back up Broadway, he felt a sense of defeat, but also a sense of calm. The hidden was not to be revealed, not yet anyway. You win a few, you lose a few — and action is better than no action. But did I win or lose? Kagan wondered. I won't be able to find out tonight unless Ozzie shows up and that's unlikely. He disappears every Yom Kippur and he's been acting pretty strange anyway. I might as well enjoy the walk back. Wherever that old guy is, he's not around here. And yet, thought Kagan, you never know, I might as well go with the percentages.

Kagan crossed the street just to be on the safe side,

with the percentages.

AT Seventy-ninth Street, he heard someone calling his name. Kagan looked across the street to find Fran waving at him. He waited as she crossed to his side.

"Did you see him?" she asked with a concern that Kagan heard and appreciated.

"No," Kagan said in a relaxed manner. "I couldn't find a trace of him."

"I didn't see him either, Moe."

"Yeah, I know."

"You do?"

They had crossed Seventy-ninth Street and were under the pool hall.

"Nobody saw him, Fran." To confirm it, Kagan turned to the two policemen, who had not moved from their post. "You fellows didn't see him either, did you?"

"No, we didn't," the younger one said, shaking his head.

"Not a trace," said the other.

"See," Kagan said to Fran.

Kagan's rapport with the Twentieth Precinct surprised her. She noted the two cops staring at her tennis shoes.

"Moe, what do you suppose they think about our shoes?"

"I don't know. I guess they take us for natural-food freaks from Connecticut."

Fran laughed and took his hand.

"Hey, lady, this is Yom Kippur!"

"I guess you're right."

She released his hand.

"That's better," Kagan said. "Now that you're behaving like a lady, you want me to buy you a drink?"

"You nut," she said, affectionately punching his arm.

"Lady, you bother me and I'll call the cops. Bothering a *cohen* on Yom Kippur is a federal offense."

"I didn't know the police were such good friends of the sneaker set."

"The young ones are. They were raised on natural foods — organic corned beef and cabbage."

"It sounds delicious!"

"No better than organic herring."

"Organic herring!" Fran said in horror.

"Oh, I forgot. You're from Connecticut."

"No," she said seriously, "you never forget that."

"Yes," he said with equal seriousness. "I guess you're right."

The last was added as an unarticulated apology, and Fran accepted it as such.

Kagan didn't look for him, but he was hoping that the man would appear since he wasn't looking for him. Isn't that how a crazy world works? So Kagan gazed about — not looking for him but prepared to recognize him at once. His attentive inattention proved difficult to sustain and Kagan was weary by the time they reached Ninety-fourth Street. He was also frustrated: no old man, no rumpled green suit, no understanding. For me, he thought, Broadway is a blind alley.

## 6

IN their apartment, they looked at the *Times* for a few minutes and gave the cat some milk.

"I told you this wasn't a Jewish cat!" Kagan exclaimed when the tawny little creature lapped up the white liquid.

"A Catholic?" Fran laughed.

"No," said Kagan, "she doesn't like champagne. She could be only one thing the way she jumps around and bothers us. This cat is Hare Krishna."

"Yvette? Hare Krishna?" Fran said in a fit of laughter.

"This younger generation is wacky, Fran. Wait and see. She'll be in Times Square in her orange fur, jumping up and down with a little bell around her neck. We'll go up to her and she won't even recognize us."

"Yvette not recognize us?" Fran registered mock horror.

"And no more Yvette either. The only thing she'll accept from us is money and we'll have to make the checks out to Maharishi Cat."

"She'd do a thing like that?"

"Of course she will, but the joke will be on her." Kagan paused.

"It will?"

"Since when have we written a check that was good?" Kagan exclaimed in morose triumph.

Not knowing how to respond, Fran attempted neutral agreement.

"I suppose so."

"You suppose?" Kagan barked. "Our check to Maharishi Cat will bounce higher than a rubber guru! And you suppose so? Since when have I written a check that hasn't bounced?"

Fran didn't answer the question. Instead, she began to cry.

Not again, thought Kagan. What is this? All Yom Kippur she cries, just because I yell at her. They're my rotten checks that are no good, not hers. My God, I can't find the old guy to wish him a *gut yontiff* and I make Fran cry. With my luck, how can I ever pick a winner?

"Fran, I'm sorry!" Kagan shouted.

"You are?" she said tearfully.

"Of course," Kagan said switching into a breezy conversational tone. "I can imagine how bad you must feel at having raised an apostate pussy cat, a *meshumed* feline — God forbid. And do you know why Yvette is capable of doing such things?" Without waiting for an answer, Kagan continued with great indignation. "Because she pisses on the couch. That's why! Any creature that pisses on the couch can't be too good."

"It doesn't smell like some cats," Fran protested.

How many times had they had this argument, thought Kagan. Either she's crazy or I am.

"That's true, Fran, but sometimes you must face reality. Cat piss is not perfume."

"It's not her fault."

"Fran, that cat has to learn responsibility. The way things are it's not good for her and it's not good for us. This cat has to go to the *mikveh* before it's too late."

Fran didn't know how to respond.

WITHOUT further conversation they went to bed. They lay quietly until Fran turned to Kagan and said softly, "I hope you find him tomorrow. I think you will."

"I hope so," he answered calmly.

After a few moments, he continued seriously, "It's a funny thing how he could get away from me while I'm wearing my old high-cut sneakers."

"Maybe you need a pair of low-cuts?" Fran chided gently.

"No, Fran, the greats wore high-tops like mine."

"I thought you told me they have better players now than they ever did?" she asked.

"They are, Fran, they're better, but they're not as great. Those old guys created the game. Without Cousy, the guys today wouldn't know how to play."

"I hope you find him."

"Fran," Kagan called softly.

"Yes?"

"I wish you a good year," he said.

Fran began to cry, but not wanting Kagan to know she called in a joking manner, more appropriate to Kagan than to herself, "Happy five — seven — three — four, Bob Cousy."

Kagan felt as if someone had thrown a switch and gravity no longer functioned. His head floated through the room. The change of state was so drastic, he couldn't quite grasp it; you mean there's no gravity?

"What?" he rasped in a voice that didn't begin to suggest the trauma he was experiencing.

"Happy New Year, dear," she said.

"Oh," Kagan whispered. "I thought you said something else."

"I did, dear. I said, 'Happy five — seven — three — four.' That's the Jewish year, isn't it, fifty-seven thirty-four?"

Kagan, sailing through the dark bedroom, felt as if he had crashed into the wall, fallen to the floor, and bricks from the wall were falling on his head. Each brick had 5734 stamped on it. The police car pulled up; the two young cops got out and walked over to where Kagan lay half-buried by the bricks. "We ought to run you in for this!" one growled. "Do these bricks belong to you?" the other asked menacingly. "Put them in the car!" the first commanded. Kagan staggered to his feet and began collecting the bricks. He dragged them over to the police car, dropped them into the open trunk, and closed it. The number 5734 was painted on the outside. The police car drove off.

"They didn't look Jewish," Kagan murmured in devastated amazement.

"Who?" asked Fran.

"The police," Kagan muttered.

"Of course they weren't Jewish," she said definitively. "They seemed decent enough."

They did? Kagan wondered.

"They helped us look for the old man in the green suit, didn't they?" she added.

Kagan got out of bed and stood up.

"I can't sleep!" he said with great conviction.

He opened the window and stuck his head out into the night. Like a bird listening for a worm high above Ninety-fourth Street, he twisted his head first to stare at the intersection of Ninety-fourth and West End and then to Broadway. The warm October night was surprisingly quiet. After several moments, the faint sound of a car horn drifted up from Broadway.

Kagan, livid with rage, screamed into the darkness, "Stop that goddamn honking; I'm trying to sleep!"

He pulled his head inside and slammed the window shut.

"It's impossible to sleep with all that honking. I can't take it!"

He opened the bedroom door, and with the light from the hall, began dressing rapidly. He put on his suit quickly, but slowed down lacing up his high-cut sneakers. Finally, he stood up and moved toward the door.

"I have to find somebody," he said.

"But, Moe, we couldn't find him," Fran pleaded.

"No, not him. Somebody who can help me."

"Pakooz?" she asked hopefully.

"Pakooz?" Kagan burst out in amazement. "Pakooz!"

"PAKOOZ, Pakooz, Pakooz," Kagan repeated in mindless amazement as he walked swiftly down Broadway. "Pakooz? Pakooz?" he muttered in rhythmic wonder. As he was saying it, he found himself adding his earlier refrain. "Pakooz, keep your shoes on. Pakooz, keep your shoes on."

"Keep your shoes on, Pakooz, I already have a pair with holes in them," Kagan laughed aloud.

Pakooz, what a crazy guy, and Fran thinks he can help me. Pakooz the cut-rate shrink — the all-hours shrink, like an all-night drugstore on the fourth floor of a West Side walkup. Pakooz had office hours from six in the morning until midnight. For an early appointment at five to six, Pakooz would drop his keys down from the fourth floor, and Kagan, sleep weighing down his bleary eyes, would tilt his head up and try to find the falling object against a dawning sky. More often than not, he stuck out a hand at the last moment to make an unexpected catch. It was a good thing, too. The sound of those keys hitting the pavement at six in the morning was clangorous and unsettling. "It's a transference problem. We'll have to talk about it," Pakooz said. At a midnight session, Kagan would lock up on his way out.

My God, Kagan mused. He's probably the only shrink in the world who has a crazier schedule than I do. Still, Pakooz only charged twelve dollars an hour when everyone else wanted at least twenty-five. Pakooz was an old socialist who didn't want to rip off anybody who couldn't afford it. The trouble was those who could afford it didn't want any part of Pakooz so the would-be psychosocialist had to rely on extrapsychological techniques. His therapy seemed to be as good as the high-priced Park Avenue practitioners' — practically worthless. "For twelve dollars an hour," he told Kagan, "you can't expect miracles." Well, it certainly wasn't any worse and it was twelve dollars.

Fran liked him since Pakooz said that Kagan was playing games with Fran's head. Huh, snorted Kagan in disbelief. The night he told me that, he had me assist him in a felony. As Kagan arrived at midnight, a security guard stepped out of the shadows and whispered, "Tell the doctor I'm downstairs." Kagan was about to get on the couch when he relayed the message. "C'mon, Kagan, hurry, he's got to get back fast." Kagan carried up four loads of bricks. "They make a beautiful bookcase, Kagan. You'll see," Pakooz explained as if that would make it all worthwhile. "Yeah," Kagan answered, "I come here to get my head together and I wind up with a hernia."

A look of sincere hurt clouded Pakooz's indefatigable brow. Kagan's was covered with sweat.

"Kagan, that's not fair. You know I give value. Take a look at these ties. They're something special."

Pakooz reached under the couch and pulled out a large, heavy black sample case. At one time or another, he had offered Kagan almost everything: ties out of suitcases, shirts out of cartons, apples by the bushel. Once Kagan lay on the couch steeped in the aroma of garlic rising from a large restaurant-sized tray of lasagne. "I can't offer you any, Kagan. I promised the friend who bought it that it would feed fifteen people. There's enough there for fifteen, isn't there? What do you think?"

Sometimes it took Kagan half an hour just to make it to the couch. It was like having analysis on Orchard Street. Kagan half expected to free associate in Yiddish. Indeed, it was difficult to free associate about anything other than what was under the couch. Pakooz, for his part, encouraged Kagan, "Don't blame yourself, Kagan; it's hard to keep bargains like that off your mind."

What was hard to keep off his mind was why Pakooz had corrupted the guard. A poor *shlepper* like that could wind up in jail while Pakooz enjoyed his new bookcase.

"Look, Kagan, I know you're not a student of politics, but I didn't corrupt him. The system did."

"And the system will put his *tuchis* in jail and not yours."

"Kagan, life involves risk."

That's great! Kagan recalled with outrage. Every day except *Shabbes* I put my life on some horse's nose only to get kicked in the ass (there must be a routine there somewhere) — and he tells me life involves risk! What the hell does Pakooz know about risk? The only thing he knows about risk is what I taught him. He was pretty good about that, Kagan admitted grudgingly. I still must owe him three hundred dollars. Yeah, about that he was all right. He never hounded me, not once. I guess those ties weren't all that bad. Everybody was wearing them and Pakooz did manage to sell every one of them before our next session. Ozzie thought they were a bargain and encouraged me to buy a couple. No, Pakooz's taste wasn't bad; the bookcase would have looked pretty good if you didn't see one like it in every West Side apartment.

Still, Kagan didn't totally trust Ozzie's opinion of

Pakooz. He couldn't, because he had never told Pakooz about Ozzie. Not that Kagan was ashamed of Ozzie; on the contrary, he felt honored to have an angel, even such an unlikely one as Ozzie. But Kagan couldn't reveal Ozzie's existence to Pakooz. He would think that it went far beyond transference. Pakooz would think I'm crazy, and then I would never get any help. Poor Pakooz can't even help me when he believes I'm only neurotic. And if he thinks I'm crazy, he'll never let me say "no" to his merchandise.

No, you can't tell anybody these days about angels. Devils, maybe; angels, no. How could I explain Ozzie, anyway? I don't even understand him myself. If I play games with Fran's head, what does that angel do to mine? Ozzie should pay Pakooz a visit, Kagan said to himself with passion. I'm always the bad guy; I always take the rap. Just let Pakooz get a hold of that horny little angel for one forty-five-minute hour. (The old socialist had converted successfully to psychotherapeutic standard time.) He would never know what hit him. And I have to put up with it day and night. Except for Yom Kippur, Kagan added, with a surge of honesty. I can take it. What the hell does Pakooz know about that? I can take it.

Kagan glanced at his pickle-green watch to discover that it was almost midnight. Where did the evening go?

Kagan looked around. He was at Seventy-eighth and Broadway. He quickly crossed the street and moved in the direction of the place where it had all begun earlier in the day.

He approached the darkened *mikveh* building. Who would be up at this hour? Kagan wanted to find out, but how could he go around waking people up at midnight after *Kol Nidre*?

I'm always late, mourned Kagan. He stood and stared at the dark building. A few cars passed, a few people. After a while, he imagined that one of the windows wasn't as dark as the others. Maybe someone was awake.

This is crazy, he thought. If you look at something long enough you can see anything. And yet, there does seem to be a little light. If I could get up to the window, I could tell for sure.

Kagan looked around. The street was quiet. He climbed up the five steps to the doorway and looked over to the window ledge that was four feet away. The ledge itself was wide, white stone. Once there, he could look into the window easily and climbing down afterwards wouldn't be a problem. He could lower himself and then jump, landing on his sturdy old sneakers. No wonder those kids wear this kind of shoes. The problem was getting to the ledge. Kagan suddenly noticed the heavy wrought-iron bracket that held the lantern light fixture. It was midway between the door and the window. He pulled up his pants leg and lifted one foot up on the metal banister. By gripping some of the heavy masonry curlicues that framed the doorway, he hauled himself up onto the railing.

Once up, he surveyed the distance to the iron bracket that jutted from the wall somewhat higher than the level of his head. He reached for it slowly and grasped it. He had hoped to test it first before putting too much weight on it, but he leaned in that direction, putting all his weight on it as he lay spread-eagled against the building. Kagan held his breath. The bracket held. He transferred his other hand to it and then with careful concentration lifted his right foot off the banister and began working it over to the window ledge. Once his foot was on the ledge, he pushed off with his left foot and brought that one over also. Then he reached for the window casement with his right hand and pulled his upper body over to the window. On the ledge, he shuffled carefully to the center and stared inside.

It was completely dark. The only illumination came from the street light above Kagan. That light reflected off the window pane, making it difficult to see anything. To reduce the glare, Kagan pressed his face against the window, cupping his hand as a blinder between the glass and his eyes.

As he was staring into the quiet, motionless room, he was interrupted by a sarcastic voice from the sidewalk below.

"See anything interesting?"

Kagan, peering intently into the serene darkness, wasn't surprised to hear a voice and answered in a natural tone of voice.

"No, I guess they went to bed."

"Isn't that too bad?" the voice commiserated.

"Yes," Kagan answered.

"Okay, peeping Tom, let's come on down!" the voice said harshly.

Kagan, startled by the command, straightened up and almost fell backwards. He grabbed the casement in a jerky reflex action. Once steadied, he looked over his shoulder only to be met by the blinding beam of a powerful flashlight. Kagan blinked and turned away but not before he caught a glimpse of the police car standing in the middle of the street.

"Now!" the voice insisted.

Kagan crouched, placing his hands on the ledge.

In a less than natural voice, Kagan apologized for the delay in his descent.

"I'm afraid I'm not very good at this sort of thing."

"I'll say," the policeman growled in agreement.

"It's not the way it looks," Kagan protested unconvincingly.

"It never is," said the policeman in a calmer tone.

Kagan managed to lower himself from the ledge and jumped the rest of the way to the ground as he had originally planned to do. Encouraged by this feat, he began to regain his confidence.

"Look," he said, "this is a mistake."

Now that Kagan was on the ground, he could see with whom he was dealing. The sarcastic officer held a billy club in one hand and a flashlight in the other. His companion held a pistol that pointed in Kagan's direction. The sight of the gun made Kagan very uncomfortable and he realized that it might be more difficult than he had anticipated to explain his actions.

"Up against the car," the sarcastic one said, prodding Kagan with his nightstick.

"Please, I think . . . ," but before Kagan could finish, he felt a hand pushing him toward the patrol car.

"Lean over, hands apart on the trunk, feet apart, no monkey business," the policeman commanded.

Feeling foolish, frightened, and uncomfortable, Kagan complied.

"Feet further back!" the voice commanded.

Still leaning on the car's trunk, Kagan took a step backwards. In doing so, more of his weight came onto his hands and he lowered his head. Not more than a foot from his face, he saw the identifying numbers 5734 painted on the trunk.

My God, thought Kagan, a shiver of recognition shaking his entire body.

"Stand still!" the policeman commanded.

Kagan stared at the numbers in disbelief and barely felt the trained, strong hands frisk him.

He didn't hear one policeman call to the other, "He's clean. Not even a wallet."

The numbers seemed to be staring out at him from the trunk, mocking him.

You win, Kagan wanted to say, but what did they win? Why did they win? Who are you, he wanted to ask. Why are you doing this to me?

"Hands behind your back!" the officer repeated.

"What?" Kagan asked.

"Hands behind your back if you don't want the club!"

Kagan leaned against the trunk and put his hands behind his back. He felt the policeman pulling his hands together and he felt something cool on his wrists, but not until the first sudden click did he realize that he was being handcuffed.

"Hey, wait a minute!" Kagan protested.

"What's the problem?" the sarcastic officer asked as he yanked Kagan to his feet by the collar of his only suit.

"I know it looks strange, but I can explain what I was doing."

The police relaxed now that their suspect was safely subdued. The quiet one returned his pistol to his holster.

"I suppose," the conversational one with the flashlight said, "your TV is broken and you were just looking for a place to watch your favorite show."

Screw you, Kagan thought. But he did not waste his energy disparaging the policeman. He was in a jam and wasn't sure that he had the strength to get out of it. Confused, Kagan wondered, what the hell was I doing? How can I explain it? The police in this town must hear some pretty weird stories, but if I tell them mine, they'll send me to Bellevue mental. *Mikvehs*, angels, superfectas, changing finish lines — these won't play very well in the Twentieth Precinct. Even if they did believe all that, they would still ask me what I was doing on the window ledge. Sure, officer, that's easy. I wanted to see the little bony-skulled refugee who runs the ritual bathhouse because I'm curious about the concentration-camp numbers on his arm. You see, I believe that they're the same numbers as those on your patrol car, which are the same as the Jewish New Year, and which would have won the superfecta at Yonkers Raceway this evening except that a missing man in a Ping-Pong-pool-table suit moved the finish line in the ladies' section of my local synagogue.

"Officer," Kagan said with great sincerity, "this is a Jewish bathhouse used for ritual purposes and I think I lost my wallet here when I came to bathe earlier in the afternoon. I thought it might have dropped to the floor when I was getting dressed. It was right before Yom Kippur and I was in a rush to get home and prepare for the fast day."

The police looked suspicious but uncertain whether Kagan might be telling the truth.

"Why didn't you ring the bell and ask if they found your wallet?" the quiet one asked.

"Well, it really doesn't make much difference right now because we are Orthodox Jews and we don't handle or carry money on the Sabbath or Yom Kippur and we don't ring doorbells either," Kagan answered.

The police looked as if they might believe him.

"As far as my climbing up to the window ledge," Kagan began with an embarrassed shrug, "that was a silly thing to do. I don't really know why I did it. I couldn't sleep tonight so I thought maybe I would find out whether or not my wallet is here. It was dumb. I'm sure I must have looked like a criminal."

"Uh-huh," the quiet policeman agreed. "I think

we'd better ring the bell after all."

"I'd appreciate that," Kagan said.

The sarcastic cop climbed up the steps and rang the bell. The three of them heard the bell ringing inside. There was no response. He pressed the bell again. No one came to the door. The policeman came back down the steps. All three stood in the street not quite certain what to do next. The sarcastic policeman looked to the quiet one for a decision.

"Technically," the quiet one said, "we shouldn't let you go without some identification. Is there anyone who could identify you?"

Before Kagan could even think about that, a voice from the sidewalk called, "Excuse me, officer, but I can tell you who dat fella is. He's one of mine customers from the Jewish bathhouse. A fine fella."

Kagan and the policemen looked up to see the small, bald *mikveh* attendant wearing a white linen shroud that reached almost to the sidewalk and a small white satin *yarmulke* perched on his hairless head. On his feet, of course, he wore white tennis shoes.

Kagan, although delighted to see the *mikveh* man, was amazed to see him running in the middle of the night through the streets of New York in a *kittel*. Good God, Kagan thought of his rescuer, he looks like the oldest living member of the Vienna Boys Choir.

"Good evening, rabbi," the conversational policeman said. "I guess that solves the problem."

He looked at his quiet partner for confirmation. His partner nodded and pointed to Kagan's handcuffs.

"Oh, yeah, I almost forgot," he said, "I may need these again tonight."

He unlocked them and Kagan rubbed his wrists.

"Sorry," the quiet one said.

"That's all right, boys," Kagan said magnanimously.

"You were just doing your job."

Seated in their police car, the garrulous one behind the wheel leaned out.

"Have a good holiday, rabbi," he called.

"Thank you, officer," the *mikveh* attendant answered.

Almost as an afterthought, the policeman stuck his head out again. "I hope you find your wallet, pal."

Kagan winced but called back, "Thanks."

The police car moved slowly towards Broadway.

"You lost your wallet this afternoon?"

"No," Kagan said with embarrassment. "I didn't lose my wallet. I told them that because I didn't know what to tell them. Listen, I just wanted to talk to you. I couldn't sleep so I walked over. I didn't want to wake you. I didn't know whether you were home or not so I climbed up onto the window ledge to take a look."

"And that's when the coppers arrived," the little man finished the story.

"Yeah."

"What can I do for you?"

"What?" asked Kagan, not wanting to ask his real question.

"What can I do for you?" the little man repeated.

What can I do? thought Kagan. I can't ask this little man about the numbers on his arm. Look at that head; only the ovens of Auschwitz could have baked the skin so tight. Look at that arm. He became a *mikveh* man in the hope that the water would wash off the numbers, but water can't wash off those numbers. Some things no bath can wash off. Those numbers, Kagan suddenly realized, don't have to be washed away. They are beyond Ivory soap and Brut cologne, beyond appearance. They are not of water, but of fire.

Kagan felt tears in his eyes.

"I came," Kagan said softly, "to wish you a good

decree. May you be sealed in the Book of Life."

"Thank you. I wish you a *chasima tova* also."

"Thank you," said Kagan.

They stood for a moment before the *mikveh* man spoke.

"That's all? Are you sure that you're not forgetting something from yesterday?"

What does he know? Kagan wondered.

"Is there something you didn't do yesterday that you should have?" the little man asked.

"Yes," confessed Kagan, "I should have called an old friend, Katzi, to wish him a good decree."

"That's all?"

"From yesterday," said Kagan with evasive honesty.

"And today, Yom Kippur?" the little man demanded.

"Yom Kippur has been a very hard day," Kagan said, shaking his head.

The old man put his hand on Kagan's arm.

"Yom Kippur," he said softly, "is a blessing, very hard — and very beautiful."

"It is?"

"You'll see," said the *mikveh* man.

"I will?" Kagan asked with fearful naiveté.

"You did the right thing." In gentle reassurance, he squeezed Kagan's arm. "You don't have to say it. You did the right thing by not asking. I'll tell you this. No bathhouse can wash off the numbers. Some things no water can wash off. But a *mikveh* is different. A *mikveh* is purity. In a *mikveh* those numbers don't exist. That's why I came here."

"Yes," Kagan nodded. "That makes sense."

They stood looking at each other in the night.

"Listen," Kagan said, "this is crazy. The cops found me poking around your place like a sneak thief. They did the right thing in arresting me. I have no business asking and you would be right not to tell me, but I'm worried about all that money. I hope you got it to a bank before the holiday. If you didn't, and as crazy as this sounds, I'll help you guard it."

The little man leaned closer and Kagan bent over to pick up his whisper.

"I don't believe in banks. I believe in *mikvehs*."

"You mean?"

The small, tightly shrunk bald head reflected the light as it nodded.

"I put it where they wouldn't think to look. That's the best place."

"Doesn't it get soggy?" Kagan asked.

"No," he said proudly. "I wrap it in those little white plastic sandvich begs my wife uses. They're wonderful. I put a few rubber bands around them to be sure. You can't see a thing."

"Oh, good," Kagan said.

"Don't worry," the little man added. "You did the right thing."

"I did?" Kagan asked, wondering what the old man was referring to now.

The little man nodded.

The superfecta, Kagan thought. That's what he's talking about.

"Say," Kagan said with all of his former verve, "are you psychic?"

"I don't know," the little man said factually. "My English isn't too good."

"Oh," Kagan said.

"It's Yom Kippur and we got a busy day ahead of us. We'd better get some rest."

"Yes, you're right."

"*Gut yontiff*," the little man said.

"*Gut yontiff*," Kagan said. "Thank you. Thank you

very much!"

"Don't mention."

They separated. Kagan turned back toward Broadway. After he had gone a few steps, he heard a voice calling him.

"Say, listen," the little man said. He was standing in the half-open door.

Kagan turned around.

"Tomorrow," the *mikveh* man said.

"Huh?"

"Tomorrow, Kagan, you'll see him tomorrow. The man in the green suit."

The little man stepped into the building and closed the door.

Kagan stared after him in a stupor of belief. He didn't have enough energy to be amazed. He accepted the small refugee's word. Why not? Kagan implicitly trusted some people. How could someone who runs through the streets of Manhattan at midnight on Yom Kippur dressed in a *kittel* tell a lie to a suffering soul? Kagan, betting man that he was during secular moments, wasn't about to bet against anything happening on this Yom Kippur. Things had been happening all day that had no right to happen. Why shouldn't he see the man in the rumpled green suit? The *mikveh* man said he would. You got to know the kvoda, Kagan thought.

Kagan walked home slowly. He didn't notice anything on Broadway, lively with its weekend revelries. His steps were slow and his head was quiet, like a horse after a long race.

*7*

ALTHOUGH he felt physically tired when he opened his apartment door, Kagan realized wearily that he couldn't sleep. He sat on the couch and stared toward the dark bedroom. Sleepily, the cat walked delicately across the couch and curled up in his lap. She snuggled, inviting affection. Kagan petted her little head gently.

"Forgive me," he said to the cat, "for I have sinned with my lips. I have slandered you, Yvette."

The cat purred and Kagan stroked her gently.

"I hope you have a good healthy mouse-filled year," he said seriously. "And please try not to piss on the couch, if you can."

Enervated, Kagan just sat with the cat and with himself in silence. Finally, he said to himself, it wasn't a lie. I did want to call Katzi. I should have called him.

"Katzi," Kagan said aloud, "have a good year, a safe year, and try to make a few deliveries on time."

The cat had fallen asleep. Kagan didn't want to disturb her and thinking of Katzi relaxed him. Katzi, there was a *cohen*. Katzi, the religious bookie. Kagan smiled. One Purim Kagan had to wait until Katzi finished reading his mother the *Megillah* before he could place a bet. It's a good thing the Knicks were on the Coast or I never would have gotten it down on time. Not that Katzi would have known the difference. Poor Katzi, Kagan reflected affectionately, he never knew the starting time and lost a fortune. Sports didn't interest him except for figuring the odds. At that he was a genius, a true scholar, but it wasn't enough. Guys would bet the game when it was in the seventh inning and the Giants were ahead five to two.

Katzi became a laundry driver; he kept all the tickets

in his head. Kagan smiled; he loved human talents —
a genius at accounts. Still, Katzi had a problem. Shirts
for Tuesday might arrive on Thursday, Friday, or even
the following Monday, but never on *Shabbes*. No sense
of time except for *Shabbes*. Most bettors were wildly
superstitious, but not Katzi. Katzi was religious. He
didn't believe in jinxes. "Unless, Kagan, the athlete
himself does. Then it must be taken into account. As
the Talmud says, 'Fate often leads a man in the direction he chooses to go.'"

Katzi, sensitive, scholarly, religious, was so unlike
most bookies that Kagan felt compelled to ask him why
he was one. When it came to himself as a gambler,
Kagan had no illusions: superstitious, impulsive, a
rabid fan — that's me, folks. But Katzi should have
been a judge, a professor, or even a rabbi. He could
have been something great. Perhaps making book gave
Katzi time to study the Talmud.

"Kagan, I won't lie to you and tell you that making
book leaves me sufficient time to study the Talmud,
although it does."

"Why then, Katzi?"

"The same reason you do, Kagan."

"No, Katzi, you're different."

Katzi shook his head sadly. "Kagan, you're a *cohen*.
I'm a *cohen*. It's in the blood."

Kagan was astonished to hear this. "You really think
so?"

Katzi nodded. "Yes, it goes way, way back."

Recalling their conversation, Kagan no longer felt so
relaxed. He looked carefully at his hand to see if he
could discern any special characteristics of the blood
pulsating inside.

It goes way, way back, thought Kagan. Past the old
neighborhood into Russia and out the other end into

Israel. Kagan decided not to trace it any further; he was very weak on the geography of the Holy Land. Instead, he considered the more immediate family for evidence of Katzi's statement. Everybody enjoyed gin rummy but that didn't seem terribly significant. Everybody outside the family enjoyed gin rummy, too. They even liked gin rummy in Connecticut. Nobody gambled that much at gin rummy. They just played it endlessly. And Kagan himself played it mindlessly. He never did enjoy card games. They seemed pointless and boring. When he kibbitzed them in the candy store, he found the players more interesting than the game. In fact, he found the kibbitzers more interesting than either the players or the game. It's true, Kagan thought, that Pa went broke several times as a furrier, but what furrier didn't? And he was trying to make a living. He just wasn't very good at it. That doesn't seem to count. Still, he never wanted to work for the post office.

Hmm, Kagan reflected curiously, I gamble like crazy and work for the Board of Education. I wonder if the post office is loaded with gamblers — paycheck poker with zip codes. Why not, a player will play anything. Betting sure as hell seems to be in my blood, and the crazier the bet the better I like it. Nobody ever accused me of being a student of the ponies like Katzi. Compared to Katzi, I bet below grade level, a remedial gambler — there must be a routine there someplace.

Katzi will give odds on anything. Two weeks on the truck, and he set odds on which buttons were most likely to be missing on a given shirt. Kagan took him on for double or nothing and wound up double, of course. Who could beat Katzi if he took the bets on time? How could Katzi be late opening a package of shirts? Kagan smiled to himself; it took them over an hour to rewrap the shirts they had been betting. It's a good thing the laundry gave Katzi some extra glued bands for emergencies or they never would have finished. While they were betting, Kagan had gotten excited as usual and started tearing them open. Katzi, not a terribly humorous guy, came up with a good line. "Take it easy, Kagan, these aren't the Academy Awards!" Hmm, Kagan wondered, I never bet the Academy Awards. I wonder who handles that action? If he put his mind to it, Katzi could do it.

A guy like Katzi should have made a fortune if he only could tell time. At Katzi's door, a line winds halfway around the block. The Giants are ahead five to two in the seventh and Katzi's still taking bets on the original odds, seven to five, Dodgers. Who could call it gambling? It was murder. Katzi lost a fortune. So did I, mourned Kagan. How could I cheat Katzi? If I didn't bet before the game started, I didn't bet. When Katzi became a laundry driver, I was the only guy who owed him money. Everybody else ran after the truck to collect. Katzi knocked down his losses pretty good with the button game. The smartest bookmaker in town is an easy touch and I can't take advantage of him.

"You can't help it, Kagan. Basic decency, it's in your blood," Katzi said.

"I've got some lousy blood, Katzi. It's costing me my life."

"I know, Kagan. I'm a *cohen*, too."

"And broke," Kagan added.

"It's in the blood, Kagan. Don't fight it."

Fight it? It's killing me, Katzi. Well, I guess Katzi isn't doing so great either. A great head like that on a laundry truck, Kagan grieved. Maybe it is in the blood. But how can you not fight it when it's killing you? Who knows?

"At any rate, Katzi," Kagan said aloud, "I wish you a

good decree. I never had a bookie I respected more. And as long as you're on the truck, drive safely, and be well. And, Katzi, try to get a few shirts back on time. It may be in your blood, but some guy might need it on his back to get a job or see a girl."

Kagan felt the cat stirring.

"Sorry," Kagan said to the little creature.

The cat rubbed affectionately against Kagan.

"I know," Kagan said to her, "it's in the blood."

The little creature walked off his lap and curled up on the couch. Kagan looked at his watch.

"Already three o'clock." As he looked at the second hand ticking over the unattractive but familiar watch face, Kagan unexpectedly said, "Only three o'clock" and quickly added, "I wonder why I said that?"

Too tired to wonder, Kagan undressed in the living room and went into the bedroom. He was asleep before he had time to consider anything.

"WHA-A-A-T?" Kagan groaned as Fran tried to rouse him.

"Moe, it's already eight o'clock," Fran insisted.

"Eight?" he managed to repeat.

"Yes, I'm going to services and you'd better get up, too, if you want to pray today."

"Yeah," Kagan agreed. "I'll get up."

"*Gut yontiff,*" Fran said as she left.

Kagan didn't hear the apartment door close. He had fallen back asleep.

IN Kagan's dream, a pitcher appeared inside a bright, airy, sun-filled baseball park. The limitless blue sky above was matched in brilliance by the vast expanse of green grass below. In the center of the verdant diamond rose the naval of the infield, elevated upon a

deep brown earthen dome, upon which a stylish left-
hander smoothly oscillated continuously and simultaneously through the motions of sign, windup, stretch,
and pitch. Although the gossamer figure was impossible to identify, Kagan knew it to be himself. Who
else could it be? (In response to Pakooz, Kagan had
once answered indignantly, "Why should I star Tom
Seaver? It's my dream, isn't it?") Kagan slept peacefully as he pitched with constancy and beauty. The
golden sun, a privileged spectator, gleamed off his
white flannels. (It was a home game.) The heavenly arc
of the fly balls drifted toward the outfield and rushed
back down to meet the green grass of life. The brilliant
white skimming ground balls. The infielders, gliding,
scooping, throwing the small delicate spheres. All the
while Kagan the pitcher continued in his rotational
rhythms, the center of the universe of light. The dugouts dipped below the horizon. The outfield walls stood
distant and serene.

Kagan rested, relishing the dream until slowly, subtly,
almost imperceptibly, the image began to change. The
outfield walls moved in toward the infield, looming
larger, darker, more perilous. The azure blue heaven
darkened and became dull; the color paled. The walls
advanced. The sun itself dimmed. The grass withered
into dark, lifeless shreds that fell on top of one another
before the enclosing walls, towering dark and uncertain. The concrete dugouts rose from the earth that had
received them and began to expand and multiply along
the encompassing walls. The walls arched above, creating darkness as the sun degenerated into a few diffuse, colorless rays. The once green carpet of life
hardened into wooden death.

The somnolent Kagan, anxious at the loss of his
once bright world, summoned the meager controls of

the realm of dreams and tried to focus on the disappearing world of openness and light. In fright Kagan concentrated enough energy to hold onto a bubble, a remembered spherical image of what the world had been. The bubble floated in the cavernous darkness of the present, and suddenly, that spherical image began to spin, rotating toward Kagan. It became dark brown and flew menacingly towards him. In reflex, Kagan raised his hands to catch it. Instantly, the dream pulled back to reveal a forty-three-year-old, graying, flabby Kagan. The real and terribly mortal Kagan of the bathroom mirror, in old gym shorts, a ragged, faded dark blue T-shirt, and his ancient black high-cut doesn't-anybody-here-remember-Bob-Cousy sneakers. Standing on the basketball floor of the old Madison Square Garden, he held a large, pebbly basketball in his hands at midcourt.

In the heavy, smoke-filled air, Kagan heard — even felt — the reverberations of the frenzied crowd. The Garden was jammed to the rafters. Amid the jumping, screaming throng, Kagan could make out Katzi. The normally reserved Katzi was screaming, "Shoot, Kagan, shoot! It's in the blood!" He saw Pakooz circulating through the aisles huckstering ice cream, soda pop, and wide, colorful ties, all from a large black sample case. "Shoot, Kagan, shoot!" Pakooz shouted. "It's not your fault. It's the system!"

High in the balcony, Fran sat crying. Higher in the balcony, in the highest tier, several fans wearing *kittels* sat quietly. Kagan couldn't identify them. He squinted, but it didn't help. There was too much smoke, not enough light, and they were too high.

As the crowd roared, Kagan looked up at the scoreboard clock. The pickle-green cube announced the score: Celtics — 100, Kagan — 99, with ten seconds

remaining in the game. The Celtics, yet, he thought; I
get all the breaks. He looked across midcourt to see
the champions in their green suits and high-cut black
sneakers. Guarding Kagan was Bob Cousy himself. Beyond Cousy was Sharman and clumped around the
basket stood Heinsohn, Luscotoff, and the greatest of
all time, Bill Russell.

"Time out!" Kagan screamed and the entire Garden
froze silent and motionless. Kagan tucked the ball under
his arm and looked around. There seemed to be no one
else on Kagan's team. And people wonder why I'm
crazy, he thought. He wandered down toward the
Celtics' end of the court. In spite of his predicament, he
couldn't help admiring Bill Russell, the great Celtic
center. (Kagan loved human talent.) Maybe after the
game he'll give me his autograph, he thought. Then his
attention turned to the situation at hand. Ten seconds
remain, I'd better play for the last shot; if I hit it, I win
the game since they won't have enough time to score.
I'll have to dribble around and run down the clock,
then I have to get off a shot. Who knows? Maybe it will
work.

As Kagan walked back to midcourt to resume the
game, he felt a surge of satisfaction and well-being.
Win or lose, I'm in Madison Square Garden. Not bad for
a kid from the old neighborhood.

At midcourt Kagan prepared to resume the game.
Although he concentrated on dribbling around Cousy,
a thought shot through his graying head — thank God I
don't have any money on this. But losing is action,
thought Kagan. Isn't action better than no action? Kagan
was troubled by the thought. This isn't action, Kagan
realized. This is murder. Kagan searched around one
final desperate time for teammates. No one. He looked
up at the pickle-green clock above the Garden floor.

"Well," shrugged Kagan, "I guess it all depends on me."

The stony silence was broken by the applause of the *kittle*-clad congregants high in the darkness.

I wonder what got into them, Kagan thought. Before he could think about it, Kagan found himself screaming, "Time in!"

The frozen world returned to its seething frenzy. Kagan found himself dribbling like crazy to stay away from the hardwood magician Bob Cousy, who advanced on him, one hand held high and one low. Good God, I'll never get near the basket. Kagan reversed his field and dribbled away, but Cousy pursued. Kagan pivoted and drove toward the center of the court. He strained his forty-three-year-old body and accelerated with the quickness and terror of a frightened prey. He managed to gain a step on Cousy only to be picked up by Sharman, but still accelerating, he kept on going and managed to get by him also. Kagan dribbled toward Luscatoff, then veered sharply away. Kagan was now streaming toward the left corner. Heinsohn was on the other side of the court; Russell was under the basket. Kagan heard the entire Garden scream SHOOT!

Kagan shot; leaping into the air, flying diagonally toward the corner, he turned to face the basket and lifted the ball high over his head for his weird, unorthodox two-hand jumpshot. Sailing tangentially away from the basket, Kagan released a desperation shot that, although possessing little chance of going through the basket, was well-nigh unblockable.

As Kagan descended slowly toward the floor, with wildly increasing excitement he watched the ball rise high in a perfect arc toward the basket. Bursting with anticipation, he stopped breathing when he realized the arc of the improbable shot was going to lead it through the hoop. (Kagan — 101, Celtics — 100!) The shot approached the zenith of its flight. Russell sprang from beneath the basket and flew toward the ball. Zooming into the air with his arms outstretched and held next to one another and his legs and feet similarly extended, he seemed to be a rocket in a Celtic uniform. He moved much faster than humanly possible. As the ball reached the peak of its journey, Russell's great strong hands clutched it into their inescapable grasp. The clock reached zero, the gun went off, and a great strangulated groan echoed from gasping throats.

Kagan, numb from Russell's defensive genius, stood in the corner of the court and watched the jubilant Celtics run in enthusiastic adolescent bounds toward their bench. Kagan felt an arm on his shoulder. The *mikveh* man was looking up at him sympathetically.

"It's not your fault, Kagan. Russell played like an angel."

Kagan glanced back to see Russell, palming the victory ball like a baseball in his huge hand and his great gap-toothed smile creasing his sweaty, triumphant face, approach the Celtic bench. His teammates hugged him, then respectfully stepped back to make room for the short coaching wizard of the Celtics to step forward and congratulate the great center. But stepping forward to celebrate with Bill Russell was not the fiery Red Auerbach, smoking his victory cigar, but a small wisp of a man.

Kagan sat up in bed and opened his eyes in wide disbelief. "Chaim Der Nechtiger!" Kagan called out incredulously.

Kagan stared about the unfamiliar room.

"Chaim Der Nechtiger?" Kagan repeated. Big Abe, the old man in the rumpled green suit, I might have expected to see them in my dream as coach of the

Celtics, but Chaim From Yesterday? What does Chaim From Yesterday have to do with anything? "Chaim Der Nechtiger!"

"Fran, you have to listen to a dream. It's crazy. It . . . ."

Kagan turned to find the bed empty.

"Hey, Fran, are you in the bathroom?" he called.

When he received no reply, he began to have vague recollections of having heard her earlier in the morning. Kagan fumbled around the night table for his watch.

"Ten-thirty," he gasped, "I'll miss the whole *davening.*"

Kagan jumped out of bed and began dressing. In the midst of tucking his shirt into his pants, he opened the apartment door. Already wearing his suitcoat, he thrust his coattails into his pants along with his shirttails. Fran always told me this never saves time.

The cat meowed plaintively from the dining room.

"A *rachmones* on the cat," said Kagan.

He dashed into the bathroom, filled the cat's water bowl, and ran back to the open door. In the doorway he struggled ferociously to free his suitcoat from his pants. His hand already on the doorknob, Kagan looked back into the empty apartment. "Chaim Der Nechtiger?" Kagan repeated. He quickly closed the door and ran down the hall toward the staircase. *Gevalt,* late for *shul* on Yom Kippur!

## 8

RUSHING down the few short blocks on West End, Kagan didn't see one Jew. I'm probably the only Jew

in Manhattan who's not in *shul*, Kagan mourned. Wait
a minute, thought Kagan. What about Big Abe and Pakooz? I guess I'm the only Jew in Manhattan who
should be in *shul* and isn't. That's not quite right
either. Shouldn't they be in *shul*, too? They aren't even
going to *shul*, Kagan mourned. "But I sure as hell am
late!" Kagan shouted definitively.

Kagan sprinted down Ninety-first Street, barely nodding to the old chimp who didn't seem to realize that
Kagan was decidedly late for *shul*.

AS he entered the *shtibl*, Kagan heard a buzz, no,
a roar of voices. Everyone was talking; no one was
praying. Kagan rapidly worked his way through the
crowded, narrow hallway to discover the reason for the
tumultuous recess. At the reading desk stood old Mr.
Isaacson auctioning off the *aliyahs*, the honors of being
called to the Torah. Except for the few bidding, no one
else could care less.

"*Fuftzik* dollars, *shishi*," the old man chanted in
singsong.

"Fifty dollars, *shishi*! Fifty dollars, *shishi*! Fifty dollars, *shishi*!"

As he quoted the highest bid, Mr. Isaacson scanned
the congregation, hoping either to discover or to inspire a higher one.

"*Fuftzik* dollars, *shishi*. First time. . . . Second time.
. . . Third time. . . . Sold, *shishi*!"

The old man's hand smacked the reading table sig-
naling the finality of the bargain.

*Gevalt*, thought Kagan, am I late! I missed all of
*shachris*.

Kagan began threading his way toward the small
room. People wished him a *gut yontiff* and he returned
the greeting. Kagan entered, but before he could speak,

revealing his embarrassment, Benny greeted him.

"Well, I knew the smart money would arrive in time to bid on *Maftir Yonah*. I guess Kagan wanted to give the little fish a chance with the small stuff."

"If I had your money, Benny, I'd buy *Maftir Yonah* and I wouldn't complain about the price."

"And if I had your money, Kagan, I'd get to *shul* on time Yom Kippur. It doesn't cost any more to say all the prayers."

Benny's tone, not as hostile as it might seem, reflected their outrageous honesty with one another.

"Yeah, you're right," Kagan admitted. "I overslept."

"You overslept on Yom Kippur?" Benny laughed, not one not to press an advantage.

Benny's idea of mercy, Kagan thought, is to ask someone if he wants to be roasted over red-hot or white-hot coals. What the hell does he know? I might have been in jail right now. I'm lucky to be here at all.

"At least I made it in time to give the Priestly Blessing," Kagan responded lamely.

"For that you could have slept until five this afternoon," Benny observed.

Danny laughed at his father's remark.

A punk like you wants to be a doctor, yet, Kagan thought.

"What are you talking about?" Kagan asked. "We give the Priestly Blessing at the end of *musaf*, no?"

"Not on *Shabbes*, Mack. When Yom Kippur is on *Shabbes*, we bless the congregation at *neilah*, right before the end of the fast."

"No kidding?" said Kagan with delight. He disliked surprises, but he loved information. "We wait to the very end of Yom Kippur, huh? Why do we do it that way?"

"Got me," said Benny, "that's the custom here. If

nothing else, it makes you rather early," Benny said.

"*Gevalt*, am I late!" mourned Kagan.

"Don't feel bad, Kagan," Schwartz falsely consoled him. "You didn't miss much, just *shachris*. Today we have *shachris*, *musaf*, *minchah*, and *neilah*. You can still hit three out of four. It's not the superfecta, but it's better than Ty Cobb."

Kagan never heard about Ty Cobb. In his embarrassment over his late arrival, he had forgotten about everything that had happened to him, even the cause of his tardiness. Kagan jumped up maniacally and turned toward the curtain for the old man in the rumpled green suit, but his seat was empty. Maybe he had switched seats. Kagan scanned the small congregation. Even the women's section — you never know. But he was nowhere.

"Where is he?" Kagan cried.

"Ty Cobb died a few years ago, but if he means so much to you, wait a few minutes and you can say *Yizkor* for him," said Schwartz.

Everyone in the little room laughed except Kagan, who spun back towards Schwartz.

"The old guy who borrowed your *machzor* last night. The guy in that crazy green suit!"

Kagan's anguish took Schwartz aback. "I don't know, Moe. He hasn't arrived yet."

"No one's seen him?"

Everyone shook his head.

"You sound like a guy who's having a nightmare," Benny said, a hint of concern entering his voice.

"I am, Benny. Don't you ever have them?" Kagan asked defensively.

"Yes, but generally at night," Benny answered honestly.

Kagan regained his composure. "You're lucky."

"Is there anything we can do for you?" Benny asked matter-of-factly, but sincerely.

"No, I'll be all right. I have to find someone. Some things are bothering me. That's all. Thanks, though."

Benny nodded.

The rabbi began *klopping* on the reading desk for quiet. It was time to read the Torah. People moved back to their seats and opened their books to follow the Torah reading.

Kagan, still standing, donned a *tallis* and began leafing through the fat Yom Kippur prayer book. It was enormous. The morning prayer, *shachris*, which he had slept through, was well over a hundred pages. As he watched the unprayed pages tumble by, he felt overwhelmed.

"Where shall I start?" Kagan wondered aloud in distress.

"Start from the Torah reading. That's what Yom Kippur is all about."

"It is?" replied Kagan, accustomed to hearing voices.

"Yes," the voice answered.

Kagan turned to find that he was conversing with Bienstock, who was coming back from the women's section, where he had been speaking to his wife.

"Read it. You'll see."

"Say, listen," said Kagan, sounding like his old self for the first time since he woke up. "Why do we give the Priestly Blessing by *neilah* at the end of the day when Yom Kippur falls on *Shabbes*?"

"Because it's our custom."

"But what does that mean?" Kagan pressed.

"That means that that's the way we do it. I don't know the reason for it. Ask Isaacson. He helped found the place, maybe he knows."

"I'd better," said Kagan.

Isaacson sat studying the Torah reading for Yom Kippur. Kagan leaned over to get his attention. As soon as Mr. Isaacson saw him, he smiled and reached to take Kagan's right hand in both of his.

"*Gut yontiff*," Isaacson said.

What a warm wonderful handshake, thought Kagan. "*Gut yontiff, gut Shabbes*," he responded.

"How are you feeling, Moe? When I didn't see you, I was worried you might be sick."

Unlike those others. But they were right, Kagan grudgingly admitted. "No, I'm fine. I overslept."

"Good, good," Mr. Isaacson said, squeezing Kagan's hand, expressing his pleasure that Kagan was not sick.

"Mr. Isaacson, since today is *Shabbes* and Yom Kippur, we give the Priestly Blessing today only by *neilah*?"

"That's right, Moe."

"Why, Mr. Isaacson?"

"Because it's our *minhag*, our custom."

"Because it's the right thing to do?" Kagan pressed.

"No, because it's our custom," Mr. Isaacson answered innocently.

"Well, why is it our custom?" Kagan pleaded.

"Because it's the right thing to do!" Mr. Isaacson answered adamantly.

They were beginning to read the Torah. Whispering "Shh," Mr. Isaacson released Kagan's hand. Kagan, smiling to himself, returned to his seat.

"What'd he say?" Benny asked.

"Some things be's that way," Kagan quoted his students.

"Isaacson reads Rumanian below grade level?" Schwartz remarked.

"Yeah," Kagan laughed. "That guy ought to write me a routine on Rumania. There's a routine there someplace."

Kagan opened his *machzor* to the exact page and wondered what the odds against that were. Although the reading had already begun, Kagan in distraction turned towards the old man's seat by the curtain. Empty, but no horses either, thank God. Kagan turned back, but before he looked inside his book, he sat listening to the reader's plaintive penitential chant. The whining tones were strangely soulful and uplifting, devoid of the undignified kvetching one might have expected from plaintive cries. Yet the sound of supplicating anguish made Kagan resonate uncomfortably to its melodic pain. To remove its keen edge, he drifted inside his book to concentrate on the quiet printed word.

Usually Kagan followed the Hebrew even though he didn't understand it. (If God wants to hear it, it's good enough for me. I'm sure he understands it, aren't you?) But today was not the usual Yom Kippur. God knew what was happening but Kagan didn't. Distressed by his ignorance, Kagan decided to read the English translation.

Everybody loves Leviticus some of the time, Kagan sang to himself when he noticed the source of the reading.

Kagan began to read about the death of Aaron's two sons. They had stepped where they shouldn't have in the Tabernacle. Now that's a pretty tough out-of-bounds play, joked Kagan.

"Hey, Benny," Kagan whispered loud enough for everyone to hear. "You read this stuff? Aaron's boys would have been better off in the National Basketball Association. There you get two technicals before they throw you out."

"Yeah," Benny agreed, "that was a pretty tough place

to work with those shop rules."

"Now maybe you guys'll have a little respect for us *cohens* when you see what we used to do," Kagan said in a normal speaking voice.

From the main room came shushing voices and disapproving looks.

"Kagan, at least they got there on time. And I guarantee you that they didn't clock out early. As for Benny, the High Priest had to believe in some of the Torah," Schwartz whispered.

"Well," said Benny, "they probably didn't have my size in those priestly linen outfits, anyway. But you never know who's cut out for what unless you give him a chance."

"Sometimes people rise to the occasion like Harry Truman and Mr. Isaacson," Kagan said seriously.

Everyone in the small room laughed.

"You think he likes *shlepping* money out of people to buy *aliyahs*?" Kagan asked rhetorically. "It's not his thing, but the *shul* needs money. So do I," Kagan added with self-pity.

"Yeah, Kagan, some High Priest you would have been," Schwartz said. "Had you been there, Titus never would have gotten his hands on those holy golden vessels. You would have pawned them long before. The Holy of Holies would have been papered with hockshop tickets."

Even Kagan laughed. "It's probably true," he admitted.

"But, Moe, you would have been great at the holy lottery," Schwartz added.

"Can you imagine?" Benny laughed, "all the side action Moe would have had going? All of Israel would have shown up to get the results."

What the hell are they talking about? wondered

Kagan. Before he got a chance to ask, the rabbi started pounding the reading desk and calling "*Nu?*" in his most anguished voice.

The group thought it prudent not to continue their conversation for the time being.

Wondering what lottery they were talking about, Kagan returned to the text. On Yom Kippur, the High Priest wears linen garments instead of gold and starts with the sacrifices. I don't know about Benny, Kagan thought, but I don't think I'm cut out for this job. It's not my thing to go running around slaughtering animals. What would Yvette think? There must be a routine there someplace. Kagan read on. Oh, yeah, the two he-goats. Kagan had an idea what they had been talking about.

Kagan leaned forward to whisper to Danny and his friend.

"You boys can see what a male-chauvinist thing the Temple was. It says two he-goats. Now with women's lib, it would have to be a he- and a she-goat."

The boys laughed.

"Or with gay lib," Kagan continued, "you could get by with just one, a he-she goat."

They laughed but Danny shook his head. "It wouldn't work, Moe. You need two."

"Oh, you do?" said Kagan somewhat defensively, vaguely recalling a lottery but not enough to understand Danny.

Kagan returned to his prayer book. The High Priest brings both goats to the entrance of the Tent of Meeting. Okay, originally Aaron did it, but in later years the High Priest in the Temple cast lots upon the goats. Kagan felt a throbbing in his temples. Action! In the Temple, with the High Priest. Aaron himself ran the game! On Yom Kippur! It was awesome, fearful, and amazing. Kagan was horrified: gambling — a lottery no less! Kagan was astonished: why is that there? Kagan was delighted: that's my boy! Kagan was fearful: five — seven — three — four! And Kagan was curious! With the throbbing in his temples, he was drawn to the other Temple. He leaned forward, put his elbows on his knees, and held the *machzor* in front of his face as if he were going to devour it.

Kagan read intently and well above grade level to find out all that he could about the action in the Temple on Yom Kippur. With burning curiosity, he discovered that the High Priest drew lots on the two goats. One lot was "for the Lord" and the other was "for Azazel." The High Priest then offered the Lord's goat, sacrificing it in the Temple and sprinkling its blood as an atonement for the Holy Sanctuary because of the impurities. But the goat "for Azazel" was altogether different. The High Priest placed his hands upon its head and confessed all the sins of Israel, then sent it to the desert "carrying all of the people's sins." In the wilderness it got shoved over a cliff.

My god, Kagan realized in astonishment, that goat, the one for Azazel, atones for all of Israel. Kagan's head ached. Gambling decides the most important event of Yom Kippur!

"Benny, what do you make out of the lottery with the goats?" Kagan inquired earnestly. And then with a rush of consternation, he importuned, "What's going on?"

Benny looked up soberly. "Mack," he said, "I can't make heads or tails out of that mumbo-jumbo. That's what God wants; that's what we do. How that little goat can drag off everybody's sins beats me. Hell, just carrying my sins it could get a hernia."

In spite of his joke, Kagan appreciated Benny's gravity. Benny addressed all of his serious theological statements to "Mack," no matter to whom he was speaking, including the rabbi. Kagan joked that Benny's blessings began, "Blessed art Thou O Mack, King of the Universe."

But at the moment Kagan wasn't searching for friendship or fellowship. He was searching for understanding.

Mumbling "Excuse me," Kagan promptly crawled over half a dozen people to Bienstock.

"Bienstock, what's it all about?"

Bienstock, following the Torah reading, looked up in distraction. He motioned with his hand for Kagan to wait a few moments until the reader reached the end of a section.

"What's the problem?"

"The problem, Bienstock, is how the goats work," Kagan demanded.

"Kagan, what are you talking about?"

"I'm talking about the two he-goats the High Priest draws in the lottery. You said that's what Yom Kippur is all about."

"Yes," Bienstock nodded. "The one for Azazel atones for all of Israel's sins, that's right."

"But how does it work?" Kagan insisted.

"It's very involved but it's all in the Talmud. They bring two white goats before the High Priest, one on his right side and one on his left. Then they bring him the box containing the two ballots; on one is written 'the Lord,' on the other 'Azazel.' He reaches inside with both hands, simultaneously grabs a ballot in each hand, lifts them out together, and the right-hand ballot, whichever it is, belongs to the goat on his right side and the left-hand ballot to the left-side goat. It's a blind lottery."

"Fine, but how does it work?" Kagan repeated

adamantly.

"What do you mean?" Bienstock asked with a tinge of irritation. "I told you that's how it works."

"No," Kagan insisted, "that's how they did it, but why did they have to have a lottery to atone for our sins? How does *that* work?"

"Because God wanted it that way."

"Yeah, but what's the reason? Why gambling in the Temple on Yom Kippur?"

"That's what God wants!" Bienstock repeated.

"Good, but how does it work?" Kagan responded torturously.

Bienstock realized that the Torah reader was about to continue with the reading.

"How should I know how it works?" Bienstock burst out in frustration. "Who cares how it works? It works! That's what counts!"

Kagan, equally frustrated, returned to his seat. He kept his book open, but didn't bother looking inside. He was thinking, but he didn't know where to begin.

All right, it works! Good, so it works. But a lottery? Why is a game of chance needed to atone for our sins? It's not what you would expect Aaron to do on Yom Kippur. And if it is there, it must be there for a reason. Everything is there for a reason. But a lottery? What's Off-Track Betting doing in the Holy of Holies? It's not right! It hurts even to see all those bingo games in a church on Saturday night. That's not right, but the Holy Temple on Yom Kippur!

Kagan sat and thought, savoring the thrill of self-recognition. Yes, folks, when he performs the ritual slaughter, Kagan closes his eyes out of respect to his pet cat, but when he draws the holy lottery, he's a genius. We've never had a High Priest who felt so at home with what Yom Kippur is all about. Most of the

time such a self-indulgent daydream would have been
protected, nurtured, developed, explored. But now
Kagan couldn't accept this escape. Something at the
very heart of it disturbed him. A game of chance. Why?
wondered Kagan. Why? Why? begged Kagan. He knew
there had to be a reason but he didn't feel very sanguine
about his chances of discovering it because he knew a
mismatch when he saw one. Kagan was about to unleash
his middling, muddled mind on a very, very heavy
subject. It would be like trying to cut granite with
toothpicks. There's a routine there someplace. Cutting
granite with toothpicks! Am I ever happy I don't have
any money on that. That's not gambling; that's murder.

But Kagan couldn't give up: how could he? The
problem was killing him. Kagan concentrated on the
High Priest and the two goats. One for the Lord and one
for Azazel.

Kagan focused on the High Priest's drawing the lots,
but that didn't provide any understanding. He imagined how the ballots felt to the High Priest's groping
fingers in the holy atonement of blindman's buff. The
awkward, blind probing inside the dark box; the strange
unexpected sensation of touch that precedes grasping
an unseen object. Kagan wondered what the ballots
were made out of. How did they feel? Were the Priest's
hands clammy, slick with perspiration? Was the High
Priest nervous? Did his hands ever slip from the ballots? What did he think about while he was reaching
for the Lord and for Azazel?

Sensing that his inquiry wasn't heading in the right
direction, Kagan decided to take another tack. What
role did chance play in the act of atonement? Kagan
was pleased with his formulation of the question. It
sounded very academic, almost professorial. You think
I smoke a pipe for nothing? Why a lottery? What is the

essence of a lottery? Kagan asked. The structure of his inquiry seemed awfully good, but to Kagan's surprise, it led only into the ballot box. He stopped formulating questions and watched the large, strong, blunt fingers (they seemed not to taper at all) poking sightlessly inside the dark, fateful box. Kagan found himself rooting "C'mon!" as the stiff joints pushed ponderously into one captive corner after another. Although Kagan enjoyed this interior drama, he was aware that his rooting didn't make much sense. Each of the High Priest's hands had to seize a ballot. The Lord would get a goat and so would Azazel. Kagan didn't care where either goat would wind up. Although that was the natural bet, Kagan was fascinated with the priestly act of choosing. The rooting was satisfying so Kagan kept up his "c'mons" and "yeahs," but not wishing to be too judgmental, he never mentioned the Lord or Azazel.

The fingers plunged close to the ballots lying lifelessly stiff on the box's floor. Yeah, c'mon baby, urged Kagan. As the fumbling fingers drew nearer to their fateful prize, another scene descended into Kagan's consciousness, unrolling like an old yellow tenement shade with a ringlike handle. A shade from the "new building." In the intruding scene, Kagan saw a small figure skating on thin ice. The scene itself was sketchy but Kagan could tell that the ice was thin from the slow, careful, fearful manner of the skater. The figure carefully slid his skates along the ice so he would not have to lift one and thereby put the entire weight on the other. He moved with his hands slightly extended as if fearful of falling. His back curved with anxiety as he stared down at his impossible path.

As the High Priest's fingers stumbled away from the ballots, the shade-skating scene came into view. The scene appeared and faded as the blind fingers ap-

proached and drew away from the ballots. Just as the
blunt finger bumped the ballot in cautious collision,
the shade completely unrolled and Kagan found himself watching the anxious solitary skater circle about
on the perilously thin ice. The sharpened image revealed just how thin the ice was. Thinner than the
delicate figure-skating blades, the ice bent beneath the
skater's heartbeats. The timid shuffling step pantomimed the uncertain footing and balance of an old
person on solid ground. As the skater circled closer,
Kagan realized that the figure was, indeed, an old man,
and after several more minutes of observing the ago-
nized motion, Kagan recognized the skater on thin ice.

"Chaim From Yesterday," he whispered. Then he
added in his normal stentorian tones of amazement,
"I'll be damned!"

"I suppose you will, Kagan," Schwartz answered, "if
you don't start praying. You have a few more hours
until *neilah* when the gate closes and is locked."

"What?" asked Kagan of both himself and Schwartz.

*"Musaf*, we're *davening musaf* now. That's why
everyone is standing except you."

Kagan looked around. Where have I been? They've
already said the memorial prayer. Thank God, Mom
and Dad are still alive — an image of the old couple
*davening* amid palm trees flitted through his mind —
or I would have missed *Yizkor* for them.

Kagan resolved to write them more frequently in the
coming year and rose to join his fellows. He looked
about again. Driven by the wavelike beat of the rocking
Jews, the murmur of prayer flowed through the *shtibl*,
filling every corner. The dancing fringes of the prayer
shawls rose and fell only to be carried upward again, as
if they floated upon the murmuring swells of faith,
woolen seagulls coasting a penitential sea with prayer

as their wake.

What a crazy place, thought Kagan affectionately. When I came in a moment ago, everyone was talking and no one was praying. Now no one is talking and everyone is praying. Everyone except for me. He opened his book to pray. His fringes began to rise and fall.

Kagan concentrated with some success. The Confessional contained fists pounding on hearts, but no hoof-beats. Nevertheless, he glanced over his shoulder to see if the man in the rumpled green suit was near the finish line. Kagan confirmed his absence and continued praying, not with great fervor, but with dedication. Through Kagan's thoughts glided the fragile figure of Chaim Der Nechtiger, circling perilously above the fine edge of sin — "For the sin we have committed before Thee" (pound) "by desecrating Thy Name." All in all, not a bad performance when Kagan considered some of the thoughts that often intruded on his prayers. You do your best and let God worry about the rest, mused Kagan.

Kagan sat down with the others and during the repetition of the *musaf* prayer made a few desultory attempts to puzzle out the High Priest's holy lottery. None of these met with much success and Chaim Der Nechtiger intermittently continued his icy shuffle. Kagan tried to get Chaim's attention to wish him a *gut yontiff* or just to nod. Kagan was forever seeking out old acquaintances in public places to say hello and rejoice in memory. Fran was forever embarrassed by it. She said that it was pointless, but Kagan relished those chance encounters. By greeting them, Kagan felt he was connecting to other places and other times, and thereby integrating a fragmented world. Perhaps it even suggested some great plan — hence Kagan's frustration at not catching Chaim From Yesterday's eye. Kagan couldn't blame Chaim

Der Nechtiger, for the little man was preoccupied with skating on thin ice.

Had Kagan been able to attract his attention, he would have said, "Chaim Der Nechtiger, *shalom aleichem.* You know, the old *minyan* on Second Street. I'm Kagan, a friend of Mr. Stein's son, Louie." If the old man's face did not light up with a smile of recognition and a hint of satisfaction (old people love being remembered), Kagan would have continued, "You remember Mr. Stein. He bought the *chometz* before Pesach." No doubt that would have done the trick, but Kagan wouldn't want to add that last part unless he had to. That was how the old man had gotten his name. It was never very clear to Kagan whether Chaim From Yesterday was very fond of it. Everyone called him that and he didn't seem to mind. Still, he never seemed to be terribly fond of it either. He bore it as one more burden along with his age and inability to get anywhere on time. Kagan, along with everyone else, had called him Chaim Der Nechtiger. What else could I have called him? That was his name ever since he appeared at the Steins' door.

Mr. Stein used to handle the sale of *chometz* before Passover. Like Louie he was a rabbi and knew how to take care of that stuff. The week before Passover, after the evening prayer in *shul*, Mr. Stein would stick around to buy any non-Passover food — mainly liquor — that anyone wanted to keep in his house over the holiday. Right before Passover, he would write up a formal contract and sell all the forbidden food to the Italian janitor of the "new building." With fascination, Kagan would watch the elaborate contractual ritual for the apparently fictional sale among the various parties, all poor.

Everyone who wanted to sell his food met Mr. Stein in *shul* at night — except Chaim. The last night before

Passover, at eleven-thirty, someone knocked at the door. It woke up the whole house. Eleven-thirty then was like two in the morning now. People had to work. In his underwear, Mr. Stein asked, "Who is it?"

"It's me, Chaim. I came to sell the *chometz*."

"It's too late, come back in the morning."

The next morning at quarter to five a knocking on the Steins' door woke us all up again. Mr. Stein climbed out of bed.

"Who is it?" he asked with trepidation. What but bad news could come at that hour?

"Chaim," a voice answered.

"Chaim who?" Mr. Stein persisted.

"Chaim *fun nechtin*," Chaim answered, and from then on he was Chaim Der Nechtiger, Chaim From Yesterday. Remembering the old neighborhood, Kagan smiled. Could Chaim still be alive?

"You think you have problems, Kagan? Take a look at what happened to these Jews," Benny said.

"What?" Kagan asked.

"I said if you want to know what *tsouris* is, read about these guys."

Kagan leaned forward to get the page number. The *musaf* service had arrived at the Ten Martyrs. Kagan remembered this somewhat: the Romans killed ten great sages. They were tortured and everything. Each year, Kagan was deeply moved. He couldn't recall, however, why they were killed.

Kagan read the English translation to find out. The Roman Emperor, who had studied the Talmudic law, had his palace filled with shoes. Then he commanded the ten sages to appear before him. "Judge these matters honestly," he said to the sages. "If someone is caught kidnapping an Israelite and sells him into slavery, what is his punishment?" The sages answered,

"The thief shall die." Then the Emperor declared, "Where are your fathers who sold their brother Joseph into slavery for a pair of shoes? You must submit to the judgment of heaven and die. If they were alive I would execute them, but now you must bear their iniquity."

Shoes, Kagan said, shoes. Where had he heard that before? Didn't it have something to do with Pakooz? Pakooz, keep your shoes on. That's it! Keep your shoes on! Kagan remembered where he had heard it first. The old man in the rumpled green suit told me that after *Kol Nidre* when I was running out to find the results of the race. Keep your shoes on, instead of keep your shirt on. "Keep your shoes on," Kagan said quietly, hoping to fathom its meaning by uttering it slowly and distinctly. "Keep your shoes on." But the pronouncement didn't yield its secret.

Kagan turned toward the empty seat as if checking a base runner in a close game; then he picked his way through the room to Bienstock.

Bienstock, deep in the prayer of the Ten Martyrs, had large wet tears running down his cheeks. Kagan rushed toward him, welcoming those tears as his own. He put his hand on Bienstock's shoulder and plaintively whispered into his ear.

"Bienstock, what's it all about?"

Bienstock, still crying, looked up at Kagan as if he did not recognize him. Then he said in a hollow voice, "The Ten Martyrs, the Ten Martyrs."

"Yes," said Kagan nodding, and he felt the warm drops in his own eyes swell as he began to weep.

Bienstock clutched Kagan's elbow and returned to reading the prayer aloud. Oh, what was done to those righteous men, mourned Kagan and he wept for the death of the righteous. Bienstock concluded the prayer with a shudder of agony.

"Bienstock?" Kagan asked after the furrier had finished. "What was with the shoes?"

"The shoes?" Bienstock said quizzically.

"The Emperor filled his palace with shoes and showed them to the ten sages."

"Oh," said Bienstock, "the shoes. On Yom Kippur, Jacob's sons sold Joseph into slavery, and with the money they each bought a pair of shoes. The shoes that the Emperor showed them were the evidence of the crime."

"Oh," said Kagan, partially satisfied, "but what about the goat?"

"The goat has nothing to do with it. That's something else."

"But the goat carried off everyone's sins," Kagan continued.

"That's right," Bienstock said, satisfied that Kagan finally understood the function of the goat.

"If the goat carried off all the sins and atoned for all of Israel, why do they have to pay for the sin of their ancestors?"

Bienstock's face twisted in discomfort. "They were very righteous," he answered.

"I don't think it's right," Kagan said.

"Neither did the angels," Bienstock answered.

"What angels?" Kagan asked.

Bienstock opened Kagan's *machzor* and showed him where the angel cried in anguish to God that it was unjust. God replied that if He heard another word of complaint from the angels, He would turn the world into water. This is His will and all who love the Torah, for which the world was created, must accept it.

"The show must go on," Kagan said hoarsely.

Kagan shook his head and wandered back to his seat.

I wish Ozzie were here, but I guess that wouldn't

make much difference. If the angels couldn't understand it, how can I? Where does that leave the little
goat? Out in the wilderness, Kagan joked. A joke that
struck Kagan as clever, but not very funny. Too much
was at stake to lose it for a few laughs.

At first I didn't know how the little goat did the job,
he groaned. Now I don't even know if the little goat did
do the job. Things seem to be going from bad to worse.
As Kagan sat perplexed, Chaim From Yesterday wearily skated into view.

"*Oy gevalt!*" said Kagan.

"What's wrong?" Danny asked.

Chaim Der Nechtiger circled on the thin ice, barefoot. Where were his skates?

"He lost his shoes!" Kagan said fearfully.

"Who?" Danny asked.

"What?" asked everyone else.

Kagan felt torn between the terror of humiliating
exposure and the desire to let them know what was
happening to him. Who would believe it?

"I said, he lost his shoes."

"Who?" they asked.

"Whoever," Kagan answered, "and the Emperor
found them and filled his palace with them to accuse
the ten sages for the sale of Joseph. I don't understand
it."

"I don't either," said Benny. "It always seemed like a
pretty weak legal case to me."

"That's life. No one understands it," said Schwartz.

"Moe," Benny said in serious appreciation, "for
somebody who came late, you're really getting into
things."

"Too deep," mourned Kagan.

"Be careful," Schwartz advised.

"Thanks," Kagan answered, nodding his head.

Kagan wondered how long Chaim Der Nechtiger could last like that.

# 9

THEY continued straight into the afternoon prayer with its short Torah reading about forbidden sexual relationships. Kagan welcomed it for he had grown extremely agitated as Chaim From Yesterday's bare feet slid across the ice. Kagan found himself stamping his own feet for warmth. The straightforward Torah reading with its old-fashioned prohibitions reassured and comforted him.

No more Bungalow Bar, said Kagan with a relaxed feeling. That's what religion is supposed to be all about: what you can't eat, who you can't screw. Fair is fair. No more Bungalow Bar, he said, not with rueful resignation but with the thrill of discovering a compass in an uncharted wilderness.

Kagan turned away from Chaim From Yesterday (what did he have to do with religion, anyhow?) and stood by the curb in the old neighborhood waiting for the little specially designed truck. The ice-cream bar itself wasn't anything special, but the truck was magic. A veritable bungalow with its slanted roof, flower-filled window boxes, and real screen door, all riding fresh as a daisy through the hot, melting asphalt streets lined with heat-blasted old brick buildings. Just watching it turn the corner, Kagan would forget that he stood on roasting pavement in front of the "new building," where heads lolled on fire escapes, risking decapitation from the old heavy windows that had been raised in a futile effort to escape the inescapable heat. Suddenly the Bungalow Bar truck appeared and Kagan thought he was barefoot in the country, the sweet meadow smells rising softly around him. The magic went beyond the mobile bungalow, ambassador of the mountains. With delicious anticipation, more pleasurable than the ice cream itself, Kagan would lick the last remnant of the enshrouding vanilla from the stick and if the word "BUNGALOW" appeared, you won another Bungalow Bar!

That Bungalow Bar made summer worthwhile — the truck, the ice cream, the search for treasure. Kagan smiled. One summer Louie heard that the ice cream wasn't kosher. They used gelatin or some other forbidden ingredient. And — no more Bungalow Bar!

Kagan looked inside his *machzor* to follow the Torah reading: "You shall not have intercourse with your father's wife." No more Bungalow Bar, thought Kagan. "You shall not have intercourse with your sister." No more Bungalow Bar, responded Kagan. "You shall not have intercourse with your son's daughter or your daughter's daughter." No more Bungalow Bar! No more Bungalow Bar!

Kagan found his rhythmic "amen" very satisfactory. That's what the Torah's all about, he thought, reveling in the rigid structure.

His satisfaction did not last long. As the purchaser of *Maftir Yonah* (Mermelstein, the not very lovable landlord) was called to read the Book of Jonah, a siren's howl on Broadway came shrieking into the *shtibl.* Unable to follow the service, everyone looked up, waiting for the interruption to pass.

As it began to fade, Benny commented, "For this, the old ladies have the windows open."

Kagan, however, didn't hear Benny's remark. He was

watching something else: Chaim Der Nechtiger falling
through the ice, a wretched look of horror on his old,
normally placid face.

Kagan jumped to his feet.

"He needs help!" he said and ran from the *shtibl*
after the fading siren.

HIS old Bob-Cousy-Celtic sneakers measuring the
even sidewalk in confident rubberized bounds, Kagan
ran down warm, sunny Ninety-first Street.

As he rounded the corner, turning downtown, he ran
headlong into Broadway's crowded sidewalk. His mo-
mentum flinging him forward, he threw his body from
side to side, but his furious slalom swerves proved
insufficient to negotiate the shifting human forest. Clip-
ping strollers, Kagan went spinning off them only to
bump others, regaining his balance in a mad whirl.
Hoping to find some room to maneuver, he sliced
toward the curbs, his cushioned feet dashing to stay
under the erratic zigzag path his plunging body pursued from point to point like a hard, silvered metal
ball in a pinball machine. Stiff-arming a knob-topped
parking meter to avoid disaster, he suddenly realized
that the fading siren was on the verge of disappearing
among the jostling afternoon sounds. Grabbing the next
parking meter, he held on long enough to pivot around
it and dashed into the street.

People stared as Kagan tore down the street, too far
behind the distant echoes of the siren's soprano shriek
for anyone to associate it with the stimulus for his
speed. Kagan maintained his wondrous form for two
blocks, but age and a day without food or drink took
their toll on his straining body. The old, high-cut black
sneakers began thumping Broadway in less than robust
bounds as the faded rubber soles slapped the decayed

pavement. Kagan, breathing deeply in lung-searing gasps, refused to slow down, and frantically tried to draw in enough oxygen to fuel the outrageous demands of his aged and ill-conditioned body. And as the high fluid pressures exploded in his head where the mad, oxygenated blood spurted toward the apogee of its circular course, Kagan understood. The goats made sense: vulnerability!

At Eighty-sixth Street, Kagan paused. His chest heaved in fractured dislocations that sent pain shooting through his lungs. But before Kagan realized how far his lungs trailed his legs, he was running again; he had sighted the revolving red light of the police car.

A T Eighty-third Street, a crowd shielded both the police car and the victim. Impervious to his pain and his unsteady step, Kagan tried to force his way through the morbidly curious crowd toward the victim. He knew who it had to be. The shoulder-to-shoulder crowd presented an impenetrable wall of backs. Seeking an opening, Kagan skirted along its murmuring fringes. "Hit and run," uttered low, deprecating voices. Kagan couldn't get in close. Standing on tiptoe, he saw that the crowd pressed forward up to the narrow island bisecting Broadway. If he circled around he might then step over the fence and cross over the sparsely grassed enclosure back to the downtown lane where the victim lay.

Following this stratagem, Kagan circled the crowd and crossed into the uptown lane where a trickle of vehicles inched forward, their drivers staring curiously across the dirty green island. Some inquired what the commotion was all about, but Kagan ignored them in his single-minded dedication to get closer. Stepping over the low metal railing onto the island, he felt the sooty grit underfoot. As Kagan glanced up to check his route, he was aware of a bobbing green patch on the periphery of his vision. More in reflex than in thought, he turned to focus on it.

Someone was waving to him from the benches at the end of the island in the middle of Broadway.

"My God," Kagan said as he waved back to the man in the rumpled green suit.

"*GUT Shabbes, gut yontiff,*" Kagan said, extending his hand. His heart trembled.

"*Gut Shabbes, gut yontiff,*" the old man said evenly and politely, standing to greet Kagan.

"May you be sealed in the Book of Life," Kagan responded.

"May you be sealed in the Book of Life."

The old man with his slightly sagging face punctuated with his caved-in features seemed friendly enough but not terribly warm. He was no Isaacson, that's for sure.

"How do you feel?" he asked Kagan.

Kagan was surprised to hear this question.

"Fine," he answered matter-of-factly. "How are you?"

"I feel a little weak."

"You do?" Kagan asked politely.

"Yes, I'm fasting."

"So am I," Kagan said, suddenly remembering he hadn't eaten or drunk anything since yesterday afternoon. "My God, I haven't even thought about that."

"Well, I have," the old man said. "Do you mind if we sit down? Besides, we might get trampled if we stand here."

Facing uptown, they sat on a green wooden bench (considerably darker in color than the old man's suit) and could see the crowd milling expectantly about the victim.

"Why?" Kagan asked simply.

"I guess they want a *mitzvah*. So they're running to help that poor fellow," the old man answered.

"No," Kagan said thinking that this might prove to be an extremely exhausting encounter; the old man might not want to discuss it. He was no Bienstock either. "Not that. Why?" Kagan insisted.

"Why what?" the old man asked in reply.

"Why are you doing what you are doing? Why did you do what you did?" Kagan asked.

"Oh," the old man said, "because it's Yom Kippur. That's why I'm fasting."

"No, not that," Kagan interrupted.

"Please, let me finish."

Kagan sat back to let him finish.

"I'm fasting," he said, "because it's a *mitzvah* on Yom Kippur to afflict one's soul. That's important. You shouldn't forget. It helps if you want to make it."

"Okay," Kagan said, not listening very carefully. "But why? Why did you move the curtain last night and change the outcome of the race?"

The old man sighed as if he were reticent to discuss the fine points of the matter.

"First of all, Moe, you must understand that I wanted to see if a lady needed a *machzor*."

"But that's not why you did it."

"Of course that's not why I did it, but that's how I did it. If it would not have been for that, I never could have done it. It's confusing, but very important. Don't forget that, too."

"But why did you do it?" Kagan insisted.

Sighing again, the old man reluctantly continued. "He didn't corrupt you, Moe."

A tenderness had entered the old man's voice. He put his hand on Kagan's knee.

"Who?" Kagan wondered aloud in confusion. "Who didn't corrupt me?"

"Whoever wanted you to bet on *Shabbes* and Yom Kippur," the old man answered.

"Ozzie? Ozzie wanted to corrupt me?"

The old man nodded reluctantly.

"But Ozzie's an angel."

The old man looked uncomfortable. A pained expression creased his sagging face.

"Ozzie is an angel, isn't he?" Kagan asked.

"Yes, he certainly is."

Kagan was confused. "Why would he want to corrupt me?"

The old man in the rumpled green suit stirred uneasily. "I'd rather not get into that."

"But he is an angel?"

"One of the most talented," the old man stated definitively.

What do you know about that? thought Kagan. One of the best. He knew that 5 — 7 — 3 — 4 was the winner, all right. He's one of the best, my angel.

"Five — seven — three — four should have won the race?" Kagan asked.

"Yes, but I wouldn't say 'should have.' I would say it 'would have.'"

"And it didn't because I didn't bet it on *Shabbes*?" Kagan said with a trace of pride. That's what I call a reward for doing a *mitzvah*, he thought jubilantly. Wait till Ozzie hears about this.

"Wait till Ozzie hears about this!" Kagan crowed.

"He already knows," the old man said quietly.

"He does?" uttered Kagan, his newfound confidence shattered. "You're sure?"

"Uh-huh."

Wait a minute, thought Kagan. "What if I bet those

numbers tonight?" he asked quickly.

"They'll win," the old man said quietly.

Kagan clapped his hands and jumped to his feet. "They'll win!" he cried. He sat down again, a wealthy man.

"I'll make a fortune."

The old man didn't answer.

"I'll make a fortune, won't I?"

The old man smiled sadly.

"Well, what's wrong with that? I can use the money. It's not against the law. What's wrong?" Kagan demanded.

The old man squirmed and shrugged.

If you act that way all the time, no wonder your lousy green suit is so rumpled, Kagan thought. "Everyone else makes a fast buck. Why shouldn't I? I can do a lot of good with the money. I can pay some debts for one thing. So what's wrong?"

Only a shrug.

Kagan, an impassioned advocate desirous of a favorable comment, plunged into the argument. "What's wrong with a little gambling?"

No answer.

"It can't be so bad. They did it in the Temple, you know!" Then he added, "That's what Yom Kippur is all about. . . ." His remark began in rapid, voluminous tones with passionate conviction but turned along the way into a quiet statement of wonderment as Kagan came to realize that he was trapped, boxed in. And he knew where, too. In the box with the two ballots where he saw fourteen, maybe fifteen thousand dollars being dragged off to Azazel by that little white goat.

"My God," Kagan said in sober awe.

"Yes."

Kagan looked at the old man in the rumpled green

suit and they both squirmed.

"Vulnerability?" Kagan asked quietly.

"I think so," the old man nodded.

"That's what the game is all about," mused Kagan, amazed at his newfound wisdom. "Either goat can wind up in either place. The goat for the Lord is no different from the goat for Azazel and it could have been the goat for Azazel. That's the name of the game, vulnerability. The human condition. The two goats are the same because there is really just one goat, me — or any man. We have the choice to turn toward either direction and that's why Yom Kippur atones, because we are vulnerable — that's our situation — and if we do *tshuvah*, return, the atonement erases the sins."

"More," the old man said soberly. "It purifies them. They become as positive acts."

Kagan sat still. "Even as good deeds?"

"Yes."

"The past is at stake as well as the future?"

"The world is at stake," the old man said with sudden conviction.

"The world?"

"Every man must look upon the world as if it is created exclusively for him."

"Really?" Kagan asked as a twinge of excitement cascaded through his sense of awe. Kagan loved information.

"Yes, because it is created exclusively for him!" the old man repeated.

"It is?" Kagan wondered.

"It is!" the old man insisted.

"It is!" Kagan understood.

"And yet. . . ."

Kagan accepted the emendation. "And yet, the world that was created for the Ten Martyrs destroyed them."

"Yes, and yet — the world was created for them; they accepted it. They sanctified and purified it. They saved the world that was created for them."

Kagan nodded.

"They chose life!" the old man added.

"I think I accept that, but I'm not sure I understand it," Kagan said.

"Few do. I've had trouble with it myself for years."

"You have?" asked Kagan.

"Yes, Moe. Even the angels went crazy and they're not given to praising man. It's like a quiz show. Someone is asked a difficult question to win a car. He gives the right answer, but when he steps out of the isolation booth to collect the prize, he discovers that it hasn't been invented yet, or the roads are destroyed, or he is blind."

Kagan looked at his pickle-green watch with tender amusement and new understanding. "Do you know how many men walked on the moon?"

"Men or astronauts?" the old man asked for clarification.

"Oh really?" asked Kagan, excited at the implication of a significant surprise.

"No matter," said the old man. "I don't watch quiz shows. They bore me."

"You watch sports?" Kagan asked hopefully.

"A little chess. Those guys are smart!" the old man said in awe.

"But don't you know who's going to win?"

"How should I know? Those guys are really smart!"

"No," said Kagan jumping back to his earlier question. "I meant basketball or baseball. I had a crazy dream last night."

"I know," said the old man.

"You do?" asked Kagan.

"Yes, but we were talking about quiz shows. Why were we talking about them, Moe?"

"You were explaining something about the Ten Martyrs."

"Well, it probably wasn't a very good explanation since I'm not so sure I understand it."

"Oh," said Kagan sympathetically.

"Sometimes it all comes together. Not so long ago I saw it all," the old man said with confidence.

"You did?"

"Moe, in the Second World War, the Nazis surrounded a town containing a small Jewish house of study. There was no escape possible, only certain death. In fear, the students turned to their rabbi for guidance. He told them, 'God has chosen us for sacrifices. We must purge ourselves of evil for only a pure sacrifice is accepted by God.'"

"Did that happen on Yom Kippur?"

"That day was Yom Kippur for the world, all right. They succeeded, Moe. To this day, all you have to say is 'Rav Hananael Wasserman' and the angels shut up."

"They do?" asked Kagan wondering about the angels' role in all of this.

"Sure!" the old man said heatedly. "Where do the angels come to something like that? What do they know, Moe? They have no staying power; they lack imagination. Man has those things. We're made in God's image, you know, and that's what drives the angels crazy. Don't worry about Ozzie, Moe. You can handle him. You have already."

"I have?"

"Moe, he hasn't corrupted you yet. Do you know how far the thing can go?"

He was slow warming up, Kagan thought, but once he gets going, this guy makes up for lost time.

"How far?" Kagan asked cooperatively.

"I'll tell you how far. The angels who were sent to tell Lot that Sodom would be destroyed said, 'For *we* will destroy Sodom,' as if they — and not God — were to destroy it. For that they were banished from heaven and had to wander the earth in humiliation until Jacob redeemed them. Not until Jacob dreamed his dream of the angels ascending the ladder could they return to heaven!"

The old man paused.

"Oh," responded Kagan politely.

"That's how far it can go!" the old man declared. "Whether it will go that far or not is another matter. Who knows?" he shrugged.

"Uh-huh. Listen," said Kagan, "the Nazi who shot the rabbi. . . ."

"May his name be erased forever!" the old man interrupted in splenetic outburst.

"Of course," agreed Kagan, "but if that act was necessary, like the death of the Ten Martyrs, can you blame him?"

"Blame him?" the old man yelled. "He's a murderer! There is never any messenger to do evil. Whoever does the act is responsible."

"But God couldn't stop the death of the Ten Martyrs without destroying the world."

"God couldn't, Moe, but man could have. They didn't have to torture and kill them. If everyone refused to torture them, the Messiah would have come!"

"But isn't there a quota?" Kagan asked. "Don't you have to know the quota?"

"No man knows the kvoda, Moe. No one can ever know, even when he is a part of it like Rabbi Hananael."

Kagan, an anguished Kagan, looked around at the uneasy crowd waiting for the ambulance to arrive.

"And yet — Moe, you must act as if the quota depends on you. For it does since it is a part of the world."

"Why hasn't an ambulance arrived to help him?" Kagan called out in pain.

The old man touched Kagan's arm reassuringly.

"Don't worry, Kagan. He'll make it. He always has. And if you want to, you can, too."

The old man stood up. "It is late. We'd better get back to *shul*. I'll wait for you there."

The old man walked into the crowd. Kagan tried to follow but couldn't. Working his way out of the crowd, Kagan heard the ambulance's siren. The police began to clear a path for the ambulance. Realizing he would only be in the way, Kagan decided to walk down toward West End Avenue.

ON West End Avenue, Kagan heard the scream of sirens announce that the victim was on his way to the hospital. As they continued to grow louder, Kagan turned to watch the police car and ambulance pass him. He caught a glimpse of the victim's limp arm above the blanket. It lay in a green sleeve, darker than a pool table, brighter than a Ping-Pong table. Kagan wasn't sure. Perhaps it was his imagination, or the motion of the ambulance, but the outstretched hand seemed to flick him a furtive greeting.

Well, thought Kagan, at least one of us will make it. I wonder who he is. Apparently, he's no angel.

WHO needs angels? Ozzie's an angel and he tried to corrupt me. A lot of good it does to have an angel if that's how they behave. What did I ever do to him for him to act that way towards me? Boy, would I like to get my hands on him — trying to corrupt me!

Kagan was outraged. The *chutzpah* of that angel —

trying to corrupt me! But he soon found himself wondering why the old man was so all-fire certain that Kagan wasn't corrupt. I gamble the rest of the week. Instead of charity, I give to shylocks. I take from the righteous poor and give to the criminal rich and I'm not even a congressman. There must be a routine there someplace!

Kagan suddenly didn't feel like developing any routines. What's going on? he wondered. All my life I'm convinced that down deep I'm pretty decent, even though most people think I'm not exactly a paragon of virtue, and suddenly someone — who is he, anyway? — someone important comes along and tells me I'm not corrupt, and for the first time I feel corrupt. Not rotten corrupt, but simple corrupt. Look at all the stuff I do: gambling, shylocking, conning people for loans, clocking out early, the lies — my God what a list — and playing games with Fran's head. Pakooz said it and it's true. He's no saint — he's got his own problems, too — but what's true is true. I play games with her head. That's a pretty corrupt thing to do. Look at all the crying she does. I know she's from Connecticut, but still she cries a lot, too much — and because of me.

Kagan began thinking about the numbers. They didn't flash through his head or anything snazzy like that. He just plain thought about them, sadly and wistfully. No great thrill and yet he knew that they would win any time he bet them. That's not gambling, he laughed ruefully to himself, that's murder. Whose murder? Not Katzi's, not any bookie's, not the track's, not OTB's. They could afford it. Statistically, it had to happen to them. Whose murder? Mine, Kagan realized. I would piss it all away, probably bet half of it in the first week alone. After having won like that, I would never believe that any numbers I bet could ever lose. My God, what that would be like! Kagan drew back from the abyss of speculation. It's bad enough as it is. "But who the hell wants to be a saint anyway?" Kagan said aloud in anger. A guy has to have some fun in life. Boredom isn't going to save the world either.

Kagan walked back toward the *shtibl*, wondering why he felt depressed in a calm, quiet manner. It wasn't like him at all. Normally, he was all fireworks, mad dashes, Paul Revere-type rides racing traffic and traffic lights in a Sixty-four Falcon. Yet he found the winning numbers a humbling experience. Why should they be given to me? All because I went to the *mikveh*? He knew that so much was involved that he couldn't blame it or place it on anything other than himself and God. It was, after all, their world, a world in which you have to know the quota and no man can. He seemed to possess some understanding, but why wasn't he in better spirits? He was fasting well. He didn't even feel hungry, but after what the old man had said, he wasn't very happy about that either. But the suffering seemed to be present, all right. As Kagan walked uptown, he still wondered what Chaim Der Nechtiger had to do with the goats. As he was wondering, a voice broke in on his thoughts. At first Kagan thought he had imagined it — an echo, maybe — but no, he was there, all right.

"Well, Ozzie, what is it?" Kagan asked in an unfriendly tone.

"Kagan, you're angry, aren't you?" the angel said in a raspy voice.

"Wouldn't you be, Ozzie?" Kagan retorted.

"Yes, you have a right to be angry."

Ozzie's voice was so very weak.

"I can hardly hear you, Ozzie. Are you fasting?" Kagan asked.

The angel burst out with a peal of bitter, manic laughter, "Sort of, Kagan!" And then he added, "He told you, didn't he?"

"Enough," said Kagan. "Say, who is he anyhow? I forgot to ask."

The angel laughed. Bitterness pierced the hilarity and Kagan felt uncomfortable.

"You do know who he is, don't you?" Kagan insisted.

"I even know who the *mikveh* man is," the angel said soberly.

And Kagan suddenly realized where he had previously heard "quota" pronounced "kvoda."

"They have the same voice," Kagan observed.

"They should," said the angel. "They are the same person."

"The same person?" asked Kagan confounded.

"He plays different roles. You know how many faces a man has," Ozzie said with sarcastic denigration.

"I guess so," Kagan agreed reluctantly, uncertain that he knew what Ozzie was talking about.

"But the one you spoke to this afternoon, that was the real one, I would say. His basic, unadorned self."

"You do know who he is, don't you?" Kagan pressed.

"Only too well, Kagan," the angel paused. "You had the pleasure of spending an hour on a Broadway bench across from your local Burger King with the Prophet Elijah."

"Really!?" said Kagan. "Me and Elijah the Prophet!"

"Yes," the angel answered.

"Are you sure?"

The angel laughed quietly, even appreciatively.

"That's not the way you pictured him, is it?" Ozzie asked.

"No, I imagined that the Prophet Elijah would be a little neater, but he's a. . . ."

"A slob?" the angel suggested.

Kagan didn't want to say it. When it came to religious stuff, Kagan was suprisingly respectful, but the truth was the truth and the day was Yom Kippur. "Yes," Kagan confessed quietly.

"That's the only thing that surprised you about him?" Ozzie pressed.

"No," Kagan admitted. "He didn't seem too sure of his understanding. I thought he would be brighter."

"And he seemed like a dunce, didn't he?" the angel laughed.

"Well — yes," Kagan agreed.

"Moe, I'll tell you the truth. I think he is a dunce."

"You do, Ozzie?"

"Yes, I do. And yet — that dunce has outsmarted more angels and won more arguments with God than you can ever believe."

"Because he's made in God's image?" Kagan suggested.

"Frankly, Moe, that strikes me as blasphemy. Whatever else you may say about God. He certainly isn't a dunce."

"Ozzie, I didn't mean that!" Kagan protested.

"Well, what did you mean?" the angel asked sharply.

"I don't know," wondered Kagan.

"Don't feel bad. Neither do I," Ozzie acknowledged. "None of the angels do. I never understood all the fuss over Adam in the first place."

"You didn't?" asked Kagan.

"How could I? 'Man is a thief,' I said. God said, 'If he weren't a thief, he would never earn a living.' 'Man is lewd,' I said. 'He has to be,' God said. 'If he weren't, he wouldn't take a wife and people the earth.'"

"And yet," Kagan said, "man is made in God's image."

"Yes," Ozzie admitted. "Now you sound like Elijah."

"Thanks a lot," Kagan said sarcastically.

"Low I.Q. or not, Moe, you should have half the success he has had," the angel pronounced.

"Why?" asked Kagan.

"Elijah has faith and humility. That seems to get him through," Ozzie said.

"No," said Kagan, "not that. Why, Ozzie?"

"Why what?" answered Ozzie.

"Why did you do what you did?" Kagan insisted.

"I was an angel," Ozzie said.

"No," said Kagan, "why did you try and corrupt me?"

There was no answer.

"What did I ever do to you to deserve that?" Kagan added in a hurt tone.

"Moe, it goes way back. It was nothing personal."

"'Nothing personal,' he says! He tries to corrupt me and he says it's nothing personal."

"You have a right to be mad, Moe, but it wasn't the way you make it sound. It was more of a class thing. I'm an angel and you're a man."

"But why?" Kagan demanded.

"You seemed like a good target. No one gets corrupted who doesn't want to be. After all, man has free will."

"But why, Ozzie? Just to be mean?"

"Look, Moe, it's like Elijah told you," Ozzie began in weak, embarrassed tones.

"I want to hear it from you!" Kagan demanded. "Elijah said that you were one of the best."

"What a cagey old guy. He always gives credit; I'll say that for him. I'll tell you, Moe, because I don't think it will make any difference now. Like I said, it goes way back. Men seemed pretty rotten to the angels and to me especially. Angels sang praises in heaven and men sinned. And yet man possessed the earth. So I asked God, 'Why do you have mercy on them?' And God answered that if I would be among them, I would fail, too. Of course, we angels wanted to inhabit the earth in place of man. Like I said, Moe, it's a class thing. 'We will sanctify Your Name,' we said; so we accepted the challenge and came down among men."

Ozzie paused.

"And?" Kagan inquired curiously.

"We failed," the angel rasped.

"You did," Kagan said in wonderment.

"Why do you think I chase every skirt in creation?" Ozzie asked in bitter frustration at Kagan's obtuseness.

"Oh," said Kagan, "that's where your hot pants come from."

"Burning hot," the angel added in self-pity.

"You said 'we.' What happened to the others?" Kagan asked.

"Every one of us failed. Some fell for theft. Some for money. Some for food. The works, Kagan. We didn't last too long."

"Where are the others now? Floating around like you?" Kagan asked.

"No-o-o," Ozzie said slowly.

"Well, where are they?"

"Back in heaven where they belong," the angel said quietly.

"Why aren't you there with them?"

"They did penitence. . . ."

"And you didn't?" Kagan volunteered.

"Uh-huh," the angel grunted.

"Why not? You were the best," asked Kagan, respectful but perplexed.

"You ask too many questions!" the angel snapped.

"Forgive my prying, Ozzie."

There was a silence.

"Ozzie?" Kagan asked.

"Yes?"

"Where are you Yom Kippur?"

The angel laughed his mad, bitter laugh. "Since I cannot return to heaven, on Yom Kippur I remain in the desert to close the mouth of Israel's accuser and to serve as a warning to others to be silent. The scapegoat is sent to me, Azazel, to remind others of my fate for I bear the sins of Israel."

The angel rasped his weird laugh.

"My God! You're Azazel!"

"Didn't Elijah tell you? No, I guess that humble old dunce would never gossip. That's another one of his winning tactics."

"But you told me your name is Ozzie," Kagan said indignantly.

"For heaven's sake, Moe, did you tell me your name was Maurice?" the angel asked petulantly.

"No," said Moe Kagan.

"Well, it's the same thing. Who wants to be called Maurice? Do you think Azazel is any better?"

"No, I guess not," Kagan admitted. "Moe and Ozzie sound a heck of a lot better. But why aren't you out in the desert now?"

"It's complicated; I am. And all of me will be back in a moment. I just wanted to say goodbye," the angel answered.

"Goodbye?" asked Kagan.

"Yes, goodbye, Moe. You're going to make it. I would bet on you."

"Why is everyone betting on me?" Kagan shouted anxiously.

"Well, you never got too righteous, for one thing," the angel said.

"But look at all the lousy things I've done. Look at all
the lousy things I do. You can't bet on me! No one can
bet, period," and he realized how crazy a thing betting
really was.

"Whose side are you on, anyway? Moe, betting is
crazy but this is more of faith."

"But I don't want to be a saint, Ozzie!" Kagan called
out in anguish.

The angel laughed, "Moe, there's not much chance
of that!"

Although still fearful, Kagan felt relieved.

"Well, I'd better say goodbye, Moe."

"Ozzie, if you came to corrupt me, why did you
come to say goodbye?" Kagan asked.

"Kagan, I've corrupted better, brighter, and more
talented than you, but, Moe, you're good company."

Kagan felt a surge of pride and satisfaction that all
those years spent hanging out in the candy store weren't
wasted.

"I enjoyed you, too, Ozzie. It's not everyone who has
an angel, you know."

"I tried to corrupt you, Moe. I probably still would if
I could," the angel said honestly.

"Yeah, I know. But, Ozzie, I'm a lousy hater. You
know that. I get hot, but I never could hold a grudge.
Say, listen, even if I do make it, maybe you'll still drop
by occasionally," Kagan said warmly.

"It doesn't work that way, Moe."

"Ozzie, you shouldn't be so hard on yourself," Kagan
said.

"No?"

"No, Ozzie. Elijah told me some other stuff, too, you
know," Kagan said proudly. "Some angels were sent to
announce the destruction of Sodom to Abraham...."

"Lot," Ozzie interrupted. "Not to Abraham, to Lot,

Abraham's nephew.''

"Oh, you know the story then?" Kagan asked, slightly embarrassed.

"Uh-huh," Ozzie answered.

"And yet," Kagan continued, "because of Jacob's righteousness the angels were permitted to return to heaven. He redeemed them in his dream. They were the angels climbing the ladder back to heaven.''

The angel didn't say a thing.

"It's true, isn't it?" Kagan demanded.

"Yes, it's true," the angel confessed quietly.

"Well?" Kagan insisted.

"Moe, it's true all right," Ozzie began.

"So?"

"Forgive me for saying so, Moe, but those angels weren't the best. I'm not Lot's angels. I'm Azazel and you're not Jacob — and — you already had your dream.''

"Say," said Kagan, swiftly changing the topic, "what's this Chaim From Yesterday business all about anyway?''

"No idea," the angel answered.

"Never mind," said Kagan switching back. "Maybe I can't help you but someone else might. You never know, Ozzie. Guys like Truman and Mr. Isaacson can fool you.''

"Maybe," Ozzie said without much enthusiasm.

"Ozzie?" Kagan asked hesitantly.

"Yes, Moe."

"I know you're in a hurry, and I have to get back to pray, but do you think you could teach me a little Torah?''

"Well, I guess a little, Moe."

"Good," said Kagan in anticipation.

"Do you remember what we talked about yesterday afternoon? The Jews had sinned with the golden calf

and Moses broke the tablets of the Law?" Ozzie asked.
"Yes," Kagan said, wondering whether Ozzie was
playing ball with him after all.

"Well," the angel said in a hollow, unemotional
voice, "not only did God say, 'The show must go on!'
but also Moses turned around and ran right back up the
mountain, hoping to get a new set. After another forty
days and nights, Moses received the second set of
tablets. This time he descended and the Jews accepted
the Torah with all their hearts. And that day was Yom
Kippur. Yom Kippur is a wedding day for it is the day
Israel accepted God's Torah."

"Really?" said Kagan, fascinated at such an interesting piece of information.

"Yes. That's why the forbidden relations are read in
the afternoon service," added Ozzie.

"I'm afraid I don't understand," said Kagan.

"Never mind," said Ozzie, "gambling was your thing
anyway."

"It's a wedding day!" exlaimed Kagan.

"Yes," answered Ozzie. "Yes, it's a true holiday
since one is confident that one can earn a good decree."
The angel paused. "Is that enough?"

"Thank you. That's fine," said Kagan.

"I'd better be going, Moe. I'm betting on you."

"Ozzie — " Kagan said.

"Yes?"

"You want to come to *shul* with me?" Kagan offered.
"It's a homey place. A lot of talking, friendly people."

"No, thank you. I'm sure it's very nice but it's not for
me. Oh, one more thing you should know, Moe. Yom
Kippur is like a *mikveh*. Do you know who purifies
Israel? God, for it is written, 'I throw purifying water
onto you and you are purified.' And it is also written,
'The Lord is the *Mikveh* of Israel.' Just as a *mikveh*

purifies the impure, so God purifies Israel. So long, Moe," the angel said, his voice fading.

"Good luck, Ozzie," Kagan called after him.

AT the corner of Ninety-first Street, Kagan glanced at his watch. The pickle-green machine announced that *neilah*, the final service of Yom Kippur, was starting.

"My God!" Kagan exclaimed, "I'm late!" and he began running down Ninety-first Street. Kagan waved at the stoic old monkey, but his thoughts were on the *shtibl*. Kagan had to pray! How he had to pray!

## 10

THE rabbi was speaking as Kagan entered the doorway to the room. "And the Gates of Heaven remain open to receive us until the final second. According to our custom, we shall receive the Priestly Blessing during *neilah*. What is the relationship between the Priestly Blessing and Yom Kippur?" the rabbi asked rhetorically.

"I'm glad you asked!" called Kagan from the doorway. "I'll be happy to tell you!"

Kagan plunged through the standees at the rear of the room. "Sh! Kagan, be quiet!" a voice whispered.

"Kagan, the rabbi's speaking!" someone reprimanded, but Kagan had rushed to the rabbi's side and started speaking, passionately, forcefully, and irrevocably.

"All priests are gamblers. It goes back to when Moses had Aaron throw down the stick in front of Pharaoh. What if it hadn't turned into a snake? In Egypt, you

were only as good as your last plague. Sure, you're a
great guy, a prince, but who have you destroyed for me
lately? Moses knew the stakes when he flung the staff.
They were playing to a pretty tough audience: the Lord
had hardened Pharaoh's heart. How long would they
have lasted had that stick not begun to wiggle? One
twitch of Pharaoh's wig and the message would have
been abundantly clear: try these two out as the base of
my new pyramid.

"But Moses and Aaron were priests, *cohens*; how
they loved action! All priests are gamblers. Moses didn't
hesitate. He put his money on the Snake in the prelims,
Blood in the first, Frogs in the second, Lice in the third,
Beasts in the fourth, Murrain in the fifth, Boils in the
sixth, Hail in the seventh, Locusts in the eighth, Darkness in the ninth, and Slaying of the First-Born in the
tenth. All winners. The Biblical superfecta! Not bad
for a kid who started out in the Soap Box Derby on the
Nile and wound up in the bulrushes.

"And the Red Sea! That wasn't a gamble? God may
not have been adlibbing, but Moses certainly had never
seen those routines before. Of course Moses had faith.
He had perfect faith — and yet — who had ever seen
an ocean split into one-way aisles like a supermarket,
heavy canned goods towering high, like vacuum-sealed
waves near the humming fluorescent lights?

"A *cohen* loves action! Anyone can make a bet, win,
and bet again. It's the losing, the love of action, that
separates gamblers from other men. Riding his impressive streak, Moses was up on the mountain forty days
and forty nights. He received the Ten Commandments
and came down to find all of Israel dancing around the
golden calf. Moses had picked a winner as usual and
nobody had backed him. Who would have believed
that a golden calf could finish out of the money? Moses

showed the Children of Israel the winning tickets but refused to cash them. Eat your hearts out! He smashed the tablets.

"Then what did he do, a man who had picked ten straight, doped out the Red Sea, and finally dropped one? Was he philosophic: you win a few, you lose a few? Did he return to his tent and take the dog for a walk? The poor thing hadn't been out in forty days and forty nights. No! What did he do? Action! He went back up the mountain for another forty days and another forty nights and not for just a straight bet either. Oh, no, although he had no business playing the same number twice, Moses decided to increase the odds. He played a parlay. He was betting that God would give him another set of tablets and that the Jews would accept them. That's a gamble: picking God and the Jews in the same event! One certainly will come through, but both at the same time? Who but a *cohen* would make such a bet?

"That bet won because it was an act of faith. After forty more days and forty more nights, Moses received a second set of tablets, just like the first ones. This time when he came down off the mountain, the Jews accepted God's Torah with all their hearts. And that day was today, Yom Kippur.

"And today is a wedding day because the bet won. We all know what a gamble marriage is. *Oy vay*, do we know! And yet, the Jews got together with God through his holy Torah. A wedding day! *Mazel Tov!* We received another chance at Mount Sinai through His mercy and our faith. We can today, also. Let us bet on ourselves. The OTB won't accept such a bet because it's a holy bet, an act of faith. But we can accept such a bet be- we are created in God's image.

"And yet — we are men. How noble is man! How frail is man! I know what a man is because I am one. I won't drink coffee from my thermos in the teachers' room like a *shmuck* who used to bring his lunch to City College in a paper sack. Why not? Because I'm a *shmuck* who used to bring his lunch to City College in a paper sack. That's why! Of course I never did! You know me. I grabbed a corned beef on rye or a pastrami club with a bottle of tonic. How could I bring my lunch in a bag like a *shmuck* who brings his lunch in a bag? Because I am a *shmuck* who brings his lunch in a bag. You see, it's the human condition. I won't drink my coffee in public, but I'll chase a horse down Broadway. That's why we can make it. Why? Because we're men. I'm a man. It's in my blood and it's in your blood, too. So much is in the blood it's a miracle the sticky stuff makes it through the heart. God knows that. After all, He created us, didn't He?

"That's why on Yom Kippur the High Priest has the lottery with the goats. We, like the goats, are vulnerable, but unlike the goats, we can bet on ourselves through His mercy and our faith. We can choose Azazel or we can choose the Lord. And don't think it means you have to become a saint. It doesn't. It means you have to become a *mensch.* A terrible choice! A fearful choice! But what choice do we really have? We must choose Life — the Lord. Let us pray, for the day is growing short. Let us pray now and let us choose now that the holiest day of the year, Yom Kippur, is drawing to a close!" And as an afterthought Kagan added, "Let us pray now because I'm starving."

Kagan's speech was greeted with the silence that follows an amazing, unexpected event. As Kagan began to make his way to his seat in the small room, tentative remarks began to probe the abyss of uncertainty.

"Listen to that!" someone breathed in amazement. "Did you hear that?" a voice asked in wonder. Finally, someone said softly, *"Yosher koach*, congratulations, Kagan,"* and that unleashed their true feelings. A tidal wave of "Congratulations!" assaulted Kagan from every direction. Benny, his kids, Schwartz, everyone congratulated Kagan. Eventually the rabbi recovered sufficiently to *klop* the reading table for order, but the only response he could get was an excited buzzing. At the moment, decorum was impossible. Anxiously looking at the clock, he raised his voice over the receding wave of voices.

"Indeed, congratulations to our good friend, Maurice Kagan." The rabbi paused. "There is nothing for me to add," he said in simple honesty. "May our prayers be accepted."

The rabbi nodded to the *chazan* to begin the final service of Yom Kippur. Everyone began to search quickly for the correct page — everyone except Kagan. He had the right page, and enveloped in his *tallis*, he was already praying. He prayed with dedication and fervor, uttering every word clearly with his lips and shaping every intention with his heart. When the *chazan* began the repetition, he remained standing under his *tallis*, following every word while pangs of hunger gnawed at his stomach. These he welcomed for they were a reminder of what was at stake — Moe Kagan.

KAGAN was surprised when Benny, his fellow *cohen*, touched his arm. Kagan removed the *tallis* from his head with a sense of uncertainty, even trembling. Although he had prayed hard and well, he knew it wasn't enough. He had more to give, more to ask, and more to decide. And time was running out. It was already time to bless the congregation!

He followed Benny and his sons into the small room which had been a kitchen before the Ninety-first Street brownstone became a *shtibl*. The *cohens* unlaced their shoes. Then the levites, Bienstock among them, poured water over the priests' hands to purify them for their blessing. Kagan extended his hands over the sink and Bienstock poured the water. Although Kagan felt the cooling splash of the water, he stared at his hands in wonderment. They seemed alien and familiar at the same time. He watched the water slide harmlessly off the knuckled backs of the strange jointed, muscular creatures. And yet, he knew those weak and invaluable fingers. The burns, cuts, and splinters they had suffered; the doorknobs they had turned, the tokens they had guided into subway turnstiles. Detached, Kagan wondered what would happen to them, and with a shudder, he worried what would happen to him, Moe Kagan. What will it be? he wondered.

In a fearful daze of imminence, he followed Benny back into the main room where they stood off to one side waiting to go before the ark of the law to give their blessing. When the moment arrived, Benny and his sons stepped out of their shoes and proceeded in stocking feet to the ark. Kagan, however, transfixed, stood motionless, wondering what would be. He saw his fellow priests step forward, but he couldn't follow.

"*Nu*, Kagan, go," someone near him whispered.

"The Priestly Blessing," a voice beseeched.

People were beginning to stare. Someone touched Kagan's elbow. Kagan turned.

"*Nu?*" Bienstock urged softly.

Kagan turned toward the ark. With a look of consternation, Benny was motioning frantically for Kagan to join him. Kagan suddenly kicked off his shoes and rushed forward. Benny's tortured expression eased, but before joining him, Kagan quickly spun around and raced back to where he and the others had been standing. Impervious to the incredulous stares and agitated "*nu*'s," Kagan began kicking the priests' rubber-soled shoes so far under the benches that no accuser of Israel — emperor or angel — could possibly find them. Having finished, Kagan ran to join Benny.

Just as Kagan arrived at the ark, the *chazan* called "Priests!" and without a moment's hesitation, Kagan flung his *tallis* over his head and face, raised his arms — hands, palms out, thumb tips touching, fingers extended in pairs. Although the priestly birdlike formation of his hands was directly in front of his eyes and under his *tallis* (hidden from the congregation), Kagan didn't see it for his eyes were closed as he intoned the blessing with fervor and belief, "Blessed art Thou, O Lord our God, King of the Universe, Who sanctified us with the Holiness of Aaron and Who commanded us to bless with love His nation of Israel."

The *chazan* then began to lead them in their three-fold blessing. Word by word they chanted the first part after him.

"May the Lord — Bless you — And protect you."

As Kagan chanted, a strange thing began to happen. He concentrated lovingly, with all his heart, on the words of the blessing, but Kagan, eyes closed, could see — and feel — his hands reaching into his own head in search of his ballot: "for the Lord" or "for Azazel." My God, thought Kagan, my fate is literally in my hands! Then he realized, at long last, there *is* a routine here, my routine. And this is it! With awe he watched his hands search his head for the ballot. He felt the spongy, sticky, gelatinous mass of his mind. Kagan held his nose; the stuff still smelled awful, no better than in high-school biology. Hershkowitz, you *gonif*, may the Lord bless you and may you protect the sick. And not just the sick. O Master of the Universe, have

pity on remedial readers everywhere. Help their eyes
to see the letters and their minds to see the syllables.
(Very important the syllables!)

The *chazan*, Kagan, and the other priests began to
chant the second part.

"May the Lord's — Countenance — Shine — Upon
you — And grant you grace!"

The fingers probed through the dark chambers of his
mind. O Fran, may the Lord's countenance shine upon
you and upon all of Connecticut. May you be granted
grace in my eyes so that I shall love you with the
respect and dignity you deserve. Fran, it will be better,
you'll see. A love of intimacy and honesty. No more
tears, Fran, no more tears. Kagan felt himself crying.
Forgive me, forgive me!

The stiff-knuckled fingers pushed toward the side
and uncovered the old Sixty-four Falcon. It's been a
good car, Lord — a better car than I have been a driver.
May it find grace, a parking spot along the curbs of
West End Avenue. Not too much of a hill either; a
*rachmones* on the transmission, Lord.

And turning back, the thumb tips brushed the pickle-
green watch.

Lord, grant your servant to see the green of life and
not the green of envy. Who cares how many walked on
the moon, Lord? Lift up Your countenance and let us
walk on earth and find grace in each other's eyes.

And Kagan knew they were about to begin the final
portion of the blessing, the blessing of peace.

"May the Lord — Lift up — His countenance —
Unto you. . . ."

Lift up Your countenance, Lord, to Your children in
this sharp-edged world of frenzy, this world of illusion
and self-deception.

The birdlike formation of Kagan's hands flew over

the shadow of memory shaped into human form.

O Lord, lift up your countenance to Katzi, my fellow *cohen*, that he may better know the redemption that is in his agitated blood rather than the anger, for Your servant Katzi loves You as few men do. O Lord, lift up Your countenance to Pakooz that he may better know what is above the couch rather than what is beneath for your servant Pakooz tries in his own way to help your suffering children at a price they can afford. O Lord, lift up Your countenance to Big Abe that he may better know the human voice rather than that of the transistor for your servant Big Abe never forgets what he hears.

The blessing continued, "May He grant — You — " and the *chazan* uttered the word "Peace," but before the priests could finish they had to chant their ancient, wordless melody.

As Kagan chanted the final notes, he anxiously watched his hands plunge into the depths to choose his fate. He believed this day to be a day of joy, but he didn't feel it. Rather, he felt something very different. He felt his whole self moving, subtly floating like the objects in his mind. His whole self seemed to be moving, but with no sense of disorientation. He felt comfortable floating, as if partially submerged in a *mikveh*. But part of him wasn't inside, and this part watched his blind fingers probe the innermost parts of his mind for his decision. My God, Kagan thought, this is really going all the way down to the wire! What a finish!

Then he heard the faint echo of hoofbeats. To silence them, Kagan willed himself farther into the purifying waters. Yes, thought Kagan, it is as Ozzie said. The Lord is the *Mikveh* of Israel. Through His unity, His oneness, we can be redeemed.

O Lord, cried Kagan, grant Azazel that he should know Your mercy for your suffering servant Azazel has taught your son Torah. And, O Lord, grant your sinning servant, Moe Kagan, forgiveness, for — and Kagan's fingers moved beyond the small, tremulous figure on ice — forgiveness, O Lord, for we leave everything to the last minute. *Oy*, Chaim Der Nechtiger, why do you leave everything to the last minute? O Master of the Universe, forgiveness, for we are all Chaims From Yesterday! Receive us!

Kagan's blessing-fingers touched something. His hands began to grasp it as he descended into the *mikveh* of his mind, created in God's image. The last voice he heard was the angel's hoarse, impassioned plea — "Kagan, choose Life!!" — and Kagan did, intoning with all his soul, "Peace!"

 Beggar Moon

THERE are too many threads. That's obvious. Our suits have too many threads, isn't one always hanging loose? Our days have too many threads. Our lives have too many threads. And stories, the stories most like our lives, certainly have too many threads. This story is about the moon and Bluma the Beggar and it has too many threads. How did I come to meet them, the moon and Bluma the Beggar? They are both Jews. So this is a story about Jews. But it is much more than just a story about Jews; it is a Jewish story. The moon and Bluma the Beggar are not just Jews; they are Jewish. And that's where the threads come in. In Jewish stories, the threads are entangled in the middle. You know the beginning and you know the ending, but you don't know the middle. You see the beginning of the threads, you see the end of the threads, but in the middle, a tangled snarl, an impenetrable mess. The *goyim* have too many threads, too. With the *goyim*, however, things are inside out. You don't know the beginning, and you don't know the end; you only know the middle.

A Jew knows where he came from and he knows where he will go, but, *vay iz mir*, can he get crazy in the middle! A *goy* has no idea where he came from or where he is going, and he couldn't care less, but he knows where he is now. He's relaxed. He's calm. Why shouldn't he be? It's a *goy*'s world. And when a Jew makes it big, he's not relaxed, calm. Look at Henry Kissinger. The man runs around like a *meshugginer*. He'd better. It's a *goy*'s world. What does Kissinger own? Nothing. He is no different from the little Russian violinists from Odessa who stood next to the Czar. Even worse, when the *goyim* tire of Kissinger's tune, he won't even be able to play weddings and Bar Mitzvahs. Nothing is new; the threads reach into eternity. And with Kissinger we know his beginning. He's in the oldest Jewish profession: an *aytza gibber*, a *dray kop*. Détente, big deal! Abraham tried to negotiate détente for Sodom and Gomorrah. And what was the result? Lot's wife: The SALT talks. A master negotiator, a big deal! When the Jews crossed the Red Sea, God opened His hand in mercy and the Jews passed miraculously through the surrounding sea. Under that outstretched hand a whole nation noodged. "*Nu*, so what's in the other hand?"

Yesterday Kissinger was a refugee and tomorrow he will be a refugee, but today he is a citizen. It's no surprise that he is Secretary of State. Who can be better at the present than the Jew? The present is defined by the past and the future. The past and the future mercilessly drive the Jew into the present. The fugitive Jew must outwit his captor, a hostile present — or become a slave. A few *goyim* may flee their pasts and dash into the present. But the future? What is that to a world-owning *goy*? No, the Jew has all the advantages. Who but Disraeli could master the present? Fleeing the past and future, what choice did the poor man have but to become Prime Minister of England?

What does this have to do with Bluma the Beggar and the moon? They were my teachers. They taught me about the threads — Jewish threads. And I'm not a very quick student or I would have learned it long ago, just by looking down at my *tzitzes*, the fringes on the corners of my spiritual serape. A Jew looks at them and they remind him of the Commandments. Look at the *tzitzes*. You can see where the threads begin. You can see where the threads end. But who can comprehend those remorseless knots and mad twinings that occupy the middle? Only He who created them. And what if He isn't talking? I looked down, but I didn't see. I had to

wait for the moon and Bluma the Beggar. Let me start at
the beginning — that I know, or, at least, I think I do.

ROSH HASHANAH is the day of judgment. Whose
judgment? Ours: yours, mine, everybody's. You don't
want to go into court unprepared, so you begin preparing the month before. How do you prepare? Prayer,
penitence, and charity avert the evil decree. They say
that even the fish in the water are afraid in Elul, the
month preceding the Day of Judgment, shouldn't you
be? What can you do in that month? Prayer is too difficult. You have to believe, really believe, and you have
to concentrate. How you have to concentrate! If you do
it right, it might transform your existence, but it would
probably ruin your whole day. It's one thing to pray, but
to Pray — talking to God all the time could mess you up.
To seek a little refuge is one thing: ten, two, and four, a
little spiritual Dr. Pepper; to fall into a bottomless pit is
another. Penitence is fine if you don't like who you are.
For a minor job, it's a great nuisance. And for a major
job, why bother? If you really don't like yourself, why
worry about what's going to happen to a creep like
you? The only thing left is charity. What else is there?

Charity is a difficult task. The recipient is not to be
embarrassed. He should receive it anonymously. Proper
charity is not an easy thing at all. In fact, charity is a
misnomer. In Hebrew, it is called righteousness, which,
as the name implies, is not just a hand in the pocket,
but a heart and head in heaven. Nonetheless, righteousness can still be charity, a coin in the cup. Who knows
if poor prayer is prayer? Who knows if poor penitence
is penitence? But give a poor person money, and that's
charity. Definitely. And thank God, too. Where would
we be without it? Prayer and penitence make for a
dull world, whereas through charity you can meet

some pretty interesting people.

In the awesome month of Elul before Rosh Hashanah, I was attending the morning prayers regularly. I'm not saying it helped, but did it hurt? What should I do in the mornings of Elul, watch the *Today* show? Do they ever blow the shofar on the *Today* show as a little Rosh Hashanah warm-up? And there's another difference. Barbara Walters couldn't care less about me. At the *shtibl*, I help make a *minyan*. The Off-Track Betting Corporation opened up an office around the corner on Broadway and we still have the best numbers game in town. Will we or won't we hit ten? And, finally, a *minyan*. "*Oy*, a *minyan*, pray, pray!" We have the hottest game in town even though the betting parlor has dozens of *minyans* who arrive early, stay late, and donate regularly. Cash, too. None of this ten-dollars-anonymous stuff. If the *shtibl* were the Off-Track Betting parlor and the Off-Track Betting parlor were the *shtibl*, the Messiah would come, because everybody would be hitting the triple: a *minyan* in the morning, a *minyan* in the afternoon, and a *minyan* at night. How could the Messiah stay away? But the Messiah hasn't come yet, and with action like that in the *shtibl*, how could I stay home and watch Barbara Walters interview a man who teaches dogs to dance? At the *shtibl* I am admired — if I am one of the first ten. At the *shtibl* I am loved — if I am the tenth. At the *shtibl* I am admonished — if I am late, eleven or higher. But that's the chance you take. You can't race without finishing out of the money occasionally. It's the best game in town. Did Secretariat ever give anyone a glass of schnapps for his father's *yahrzeit*? And his father was a somebody, Bold Ruler.

The action, however, occurs at the beginning of the service. By the time the final *kaddish* has rolled around,

it's out the door, get a paper, a cup of coffee, and off to
work with the reproachful call of a poorly blown shofar
pursuing me. During one such hasty exit, I met Bluma.
She sat in the back at the bare *kiddush* table. A dark
wooden cane rested against her leg. She was lost in
reverie. As I approached, however, she snapped out of
it and stood up.

"My dear man, can you help me for Rosh Hashanah,
the New Year?"

She had a supplicating tone, but the major tone was
one of inquiry. I gave her a dollar.

"God will bless you."

"God bless you, too."

"You'll see," she insisted.

THE average gift in the *shtibl* is fifteen cents to a quarter, but everyone gives. How can we not? There are so
few of us; we barely have a *minyan*. The poor woman
has been waiting. And sometimes she really must wait.
We start later than other synagogues when we start on
time, and most of the time, we only start looking for a
*minyan*. And then we have to pray; there is, after all, a
reason why we go through all this. So by the time the
poor get to us, they have put in a hard day chasing after
the more punctual and populous. Can you imagine
what Elul must be like for those genuinely poor people,
screaming about Rosh Hashanah and streaming from
one synagogue to another with the interminable still-
born wail of the aborted shofar calls assailing them all
over the West Side? It's a wonder they bother to come
to our *shtibl* at all. So I gave her a dollar. I never give
enough charity anyway. The checks never get written.
Like the shofar blasts, they come out only for Rosh
Hashanah. Yes, of course I'll give. It's a worthy charity
. . . before Rosh Hashanah.

I went out the door as she remained at her post. I had gotten a good look at her. Gray hair closely cropped into short tufts gave her strong round face a mannish look. The plastic-rimmed glasses she wore did not detract from this impression. Nor did the neat, short-sleeved khaki tunic. Under the tunic, a simple dress. A clean, uniformed appearance. But Bluma wore something striking which both enhanced and enlivened the sense of uniform. She had on long, bright red socks originating somewhere in her low-cut white tennis shoes and terminating just below her knees. Yet it would be a mistake to think that from the waist up Bluma suggested a Foreign Legion sergeant and from the waist down a utility infielder for the Boston Red Sox. No, from head to toe, it was all Fenway Park. Her haunches angled casually onto her dark heavy cane the way old sluggers, the true students of the game, lean on their sacred allies around the batting cage, while inside at bat some young kid mercilessly tears at the ball with his impersonal stave, using only his lower nervous system. Great reflexes, but no glimmering that hitting is an intellectual art and a social one; be good to your bat and it may be good to you. Even Bluma's eyeglasses seemed oddly reminiscent of baseball. And so did her stature, too small for her size. Not stocky, although she was, so much as the suggestion that she might have been bigger. And, too, she might have been better, or at least more successful. Although her career wasn't going to put her into the Hall of Fame, someone else in her family had made it. Who else could she be? Oh, those Red Sox! How could I not be taken with a beggar who looked like Dom DiMaggio? Barbara Walters — feh! feh! feh!

So I left the *shtibl* with a light, airy feeling: Rosh Hashanah at Fenway Park with a good, a very good, an excellent — but not a great — cantor in center field. Let the Young Israel, the Jewish Center, crowd have Yankee Stadium with the world-famous, nonpareil, *vunderbarisher* cantor, Joltin' Joe DiMaggio, the fifty-six game angel, chanting under the pagan, funereal monuments. (This stadium made possible through a generous donation of the Sultan of Swat.) You don't want to look too good on Judgment Day, the Judge might get suspicious or jealous. Better a smaller scale with a little intimacy, a crummy Fenway, where fans attend for only one reason, love. And when God looks down hurriedly (He has to look everywhere on Rosh Hashanah), our good deeds can fill the *shtibl*'s small room. In Yankee Stadium our good deeds wouldn't make it to left center field, much less to the monuments. And in the Jewish Center, they would smolder restlessly below the stained-glass windows. And you don't want to leave all those stains uncovered on Rosh Hashanah. If it weren't for crime in the streets, it would be theologically sound to squeeze a *minyan* into a telephone booth for Rosh Hashanah. Stuffed with good deeds, crammed with prayer, and direct dialing yet. Yes, Fenway Park for Rosh Hashanah and Yom Kippur; Yankee Stadium for Hanukkah and Passover.

THAT'S how I met Bluma. It was a Tuesday. The following Tuesday I looked up from my prayers to see her sitting at the empty table by the door. I got up and walked over to her. As I began to reach in my pocket, she waved me off.

"Finish praying first. It's good for you."

I returned and finished praying. On my way out, I gave her a five-dollar bill. She took it and began to thank me, but as she drew it closer, she suddenly stopped.

"Hey, this is a five-dollar bill. You know that?"

"Yes, it's for you."

"You sure?"

"Take it. It costs a fortune to make Rosh Hashanah . . . chickens, wine, fish. . . ."

"I don't eat all that stuff," she said, but she put the money into her pocket. She looked back up at me.

"Say," she said, "you should have a happy New Year."

"Thank you. You, too."

"Don't worry about me. God is good." She paused a moment. "Say, are you married?"

"Yes."

"Your wife should have a happy New Year."

"Thank you."

"Any kids?"

"One."

"Your baby should have a healthy New Year. Healthy, that's the main thing."

"Thank you."

"Is it a boy baby or a girl baby?"

"A girl."

"Don't feel bad," she commiserated. "Maybe the next one will be a boy."

"Be well," I said as I went out the door.

I descended to the street and had gone a few steps when I heard a voice calling, "Say! Say, you!" I turned around. Bluma was at the top of the stairs, her red socks reverberating in the clear morning light.

"Be well, too," she called. "And be careful!"

The following Tuesday, again Bluma in the red knee socks. Bluma, however, is not the only individual who needs the help of the community. Some come more regularly, some less regularly. We get a mixed crowd: men, women, observant, unobservant, old, not so old.

Why not? Along with the individual donation, the *shtibl* contributes institutionally. On the table where the Torah is read stand several *pushkes*, alms boxes. The two are complementary. What is Torah if not righteousness? The largest silver-colored alms box goes to our own local poor. Mr. Isaacson enthusiastically dumps the entire contents into the outstretched hands. Some don't even wait for Mr. Isaacson. It's their money, isn't it? Why should they wait for him? No one dropped a coin into the box just to hear a clink or a clank. Mr. Isaacson lets them take. It is theirs. He lets them take — unless there are others who are entitled as well. Then it must be divided equally, and no thief Fagin ever trained could beat Mr. Isaacson to the *pushke*. Mr. Isaacson has good moves and, more important, great recovery. When his prayer shawl hoods his head, his phylacteries entwine him in holiness, and his whole being Prays, yes Prays; let someone surreptitiously and unfairly lift the *pushke* and Mr. Isaacson comes from nowhere to put a firm, guiding hand on the *pushke*. Jangling and unplundered, it returns to the table. It makes no difference whether Mr. Isaacson must come from behind, go over the top, or dart in from the side. Mr. Isaacson touches only the *pushke*, never the person. Touching the man would be a two-shot foul since you really cannot blame the poor cadger; he has to eat too. It's a game attempt; it's a clean block. No score; no foul. Isaacson is a defensive specialist. He never offends. The Bill Russell of the National Pushke Association. And Mr. Isaacson always enjoys the home-court advantage. Drive on Russell in Boston? Empty a *pushke* on Isaacson in the *shtibl*? You've got to be kidding!

That Tuesday someone was kidding. He's always kidding. Sometimes he kids that he's blind, sometimes lame, sometimes deaf. A real sense of humor! Mr. Isaacson had him covered before the *pushke* started to move. Bluma was waiting patiently in the back by the door. Mr. Isaacson gave the culprit a dirty look. This fellow has *chutzpah*. When he feigns blindness — white cane, cup, sigh, and all — on the IRT, he never even bothers with the local, only the express! I should see as well as he does. He begs real bread for imaginary children. He poses with bandaged hands, broken arms, crutches. You name it, he has faked it. No shame whatever! A scandal. But he gets. Not from me, but from Mr. Isaacson and the others.

"Mr. Isaacson, did you ever see him as a blind man in the subway?"

Mr. Isaacson laughed. "And he doesn't even need eyeglasses like you and me."

"Why give him anything?"

"Just because he's not blind doesn't mean he's rich, does it?"

He didn't need from me. The morning service, *shachris*, ended. The phony started his routine as everyone wound phylacteries and folded prayer shawls. I headed for Bluma.

"Good morning, how are you today?" she asked.

"Fine, how are you?"

"Thank God," she answered.

Why hadn't I thanked God? I offered her another five-dollar bill. She wouldn't accept it. I insisted.

"No, no, it's not right," she protested.

"Why not?" I queried.

"You can't afford it," she said mercilessly.

"How do you know I can't afford it?" I demanded.

"You're not rich," she stated with such conviction it was almost a taunt.

I was amazed that she wouldn't take my money. A

beggar not taking a five-dollar bill! What was the world coming to! I thought her obstinacy might be caused by my appearance. Sartorially, I am the Jackie Robinson of *shachris*. I broke the color line: I wear blue jeans. I also broke the collar line: I can't believe that God turns away because in ninety-degree weather I wear a polo shirt from Alexander's.

Indignantly I asked, "You think I'm not rich because I don't wear a coat and tie and my hair is too long?"

Bluma's eyes grew fiery with frustration. I had offended her.

"You're not a hippie. I can see that."

"Then how do you know I'm not a rich man?" I demanded, my voice rising.

Bluma practically rolled her eyes in frustrated horror at my obtuseness as I stood there proferring the five-dollar bill. Then she stared directly into my eyes with what I was to come to know as one of her use-your-head looks.

"Because you give and the rich don't give!"

What could I say? She had proved her point. I was overwhelmed. So I said nothing. I felt a little foolish. That always happens when I try to do a *mitzvah*, a good deed. I had embarrassed Bluma. I should have known that an old Jewish woman who travels the synagogue circuit dressed like Dom DiMaggio would not be a stickler for style.

Gently pushing my money away, she said softly, "Save it. You might need it, too."

What could I say? I decided to tell the truth.

"Listen, Bluma, you're right. We're not rich."

"See," she gloated, "I could tell. Bluma knows."

"Yes, but I never would have offered it to you if we couldn't afford it."

Then Bluma was a little perplexed.

"If you don't take it, Bluma, I'll have to find someone else to take it."

"You sure? You wouldn't be tricking me now?"

"No, I promise you. I brought it for you. Please. . . ."

"Only if you're telling the trute." Bluma isn't too good with "th."

"I am."

She accepted it. As she put it into her pocket, who came running our way but the phony. He's blind on the subway, but in the shadows of the *shtibl*, he can identify a five-dollar bill at a hundred paces. He came dashing down the corridor. As he approached, he simultaneously increased his speed and his suggested ailments. His pumping legs fell lame, his eyes grew dim, his shoulder sagged, his back buckled, his arm slackened, and he hurtled forward! Bluma and I sensed we were watching medical history. Another twenty yards and approaching the speed of sound, he would have buried himself alive. No mean feat. In spite of what we knew about him, we were awed by such a performance. How Isaacson beats him to the *pushke* is beyond me! The joker slammed on his brakes. He didn't waste any time.

"A little bread for the children," he moaned. "*Oy*, a little something?"

After a performance like his, even I was inspired. I became a disciple and played dumb.

"*Oy*, a little bread for the children," he moaned.

"Okay," I said to Bluma, "be well."

"You be well," Bluma responded.

"*Oy*, the children aren't well and no medicine. A little bread at least." He paused and then took up his wail, "God should curse anyone who would let a sick child starve."

The fire returned to Bluma's eyes. All the DiMaggios

have been dynamite in the clutch. Waving her cane, she stepped forward. And from there, it was all Elijah and the Prophets of Baal. And the Prophets of Baal were even blind to what they could see.

"God should bless you." Bluma raised her voice.

"A curse on a man who lets the innocent starve."

"God bless you and your wife!"

"*Oy*, letting children die. Letting a baby die!"

Bluma screamed, "God bless your baby! The baby should be healthy, that's the main thing."

"No bread for a baby. A curse, a curse."

Bluma, still staring at me, asked frantically, "Is it a boy baby or a girl baby?"

"A girl," I answered.

Back on the track, she started rolling now. "A good healthy, happy, sweet year for your little girl!"

"*Oy*, what kind of year can it be when the Jews let children starve?"

"Feh! Feh! Feh! The devil should starve — but the Jews and your little girl baby should have a good year."

"A curse on such Jews."

"A blessing on such Jews, all the Jews. A curse on our enemies, may they rot."

"*Oy*, the Jews bring on their own suffering when they are not good to other Jews."

"God is good, so are His people. He'll save us. God knows the trute! God loves the trute! God searches for the trute! He knows the hearts of everyone. God is good and so are His people and that's the trute. A happy New Year!"

No contest. The phony, uninvolved and unenriched, turned to hustle some other worshipers. What a day for him! The poor faker ran into the Bill Russell of *pushkes* and the Dom DiMaggio of blessings in the same hour. (Could that Dom field those long, center-field curses and get the blessing back to the infield!) What a day. He turned into a flying pretzel only to smash himself into crumbs against the Western Wall of Bluma's passion.

"A happy New Year," Bluma calmly remarked to me. "Say, what is your name?"

"Harold."

"Say, Hal darling, I gotta talk to you."

"Bluma, I'm late for work," I begged off.

"Nobody's got time for Bluma. Run! Run! Run!"

"I'll see you Thursday."

"No, Thursday is no good. I gotta go to the butcher. I gotta million things to do. . . . Okay, Hal darling, be well."

When I reached the sidewalk, a voice called after me. "Take care of that girl baby."

As I passed the OTB parlor on Broadway, it looked as if everyone inside was taking the rest cure. Staring at a sheet, what kind of action is that? They don't even see the horses! Maybe one is missing a leg. Every gambler thinks it's his lucky day. How did I know it was my lucky day? The phony one left the field. The blessings remained. Nothing is new. Mount Gerizim and Mount Ebal — the mount of blessings and the mount of curses, and as usual the Jews in the middle. It was a heady experience, all right, but I grew up in a family where everybody was alway yelling. No, I was impressed by Bluma's *svora*: you give and the rich don't give. That's a *svora*, logical analysis! *Svora* is *kop*, a good mind. Knowledge is power and *svora* rules the world. The mind is the true reality. It is written, "God gave man dominion over all creation," yet the lion is king of the jungle. But only Adam knows why the lion is king, even while he is being eaten. That's *svora*. I ask you, who is really the king of the jungle? Kissinger. Kissinger is a practitioner of *svora*. He practices power politics, yet he would get a hernia if he had to carry his own briefcase. Kissinger made it on *svora*. Not a Jew was at the Congress of Vienna in 1815. Not a Jew orchestrated the Concert of Europe. Metternich was there. Talleyrand was there. But not a man understood the score until Henry Kissinger put down his soccer ball and became a professor. Who is really the conductor of Europe? It's nothing new. Look at Einstein, who knew more about the world than any other man. There was a master of *svora*. Relativity, light, gravity, the atom. He knew it all. Einstein understood how to split the atom, turn matter into energy. Who cares if he had to flee Europe to prevent the Nazis from splitting the atoms of his head on the anvil of Auschwitz? Who is the master of the world? Einstein or Hitler? Einstein — *svora* rules the world. Einstein is a *kop*, a great intelligence. Hitler was a wolf in lion's clothing. Ah, *svora*, it is a great consolation for those who don't own anything. What does an animal or an owner have to understand? "Mine" is his total understanding. It's mine: owner-ship — that's it. Who has to understand? Adam the outcast, the oppressed, the cursed, the poor, the Jew — Kissinger, Einstein, and Bluma the Beggar. Oh, that Bluma! The body of a DiMaggio, the head of an Ein-stein, the heart of a. . . . That I didn't discover until after Rosh Hashanah.

I saw Bluma one more time before Rosh Hashanah. She told me that enough was enough. She couldn't accept any more money from me. And then she told me what she wanted to talk to me about. She was going to bring me a few things — clean, like new — for the wife and baby, too.

"But I don't know about your arms," she said. "Maybe your arms aren't as long as they look."

"Bluma, that's kind, but we don't need anything,

really."

"Everybody needs something!"

"Bluma, please don't. We don't need it."

"Don't be stubborn. I don't like it. I'm stubborn; Bluma's stubborn. You'll be here Tuesday after Rosh Hashanah?"

We made it through the month of Elul to that Rosh Hashanah. Had I prepared? A little, I guess. Not enough. We dipped slices from the round holiday loaves into honey for a sweet year. We ate the head of a fish. "May it be God's will to make us the head and not the tail." Powerful but perfunctory. Then I didn't understand that Jewish fish do not have a middle. Talk about threads! Nor did I understand that *goyish* fish are all middle, without either head or tail. But I shouldn't be too hard on myself. I had prepared, and progress is not altogether obvious at the time. The entire month of Elul, I seemed to hear nothing but mangled, miskeyed, strangled failures on the shofar. How could it be otherwise on the Day of Judgment? But it was. The same man. The same shofar. But a different day, and a different sound. A full-throated sound whose staccato cries and low-sighing wails did not assail the ear, but, rather, through the ear infused the listener with the venerable mystery of anguished joy, comforted sorrow, penitence, and hope. The tones are not of the mind. We hear them, but we do not listen so much as we feel them. The shofar forms its notes in its own image. The curved creatures invisibly penetrate and hook our hearts. The hooked messengers tug upon our insides to heed the call: their presence and our receptivity. A call from past Rosh Hashanahs: the creation of Adam, the Binding of Isaac, our own actions. A call from future Rosh Hashanahs: the redemption of the Messiah. But the shofar curves upward, its mouth to heaven. Talk about threads!

The shofar's timeless supplication rises to heaven, where the angels, whose names it is even forbidden to mention, weave the ethereal filament — threads of penitence — into the Holy Veil. Talk about threads! Some threads — the heavenly Garment District.

And the Ten Days of Penitence had fallen, Rosh Hashanah to Yom Kippur. And the Jews in the middle. Also in the middle was my appointment with Bluma. She sat in the back.

"How are you?" she asked, and without waiting for an answer she continued, "Wait here a minute, I got some things out there in the hall for you. It's not their business. They don't have to know."

Bluma moved away to take her professional post. As the congregation filed by, she wished each of the *minyan*, "Be inscribed in the Book of Life on the impending Day of Atonement, Yom Kippur." She put the change into her pocket. I offered her a five-dollar bill.

"Will you stop it!" she snapped.

"Here, Bluma, it's before Yom Kippur for me, too."

"You gave and you need it." She looked at me with a smile. "You work and your wife works. She teaches."

Bluma paused to savor my reaction. I was surprised. She smiled widely.

"I've been doing some checking on you. You're not dealing with a fool. Come, I've got some good stuff for you. You'll see about the arms."

We stepped into the narrow hall. Two enormous shopping bags bulged with neatly folded clothes. The two, double-bagged, almost blocked the passage.

"Listen, Bluma, I just can't take this."

"What's wrong with you?" she snapped.

"It's not right."

"Don't you understand? I'm giving *you* something.

See! You give me money, right? It comes back at you. It comes back at you, doesn't it? Whaddaya say?"

"It sure does."

"Whaddaya say? . . . I'll help you with it. I know it's heavy. I could hardly *shlep* it up on the bus."

"Bluma, where do you live?"

She looked up in aggravation.

"Feh! Feh! Feh! Right away he wants to know where I live. I live. I live. That's all."

"No," I said reaching for the bags. "I'll get them."

As I picked them up, we heard someone coming. Mr. Isaacson had stayed behind to recite Psalms. He clattered down the corridor toward us.

As he approached, she barked at me, "Boy! Help me with these packages!" And as an afterthought: "I have to take them to a poor old woman."

The sharp command stunned me into my past, and out of a respectful St. Louis boyhood I mumbled, "Yes, ma'am."

Mr. Isaacson smiled as he squeezed past. As I lugged the bags down the steps, I was grateful that I didn't have to *shlep* them up on a bus. I looked over at Bluma hobbling down the hard, stone stairs. Boy, help me with these packages. And I wave five-dollar bills in her face like Yankee Doodle on the Fourth of July. Some charity. Can't I give it in private?

"Bluma, you know this isn't fair."

"Hal darling, what's fair got to do?"

"I gave you a little and you gave me a lot. I have to give you more."

"Now shut up! You don't argue with your wife, do you?"

"Yes," I answered.

"You do? That's no good. She's more intelligent than you. She won't like it."

"She doesn't."

"See! Bluma knows."

We walked up Broadway together. I stopped to turn off at Ninety-third.

"Thank you."

"Be healthy. That's the main thing. There's good stuff in there for the baby. I folded it neatly. I don't know about your arms. You'll see."

"Where did you get so many nice things?"

"Leave it to God and Bluma," she beamed.

I left it to God and Bluma — and my arms were too long. The only item in both bags for me was a maroon sportscoat. It wasn't bad at all, but I didn't even have to look into a mirror. I knew I was in trouble when the sleeves didn't reach down to my elbows. *Nu*, God and Bluma make better friends than tailors. My wife was amazed to see my bundles. She couldn't believe it. But she couldn't refuse Bluma's gift either, until the roaches walked out. The roaches didn't walk out, however, until she already had chosen a green coat for herself and a dark blue pullover for the baby. After the roaches appeared, I had to take the bags down to the basement since nothing, according to my wife, can atone for roaches. Although the little creatures had destroyed much of the charm for her, she was fascinated at my departing to make a *minyan* at seven-thirty in the morning and my returning at eight-fifteen with a pile of used clothes. She saw in this occurrence some strong atavism exhibiting itself. Immediately before Yom Kippur, we called my folks in St. Louis to wish them an easy fast. My wife spoke first and introduced me as the competition. At the end of the conversation I asked:

"Say, Pop, how's business?"

"Slow."

"What's slow mean?"

"Slow means we have a million pounds of used clothes, winter goods, that should be moving by now."

"Yeah, I know the feeling," I said.

Bluma the Prophet. In the first grade, the roving reporter for the *George Washington Bugle* asked me what I wanted to be. "A ragman like my father," I answered, embarrassing the family. You never know when you leave it to God and Bluma.

THE next time I left it to those two, I found myself in an even stranger situation. Several weeks after Yom Kippur, Bluma announced that she wanted to give me some "nice things." My wife suggested that they couldn't come into the house without her leaving it. "We paid to get rid of our roaches. It's insane to accept hers." She had a point. Bluma said that she was smarter.

"Bluma, I can't."

"Feh! Feh! Feh! Whaddaya mean, 'I can't'?"

"I can't."

"Did I give you good stuff?"

"Yes."

"Did your wife like the coat?"

"Yes."

"Sure. It's a good coat. Wasn't the baby's stuff nice? I folded it special."

"Very nice."

And then she softened, and said quietly, "Hal darling, don't be so proud. It's no good. I know."

I had an inspiration.

"Bluma, I'm not, but it's too far for you to *shlep*!"

"That's the trute," she conceded.

"So it's not fair. We'll manage."

"Are you busy Sunday?"

I trembled. "What time?"

"Any time. How about the morning?"

"I have to take the baby to the park."

"The afternoon then."

"We may have to go somewhere."

"When does the baby nap? She's gotta nap."

"Around one."

"I'll meet you in front of Two-fifty West Ninety-nint'."

"Is that where you live?"

"Live. Live. Live. That's where I'll be."

That is, of course, where I was. My wife wanted to know why I couldn't say no. I couldn't. And I didn't want to say no. How many people can you respect these days? Very few. Bluma was one. And Elul is only one month of the year. We always need to hear the shofar at Rosh Hashanah, but that doesn't mean we should prepare for the rest of the year by becoming deaf. On the contrary, it means that we must prepare by improving our hearing the rest of the year so that we can hear it better. And what was I supposed to tell Bluma? "Happy New Year, kiddo! See you next time round!" Of course I enjoy Elul. I also fear it. Elul is the homestretch, the final games of the season that can decide a pennant. Elul-Rosh Hashanah-Yom Kippur is the name of the game. Judgment-Atonement-Life. The final games are more dramatic, but all the games count in the standings, even the ones played in April, cold and rainy. And what about God? We relax a little after Yom Kippur. Why not? We have to, we're only human, but He's not. Does God go to Florida for the winter and the mountains for the summer? Of course not! And there was another consideration. I had started it. I was responsible. I gave her the five dollars. It was my corny Yankee Doodle stunt. I played friend and hero. Didn't she have a right to reciprocate? Couldn't she be a hero and friend? It could come back to me, see! Reciprocity

is the trute! How can I give, if I can't receive? Righteousness, like Broadway, is a two-way street. Let it be
well traveled. If you can *shlep* it downtown, you can
*shlep* it uptown. And anyway, I liked her. And I feared
her.

I turned the corner on Ninety-ninth Street and for a
moment I didn't see Bluma. She was almost halfway
down the block, seated on a standpipe projecting from
the building. If not her residence, at least her office.
The bright red of the standpipe perfectly matched her
socks. All were the same height, too, as if they were a
matched set. Bluma saw me and waved her cane to
attract my attention.

"Good. I didn't think you were coming."

"I said I would be here."

She leaned on her cane and stood up.

"Here," she said, "you sit down."

"Oh, no, Bluma, you sit."

"No," she insisted as hostess, "you had a long walk.
You must be tired. Sit."

"I'll stand. It's good to stretch my legs a little."

"Sit. You'll see, you'll like it. And I have to get the
bags."

I noticed that there weren't any bags. None. Just
Bluma and the standpipe, which I now could see was a
Siamese fitting; at the top, the seat of Bluma's chair, the
pipe branched out into a V-shape. I sat down. It was
surprisingly comfortable. I leaned my back against the
building and relaxed. A little low, but after all, if my
arms are too long, why not my legs, too?

"It's nice, no?" she smiled.

"Yes, it really is comfortable."

"When it's hot and the days are long, I like sitting
here. It's nice. There's a breeze sometimes."

"Yes, I can see."

"Okay, relax. Wait here. I'll get the things. You like tea?"

"Bluma, can I help you get the stuff?"

"Bluma can manage. It's not for you."

"Bluma, you live in the Whitehall?"

"Feh! Feh! Feh! My dear man, could I live in a place like that?"

"You're sure I can't help?"

"I'll be right back."

Bluma slowly hobbled to Broadway and turned uptown. Just before she turned the corner, however, she turned back and waved. She smiled, but I suspected that she was happy to find that I wasn't following her. I wasn't. I was sitting on the standpipe watching Ninety-ninth Street. I felt foolish all right. Bluma, at least, had the legs and the socks that matched the pipe.

Sitting there, I saw Ninety-ninth Street in a way I had never seen it before. A cousin of mine used to live at the corner in the building with the letters missing — THE AL NDA E. I must have looked at that sign a dozen times. If the building's owner would sit here for a minute, he would fix that in an hour. We are all running with our eyes wide open, but until we are forced to stop, we really never see anything. I saw the shapes of the building and the texture of the entire block. I looked the other way and saw a clock on a church steeple. An enormous, gargantuan clock was up there, and suddenly it seemed a peculiar thing for a church to own. An incredible, monstrous clock! What were they doing with it? Advertising? What? I wasn't even sure such a large clock could be so benign. Certainly it was strange. I saw green plants in a window across the street. I wondered who watered the hanging vine and if they spilled water on the floor when they did so. And I saw where the old, tired cement of the side-

walk had buckled and fled on an incurable slant toward
its weathered, crumbling edges.

After a while, I had seen Ninety-ninth Street and
still no Bluma. Even though it was comfortable, I felt
more than a little incongruous, like a crumpled stalk
of celery on top of an ice-cream sundae instead of
the compact maraschino cherry. When a law-abiding
citizen is the celery in the sundae, he fears the law.
What's wrong with celery on a sundae? Nothing! It's
healthier, seething with vitamins, and won't rot your
teeth, but it doesn't look right, and because our hearts
are corrupt, we judge only with the eye. Corrective
lenses can make us all retinal chief justices: regular
appearance is propriety. Strangeness is guilt. And there
I sat, fearing what a policeman circling about the drug-
infested, crime-related, alcohol-inebriated, homicide-
saturated Upper West Side would think of my 44-long
sprawled on the Siamese standpipe of Two-fifty West
Ninety-ninth Street. As the patrol car pulled to the
curb, I would take the offense, "Officer, righteousness
is a two-way street." "Yeah, pal, a two-way street. No
loitering. Get moving." "Officer, do you believe in
God?" "Not north of Ninety-sixth Street. Let's go." The
cop car that does roll down Ninety-ninth Street doesn't
bother to slow down. The cop does look at me. What is
he thinking? He's probably thinking that if he had a
dollar for every German shepherd who pissed on that
standpipe, he'd be a millionaire, a thought which has
crossed my mind from time to time even though, thank
God, the standpipe has been freshly painted.

And there I sit, hoping that nobody I know will come
walking down the street. What would I tell them? I
don't have to tell anyone else anything at all. People
stare at me from a distance, but they give me a wide
berth when they pass. And when they pass, they don't

look at me; I look at them. A few even cross the street.
Shuffling past, the junkies and winos smile fearfully at
this ungainly, sedentary invasion of their glass-eyed
world. If strangeness is guilt, it is also fear, the most
negotiable commodity on the Upper West Side. I explore
my newfound power and even stare at people with
dogs large enough to fool the parlor-bound Off-Track
Betting crowd: my, that's a hairy horse. Big deal! Two
St. Bernards later I'm bored. Where is she? Where's
Bluma? What's taking her so long? A panicky feeling
creeps over me. What if she never returns? I'll have to
sit on this pipe forever. What choice do I have? None. I
sit. They stare. They fear. They look away when they
pass. They tug on the leashes to save the beasts from
me. I wait for her, and as I do, there is something
familiar about the strangeness. Something similar to
stepping (or in this case sitting) outside the realm of
normal — that is to say, identifiable — behavior. Where
else could it have been? It had something to do with the
*shtibl*. But where was Bluma? I keep my eye on the
corner of Broadway. It's a two-way street. She has to
return. The baby can't nap all afternoon.

As I stare intently toward Broadway, I hear a voice
call, "Hey, Hal darling! Over here!" I swing around to
discover Bluma standing in front of the AL NDA E
near West End Avenue. Bluma as Daniel Boone. At her
feet are one shopping bag and one old beat-up suitcase.

"You drink tea, Hal?"

"Yes."

"Good. You got a box."

"Bluma, you want this back?"

"Bags! Bluma's got a million bags!"

"No, the suitcase?"

"Suitcases, too!"

We walked to Broadway together.

"Thanks, Bluma."

"Don't mention."

"I'll see you in the *shtibl* Tuesday."

"We'll see. . . . Now I gotta go over there and sit down. It's comfortable, no?"

"Yes, it is. You could use a rest."

"I'll say. Be well, Hal."

"You, too. And thank you."

I *shlepped* that suitcase down Broadway. Daniel Boone only had Indians to worry about. I had roaches. I knew I was in trouble when I put the bag down to wait for the light at Ninety-sixth, and the bag started running home by itself. I was tempted to follow it to find out where Bluma lived, but that hardly seemed fair after all the trouble she had taken in circling the block. Bluma definitely had uptown roaches who had no interest in exploring Ninety-third Street. I had to carry them the whole way. They just wouldn't walk in my direction. As I spotted some moving about the bag, I was tempted to throw everything into a large wire litter basket on the corner. I fought the off feeling. It would be too dangerous to have a wire basket careening riderless uptown. And how did I know Bluma wasn't watching me now? But I did know I couldn't bring those things into the house. When I got back, I took them straight to the basement and gingerly examined their contents next to the collected refuse. The infested clothes were out of the question. The tea looked pretty bad, too. The Jewish calendars were in good shape, but the most recent one was four years old. We had a current one upstairs and how many garish pictures of Moses coming off the mountain with the golden rays of light hitting his head could one apartment tolerate? Then I came across a short, ugly metal lamp. Maroon, without a bulb or lampshade. It seemed difficult for a roach to penetrate, so I decided this was the object to cherish. I also kept an old coffee pot. I didn't want the lamp to feel alone. Stamping my feet in self-defense, I backed my way onto the elevator. Upstairs, I also washed the gifts. By the time I finished, I needed a rest. I sat down — on a chair.

Several Tuesdays later, I waited for the others to leave before I offered Bluma an envelope.

"No. Keep it."

"It's for you."

"Listen, Hal, you keep it. If I need it, I'll get in touch."

"How can you get in touch, you don't have my number?"

"Yeah, good idea. Write it for me."

I put the envelope back in my pocket and gave her my number.

"What was it? A five-dollar bill?" she asked.

"Yes."

"That's good."

We walked outside together.

"Hal darling, during the winter, you'll miss me."

"Why?"

"My dear man, I should slip and fall on the ice? Feh! Feh! Feh! What are you talking about? I've got to be careful."

"I'll miss you, Bluma."

"Of course you will."

I didn't see Bluma all winter. Nor did I hear from her. I thought it strange that Bluma should disappear for the winter like a bear because she couldn't hibernate. She had to awaken every morning. Well, I figured, that's how Bluma wants it. I thought about her from time to time, especially when my daughter wore the blue pullover or I turned on the ugly maroon lamp.

Something else reminded me of her. I finally recalled the activity outside the realm of normal public behavior that had haunted me when I was camped out on Bluma's standpipe. It involved the moon. Let me explain.

The Jewish calendar is a lunar calendar. The first day of the new month is celebrated as a minor holiday. During the Sabbath service preceding the new moon (new month), we intone, "Let it be Thy will to renew us for a good and blessed month." And "May He who miraculously redeemed our fathers from slavery to freedom, quickly redeem us and gather us from our Diaspora to the land of Israel, for all Jews are brothers." The Blessing of the New Moon is performed outdoors at night. The new moon, a fragile crescent, can be blessed during the period of its renewal, from the time it is easily seen until it becomes a full moon. Traditionally, it's done on Saturday night after the evening services because when we bless the moon, we encounter the Shechinah, God's Holy Presence, and consequently Sabbath attire is appropriate. Immediately following the service, every one of us in the congregation grabs a prayer book, and we go piling down into Ninety-first Street in search of the moon. Depending on the season, sometimes we simply cross the street; other times we must go all the way down the block and even cross West End Avenue to get an unobstructed view. "C'mon! It's over here!" And the properly attired horde goes racing down the block and across West End Avenue to glance quickly at the crescent moon. After a quick glance at the moon, everyone hastily opens his book and begins furiously chattering away.

How can we read the blessing so quickly in the dark? The Blessing of the Moon is printed in extra large letters because of this difficulty. Indeed, all large let-

ters are referred to in Hebrew as Blessing-the-Moon
letters. And we read quickly. "The heavenly bodies are
ecstatically happy to do the will of their Creator, the
true Producer, whose production is truth. And the
moon was commanded to renew itself as a glorious
crown for those not yet born, for they are to be renewed
in the future as the moon is, and they will glorify their
Creator for His glorious majesty. Blessed are You, O
Lord, who renews the months!"

Normally, a prayer service in the *shtibl* is a free-form
event, but there is some structure. Under the moon,
however, it is completely unstructured and each of us
takes off helter-skelter for himself, but there is some
group interaction. At a specific point in the prayer,
each worshiper must exchange greetings with three
other individuals. He looks up from his prayer book
and taps someone. "*Shalom aleichem*, Peace unto you!"
The other must interrupt his prayer to respond, "Unto
you, peace!" In turn this individual will address three
greetings and receive three responses. The threefold
exchange washes through the group like a mad tidal
wave of greeting, leaving eddies and lone swells of
peace in its murmuring wake. One of our less learned
congregants refers to the ceremony as "praying to the
moon." This is, of course, blasphemous. In fact, when
one utters the line "As I dance opposite you, O Moon,
and I am not able to touch you, thus may my enemies
not be able to do me harm," we are adjured to dance in
a manner that clearly suggests blessing of the moon
and not worship. Monotheistic choreography dictates
that one leap stiff-legged so as to avoid any bending of
the knee that might be misinterpreted as idolatrous
worship. This admonition is carefully respected. The
effect is a mad, stiff-legged happening that looks like a
Buster Keaton movie run at twice the usual herky-jerky

speed. With one notable exception — Reb Meir Hurwitz is so inspired by this line in the service that he plants each hand on the shoulder of a tall neighbor and with a quick thrust of his short, powerful arms goes sailing above the throng, almost launching himself into lunar orbit.

How do we appear then, on a dark street corner in the middle of the night? An unshaven (we have not been permitted to shave since the Sabbath began) but well-dressed group of Jews rocking and chanting cacophonously, lickety-split as they tap each other while they leap about like stiff-legged kangaroos with the exception of one, Reb Meir Hurwitz, who sails over the group like an ecstatic, lock-legged version of Rodin's statue of Balzac, and all this directed toward the banana moon rising a quarter of a million miles above Daitch Shopwell supermarket, where hordes of real bananas can be had for seventeen cents a pound. Passers-by tend not to cross at our corner. Those who must pass us often step into the street and rarely look directly at us.

We all read as quickly as we can for the obvious reason: the hapless *shmendrik* who finishes last will have all the prayer books foisted upon him, and he must *shlep* the towering, heavy stack across the street, down the block, and up the stairs into the *shtibl*, opening two doors unaided. But that is only the obvious reason; there is another, even more powerful one. Who wants to look and feel like a fool? Strangeness is guilt. Blessing the moon might put us in the presence of God (certainly a good deed), but it also exposes us to people's fearful faces. And that calls for a fast finish. This is the Diaspora, baby!

After that realization, every time we blessed the new moon, I thought of Bluma and my having sat on her standpipe amidst the incredulous, fearful stares. Bluma and the moon both moved me from the realm of the inconspicuous, the dwelling place of the complacent. The stubby thumb had better be more powerful than any camouflaged finger. It has to be, to survive. So Bluma and the moon began to be associated together in my mind — a vague enough but real sort of relationship. Initially, I simply considered it a curiosity.

As I performed this *mitzvah* month after month, something was happening. I was finding a pleasure, a sense of satisfaction in it. More often than not, I was the *shmendrik* who *shlepped* the prayer books back to the *shtibl*.

Bluma reappeared one raw spring day. Not in the *shtibl*, but across the street.

"Hal darling, over here."

"Bluma, how are you?"

"Don't ask, a single person should never be born."

"What's wrong?"

"Use your head!"

We stood there a moment.

"Bluma, why didn't you come into the *shtibl*?"

"Who needs them? Hyah! Hyah! Hyah!"

Horselike, Bluma tilted her head and chomped her teeth to utter the cruel, neighing "hyah." I looked at Bluma. The red socks had not made it through the winter. The cane was gone, too. Bluma leaned on a baby-carriage axle that looked harsh and vicious. Held vertically, it also resembled a degenerate ski pole. The presence of one broken ski pole suggested instability. Bluma spoke rapidly, punctuating her remarks with the explosive neighlike hyah-hyah-hyahs! She spoke against people.

"The rabbi's no good! A beard for people, but not for God! American rabbis! Feh! Feh! Feh! I give him three dollars for a big mezuzah like the *shtibl* has — and he gets me a little one. I told him I didn't like it, but did he give me the three dollars back? What kind of rabbi is that? A *gonif*! A thief! A *gonif*! You're not like that. You're from the other side. Rabbis aren't like that on the other side, are they?"

"Bluma," I explained, "I'm not from Israel. I'm from St. Louis." ·

"That's not around here, is it?"

"No."

"You're from the other side. . . . See!"

And I heard about legal actions — falls, insurance, lawyers. I could never understand any of the stories. I would ask why a lawyer had taken a particular action:

"Why? A farmer puts an egg under a chicken! You know what that means? You don't know? It means he takes two. Shut your mouth! You got to be intelligent! Hyah! Hyah! Hyah!"

Bluma, who had always guarded her private life and personal history so closely, was suddenly revealing things inadvertently and not caring.

"How do I know so much about courts?" she would yell. "That Irishman I married. He changed his fait' for me, the alcoholic. I was always in the court for non-support. I used to sit and listen to the other cases. You can learn a lot."

And I heard about her dog for the first time.

"Bluma, you have a dog?"

"Yeah, what's wrong with that? She's good company. Shut your mouth! She's intelligent; she listens. Brownie understands Yiddish. That's better than you."

Still, I heard the old Bluma. "God is with the righteous. Don't worry about God." But I was most moved when I asked if I might give her some money.

"Money's not everything. What about *yener velt*, the world to come?"

"You're right, Bluma, but can I help you a little?"
For the first time that morning she softened and
some of the frantic tension left her.

"Hal darling, I retired. I got another check, a little
money. Others need more than me."

"That's wonderful."

"We'll see. Maybe from time to time you'll give me a
little something. I know some very poor people and,
after all, Bluma has to give a little 'righteousness,' too."

"Sure, Bluma."

"But, Hal darling, we'll still talk. You gotta talk to
people. You know that, Hal, don't you?"

"We all have to talk."

"Now shut up and listen. Don't interrupt all the
time. It's not right!"

BLUMA had returned, but the winter of loneliness
had taken its toll. Much of her charm and style had disappeared with the red socks. Spring, a new season, and
even the DiMaggios can't play forever. Bluma could
not move as well, the legs heavier and slower. Apparently our relationship had changed as well. I had
survived her brutal winter. Now we were old friends.
We talked. How we talked. For Bluma, I became a
chance to converse with a world which wouldn't see,
which wouldn't listen, which wouldn't care.

"Look at me. Only the police look me in the eye.
They understand me. They laugh. Are you observant?
Do you study people? I observe them. The policeman
said to me, 'Bluma, you should be a detective!' I study
people."

We began speaking on the phone. Everyone in her
building was an addict or an alcoholic or a thief or
murderer. The manager was no good. The super was a
sex maniac. I believed all of this. A welfare hotel offers

more human degradation than hell ever could.

"It's terrible, my dear man, I can't stand it. . . . Yes,
I live in the Whitehall. You guessed. You're not as
dumb as you act."

She would no longer take any money, but she still
insisted that I take from her. What I didn't drag home!
My pregnant wife could not believe it. What could she
say? Nothing.

In the summer during my vacation I had agreed to
pick up a load. It was humid and in the nineties. It
struck me as madness. What in the world could come
out of such a project? I went out the door and was met
by the wall of brilliant, sticky heat. I headed uptown.
At ten in the morning, the harsh heat and heavy air
hung over Broadway like a motionless, fly-covered
beast. As I walked, I wondered how in blazes I ever got
here. Something must have gone wrong with my life
somewhere.

When I approached Ninety-sixth Street, I saw a very
tall young woman with a dog. They were walking in
the same direction as I was. I could see her legs. I
thought it must be the mind-joggling heat. Those legs
looked like they belonged to Peggy Hartridge, my fresh-
man flame at Harvard. She had nice legs all right. I
walked behind her for a block. The woman seemed
very young; too young to be Peggy. It had been years. So
I just walked behind her, focusing on those lovely
young legs and basking in memory to escape the insuf-
ferable heat.

Peggy Hartridge. What an unrequited relationship
that was! Calculus class, homework together, walks in
the snow together, and countless ice-cream cones.
Almost six feet tall, blond, blue-eyed, and bright. Everything you could ask for in a math partner. I got a B-;
she got an A. Bluma would believe that part, all right.

There had been no chance that Peggy was going to change her fait' for me. Our relationship never blossomed. I had the inclination, but not the courage, and she was always falling in love with someone else. A sophomore who looked like a Swedish lumberjack, straight A's in linguistics. A German, unlike Henry Kissinger, a real one, who took her sailing at night on an African lake (her father was a Peace Corps administrator) where the waves were so high they blotted out the brilliant stars, and who during the day casually shot king cobras. What did I have to offer? By day, I took her to the bleachers in Fenway Park and explained why the left-field wall was called the green monster, and by night I took her to see a thirty-year-old subtitled film, *The Dybbuk*. But what I found most attractive about her was the way she received a compliment. With absolute grace and charm. She wasn't embarrassed or thrilled, but very direct and appreciative. I don't think Peggy Hartridge knew about the Evil Eye the way Bluma did.

"Bluma, you're a wonderful person," I had said.

"Shut up! Whaddaya want to do, give me the Evil Eye?"

What did Peggy know about the Evil Eye? The boat never capsized, the cobra never bit her, and every time I came close, a Swedish lumberjack walked into her life. The worst thing that ever happened to her was when she caught mono. Some Evil Eye! She went to the infirmary for two weeks, studied for finals, got all A's, and fit as a fiddle flew off to watch the snake charmer.

Enough was enough. I walked ahead of the lady with the dog and looked back, fully expecting to find myself staring into a strange, terrified face. Even if it were Peggy, how could she recognize me with a beard and long hair?

"Hello, Peggy," I said, somewhat surprised.

"Hal, how are you?" she answered coolly.

"Fine, how are you?"

"Good, thank you."

"Peggy, what are you doing here?"

"I'm coming back from the vet on Seventy-ninth."

Along with a charming dog, Peggy had acquired a Ph.D. in history and was teaching at City College. She certainly hadn't aged. We talked about what we were doing because Peggy did not seem to remember the past very well, a strange failing for a history professor, I thought. We arrived at Ninety-ninth, and there was Bluma at the corner. I introduced them.

"Bluma, Peggy."

"What's your dog's name?" Bluma asked Peggy.

"Duncan," Peggy answered.

"Duncan?" Bluma queried.

"Yes, Duncan," Peggy repeated.

"Duncan," Bluma said. "You'll forgive me, my dear, but Duncan is a stupid name for a dog. It's a person's name."

"What's wrong with that?" Peggy laughed.

"He's not a person. He's a dog," Bluma generously explained. "When I got my dog, her name was Lady, but that was stupid. Lady is what you call a person, so I changed her name to Brownie because she's brown. See!"

"I guess so," Peggy said pleasantly.

"No, you don't," Bluma said. "Why not call him Blackie, he looks kind of black?"

Peggy did not respond.

"Call him Spot," Bluma suggested by way of a compromise for the solid-colored dog. "Maybe he's got a spot."

"I like the name Duncan," Peggy said.

"It's a nice name, but it doesn't make sense!" Bluma
explained.

I switched the topic, and after a little small talk
Peggy excused herself. We watched the six-foot, blond,
blue-eyed creature walk toward West End with her
large black dog.

"She's a *shiksa*, isn't she?" Bluma said matter-of-
factly.

"How could you tell?" I asked.

"Duncan is a *goyish* name," she answered. And then
she said, "Wait around the corner. I'll get the stuff."

"Can't I get it for you?" I offered.

"Shut up! Nobody should know our business."

Bereft of Bluma, Peggy, and Duncan, I waited on
Broadway in hot steamy misery, thinking what a
strange coincidence that had been. As I was daydreaming in the heat, Bluma arrived with the packages. In
some ways, she hadn't changed. Bluma still would not
embarrass me. She put the packages down in front of
Cake Masters' bakery and crossed to the curb where
she pretended to greet the man delivering magazines
and newspapers.

"Oh," Bluma called merrily to him, "how are you,
my friend?" And then still walking toward him, she
spun her head in my direction and said vehemently,
"Use your head! Use your head!"

I ran over and picked up the packages and started to
*shlep* them downtown. What a strange day! Talk about
threads! Ageless Peggy Hartridge comes looping back
after all those years. But Bluma was right. God is good; I
could have gone the way of Henry Kissinger and Bluma.
I could have thrown my life away, cut myself off from
my roots — and what for? A woman who names a dog
Duncan! It's not even a nice name.

And in that bundle was an army trench coat, the

arms right. My wife admitted that the long green com-
bat coat fit me better than anything I had ever had
tailored. I wore an army coat in a time of peace, but
Bluma maintained her war, battling in the trenches on
a hundred different fronts. Her words remained a ver-
bal feast, but I did not have the stomach for them. Not
with all the pain and hurt that was served with them.
And strange things began to surface. One day Bluma
rang our bell, but I could not hear over the intercom so I
went downstairs to see who it was. I invited Bluma up,
but she refused. We talked in the lobby. After a while,
my wife came down to see what had happened. She
joined the conversation. After we had spoken for a
while, I escorted Bluma to the corner.

"You got problems, Hal. Your wife is a jealous
woman."

"You think so, Bluma?"

"C'mon! Why did she come down?"

"She just wanted to see who it was," I answered.

"Use your head. Be careful! Hyah! Hyah! Hyah!"

"You are a remarkable person, Bluma!"

"People love me. The world loves me. I have a
remarkable personality. It's a gift," she said with pride.

What could I do for Bluma? I turned to the moon.
The moon had the answers, for the moon and Bluma
were sisters. The answers were in the Talmud. In Gen-
esis it is written, "And God made two great lights."
Later it calls them "the greater light and the lesser
light." What happened? Originally the sun and the
moon were of equal magnitude. The moon came to God
and asked, "Can two kings wear the same crown?"
*Svora*! The moon was right, but God commanded the
moon to make itself smaller. The moon asked, "Since
what I have suggested is a good idea, why must I make
myself smaller?" God heard the moon, and decreed

that the moon will rule by day and night. The moon asked, "What good is a candle (the small moon) in broad daylight?" God said that Israel will count the days and years according to the moon, but the moon answered that the sun was needed for this, also. And when God saw that he could not console the moon, the Holy One commanded Israel "to bring an atonement for Me because I have made the moon smaller."

And Israel brought a sacrifice for the Lord on the New Moon until the Temple was destroyed. And Israel blessed and still blesses the moon in its renewal, for in the moon's renewal we see the symbol of Israel's renewal. Every nation has a heavenly advocate. Israel's is the moon, that pale creature of *svora*. Esau's is the sun. It is written, "Esau hates Jacob (Israel)." But Jacob does not hate Esau because the moon has forgiven the sun since God is good. To demonstrate this — and to emulate this freedom from jealousy — we say "Peace unto you. Peace unto you. Peace unto you," as we bless the New Moon.

And every month the moon begins its heavenly renewal in the hope that this renewal will be the ultimate and final renewal, for God is good. And Israel below chants as it blesses, "The throne of King David is established forever!" For the throne of David, the dynasty of David, the Messiah of David shall, "like the moon, be established forever." And the renewal of the "New Month" and "King David of Israel lives and endures" possess according to the numerical values of their Hebrew letters the identical sum, eight hundred and nineteen. The ultimate numbers game — eight hundred and nineteen — redemption — the Messiah.

And yet we who attempt to bless the moon from West End Avenue and Bluma on Broadway stand isolated and ashamed as we reach to grasp a wanderer's hand. Bluma and the moon: both had been wronged, both remained faithful, and both pursued subservient, but never servile, circuits about other bodies, heavenly and human, no grander in creation but less diminished in an everyday, material world. The moon chasing about the earth to catch the fire of the sun and Bluma looping through the Upper West Side to catch the coins of undiminished human fortunes. Bluma and the moon awaiting the shofar's final, redemptive blast.

What does that leave for the moon maiden, Bluma, on the Upper West Side? What could I do? Bluma made greater and greater demands on my time. Bluma expressed her love — the power to control. Perhaps I did not love. Perhaps I did, for I countered with demands that Bluma could not meet. I invited her for the Sabbath meal. I invited her for any meal. I invited her to visit. Once, when she was in the hallway outside our door, I asked her to come in for "at least a cup of tea."

"Hal darling, I remember a woman who was very good to me. She begged me to come into her for a meal. Finally, I came. She put the food on the table. When I sat down, she moved over to the window sill. See! I am observant. The policeman said, 'Bluma, you should be a detective.' See!"

Everything she said was true, but I invited her for Rosh Hashanah anyway. Can't we learn? And it was our anniversary of sorts. No, she wouldn't come. I told her that we would be expecting her and if she could not make it, not to worry, we would understand.

"What are you having, Hal?"

"Turkey."

"Turkey is *goyish*."

I heard the shofar — the calls of creation — and I thought of the moon — the calls of the Messiah — and I thought of the moon and Bluma. I knew that the heavenly threads being woven were for Bluma. We returned from the *shtibl* for lunch and, without Bluma, we ate the *goyish* bird.

Yom Kippur arrived and I donned my shroud for the Day of Atonement. White shrouds, for white is the color of the angels. Shrouds, for life is the name of the game. And in the morning, a man walked in and told us that the Arabs had attacked Israel. And we turned to pray, as is the custom, for we wear shrouds, and they do the dying. We prayed. And after the Day of Atonement, we ran to Bless the Moon. How quickly we blessed the moon before we dashed home for news. "What is happening? Have they stopped them yet?" And the news was not good. The war dragged on for too long. The nation is small, the wound is large, and the precious blood flows quickly. And the relentless, steely cold fear of destruction hovered over a small people of flesh. And the threads were soaked in blood. The holiday season continued and so did the blood. It was a fear such as I have never known. How could we rejoice? Yet we tried. Talk about threads! An impenetrable snarl! And I repented of my arrogant sin. The threads were not simply Bluma's and the moon's, but the threads of an entire nation. And in the middle of it all — the war, the fear — there was a pennant race. Who could care? And for the first time, it dawned on me that someone led the National League in batting the year two million Jews died in Auschwitz. Who can comprehend the middle?

In the incomprehensible middle, where could I turn? To the beginning and to the end. The threads are Bluma's, the nation's, the moon's, and mine. I turned to the moon. For the moon is memory, and we are a people of memory. The sun has no memory. The sun does not need one. It is ageless and always shining.

Peggy Hartridge cannot remember her past. For her, it is always the present. Bluma the Beggar has no present. She possesses the past (she has never forgotten anything) and the future. Memory is the curse of Bluma and the Jews, and it is our salvation. We live in the past and rebuild the future. The world compresses us into the present. Either we transcend it, or we go crazy. The acquisitive millionaire in Scarsdale and the ascetic Talmudist in Brooklyn are two sides of the same coin. Both are driven by the past and the future. One rejecting. One accepting. But it's the same fuel — higher octane than lies under any Arabian desert.

The sun is Esau. The sun is the present. The sun is obvious. The sun is hairy. Nothing is hairier than the sun. One sees it in all the pictures children draw. When the sons of Esau landed on the moon of Jacob, what did they do? They took pictures and flung Hasselblad cameras over the face of the moon. The moon remembers. The sun is static. The moon is born, grows, and dies, only to be reborn. It is no mistake that the moon affects the tides. For the seas are the insensate potential of creation. The great tremendous unstructured and unchartable mass — chaos and creation. The moon tugs invisibly only on those liquid currents of immutable repose and fathomless desire — the pulsating sea and the immeasurable human heart. The moon is the tide of the Diaspora — a self-contained wave sweeping the face of the earth in bitter greeting.

The bitter tide sweeps through the incomprehensible present. The threads are tangled. The sorrow is real. Bluma's complaints grew. Bluma couldn't live there. What could Bluma do? She gave to help Israel.

"Hal, they got trouble on the other side. If we don't help 'em, what'll be?"

What could I do? I went to the Whitehall with a

lawyer, a Spanish-speaking rabbi, and an old Lower East Side hand, all from the *shtibl*, to see if we could help. We couldn't. Bluma's horrors — junkies, winos — were real, all right, but her complaints — a leaky sink, a broken toilet — were imaginary. Brownie was lying on the bed because the room was filled with boxes, suitcases, and bags from floor to ceiling. The lawyer asked why she kept all that stuff.

"My dear man, everyone has something."

We had failed. Bluma said we had made things worse. Perhaps we had. For the first time, I *shlepped* downtown from Bluma's unencumbered by a material load. I carried a heavier one: Bluma was in pain and I could not help. On the way back, I saw the phony, arm in sling, at Ninety-sixth Street. People gave to him. The Talmud says, thank heaven for the phonies, or we would have to give to all who asked. In the middle, God bless him.

I was depressed. The Yom Kippur War. Bluma. Myself. Then my wife gave birth — another girl baby. I was ecstatic. I called and told the good news to Bluma, who told me that I was no good. She said that I never called, I made things worse, I would have destroyed the world except for God. "God is good."

I hung up less ecstatic, but understanding, for I had a wise teacher. The disease contained its cure. We shall arrive at the ends of our threads because of our gladness. The Talmud tells us that "The Divine Presence dwells among Israel only in gladness," and I know that gladness is from man, who knows that God is good. How could we not be glad? I have my teachers of gladness, quieting the terror-crested wave of bitterness. The Messianic moon renewing the throne of David. Then we shall all be on the other side, dwelling in our land of peace. It will surely be. The Messiah! Although

I weep now for Bluma, I am glad, for that day will come when everyone has something. Oh, that Bluma, will she have something! She will have the shofar's calls — the Holy Threads — which will hang in the windows of her room, shielding her from lunacy. For lunacy will be the moon shining by day and night as brilliantly as the sun. And I shall stand to honor my teacher when the door to her room opens. . . . Room 819.

*Building Blocks*

I ARRIVED late for the afternoon prayers on Shivah Asar be-Tammuz. On the Seventeenth Day of the month of Tammuz, a fast day, one laments the breaching of Jerusalem's wall by Roman legions in the final days of the Second Temple. Shivah Asar be-Tammuz is not your average fast day by any means. It kicks off the whole mourning season that runs for a full three weeks culminating in Tisha b'Av, the day the Temple itself was destroyed. This period is known, in fact, as the "Three Weeks," "*Drei Vochen*," or "*Shalosha Shavuoth*," all of which literally mean three weeks. During this period one observes customs and laws of mourning (with the exception of the intervening Sabbaths when all mourning is forbidden). One does not listen to music, have one's hair cut, or get married. Additional strictures for the final nine days demand that one does not eat meat, drink wine, go swimming, or wear new clothes. And on the fast of Tisha b'Av one does not wear leather shoes, sit on chairs, or even study holy subjects. In other words, starting with Shivah Asar be-Tammuz you can really mourn your head off.

It's not exactly a picnic, definitely not my best season, and I come from a family that loves to mourn. And not just at the chapel or grave — tears, stools, ripping clothes, *kaddish*, the works. Sorrow, bitterness, anguish, indulgence, sweetness — real mourning. And not just for seven days — for years. And why not? How many sensual things in life are there? But when my family mourns, we are mourning for someone — a father, a sister, an uncle. We shriek "Rachel," "Morris," "Menachem the son of Lazar." It's all very intimate, personal. When Shivah Asar be-Tammuz comes and you mourn your head off, who is it for? The whole world! A pretty tall order. Who even knows the name of the world? Earth? Universe? Did you ever try and mourn for the whole world the week Hank Aaron hit his 700th home run? It is a confusing experience. And if the Temple had not been destroyed, what would Einstein have been, a camel driver in Beersheba? The Budapest String Quartet, olive pickers in the Galilee? It's true. Yes, and if the Temple had not been destroyed, we would not have been around for Hitler and his ovens. That's true, too. All the years of blood. If only the Jews had been good. If only we hadn't hated without cause. If only we hadn't transgressed His Sabbath — our Sabbath. If only we had minded our own business like the Italians and Greeks and all the other short, swarthy races of antiquity. What can you do? Mourn — from Shivah Asar be-Tammuz through Tisha b'Av, and who can be so certain Sandy Koufax is so happy anyway? But the man did pitch four no-hitters, so is it any wonder that I was late for *minchah*, the afternoon prayer?

Of course, I had been present for the morning prayers. At their conclusion the *minyan* attempted to find a time for *minchah*. Eight o'clock? Too soon! You can't eat till nine o'clock!! Eight-fifteen? Too late! At nine o'clock you can eat already! Eight-ten? Eight-ten? Good!

No, they couldn't start *minchah* late enough for me. My goal is always to avoid the business of the day. I was annoyed that we would have to wait so long between the afternoon and evening prayers. Waiting for a fast day to end is the deadliest, dullest waiting of all and not simply because one is hungry. That's the least of it. You want the day to end and to get back to your normal, confused life. Of course I eat when it's over. I overeat, but not because of need, rather it's the principle of the thing. Why not eat when you spent a day not eating! It places the day in perspective; you were famished. What an ordeal that was! No, it is not the eating.

It is those final moments when the day is technically
over, when the darkness begins to descend, the bright,
harsh light relaxes, and the true, luminous inner nature of the day emerges. The barest moment before the
screen door slams against the frame when the agitated
smidgen enters, unintimidated, unhurried, unavoid-
able, and one is faced with the reality no architect
ever envisioned: a fly is in the house. And it is His
house. You are trapped.

So it is between *minchah* and *ma'ariv*. When you are
standing in the comfortable little wood- and book-lined
room staring at the impending darkness or checking
the liturgical calendar to see when it is time to pray or
even wondering why your shoes get scuffed the way
they do, the day rises up from the worn wood floor,
comes over the heavy wooden benches, and taps you
on the shoulder, whispering, "The night is for hiding,
do you think you can hide from the day? Here I am, all
twelve sun-filled hours of me." And what can you do?
You turn around to face the day, all of it. So when the
*minchah* prayer was finished (it went quickly since I
had missed the first part) and Mr. Isaacson sat next to
me at the little table in the back, I welcomed him. A few
pleasant words with a charming man, a righteous man,
and the day would be over. Who wanted to look Shivah
Asar be-Tammuz in the eye?

He turned to me and said, "Some things come to
mind, you mention Russian."

I had mentioned Russian because Mr. Isaacson is the
man who makes the *minyan*. He's not the tenth man,
but he is responsible for him and for seven, eight, and
nine as well. In the summer it is hard to find a *minyan*,
and when it becomes apparent that no one is going to
walk in the door, Mr. Isaacson takes his *tefillin* off and
goes out to help numbers seven, eight, nine, and ten

find us. He shanghais the unwary up and down Ninety-first Street. He cadges them on the corner of Broadway. He plunders other *minyans*. This last is like asking Othello to lend you his wife, but Mr. Isaacson is a hard man to say no to because what's in it for Mr. Isaacson? Is he paid for it? No, thank God, he has a good business. Does he have to say *kaddish*? No, thank God, his family is fine. Does he have to run around like a *meshugginer*? No, he could pray anywhere. Who would want to start his day by saying no to Mr. Isaacson? Not numbers seven through ten. And so when I didn't attend regularly, I wanted Mr. Isaacson to know why. Why? My wife was taking a Russian course which started quite early and I had to get the baby dressed and over to her play group. And who gives the baby a lollipop on *Shabbes*? Mr. Isaacson. So I understood his mentioning my mentioning Russian.

He had a distant look in his eye. He was clearly moved by the long summer fast day — waiting for the sun to set.

"I was in the Fourth Russian Army; we hadn't eaten for days. They were shelling us something terrible and then on the fourth day they told us to move forward. So we began climbing this hill. It was a big hill and we were carrying everything. They had even given me a big, heavy ammunition box to carry, too. I struggled up the hill and they told us to dig in so I dug a trench and when I finished a sergeant or an officer would say, 'You with such-and-such a group?' And I would say, 'No, I'm with the Fourth Russian Army,' and they would say, 'They're over there.' And I would move over there and I would start digging again. I would dig in and they would ask, 'You with such-and-such a group?' and I would say, 'No, I'm with the Fourth Russian Army,' and they would say, 'Oh, they're over there.' And I would move over there and dig in again and the same thing would happen. 'You with such-and-such a group?' 'No.' 'Go there.' It wasn't like today; you didn't ask questions. You did what they told you."

He shrugs his shoulders, *nu*, and holds his hands out palms up — what can you do? He lifts his eyes in a perplexed look. What can you do? And what could the sergeant or officer do? This man, Mr. Isaacson of the Fourth Russian Army, is digging. He is honeycombing half of Rumania.

"I went from here to here to here." He points to various positions on our table, the Rumanian hilltop, in front of us.

"Finally I found where I was supposed to be. I was digging in, it must have been near dawn because I looked down and saw water. There was a stream at the bottom of the hill. I went right down there. I didn't walk. I ran right down and threw myself in. My head and arms and everything right into the stream."

He pantomimes his immersion. He smiles: it is refreshing.

"It felt so good. We were so thirsty and tired. The others saw it, too, and they started coming down. Pretty soon the whole army was in the stream. Then they told us to get moving so everybody got up and we started marching along. I felt something under my foot, kind of unsteady, and looked down. We were walking over trenches. We were supposed to replace the garrison. We moved up and took their places and they started bombing us. It was terrible. For three days nobody moved and then in the morning they told us to attack. We went running out a little way and dug in. I started digging. They were shelling us awhile and stopped. I was so tired, I hadn't slept in several days. I guess I fell asleep. Just like that. And the next thing I knew, everybody was running over me. They had given the order to attack and I was asleep."

Mr. Isaacson laughs at this. What kind of soldier is that? The Angel of Death yells "Forward!" and he is asleep.

"So I jumped up, too, and started running. It was terrible. We were attacking toward the north and the Germans were to the east on our flank, so they opened up their machine guns and caught us in a crossfire. We had to turn the entire army to the east."

On our table Mr. Isaacson has the entire Russian Fourth Army wheel ninety degrees to the right to face the darkening windows and the entrenched Germans.

"I saw that they had us in a crossfire, and instead of going east I got down and ran south to the other end of the battle. People were dropping and I was running low. I saw this ditch filled with dead bodies and I thought to myself, '*Moishe, men ken geharget vern*,' so I jumped in and lay down. The whole thing kept going on. After a while a Yettaslav jumped in and said, 'What are you doing?' and I said, 'I don't know.'"

Mr. Isaacson shrugs his shoulders for both of us, the Yettaslav and me. What can you do? I asked who the man was.

"The Yettaslav was a big, strong fellow."

Mr. Isaacson straightens up and thrusts out his chest and shoulders. "He was from Yettaslav, a town near Odessa where all the men are big and strong. He said, 'Let's shoot at them,' so I took my rifle and put a bullet in and shot, but the bullet wouldn't come out, so I tried pushing it through, but I could not do it. I put another bullet in and shot and pushed. Again nothing, but that must have done it. It didn't work. I didn't know what to do, so I picked it up and gave it a *klop*."

The bullet-stuffed rifle comes crashing down on our

table.

"And it broke in two. It fell apart."

We stare in astonishment and dread at the two pieces of the no-good Czarist rifle before us.

"I didn't know what to do. I looked over to the Yettaslav to see if he knew what happened, but he was right next to me shooting away. I was afraid if he saw, he might kill me. He might think I did it on purpose."

"Did he know you were Jewish?"

"Yes, he knew."

"How could he tell?"

"He was from my unit of the Fourth Russian Army. He knew me. 'Jew, dirty Jew,' he would yell and shoot at me. So I leaned over the broken rifle and pretended I was shooting."

Mr. Isaacson leans over the broken rifle, resting his extended rifle-cradling arm on the *chumashim* stacked on the table. The Yettaslav and I are to the left shooting away at the Germans and can't see what is really going on — nothing. Mr. Isaacson continues to hide from us. I can only hear his voice.

"I was like this a long time. The longest time. I didn't know what to do. I was afraid to look over and see what he was doing. The whole battle was going on and I was afraid to look over at the Yettaslav. Finally, I looked over a little."

Mr. Isaacson twists only his head around for the briefest glance before returning to his hiding.

"I couldn't see anything, so I turned around again. And this time I looked."

He looks.

"And you know what? I saw the Yettaslav just sitting there. He wasn't doing nothing. Just sitting there like this."

Mr. Isaacson, still using the table as the wall of the

trench, places one fist on top of the other and on top of the upper fist he places his chin so he sits there bent over and bemused, staring directly ahead like a stone monkey on some Asian temple frieze.

"So I sat up and said, 'Hey, are you all right?' And he didn't say anything so I reached over and touched him a little."

I feel a small tugging on my elbow.

"His head turned a little, and his hat fell off. I saw a red spot on his forehead. He was dead. He had been shot right through the head. I thought, what do you do now, and I took his gun and gave him mine. And then our sergeant came running along and jumped into the ditch. And we lay there for a long time with the whole thing going on. Along about evening it got quieter and he said, 'I wonder what's going on?' I said, 'I don't know.' And he said, 'Take a look.' So I climbed up carefully and looked around. I couldn't see anything and I jumped back down. Then he got up to take a look — nothing. And after a while he said, 'Take a look.' So I got up — nothing. I got down. Then he got up again and nothing. So we were getting up and down and nothing happened but he was a little short fellow and I guess they couldn't see him because he told me to get up again and I got shot, back in my side. It felt like somebody hit me with a strong iron rod. I bent over like this and fell back into the trench. I heard the sergeant say, '*Probalt*,' finished."

"*Nu*," someone calls out, "*ma'ariv*." The evening prayer. Shivah Asar be-Tammuz is over. What! Not yet! I'm in the middle of a story. Wait a minute! But someone begins leading the evening prayer. I turn back to Mr. Isaacson, but he grabs a *siddur*, and jumps up with fervor in his eyes. He draws closer to the pipe that runs from down below and up to heaven. I hear him implore.

"He is merciful, He shall forgive iniquity, and He shall not destroy. Often He turns away His anger and shall not stir up all His wrath. Lord, save us. The King shall answer us in the day we call."

The leader calls, "Bless the Lord Who is blessed."

We answer, "Blessed be the Lord Who is blessed forever and ever."

And I bless the Lord Who makes the evening. I glance up. Mr. Isaacson's eyes are closed as he blesses the Lord Who turns the day away, Who evens the evening, Who turns His anger away and answers us in the day we call Him. Even then it is dark. Shivah Asar be-Tammuz is over, but the fast is not. Hungry supplicants rush through *ma'ariv*. For me the evening service after a fast is an anticlimax emotionally, but necessary intellectually. This service has always been a test of faith; one I rarely pass. I am purposefully, willfully patient. I thrust the day of affliction into the past in order to turn the day, bend it into experience, but the vanity of affliction rises hungrily from my stomach, disintegrating concentration. Have I not done enough? Only Mr. Isaacson entreats, blesses with the fervor of the day.

The day of affliction is over, but what about Mr. Isaacson? We have left him *probalt* — finished. I see him lying in a Rumanian ditch on a Russian battlefield, bent and bleeding as the day turns into evening, a new day. Sorrows are never as discrete as the fasts that follow. How can they be, you can't fast forever. The service halts. No one intones the mourner's *kaddish*. Everyone looks around. Are you a mourner? Are you a mourner? No familial mourners. A voice calls to the leader, "*Zugt kaddish.*" A dispassionate *kaddish* pours forth. The rhythm tumbles forth — the building blocks of the universe rumbling against one another as their

names are called. The roll call of cornerstones —
granite of existence. So fleeting the call, so light the
touch in this hurried, famished *kaddish*, yet they remain
granite and radiate their power when called.

It is over. We are standing. I turn to Mr. Isaacson.

"We can't leave you there, lying there like that," I
joke in fear. Fear of what? Fear of death? Fear of the
day? Fear of the story? Do not give Satan an opening.

Mr. Isaacson does not hear the joke, does not feel the
fear, but his eyes are open and he desires to tell the
story. People turn to say goodnight. "On the way home,"
he explains, "I'll walk with you."

The men who are studying the *daf yomi*, the page of
the day, drift toward the room with the long table and
the large books. A page a day and in seven years you are
finished, done.

A student of the entire Babylonian Talmud. What
could be easier? What could be faster? Ah, but there is
the Jerusalem Talmud! No matter, never mind. One
thing at a time. And when you have completed it, what
do you have? You have one. You have earned the
privilege to start two. Begin again. What could be
simpler?

Mr. Steimatzky approaches and asks me if I have
been fasting. "You have? Good. Here!" He thrusts a
strange, artificially green bag toward me.

"Take."

I peer inside the long, distended bag to see nectarines gathered in the bottom like refugees. If I hadn't
fasted, they wouldn't be mine. Mr. Steimatzky is not
in the catering business. I gaze at them, their green
splotches all the paler and purer in the chemical green
dye of the bag.

"*Nu*, take." Mr. Steimatzky has a presence, a bearing. He did not flee two countries, two worlds, learn

three languages only to hand out pale nectarines in poisonous bags. He is, in fact, a diamond dealer who enfolds his natural gems in conservative custom-made shirts, soft and natural, nothing like this garish sack with its bastardized New World hybrids from Key Foods. I stand there. I am keeping a man waiting with his arm extended as if he were a beggar. A man who shuffled through the express line, eight items or less, with its clanging cash register and garish, chipped fingernails prancing madly about its keys to register the value of his own garish sack — all in a custom-made shirt — just so his fellow congregants who fasted (when you flee two worlds you only bother about the very righteous) can rejoice a little sooner. I stare at the awful color of the bag. Who cares what color the bag is? "Though your sins be as scarlet!" It is a matter of respect. Of generosity. Of brotherhood! His arm is extended. Shall I refuse his kindness and take from him his good deed instead? Shall we both return empty when we both can draw back together filled and fulfilled; he with his *mitzvah* and I with my nectarine?

"No, thank you," I say. "I'd better wait until I get home."

He draws back his gift, offended.

"No, I'd better wait for some juice, that's easier," I remark.

What am I saying? I, who used to break the twenty-five-hour Yom Kippur fast at Glaser's Drug Store on two vanilla shakes (and in those days they gave you the whole, cold shiny canister with its two-plus glasses lying thick and frigid inside) and an ice-cream cone kicker.

"I bought them for you," he entreats.

"No," I say touching my stomach apprehensively. "I'd better not. Thanks anyway."

"Awright," he turns away hurt.

I feel embarrassed, foolish, and I owe him an apology, at least an explanation. But how can I explain that the day isn't over, that it is twilight and Mr. Isaacson is lying broken in a corpse-strewn Rumanian ditch, when outside the very windows of the synagogue Mr. Steimatzky sees darkness and inside he sees Mr. Isaacson saying goodnight to Mr. Sobel? How can I break the fast when the day has not turned? How can I do a good deed with nectarines when the greatest of all *mitzvahs*, the saving of a life, lies before me? And anyway, they aren't washed. God knows what is on them.

Mr. Isaacson and I are together again.

"We can't leave you like that."

We are the last in the room. I am standing prepared to stay and listen.

"No," Mr. Isaacson motions toward the door. "Come, I'll walk you home." He takes my arm. We are in the narrow hallway moving toward the door.

"No, please, let me walk you home."

"No, you're hungry. I'll walk you home."

"Please, Mr. Isaacson, it's not right."

"Why?"

Why? Because he lives nearby, down the block in the other direction. Because Broadway is unpleasant and unsafe. Because I should escort you and not you me. Because. . . .

"*Kuvid*, respect!" I cry, hoping to understand the meaning of the words, in a high croaky voice sounding and feeling like a bilingual frog, and having no more understanding than the Egyptians of the plague of those croaking amphibians. If I can't whisper the words intelligently, why do I think I can understand by yelling them? Mr. Isaacson drops my arm.

"Respect, *kuvid*!" I cry again uselessly and doomed.

But, after all, the nectarine man gave me three chances with his green bag, shall I deal more harshly with myself than Steimatzsky did? What kind of respect is that? Yes, I feel like a fool screaming at Mr. Isaacson. I had hoped that when I intoned *kuvid*-respect it would be as a shofar blast up above and Gabriel would take not one but two unwashed nectarines (in the World to Come nothing can hurt you), place them in a green Key Food fruit-and-vegetable bag, check them to make sure they're good ones (69¢ a pound, not the ones in the window), staple the bag closed, and write with a heavenly fat grease pencil "World To Come — Heavenly Reward — Pays Double." Instead, Mr. Isaacson is intimidated by my outburst and says, "All right."

Now what's going to happen up there? A voice can come down at any moment and Gabriel hollers, "*Shmuck*, you yell at Isaacson who doesn't need it and you don't take a nectarine from Steimatzky who doesn't need it either. *Shmuck*, you don't know how to give and you don't know how to take." It's true Mr. Steimatzky's custom-made shirts have quite a bit of cloth in them. What can you do? Go home and eat yourself sick?

Mr. Isaacson and I descend the stone steps onto the sidewalk. We turn left toward his building. Respect!

Ninety-first Street glows pink under the high-crime street lights. Cars are bumper to bumper alongside the curbs. Heavy brownstone staircases crowd down onto the quiet sidewalk. The buildings small (a bay window, a fancy balustrade), the garbage cans few, the trees scraggly. And all is soft and close in the pellucid pink of the sodium arc. You could touch it and it wouldn't be rough. It is unreal and very intimate. Mr. Isaacson takes my arm. Behind us we hear a stammering of farewell. We turn to acknowledge Mr. Sobel's third

goodnight. *"A gute nacht."* And Mr. Sobel plunges off
down the street in a stuttering motion, for every step
taken, three starts.

We return to our direction, but Mr. Isaacson pauses.
The mood has been broken. Mr. Sobel has limped into
the night trailing shreds of Rumania, fibers of time,
moans of agony. We stand exposed on Ninety-first
Street. Mr. Isaacson the righteous and I.

"Let me walk you home."

"No, you live right here."

"You must be hungry,"

I must be hungry. And not you? Could it be Mr.
Isaacson didn't fast? The righteous? But in years he is
an old man. I look at my old friend. It has been over fifty
years since he turned the Little Father's weaponry into
bullet-choked kindling. Why should I be disappointed
that he didn't fast? Will it affect the purity of his message? Must righteousness exclude common sense? Over
seventy! Until a hundred and twenty! I take his arm to
guide him.

"Let me show you a little *kuvid*," I implore.

It is the night of threes. Three offerings. Three good-
byes. Three weeks. Three *"kuvids."* And in the street
my *kuvid*, my call for respect, is heard and does not
sound strange. And why should it? What are the upright
founts channeled above us bathing the scene in a sea of
pink but respect? Pellucid preventive pink: respect for
the power of evil. *Kuvid* for the *gonif.* The wall has
been breached; the sea enters. Arm in arm we negotiate
the floodlit street. We make our way to the refuge of
shadow near the corner. One tree on the block is capable of shelter. We are under it. The pinkish rays do not
bounce; refuse to diffuse. Incapable of dusk, unable to
dawn, how dull is their reflection. Like their inspirers,
the evildoers, they leave nothing after them; powerful

but shortsighted, they wither against the simple green leaves of our shelter. And we stand in darkness. Unable to see each other, steadfastly we gaze together upon the sea of carnage. We are returned.

"THE bugs. It must have been the bugs around my face that woke me. I was alone, lying there in the dark on my back. I knew I was injured, but I didn't know where. I checked my hands — I brought them together. No, they were all right. I felt my legs; no, it wasn't them. I felt my face; it was all right. Then I felt my stomach. It was okay, but as my arm came down from my stomach, it felt something soft and sticky on the side. I knew where I was hurt. In the side toward the back. I took my hands away. I didn't know what would be. I lay there. After a while I thought to myself, 'There's no *tachlis* in this,' so I tried to get up. It hurt but I managed. I took my coat and cigarettes and a kit like kids have now and started climbing out."

"How did you know where to go?"

"I didn't, but there was a well nearby and I heard a bunch of Rumanian soldiers singing, so I thought I would go there and they could help me. I got my things together and I took a few steps. I was uneasy."

Mr. Isaacson balances himself delicately using the darkness for support.

"But I saw I could make it, so I kept going. And when I got near, crossing a field — boom! Shells started coming in and I was knocked flat and I went out again."

In the darkness Mr. Isaacson must be shrugging his shoulders, what can you do?

"After a while, I came to again and I didn't hear any more singing. They must have left if they didn't get killed. I knew I wasn't getting anywhere in the middle of the field, so I got up again and tried walking. Same thing — I felt unsteady but I went very slowly. After a while I got to the well, but there was no one there. I took a drink. I felt a little better. I was leaning against the well and I thought I could use a smoke, so I reached for a cigarette."

"But you didn't have any."

"No, I had my cigarettes. I left my gun. What did I need that for? I didn't feel like shooting anyone and they were lousy guns. But I took my cigarettes. So I lit it and inhaled. . . ."

I hear Mr. Isaacson inhaling and relishing the sweet smoke after crawling around for half the night like a wounded beast.

"And. . . ."

Although it is very dark, my eyes have been adjusting and I can see Mr. Isaacson. He is standing next to me, his chest uplifted inhaling the cigarette — his act of life, returning to normal. A well in a deserted field, a cigarette in the hot, summer night.

"And. . . ."

MR. ISAACSON'S hands rise to his shoulders and as he exhales they choreograph in quick wavy descent consciousness sinking away, below the surface. Mr. Isaacson's head has bobbed and sunk onto his chest, his lungs empty even of smoke. We leave him there, but my Mr. Isaacson, the one I know, slips out from behind the collapsed one and tells me, "I was weak and I wasn't used to it."

He laughs. Some cigarette ad! He laughs and stops speaking. We stand there silently. The Surgeon General should have spoken to Mr. Isaacson, he could have told him. And yet, I know his daughter. I don't really know his daughter, but I have seen her. A beautiful woman, a model. Mr. Isaacson once told me with pride

that she was in one of the most popular cigarette ads.
You saw her everywhere. You couldn't avoid her. Was
it Marlboro? Kent? What difference does it make? But
there she was gaily smiling on this seesaw from the
back of slick magazines, down from tall buildings,
inside subway cars. Young, beautiful, refreshed, and
alive! Amazing! After what a cigarette did to her father!
Did she even know? Could this be what Mr. Isaacson is
musing about? His daughter on that smoky seesaw and
the cigarette that almost killed him? No, ridiculous!
Mr. Isaacson can't be thinking of that. The righteous
don't tie knots, they untie them.

"I lay there I don't know how long. I was lying there
and they came around and found me."

"How did they know you were alive?"

"I guess I was moving a little or something. I had
some dreams."

"Do you remember them?"

"Like it was today. Like it was now," he answers
fervently.

"What were they?"

"I dreamt I was lying there worried and frightened. I
didn't know what to think. It was like the world
disappeared. And then my grandfather appeared, a big,
handsome man with a beard. A religious man, a saintly
man. I remember him very well. A good person. He was
standing in front of me."

And he is standing there in front of me, too. Mr.
Isaacson is straight and tall with his right arm raised
and his curved but open hand rocks forward and back
ever so slightly in benediction, strength, and forbearance. And Mr. Isaacson's face has become firm. Capable of joy and comfort, but now it is set firmly. We must
wait for another day, it is saying. And to wait for
another day we must live through this night. Benedic-

tion, strength, and forbearance. Yes we will.

"And he said to me, 'Moishe, it will be all right, don't worry.' And I knew I would be all right. I opened my eyes and I saw a figure where he had been standing. It was very dark, but I could see it had an arm extended and in the hand it held a gun. It said, '*Nyemetz* or *Rooski*?' German or Russian? Since it said *Nyemetz* or *Rooski* I thought I'd better say *Rooski*, so I said, *Rooski*.' — '*Rooski*? — '*Da! Rooski*.' And he put the gun down and they came forward to help me."

"Who were they, soldiers?"

"No, they weren't soldiers. They worked for the army. For two weeks the battle was going on and the bodies were just lying there. When the battle ended, the army hired men to go around and collect the bodies and the equipment that still might be good. They were looking for the dead, but found me instead.

"They came over to me and saw that I was wounded, but by then I couldn't walk, so they took my overcoat. They gave us great, heavy overcoats, very strong, so they took that and I was lying on it like a stretcher. I couldn't keep conscious. I was going in and out and we were moving slowly. It wasn't easy for them."

Under their heavy burden — a wounded man on a Russian greatcoat without handles or rods, the rough wool tearing at tired hands fighting to maintain a grip — we pause. They came seeking death but found life and it's enough to kill them. See what happens when you don't follow orders. Hired to collect the dead, they freelanced a little and slipped a live one in on the Czar. Little Father, we heard you say dead, but look at him with your Holy Russian eyes, he's as good as dead, isn't he? Merciful Patriarch, and if he lives, you won't have other wars to swallow him alive, like a frog, a beetle? And the Czar of all the Russias, irate, all his hemophilia genes dancing a *kazatzke* in Slavic disgust, squeals, "Fools, if you wanted to take something broken, take the Holy Russian rifle Isaacson broke, and if you want to give me a present, why give me a suffering Jew? Of those I have plenty." And the human garbage collectors quake in fear, but a voice comes clapping down like a shofar from the heavens above. "These will eat nectarines in the World to Come with the righteous!" Justice! It is Gabriel! He has spoken! The nectarines are redeemed. Mr. Isaacson is saved. The day has turned. It is time to say amen.

"And so you were saved," I return in a response of faith, God is a faithful King.

Mr. Isaacson does not answer.

"They took you to the field hospital?"

My wife must be worried by now.

"It must have been something to know it was over."

"I woke up in the forest," Mr. Isaacson is saying. "The light was coming through the trees; it must have been dawn. They had stripped me bare. They even took my boots. I didn't have a thing. No coat, no cigarettes, nothing. They did a good job all right. They took everything."

Everything? I draw further under the tree to avoid falling nectarines. Their crash will bury Ninety-first Street, beating the high-crime lights into the ground like mangled hangers writhing in darkness among fluorescent shards on a closet floor. Everything.

"*Gonovim!*" Thieves! I spit accusingly at those two who have stripped Mr. Isaacson. But Mr. Isaacson doesn't share my bitterness.

"Weren't they *gonovim*?" I ask intensely.

"No, I don't know. I guess they thought I was dead, so they left me," he says understandingly.

I feel confused and foolish. If they thought he was

dead, they shouldn't have let him go. They were sent to
collect the dead. That was their job! With all the Hitlers
in the world, I get mad at two foolish, doddering old
drunks (they must have been drunks! Weren't they
*goyim*?). Two old drunks who tried to save a man's life,
and when they found that impossible they rescued his
valuables. Dust to dust was not decreed on valuables,
just flesh. Yes, just flesh, but I feel something else. I feel
anger. Yes, anger.

Why shouldn't I feel foolish, I am angry at Mr.
Isaacson. I want to ask him, Mr. Isaacson, how can you
be so naive? All right, they were exhausted, they could
carry you no farther, their hands raw and bloody from
the unequal tug-of-war with your coat, all that may be
true. . . . Mr. Isaacson, hate them! Hate them as I hate
them; it will do your heart a world of good. Oh, torn
confusion, a world of good? I feel my heart constricting,
mean and small within me. Of course, one should have
a big heart. A big heart to live. A big heart like Mr.
Isaacson's. And maybe, that is why he is here now. The
day has turned, but what about the Three Weeks?
The day had entrapped me, but what about the night?
The Three Weeks have nights, and I feel the dark, in-
visible cords circling about me. I who would run home
to supper am held by the night to a dawn. Mr. Isaacson's dawn. I cannot struggle against the unseen cords
of night. I am resigned, but I am not righteous.

A part of me wants to race down the street. I raise
only my eyes to glance down the still street. I can see
Mr. Isaacson on the prowl for our *minyan*. Mr. Isaacson
collecting bodies all up and down Ninety-first Street,
and I know what they feel when they encounter the
holy collector, enmeshed in his net of righteousness. I
know their torn hearts. Part screams, "Isaacson, drop
dead!" But part fervently petitions, "O Lord, make

me like Mr. Isaacson." Part pumps like mad for the
subway on Broadway, but part beats with fervor,
"Where are my brethren? Let us pray together, 'May-
His-Great-Name-Be-Praised-for-Ever-and-Ever.'" And
so a *minyan* is made as an IRT express slides out of the
station with one fewer passenger than it would have
carried. But even at that the subway car is jammed;
people mashed together like the bullets in the rifle that
wouldn't shoot. So where should he be? The refugee?
Number ten, the *minyan*. I turn toward Mr. Isaacson
but over his shoulder I glimpse my phantom local
disappearing down Ninety-first Street. Part of me hun-
gers for that frantic train and not for heaven where the
angels remark on weekdays that the righteous can drive
you crazy.

Yes, they can drive you crazy. The righteous do
whatever they want with you. They control you. Who
knows where his story is going? Where his tale is
leading us? But his story has become my story, so I take
his hand and ask, "What happened?" What happened
to you? What happened to us? To all of us? And I am
fearful, for I am not sure we will make it.

And we stand together under the nocturnal shade
tree to discover our fate. He talks and I listen. He was
discovered and carried through the deserter-filled forest on an empty gun carriage to a dressing station in an
orchard where his wound was cleaned. I hear of the
journey to the field hospital by wagon, too painful — by
ambulance ("a real automobile"), too painful — and a
roadside conference that elects to carry him all the way
by stretcher. And so he arrives at the hospital in the
hands of men, but fears to place his fate in their hands
again after a young Jewish soldier dies under the knife.
An ugly nurse begs him to consent, but he refuses. For
days the world has been conspiring to destroy him, but

never with his consent!

That night a Russian Orthodox priest appears in the ward and bed by bed draws near with his huge uplifted cross. Mr. Isaacson, exhausted, lifts the fringes on the corners of his garment and the priest halts. The others he blesses with his cross, but Mr. Isaacson he kisses.

"I got through the night all right, but the next day was bad. I couldn't keep it from hurting. No matter how I lay, no matter how I turned, it hurt. They wanted to operate, but I wouldn't let them. And how that nurse cared for me and comforted me. What a good person! But she was ugly! Ugly as sin. She cried over me and begged me to let them operate. Oh, she was good to me. What a good person. Finally, it hurt so bad, I figured it didn't make much difference, so I told her they could operate.

"The doctors had finished, so she ran to find one. I thought that was the end, but it wasn't. They opened up the wound and found a piece of shrapnel stuck between two ribs. They just took a pliers and pulled it out. It was simpler than anybody had guessed. As soon as they pulled it out, I began feeling better."

"I bet the nurse was happy, too."

"She was thrilled. How she cried over me! What a good person — ugly as sin."

Mr. Isaacson smiles, enjoying the paradox. And what did she think of Mr. Isaacson? Could she see into his heart where he called her a good person? Could she for once see her inner beauty mirrored in his eyes instead of the ugly-as-sin glances that well men unceasingly cast? Or was she herself the righteous and in her eyes Mr. Isaacson learned?

"Without her you might have been lost," I venture in appreciation of her good deed.

"Yes, and not just then," he answers.

"Another time?"

"It must have been the next day or the day after. The Germans started shelling the hospital. The bombs were falling right into the building. I thought I was going to get killed. I begged her to save me. She ran and got an officer's jacket and put it on me. And when they came running in to evacuate the officers, she shouted at them, 'He's an officer!' 'Officer?' they ask. 'Yes,' I answer, 'officer!' They look at my jacket — an officer's — and carry me right out of there as fast as they can. She saved me."

"What was her name?"

"I don't know. We just called her Nurse."

"Did you ever see her again?"

"No, a few days later they moved me farther back and I never saw her again."

"Was she Jewish?" I ask.

"I don't know," he answers. "I don't think so. I think she was Russian."

She is what she is — and that is righteous. And I am curious about the righteous. The righteous are not just nice; they are essential. Thirty-six Righteous sustain the world. If it weren't for them the world couldn't keep going. It would stop right in the middle of no place — like a Yo-Yo with no more energy-feeding string to tumble down. *Kaput* — finished! And since they are righteous they are anonymous; otherwise, they would never get any sleep. Anonymous, but when I come across one of them, I am curious to find out who they are. What is her name? Who is she? The righteous, it turns out, are who they are. I confess I wouldn't mind her being Jewish, but whoever she is she does her good deeds anonymously, the Yo-Yo spins, the world turns, and we go from year to year lurching like a blind man at noon. For at noon, the righteous can help the sightless find the path. At night we are lost. The righteous aren't cats; even they can't see in the dark. But she is not entirely anonymous. We know what she looks like. She is ugly as sin. The nectarines are served in the World to Come in an ugly green bag. Ugly as sin and never sins. Ugly? No, unscarred by beauty.

"And so you were saved," I conclude.

"Yes," he answers, "thank God."

And for this evening we are finished. How can we go beyond the righteous? We stand a while, quiet and reflective. Mr. Isaacson breaks the silence.

"Regards to the family."

"Thank you, regards to Mrs. Isaacson."

"Good night."

I watch Mr. Isaacson cross the street and turn to retrace my steps down Ninety-first Street past the *shtibl* staircase crowding onto the silent sidewalk. It is warm and humid. As I cross Broadway I hear a faint rumbling that might be mistaken for a distant sound from the heavens above, if beneath, the subway, hot and empty, weren't pursuing its predetermined course.

I turn onto my street and see a squat, heavy-limbed figure moving deliberately through the pink light showering down upon him. The page has been learned for the day. Why hurry? A page a day.

I am by his side.

"Are you still fasting?" he asks.

"Yes."

"They were for you."

"Yes, thank you. The Three Weeks, a very difficult period," I explain.

"Yeah, but we'll make it."

"Yes," I answer. And I open the door for the nectarine man because we'll make it, and not to would be . . . ugly as sin.

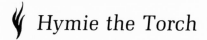 Hymie the Torch

ALTHOUGH people lead normal lives, there are no normal people. This is understood by people who once led normal lives and by no one else. No corporation, government, or religious group can insure safe handling in transit. You take your chances.

Hymie Grosbart led a normal life. He drove the appropriate direction in one-way streets; he paid when he was served; he was an officer of the temple. All the while, he was an incipient arsonist. That an officer of the temple should be an incipient arsonist is not so surprising. There is something about fire that tickles the Jewish soul. Moses had his burning bush, the wandering Jews their pillar of fire, Elijah his fiery bolt from heaven, the Maccabees their twinkling menorah, and Hymie Grosbart his dancing flame of *havdalah*.

Hymie had discovered that thrill as a child. After the sun set on Saturday, the family gathered in the kitchen to hear *havdalah*, the ceremony ending the Sabbath. His father blessed the cup, blessed the spices, and blessed the fire. Hymie always asked to hold the tall, braided candle. When the ceremony was over, his father would take the cup, pour a little schnapps onto the slate counter, and light it. The shimmering vapors clothed in flame leaped above their tremulous disappearing base. Hymie loved it.

All right, fire tickles all Jewish souls. So what if it positively regaled Hymie's? He still had to go upstairs, brush his teeth, put on his pajamas, and go to bed. Other children dragged sugar-plum fairies onto the pillow of imagination. What's so harmful that Hymie had a dancing flame?

He was a normal kid. Picked his nose as much as most, teased his sister less, burned more leaves, and always asked for vanilla instead of chocolate. Pleasant, polite, but not talkative, he made it to high school and assumed that he was receiving an education. On Saturday nights, he himself lit the dancing flame. Of course he loved its magic. Magic that released energy locked inside Creation. That wasn't the only energy. On Saturday nights he also discovered kissing girls, drinking beer, and playing cards. He grew up.

When graduation approached, Hymie had no definite plans. College was mentioned. Hymie's cousin in law school advised it. A trade was talked about, too, but all discussion ended when Sukenik, a bachelor cousin who often joined the family for holidays, offered to take Hymie into his successful hardware store to "teach him the business." The implication — inheritance — was clear, and the offer was accepted. Hymie had always liked the cousin, a small, thin man who channeled great stores of nervous energy into his business. Hymie wasn't lazy either. Soon, he too knew the entire stock and could reorder without having to examine the dense array of shovels, brooms, hammers, and fly swatters that shrouded the surfaces of Sukenik Sales. His contributions did not go unappreciated. Over Hymie's objections, Grosbart was added to the store's name, and Sukenik and Grosbart — S & G, as it was called — became one of the leading firms in town.

Aunts suddenly became interested in marrying their nieces to Hymie. He rejected the wealthier, high-powered matches and chose Sarah, an attractive and unassuming girl. They bought a spacious old home in the neighborhood and promptly insured it along with Hymie's life against any untoward event. The temple chose Hymie as vice-president. He sat on the stage next to the president. His children sat on his lap and marveled at the large, gold-fringed American flag that stood next to their father's great chair. Poker Mondays, folks

Wednesdays, temple board Thursdays. A dish of vanilla ice cream after *havdalah*.

The Depression did not affect Hymie immediately. With his money in bonds, he was not hurt by the stock-market crash. Not financially, but he saw the haunted, fear-stricken eyes. He extended credit where he could, but for those who had been wiped out in the precipitous, swift collapse, there wasn't much that anyone could do. As the Depression ground on, smaller businesses failed, but there was business enough for the few that survived. Few survived better than S & G.

One night, driving home, Hymie noticed a neighbor walking. Shapiro's herky-jerky gait caught his eye. Hymie pulled up at the curb and waited for his friend to catch up. Hymie rolled down the window and called to him, but not until he honked the horn did the distracted man realize that anyone had stopped for him. Hymie asked whether something was wrong.

"Wrong?" Shapiro said, as if Hymie had made the greatest understatement of all time. Hymie smiled his shy, trusting smile; Shapiro opened the door and slid into the seat next to Hymie.

"Wrong?" Morris Shapiro repeated, shaking his head, and he began to tell Hymie just how wrong things were. Shapiro had owned a successful camera store, Federal Photo Supply, but in the Depression what was there to photograph? Men standing on street corners? Thousands of dollars' worth of cameras in stock, a good building, and no sales. Shapiro had believed that the Depression couldn't go on. Everyone had believed that it couldn't go on, but it had. So had his mortgage payments on the building and he stood to lose everything. A lifetime of work. What choice did he have? To stand back and watch thirty years go down the drain like a dirty bath? He couldn't do that! What could he do? He had a wife and kids, didn't he? It wasn't his Depression. He didn't want it. He didn't cause it. What did he have left? One thing, insurance. Of course, he knew it was wrong, but what choice was there? He called the "burner."

"Burner?" Hymie inquired gently.

"Yeah, for a price, he burns your place down. But listen to this. I make up my mind. I get in touch, make a deal. I get the stuff, set everything up for tonight, and I just got a call. The son of a bitch is in jail. He got himself arrested this afternoon. If that don't beat all!"

"Hmmm," Hymie said.

"And the insurance expires tomorrow. If that don't beat all!" Shapiro called out in amazement.

A strange thirsting itch worked deep in Hymie's throat.

"What stuff did you get?" he asked softly.

WHAT was done first as a favor for a distraught friend developed into something more as the Depression worsened. When normally honest men become criminals, they crave someone who is discreet. But, above all, even in the terminal act of their commercial careers, they remain businessmen. Results! The warehouse must burn fast. The drugstore must burn completely. The gutted restaurant must contain no evidence of its unnatural destruction. And the more humane did not want their self-inflicted flames to consume their neighbors. God forbid that lives should be lost and innocent blood be on their hands along with the insurance benefits. In short, they wanted an expert. They found him.

At first a few came. Shapiro must have mentioned it. Hymie never did. Then others, until in no time almost every fire downtown belonged to Hymie. Anyone who needed a burner naturally thought of Hymie, Hymie the Torch. No more poker, no more temple board, hardly time for the folks. Only the vanilla ice cream remained. He needed no one and he trusted no one as his movements became unaccountable. For the first few arsons, Hymie stayed to view the illuminating fruits of his labors. His eyes sparkled as the first bloom of flame poked through its nurturing shell. His soul laughed as the entire fiery bouquet burst forth with its luminous petals, showering the building in sparks. The luxury ceased as Hymie the Torch became better known. Eventually, his house came under surveillance and every night he was followed, but Hymie always found a way. When Hymie the Torch took on a contract, the sky glowed before morning.

Until the arson squad realized that the Torch never flamed on the Sabbath, Hymie was followed to the temple and back on Friday nights. The detectives waited respectfully across the street in their black Chevrolets. Hymie retained his generous nature. Some of the older, poorer congregants lived in dark tenements on streets that were no longer safe. With his detectives in tow, Hymie escorted them home, all enjoying the protective scrutiny of the city's finest. It was the only night of the week that Sarah did not worry. Not that she ever discussed his new activity with him. Nothing was said, but she knew, and to tell the truth, she was confused. The more notorious her husband's reputation, the kinder and more thoughtful he became.

Not everyone found Hymie so appealing. Those who sought him at night spurned him in the morning. Hymie knew more than their sins. He knew their fears and weaknesses. He was the repository of shrouded voices they couldn't silence. Exhausted and fearful, with red, sleepless eyes, they had come to him in their shame. Refugees cast forth from a secure land onto a

beach of chaos where tides of disintegration threatened
to inundate them. The only means of staying afloat was
that relic from a world when risk was shared — their
insurance. By destroying that last vestige of trust they
could cling to their homes as their businesses were
swept away in a sea of flames. They did it in the dark of
night when shadows sleep and stars shine silently. But
they could not do it alone. They needed a torch. By
night they begged Hymie; by day they despised him.
"When Hymie the Torch smiles, insurance companies
sit *shivah*," they smirked. And what was in them a
virtue in him was a vice. "What choice did we have?
Could we let our children go homeless and starve?
That he, a rich man, should do such a thing is a scandal!"

How did Hymie react? Not at all. He became more
religious. Hymie knew that there were many more
learned than he, but he felt that few better appreciated
the Sabbath. For him the Sabbath was perfect peace.
Who but a master of fire could deeply appreciate a
flame-free respite from mastery over Creation? Hymie's
fingers did not touch a match nor flip a switch. At the
Sabbath's conclusion, when the *havdalah* candle
burned in braided flame and he chanted, "Blessed art
Thou O Lord, King of the universe, Who distinguishes
between holy and profane," Hymie felt that he understood better than anyone else. Not that Hymie was
holier, but who was more profane Sunday through
Friday than Hymie the Torch?

When funds were needed in the community, he was
never forgotten. Hymie the Torch might not be welcome on the eastern wall next to the flag, but his
checks were always accepted. Checking accounts know
no scandal — only insolvency, and Hymie was far
from that.

From his after-hours proceeds Hymie filled a safe-deposit box with cash. Although he didn't like to think about it, he knew that he might need it. The business could run without him, but if he had to become a guest of the state, well, at least Sarah and the children would be well fixed.

Hymie was careful and Hymie was patient. He didn't take every job that came along. If something wasn't right, or contained a hint of not being right, he wouldn't touch it. No one was ever hurt in his fires; he feared that more than jail. And he never promised specific dates. If someone was in a hurry, Hymie wasn't his man. There were some close calls, but his luck held.

The authorities never bothered Hymie, not in person. Well, almost never, and even then it wasn't official. Once a peppery battalion chief came into the store and asked to see Hymie. Hymie asked him what he wanted.

"My name's Bannion. I'm a fireman and I just wanted to see the guy who's burning the city to the ground!"

It was pugnacious, but not without respect. Hymie didn't expect the firemen to be pleased with his actions. After all, they had a job to do, too; he just nodded.

"You're good, Hymie, but we'll meet again."

Hymie, neither acknowledging nor denying, just smiled.

The battalion chief turned to leave, then stopped with a wave of his hand. He motioned to all of S & G and asked in quiet wonderment, "Why, Hymie? Why?"

Why? Well, some things just can't be avoided. Hymie never claimed it was right, but if he, Hymie, didn't do it, someone else would. Someone not nearly as good. Why? To tell the truth, because Hymie loved doing it. You can't beat that for motivation.

The economy improved. Over the years there were

fewer and fewer requests for his services. By the end of the decade, his skills lay dormant, but his memory was active and, of course, the dancing flame of *havdalah* — Hymie's own miniature burning bush — glowed weekly. He was philosophical — he wasn't as young as he used to be. Night entries, dark stairwells, exiting through windows. Fire was a young man's game. No, he was no youngster; his children had married. A son and son-in-law were in business with him now. No regrets. They had been good years.

Hymie had just become a grandfather when Pearl Harbor was attacked. His son and son-in-law were drafted, and Hymie was kept busy with the store. There was a great demand for everything S & G could stock. There could be no question of burning anything now; it wouldn't have been patriotic. And Hymie was a patriot; while the *havdalah* flame danced, Hymie uttered a special prayer that in the coming week God should protect all the soldiers and sailors.

When the war ended, his children returned. His son limped, but thank God it wasn't too bad, and the family was together. The boys returned to S & G and together they branched into manufacturing. The company rapidly expanded from a single prosperous store into a large chain that sold many items of its own manufacture. Hymie still had the final say, but he nearly always agreed with his young partners.

Others who had previously envied Hymie for his wealth now envied him for something else. He got along so well with his children, and not just in the business. The families all lived in the same neighborhood. The younger ones often came to Hymie for Sabbath afternoons. Often after *havdalah*, the young couples would go downtown to take in a picture show while the grandparents did the babysitting.

One Saturday night, however, Hymie's daughter didn't feel well. Why didn't Hymie and Sarah go with her brother and sister-in-law instead? Mom might enjoy it, the son urged. Hymie had no desire to go. It had been years since he had seen a movie, but Sarah seemed intrigued by the idea. Certainly she was flattered by the invitation. "Well, if your father wants to. . . ."

So Hymie went to the movies. Under the brilliant marquee's dazzling bulbs and in front of the brightly lit shop windows that sent colored light cascading past elegantly clothed mannequins, Hymie and Sarah felt like tourists from a small town. The early show let out; the line surged forward. Hymie and his wife were impressed by the opulent velvet hangings that framed the lobby; things had changed.

The lights dimmed, the plush curtain parted, the crowd quieted, the screen came to life with a cavalcade of the news. Well, thought Hymie with satisfaction as the familiar booming, resonant voice launched into its documentary accompaniment, at least some things haven't changed: lively and upbeat — a beauty contest; heraldic — a visiting dignitary; respectful — a centenarian Confederate veteran's funeral; celebratory — the annual Pennsylvania Dutch Apple Butter Festival. The music then switched to stark chords and the announcer's voice became grave and ominous as he intoned, "Recently obtained enemy films show the savage horrors suffered by civilians in the last war."

Hymie sat up and quit munching popcorn. The screen showed scenes of a Nazi concentration camp: the long line of bewildered arrivals, the gas chambers, the stacks of shoes, the mountains of corpses. And the thing that pierced Hymie most deeply — the flames, the bright flashing flames from the chimneys of the crematoria. As suddenly as it had appeared, it disappeared, giving way to a bouncy story about ladies' fashions.

The war had been over for more than a year and the unbelievable facts had trickled slowly into everyone's consciousness until they were undeniable. Although, even then, who could really believe that it had happened? Never had he seen pictures! Hymie sat, refusing to believe. No, no — no! He wanted to scream, but he just sat there staring silently with everyone else as the feature came on — Fred Astaire began to dance.

Driving home, no one mentioned the concentration camp, but even Fred Astaire's magic feet had not tapped it out of their minds. When Sarah and Hymie got out of the car, they thanked the children for a lovely evening.

Hymie waited for Sarah to fall asleep. Pajama-clad, in the kitchen, he burned through a book of matches. Brilliant phosphorous burst, steady crawling, consuming white flame, curled black ashes. One after another. With every one, his bitter anger struggled to prove possession. In the morning he went about his business as usual.

Life went on as before until a year later a grandchild became ill. Fitfully gasping for air, the child lay in an oxygen tent. Hymie joined the family vigil at the child's bedside. The nurses continuously reminded them not to smoke because of the highly flammable oxygen that was flowing with a hissing swish through the rubber hose attached to the large indestructible metal cylinders. The smallest spark, they explained, could be disastrous. They had no idea who Hymie was.

The second night he stood the lonely vigil and the warnings were repeated. Hymie sat and watched his grandchild's distended mouth and quivering chest struggle to get enough air. For a brief moment, thinking that he had seen something amiss, Hymie quickly leaned forward. Reassured, he sat back in his chair. It reappeared; Hymie purposefully looked away to dispel the pale image, but when he turned back, he still saw the faint flames burning above the child's mouth like a refinery flame burning off the excess gases at the top of a high smokestack. Hymie imagined his grandchild consumed in the faint flickering. The disintegrating body of caked, black ash somersaulted slowly in the tent and was sucked through the tubes back into the hermetically sealed vacuum of the cylinders coating the metallic sides with a fine shadowy powder visible only through that powerful microscope known as the eye of God. The only thing remaining was the small pair of tennis shoes in the closet that the child had worn into the hospital. Crazed with fear, Hymie slipped his hand under the flap to grip the child's leg so that he could not be sucked away. The child gasped when touched but Hymie did not draw back. He held him firmly.

In the morning, the child breathed. His color slowly began to return. Hymie kissed him and cried. He went home, but he could not sleep that night. When he lay down and closed his eyes, he saw the hated flames. He opened his eyes and sat up. The light filtering into the bedroom drove him to distraction. He lay down but the flames, fueled by death, soared. Hymie wanted to reach into his head and tear the image from his mind. He leaped out of bed, showered, and read until morning. He didn't feel the least bit tired. No one suspected that he hadn't slept in two days. But he knew; Hymie the Torch knew.

Sarah thought that he was overtired from his sleepless night in the hospital. She called the doctor; the physician prescribed sleeping pills. Even with the pills Hymie couldn't close his eyes without seeing the fire rushing from the chimneys as the bodies were sucked in below. He took twice the prescribed dosage, and when that failed he tripled it. He slept. He finally slept. The flames disappeared. The next night he took the pills again.

After a week, the flames returned. Not continuously, but randomly, often at unexpected moments. Hymie would suddenly realize that he was seeing them as he was looking at a stop light, glancing to find where the paperboy had thrown the paper, or signing his name to letters. At first this didn't bother him very much. After his difficulties, it seemed reasonable that his problems shouldn't disappear instantly. But after some time, he realized that the cremating flames flickered in his mind absolutely every day. From that moment, the horrible scene surfaced unfailingly every day with its barbaric and hideous brilliance. On the Sabbath it was even worse. Even when Hymie closed his eyes to pray, he saw them. He began to despise the Day of Rest.

Hymie came to loath fire. He hated the sight of it. He despised even the idea of it. He couldn't imagine kindling it — not even for *havdalah*. Not even the candle for the blessing, "Who creates the lights of fire," much less the dancing flame. When the children came over, much to their surprise Hymie insisted that his son or son-in-law perform the ceremony. Hymie smelled the spices but he turned away from the candle. The grandchildren asked Hymie to create the dancing flame, but he had others do this, and before the flame began to glow, Hymie would leave the room. No more vanilla ice cream either. When Hymie and Sarah were alone, Hymie would not even intone *havdalah*. She didn't ask — it wasn't their way — and he didn't tell her. How could he tell her that the thing he had loved, the thing that had thrilled his soul, was now hateful to him? More than hateful. An abomination. Fire had been so pure, so sweet, so true, and now it was ugly, shameful, and vulgar.

Hymie was confused. He seemed to be the same person he had always been, and that mystified him. He had loved something and now he hated it. Could he have been Hymie the Torch? But above all, Hymie was depressed because he felt that he had been a fool. A God-awful fool. His love had betrayed him! What a fool! The image of his love's betrayal flamed before him daily — the unfaithful, consuming flames seared his brain. Hymie the Torch? Hymie the Fool!

People seemed more distant and more foreign. They had no idea that he was in pain, and he didn't want them to know. They couldn't help. What could they do? They would only know what a fool he was. All the while the flames never lacked fuel. In grotesque heaps the bodies continuously entered the ovens.

Only one thing — well, two: it was true that Hymie no longer said *havdalah* — changed in Hymie's routine. Although he regularly attended synagogue, Hymie began attending a different one, a new one. Among the refugees who had arrived in town was a Rabbi Mendel Myers. Once an outstanding student of the Great Warsaw Yeshivah, the refugee had been invited to the city to teach in the local seminary. On his own he opened a small synagogue in the basement of an apartment building. A few tables, several benches, a velvet ark covering that in spite of its recent dedication was already faded. A small subdued group. Refugees, old men who never felt comfortable in English, a few who had real or imagined ties with the Great Warsaw Yeshivah — and Hymie. No other "real" American would come near the place. No one disputed Rabbi Mendel's scholarship. It was vast and precise. No, it wasn't that. It was — well, he was a refugee. Not that the community hadn't welcomed those people and not that they hadn't understood that such people would need time to adjust. Still, when a policeman approached, the rabbi fled across the street. In America! And the old briefcase he dragged around? One or two books were in it, but it was mostly filled with hunks of stale, crumbling bread that he would take out to gnaw upon at the most inopportune times! Not just on the streetcar. He did it once on the dais of an interfaith discussion in the presence of an Episcopal bishop and a Catholic monsignor! And his eyes. It wasn't a look that inspired confidence, but it was a look of someone who had been through Auschwitz and had seen the flames, so Hymie attended the dilapidated little synagogue.

As much as Hymie hated the flames, he still wanted to know the details. How? Why? Hymie sat on the bench, watched and listened. It was not very comfortable. He watched a lot of stale, crumbling bread consumed in long, ruminating, salivating chews and he listened to some very brilliant lectures, but what he learned about the flames he learned from Rabbi Mendel's eyes. And the flames were as horrible as Hymie had imagined.

After the war, marginal companies that had thrived on the war-fattened boom faltered. Some adjusted to the harsher economic climate; others contacted Hymie, Hymie the Torch. To their amazement, the Torch, who had neither been arrested nor had payment denied on any of his fires, refused. How could Hymie the Torch refuse? Would-be conspirators met Hymie in the dark outside his office. They stopped him on his way to the synagogue. They begged — "Hymie, our lives!" They implored — "Hymie, our kids!" Hymie just shook his head. "Why, Hymie? Why?" But Hymie just shook his head. He was out; that's it. Sorry.

Hymie's family heard reports of his refusals and were pleased. Everyone in the family felt a little more secure. Everyone but Hymie. The spurned offers only fueled the terror that blazed endlessly in front of him — one, two, three, four, five, six million.

His would-be customers found other torches. Some failed to collect; the mismanaged fires were obviously fraudulent. Some went to jail; their burners were careless and indiscreet. And worst of all, some killed. Hymie felt accusing stares. Not that anyone actually blamed him, but Cohen was broke, Shakowitz was under indictment, and firemen's funerals were held with frightening regularity. Of course, no one thought that Hymie should have announced his retirement in the newspapers; still, as the saying goes, you don't close the synagogue on the eve of the Sabbath.

No one said anything to Hymie's face. Well, almost no one. One day he received a call in his office.

"I want to talk to you. It's very important," a voice insisted.

"Who's speaking?" Hymie asked.

"Hymie, please drive through the park today. I'll be standing by Custer's monument at noon."

"Yes, but how will I know you?"

"Don't worry, Hymie. Just be there. You'll recognize me all right."

Hymie was intrigued. He had a memory for voices and he suspected that he had heard this one before, but he just couldn't place it. The flames vanished as the mysterious caller's identity occupied him all morning. Nor did they bother him as he drove through the park, but when he arrived at the monument and saw who was standing there in a uniform with a double row of bright brass buttons, he remembered the voice and again saw the infernal flames.

"Good, you came," said Bannion nervously as he got into Hymie's car.

Hymie drove through the park.

"Do you remember me?" the passenger asked.

Remember him? Ever since his unannounced visit to Hymie's office, Hymie had been following his career. Bannion had risen all the way to the top. He ran the show now. Chief of the entire department.

"You came to my office once," Hymie said.

"Yeah," Bannion said with embarrassment, "that was a while ago. Times have changed."

Hymie nodded. How times have changed, he thought.

"Look," Bannion said with his old aggressiveness, "I'm not one to beat about the bush. I want to talk to you."

"I don't know anything about them," Hymie said. "I'm out."

"Yeah, I know. That's the point. I want you to go back in."

The last was said quickly, as if the chief had to say it, but didn't want to have to hear himself saying it.

Hymie looked at Bannion. The car swerved.

"Maybe you'd better park while we discuss this," Bannion suggested.

Hymie parked.

"Hymie, the guys who are doing the jobs today are no damned good." The chief's voice was rising. "Every jackass who can light a match thinks he's a torch. We picked up a Dago last night. It was his first blaze; he tells us he's sorry. We buried three good firefighters because of him and he tells us he's sorry!" The chief was practically shouting.

"Sorry, I guess I got pretty loud, but Hymie, my men are frying. Those guys aren't running into burning buildings; they're running into death traps. You know how many firemen died in those fires?"

Hymie nodded. He had followed it all in the papers.

"Twelve, Hymie. Twelve in two months!" The chief's voice cracked as if he were on the verge of tears. He paused to regain his composure. "I got to protect my men; I'm the chief. That's my job. Hymie, I can't do it just by catching those amateurs. They crop up like weeds. We got the Dago last night. The week before we got the Polack who was worse than the Dago. The Polack set the cold-storage fire that spread to the bakery where six of my men went through the floor. And now that we got the Dago, some other half-ass fool will think he can make an easy buck and print a card that says 'torch.' Maybe it'll be a dumb Mick like me or a fast Sheeny like you or a crazy Nigger. The Lord knows! But some bastard will kill my men for sure."

Bannion paused.

"Can't you get back in?"

Hymie sadly shook his head.

"Hymie, I'm begging you with Jesus as my witness. My men are dying. You can save them."

"Sorry," said Hymie, his voice cracking.

Bannion heard Hymie's anguish.

"Look, I know it's not any easy thing I'm asking. If you promised the wife or somebody, I'm willing to talk to them."

"It's not that," said Hymie.

"You're not so young. You let me know in advance and I'll see to it that the coast is clear."

Hymie shook his head.

"Almost thirty kids," the chief said in a hollow voice. "Orphans."

"I can't. I can't," cried Hymie.

Hymie looked Bannion in the eye.

"I wish I could, Chief. I wish more than you can imagine." A puzzled Bannion looked at Hymie.

"Why not, Hymie?"

"God," said Hymie.

"Religion, huh?" asked Bannion.

Hymie nodded.

"That bad?" commiserated the chief.

Hymie nodded again.

"Well, we'll see," Bannion said sympathetically, but Hymie just shook his head.

STUDYING the Talmud, Rabbi Mendel sat next to the tattered ark. Hymie entered and sat down across from him. The rabbi finished a sentence and closed his thick volume. He continued rocking and squinted into the air as if he were trying to focus on some elusive thought. Then with embarrassment, he lowered his gaze and looked at Hymie. They exchanged greetings. They had always gotten along well. Hymie appreciated the rabbi and the rabbi appreciated Hymie. As the only "American," Hymie suggested to the rabbi that he might not be quite as warped and scarred as he thought he was. Hymie was, after all, a successful American-born millionaire businessman who wasn't very learned. He smiled at Hymie.

"Hymie, I have asked you to come in because I promised I would. I had a visitor who spoke to me about you. I would not have told him that I would, except that I didn't want him to go away angry. He is an important man who could hurt our people. Fire Commissioner Bannion."

Hymie was dumbfounded, but he managed to utter, "Chief, not commissioner. Chief."

"Yes," said the rabbi, uncomfortable at not understanding the difference.

"Bannion was *here?*" asked Hymie.

"Yes, last week. No uniform. Rabbi Drillstein asked him to. It was very nice of Rabbi Drillstein. You do know that I'm afraid of uniforms, don't you?"

Hymie nodded.

"Rabbi Drillstein didn't have any choice either. A high church official asked him to set up a meeting for the — chief — with your rabbi."

Rabbi Mendel looked to see if he had gotten the fireman's title correct this time, but Hymie just stared in amazement.

"Forgive me, Hymie, for having listened to the 'evil tongue' about you. I do not enjoy gossip, but he was a high officer and an official of the church sent him, so I didn't want to offend."

"It's all right, rabbi. It's all true," Hymie said.

"Still, it remains 'evil tongue' even if it's true. Forgive me," the rabbi said.

"I forgive you, Rabbi."

"Thank you. You already know what he told me, but I would like to tell you what I told him. I said that he could not be sure that your fires would not kill anyone. No matter how good you are, it is impossible to know. I told him that if you were to go to jail, neither he nor I could replace you in your home. Oh, yes, and I told him that I would talk to you."

"What do *you* think, Rabbi?" Hymie asked softly.

"I sympathize with that man. He cares about the people he commands. And he is confused, for life and law seem to be in opposition. But you are not responsible for their deaths. It is tragic and he cannot accept that. His complaint is not against you."

"Rabbi," Hymie said slowly, "do you see the flames?"

"The flames?" he asked, uncertain what Hymie was talking about.

"Yes," repeated Hymie, "the flames."

"Well," the rabbi said, "I don't know very much about burning buildings."

"No," said Hymie, "not those flames. The flames of Auschwitz. The crematoria."

Rabbi Mendel Myers stopped rocking. He sat up straight, with a stunned, hurt expression, and stared at Hymie.

"Yes," said the rabbi with resignation. "I see the flames. I smell the ashes as the flames propel the souls to heaven. Yes, I see them, but why do *you* ask?"

"I see them too," said Hymie with the same weary resignation, and Hymie began to rock.

The rabbi heard Hymie's anguished weary horror, and he knew that Hymie, indeed, did see the flames.

When the rabbi spoke again, it was directed as much toward himself as to Hymie.

"It is taught that all of Israel is one body. When I suffered, I found solace in the knowledge that other Jews were living peaceful lives while we were being degraded and destroyed. I thought that although the one hand was being burned, the other hand felt no pain. I had no idea what is meant by one body. It means a living body. In one body, if one hand is being burned, the entire body tightens and tries to tear itself away from the fire. The mouth opens, the throat screams, the eyes widen, the legs kick, and the other hand flails the air in pain."

The rabbi looked up with the awareness that his suffering had caused others pain. He turned to Hymie and said with concern, even embarrassment at not having known, "How, Hymie? How?"

After his long, lonely torture, Hymie poured forth his story — from the first *havdalah* with dancing flame and vanilla ice cream to the night at the movies and all that had followed. Rabbi Mendel Myers listened with the sorrow that Hymie was one of them. Sorrow that the flames consumed so far from their source. Sorrow that there was no real American in his congregation. Above all, the sorrow that there might not be any real Americans, after all, anywhere.

Hymie cried for the first time since he was by the child's hospital bed. He leaned his head onto the table and he wept.

Hymie remained there until he felt the rabbi tapping his arm. He pushed himself off the table and sat up. The rabbi handed him a piece of stale bread. Hymie accepted it and began to gnaw the hard, cellular surface. The dry flakes gathered on his tongue, gently coated his mouth, softly cushioned the choking void of his throat. With relief his teeth ground against the rough, dessicated bread. Without acknowledging one another, they sat, slowly grinding their meal in the empty house of prayer. Then, without interrupting his monotonous gnawing, the rabbi spoke.

"Hymie the Torch, you know a great deal about fire," the rabbi said, "but you must learn more."

Hymie, not comprehending what the rabbi meant, stared at him in confusion.

The rabbi spoke quietly but with a powerful narrative force.

"In the beginning, man was in the Garden of Eden; he had no need of fire. Food was plentiful; every tree had fruit. The climate was perfect. And it was never dark because the sun, the moon, and the stars were brighter than they are now. Man had no fire because he had no need for it. But man sinned."

The rabbi paused, then repeated slowly, "Man sinned."

He continued speaking normally, "Man sinned and he had to be punished. Man sinned on Friday before the Sabbath and in punishment God wanted to dim the luminaries, but out of respect for the Sabbath, He did not do so. Throughout the Sabbath, the luminaries shone and there was no darkness, but when the sun set, ending the Sabbath, all were dimmed to one forty-ninth of their former brilliance.

"Adam feared the darkness caused by his sin. 'Night will overwhelm me!' he cried and he even feared that the serpent would bite him. God, in His mercy, gave him two stones and granted him divine inspiration. When fire burst forth, lighting the darkness, Adam spontaneously recited the blessing, 'King of the Universe Who creates lights of fire.'

"We recite the same blessing over fire at *havdalah* every Saturday night because that was when fire was created. Adam kindled fire and survived the darkness of the night. The next morning, on the Eighth Day, the sun rose, dimmed, but once again daylight followed. We, too, have passed through a night of terror. And our night was made darker by fire. The tall chimneys' flames darkened the day unto death as they preyed upon the flesh of Israel.

"Night's terror is not easily forgotten. Every sunset reminded Adam of his fear. For many of us, every flame recalls our own dark night in which six million loved ones perished. Adam knew his sin. We do not know ours. We sinned, of course, but we do not know what we did to deserve what we received."

Tears had formed in the rabbi's eyes and they began slowly to descend onto his pale cheeks.

"But, Rabbi, that might apply to Adam and to me because we sinned," Hymie began.

"No," the rabbi said, "yours was not so bad, Hymie."

"It was a criminal act, Rabbi," Hymie insisted.

"The world is very cunning. It devises different ways to drive us mad."

"But, Rabbi, what did those people do to deserve such a fate?"

"God knows," the rabbi said softly.

"Do you believe that?" Hymie asked, revealing his deep hurt.

The rabbi gagged as the tears fell onto the hard bread before him.

"*You* must believe that!" he commanded.

"Why me?" Hymie asked.

"Because if one hand is burned and cannot eat, the other must feed the body," the rabbi explained.

Hymie chewed on his stale bread and thought for a moment.

"But you're a rabbi," Hymie protested.

The rabbi averted his eyes from Hymie for a moment and then brought them back to focus directly on him.

"Then listen to me," the rabbi pleaded. "I am a refugee. Don't ask what I do believe and what I don't believe. I don't know that myself. I study the Talmud, Hymie. You know why a man would run away from uniforms and eat stale bread — or why a man who loved fire would be afraid to touch a match."

The rabbi paused. "Or why the genius of Warsaw would be afraid to touch a volume of the Talmud."

Hymie knew. Oh, how he knew, and when he saw the rabbi's fingers rise from the table and move toward the Talmud, he cried out.

"No, don't! Not because of me!"

"I must because of you," the rabbi said with a firmness that had not been present in his voice.

Why? Hymie asked with his eyes.

"The body of Israel must be nourished," the rabbi explained.

The rabbi thumbed through the large folio pages — love in his touch, sorrow in his eyes — until he found what he wanted. He began to chant, first in the original Aramaic, then in translation for Hymie. It began as a somber, funereal mourning chant.

"There are six kinds of fire. There is a fire that eats but doesn't drink: this is our common fire. There is a fire that drinks but doesn't eat: this is the fever of the sick. There is a fire that eats and drinks: this is the fire of Elijah the Prophet that consumed sacrifices and water. There is a fire that eats wet and dry: this is the fire that the priests had on the altar in the Holy Temple."

The rabbi's chant had become increasingly less mournful until it was on the verge of joy.

"There is a fire that quenches fire: this is the fire of the angel Gabriel that he used to save Hananiah, Mishael, and Azariah from the fiery furnace. And there is the fire," the rabbi chanted triumphantly, "that consumes fire: this is the fire of the Shechinah, the Divine Presence."

The rabbi looked at Hymie and asked him in direct, nonmelodic tones, "Hymie, did you love them all?"

"No," said Hymie shaking his head.

"Which one betrayed you?" the rabbi demanded.

"Only the first, common fire," said Hymie tortured by memories as he mentioned the thing he once loved.

"Still," the rabbi said, "there are other types of fire

that have not betrayed you."

Hymie chewed on his bread.

"Rabbi, I am only a man of common fire," Hymie stated.

"Yes, now you are, but if you have been burned by it, don't you think it is time you learned to work with another kind?"

"You don't understand," Hymie protested. "I'm a plain arsonist. I'm Hymie the Torch."

"No, you're not," the rabbi answered.

Yes, thought Hymie. I'm not even that anymore.

Hymie was confused.

"Rabbi, you don't believe this. Why should I?"

"Because we are facing the same question, Hymie."

"What question?"

"The question is who we shall become. I am trying to become a rabbi," the rabbi said with his strangely quivering dark eyes staring at the man who had been his only American.

Hymie turned away to avoid the gaze for he saw in those eyes the vulnerability of the heart and the will to live. Hymie remembered hearing his grandfather say that it is better to throw oneself into a fiery furnace than to shame someone publicly. He shuddered in horror at the image. Hymie impulsively licked at the dry bread. He felt a surge of love for this weird, vulnerable former genius and wished that he could put him in his own pocket and protect him from the things that pained him so. Hymie reached across the table, lifted the rabbi's hands off the Talmud, and rested his own on the strange block print instead.

"You are my rabbi," Hymie said.

Rabbi Myers blinked and experienced a surge of hope for the body of Israel whose survival was a divine promise. Rabbi Myers smiled at Hymie.

Hymie squeezed the rabbi's hands and said, "We are in this together, aren't we?"

The rabbi nodded.

"Hymie, it is Monday night; if one does not perform *havdalah* immediately after the Sabbath, it may be said until Tuesday morning. I am going to make *havdalah* for you and then you are going to recite it for me."

He looked at Hymie. Hymie didn't know what had happened but he did know that they had come too far to do otherwise.

The rabbi went to a closet and returned with a wine bottle, a silver cup, a spice box, and a braided candle. He handed Hymie the candle with a box of matches. Hymie lit the candle and the rabbi began to chant. Hymie was overcome. He heard the rabbi and he saw the flame, but he was dwelling in sadness and in destiny. He saw himself and the rabbi both standing in a dark cave with no chance of returning to Eden and with no choice other than to wait out the long, dark night.

The rabbi finished. He drank from the cup and took a candle from Hymie. He extinguished the flame in the wine-dampened saucer.

"It's your turn, Hymie, to recite *havdalah* for me."

Hymie reached for the wine cup, but the rabbi stopped him.

"No, Hymie, not here. We must get our coats."


THE Dairy Maid waitress didn't know what to make of it, especially the one with the beard, but the two men were eating vanilla ice cream and rocking slowly back and forth as if their counter stools weren't bolted to the floor. What was strangest of all — they had brought their own thick chunks of toast. Toast and ice

cream — what kind of meal was that? But Hymie knew
and he ate even though he wasn't hungry because he
knew that it was still several hours until the sun rose
on the Eighth Day.

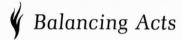 Balancing Acts

I RETURNED to Jerusalem and it wasn't easy. It wasn't easy because time is different here. Time may move as quickly as it does in other places, but it doesn't relinquish its past as it advances. Other cities may be eternal, but only Jerusalem's eternity is an active part of its present. No visitor is a stranger in Jerusalem. With the past so near, his roots are apparent. When I came as a tourist, I, too, felt at home, and an awareness stirred that this, indeed, should be my home because not to be in Jerusalem is to surrender part of yourself. I am an American and we never surrender! So with my family and my paints I came to live in Jerusalem.

I returned to live in Jerusalem, and it wasn't easy, because to live in Jerusalem is to surrender part of yourself. The nearness of generations makes the transient feel permanent and the permanent resident feel transient. All-encompassing Jerusalem. You are in the middle — small, minuscule, and a creation of Jerusalem itself. It is even more complex for you are also, potentially, an essential part of Jerusalem. Surrender is victory! With so much at stake, the tension is dreadful and exhilarating. You can't go home because you are home. You can only run away — or be driven out — and that is hardly new. That's how you got where you came from in the first place. How can you make what is permanent temporary? And how can you make what is temporary permanent? You can only tell the old stories, but can you tell them any better? Or in my case, paint what is already perfect? It's a privilege and a punishment, which is the way it has always been. God had to hold Mount Sinai above the Jews, threatening to crush them with it if they wouldn't accept the Torah, because everyone knew the score: being the Chosen People is a mixed blessing. With the light of Torah under the shade of the mountain, who could postpone the game because of darkness?

At first I thought that I was not painting because of all the aggravations and tedious chores of adjustment in the Holy Land. Of these there was no shortage: the plumbing alone would have defied Neptune. The toilet leaked onto the floor, the bathtub leaked onto the neighbors, the pipes refused the washing machine's pump-driven discharge. And waterworks were once His specialty. He split the Red Sea to bring us into this land! But, after all, I as an American hadn't been chased by Pharaoh. Would I have surrendered?

As these problems diminished, I still did not open my paint box or pick up a sketch pad. Earlier, running errands around the city, I had been struck by Jerusalem's overwhelming beauty. If that didn't inspire me, what would? Later, however, after I had no errands, I continued to walk the streets. The beauty increased. I saw modest, unadorned hills baring themselves in humility and resignation before higher elements of sun, rain, and wind. I saw the gray stone's durable hard edges of eroded harshness, still strong and intolerant, surrendering nothing without prolonged, unrelenting struggle. After a rain I felt the passion of ancient earth's moist hot breath in its cycle of renewal. The rocks remained cool, hard, but infinitesimally less; for each soft drop had made its slight, disintegrating mark.

How I wanted to capture the colors of fertile barrenness! I stared at the ancient olive trees with their hidden roots, gnarled, flinty trunks (surrender!), delicate, curved crowns of small, stiff oval green leaves (victory!). How I longed to capture their gentle, patient life. I watched the faces at a bus stop, reflecting a thousand places; for even the four corners of the earth have four corners, and these people had been to every corner — and to Jerusalem, too. Yes, I was inspired, but

I was overwhelmed. The beauty increased, but I was diminished. My steps were merely the most recent echoes. When I arose, the day seemed too long, and when I retired, the day seemed too short. The minutes had different shapes, the hours had different textures. In Jerusalem I stared at my watch in disbelief and wondered where my day had gone. In answer, it ticked; the game had not begun and we were already in over-time! And what was the contest?

I began to wish that I was back where time made sense — in America, where the National Football League played an exciting game in four discrete quarters that anchored a comprehensible Sunday afternoon, with announcers to guide me through every play and replay. On Sundays I found myself wondering how the Jets were doing. I began to wish that I was back where things weren't nearly as complicated nor as beautiful — in Manhattan, where great things were obvious and small things were plain. Where a pigeon was a pigeon. A plain, dirty pigeon on a pebbly, granite-grained side-walk. No big deal, but if handled right, the stuff of art. Interesting perspective — unsettling, off-angle view from above; good composition — discarded sidewalk refuse; rich subject — the stupid, goggle-eyed bird, weirdly realistic. And eight red toes. What I could do with color and design on those eight toes. Thank heav-ens, Manhattan is for the birds!

In Manhattan they were ordinary pigeons — scav-engers, hangers-on, Broadway bums who parked on grimy cornices, descending to peck Burger King crumbs off warped, half-destroyed benches, but in Jerusalem they were doves, cherished residents of the Western Wall, sole remnant of the destroyed Holy Temple, God's House on His Holy Mountain, in His Holy City. The Western Wall — silent, eroded, abused by millennia

— but now its gaps, holes, and harsh fractures are sheltering spaces for harbingers of peace, and the long-silent Wall has a live voice dwelling inside.

The delicate masters of this voice emerge from the Wall and ascend on rhythmic, thrusting wings to circle above the Holy Mountain. Soft, beating wings catching the slanting light, reflecting, shaping, transfiguring the radiant particles streaming from afar onto His Holy Mountain. As they soar, they thrust into the radiance other voices from below. The thick primordial silent voices of the stones of the Wall itself and the earth of the mountain. The joyous wailing melodies of the seed of Abraham, seed of Isaac, seed of Jacob, reciting the psalms of David, purchaser of the holy site. The small fleeting feathered specks wheel and break about in the stream, creating sheltering feather-lined bubbles to convey all the voices and prayers upstream to their Source. Thank *heavens*, Jerusalem is for the birds!

All this seen on Friday evenings when Jerusalem welcomed the Sabbath. The light emanated from the stones too. It was no reflection. Only on the Sabbath did it emerge from its stony, silent vaults. All celebrating sanctity and peace.

Paint that pigeon! How was I to paint any pigeon without painting those doves, stones, Abraham, Isaac, and Jacob, the feathers, the radiant stream of light? The permanent and the temporary, the hard and the soft, the loud and the quiet, the speakers and the speechless, the large and the small, the heavy and the light; the earth, the earthbound and flight-blessed, all chanting in unison to the Indescribable, Eternal Creator, "Why not now? Why not rebuild Your House, Your Holy Temple, now?"

I couldn't untie the rope that I had wound protectively around my box of paints. Confused, I wandered as if I were a small tile floating in a great eternal mosaic. I sat on my roof in the Old City's Jewish Quarter and watched the light change during the various hours of the day. I enjoyed looking across at the Mount of Olives and staring at the gravestones. As my mind was hopping from stone to stone, surprising thoughts intruded: the New York Giants, El Greco, and most surprising of all, my Uncle Maxie. Perplexed, I nevertheless enjoyed the view. It was, after all, Jerusalem — stone-confusing-beautiful. I had a bleacher seat, but what was the game? Uncle Maxie didn't have a uniform and I didn't have a scorecard!

I walked into town and bought a *Herald Tribune* to find out the results of the Superbowl, a game I understood. I read it avidly, like a letter from a very close friend. The Raiders finally had won. The Vikings had lost again. That was reassuring; I wasn't missing much, but I had a sense of loss. I wished that I had seen it. I put down the sports page and looked across at the timeless cemetery. Did I have a season ticket?

I walked. I met my neighbor. He was pleasant and asked how things were going. Just fine, I replied, wondering what I was doing. I made frequent trips to the post office.

I answered letters. I talked about the weather, the agonies of Israeli bureaucracy, the kids in new schools. What was I doing? "Not much, but it's very beautiful here," I wrote, as if the beauty alone could sustain me when, in fact, with all the loose ends of time, it was strangling me.

My neighbor's father died. The funeral was on a Friday afternoon, a most inconvenient time. There is never enough time on Fridays to prepare for the Sabbath.

Attending a funeral wouldn't improve our chances any. Since I had never met the deceased, I thought I would walk in the funeral procession that left from the hospital and then return home without going to the cemetery.

Another friend and I accompanied my neighbor to the hospital. On the way, I realized from their conversation that my neighbor was not going to the cemetery either but, instead, he planned to go straight home. When I expressed surprise at this, he told me that according to the custom of Jerusalem, children and grandchildren do not go to the cemetery to bury a father. Not wanting to bother or distress him in his grief, I didn't pursue the subject.

Later, however, I sought an explanation among the crowd of mourners waiting for the procession to begin. Most people I approached either didn't know or, if they did, didn't want to discuss it. Embarrassed, staring at their shoes, they would shift their weight, kicking at the ground the way you might at a wedding if a child asked you what the married couple do after the festivities.

I persisted. Finally, a neighbor turned away from the crowd and told me under his breath and out of the side of the mouth — not just from embarrassment, but from fear, too — that, according to the mystical teachings of Kabbalah, a man's seed that goes to waste results in the creation of demons and other impure spirits. If the children, the legitimate seed of the dead man, attend the burial, then all that a man has created, including the spirits and demons, might attend also. The soul rises for final judgment at burial, and these evil creations might damage his case. The children therefore do not attend because it is better to have no witnesses rather than some who would certainly be damaging.

Such an idea struck me as fantastic and cruel. Fantastic because who could believe such a thing! Cruel because the children should be at a father's burial. For their sakes — to avoid denial, and for his sake — to show respect. Although I was shocked, I was also fascinated by the novelty of the concept.

Still, once the premise is accepted, then the children's returning straight home makes a certain amount of Superbowl sense. If you can't rely on execution the way the old Green Bay Packers and Cleveland Browns did to run straight over the opposition, then you have to employ a little deception: if your angelic fullback can't destroy the demonic middle linebacker with a crunching head-on block, then you have to get the accusatory devil to take himself out of the play through a few good fakes. More your Dallas Cowboy multiple-set offense. Although what happened should be termed a naked reverse; for after the sons had approached the father's body at the mortuary and had placed dirt upon the closed eyes, they went rambling home around left end with their half-brother spirits in swift pursuit. While they were heading that way, the real funeral procession plunged off right tackle and angled for the cemetery on the Mount of Olives.

Once I understood how the play was shaping up, I had no choice. Since my neighbor couldn't attend, I had to do it for him, and given the nature of this Kabbalistic offense, I was all the more important. You can't tell the players without a scorecard, as they say, which is true enough, but as I had never met nor seen his father, even if there were a scorecard in the pressbox of the impure my name and number wouldn't be listed.

So I arrived at the cemetery ready to play. And I did,

too. After the members of the burial society removed
the prayer shawl, lowered the body into the grave
(wrapped in a simple muslin cloth — anonymous and
white; no uniforms here! — let the impure spirits guess),
placed the thick concrete tiles above him, and began
quickly to shovel the dirt back into the grave, I, who
wasn't in anyone's game plan, stepped forward to shut-
tle in the first play. I grabbed a mattocklike shovel and
went to work pushing the dry, heavy clods over the lip
of the narrow grave, reaching and pulling the farther
earthen remnants back into place, though this time
with Shraga Feivel Tsur né Glattstein tucked humbly
beneath, and finally scraping, broomlike, the loose
pebbly soil along the ground into the rapidly diminish-
ing pit. Others wanted the merit of helping bury a man
who had been a brother, a friend, a companion, an
acquaintance, but to me he was anonymous, and in this
Coliseum of Kabbalah I knew I had Shraga Feivel on
the road to glory. Let them stare; I kept on: four yards
and a cloud of dust.

Finally, I surrendered the shovel and stepped back
to watch the second team bury the Devil's chances and
end the terrestrial appearance of a man from Jerusalem.
If he hadn't made it into the end zone, he was mighty
close. I felt confident that our brilliant burst down the
sideline had succeeded and there would be no undue
criticism in the postgame interview.

Feeling more relaxed as the clock ticked off the final
seconds — time had become intelligible! — I looked
around, first up at my roof on the hill across the valley.
From that distance the stones seemed to blend together
and I couldn't quite pick it out of the crowd. I turned to
examine the cemetery that I had constantly viewed
from afar. It was both very personal and very commu-

nal, the stones worn, the ground ungraded, the weeds natural and profuse. The graves lacked that perfect Euclidean geometry that we associate with our average American right-angles-only approach to death. The Mount of Olives offered more freedom of arrangement, a random mumbo-jumbo that followed the lay of the land. All very surrealistic. Almost planned in a dilapidated, slightly chiseled, slightly eternal way. All very comfortable.

And the view! The view was magnificent: the east side of the Temple Mount with olive trees nestled at its base; down to the left the Kidron Valley; directly across the valley — the Jewish Quarter inside the Old City walls.

I'm not saying I was in a rush to join Shraga Feivel, but I did feel a debt of gratitude to him. Tradition has it that the Messiah will first restore the dead to life on the Mount of Olives. Standing by the nearly filled grave, I suddenly realized that the tradition has it right. I resolved to thank the deceased at the first opportunity — after one hundred and twenty years, of course.

That cemetery is just not like other cemeteries. It really is a wonderful place. If you have to die, that's the place to go under, especially with the resurrectional talents of the Messiah. It's dust to dust, but in that earth on that mountain, I sensed that a physical joining occurred simultaneously with the physical departure. I felt sorry for those poor souls whose bodies were lost at sea or left without proper burial. No doubt the Messiah can take care of all his customers, but in the interim they are missing a lot of the fun, if you know what I mean, because the old, decrepit Mount of Olives radiated anticipation. It was three steps above hope. It was high up on the ladder of anticipation. The only question was when? When was the Messiah coming?

I SUPPOSE I had always believed that the Messiah
was coming sometime or other. His arrival is an article
of faith, as they say. I was never one to go out of my way
to deny an article of faith. So far as I can remember,
when I was growing up in St. Louis, no one worried
very much about the Messiah. There were always
enough other things to worry about. Personal things
like how to make a living, what car to buy, whom to
marry. Things that can take up most of your day.
Communal worries: synagogues, the St. Louis Cardi-
nals, hospitals, schools, old folks homes, the price of
kosher chickens, and the poor Jews of Israel.

No, the Messiah's coming was not a pressing matter.
Had it not been an article of faith but, say, an article of
clothing, it might have been an old leather aviator's
helmet dragged home by someone's father or uncle
from World War II and promptly relegated to a dusty
attic. The kind of thing no one would ever throw out
nor know exactly where it was. So it was with the
Messiah.

The Messiah, however, unlike an aviator's helmet,
was — is — an unknown quantity. After the Depression,
the Second World War, the Holocaust, people everywhere, including the Jews of St. Louis, were fairly
burning for known quantities: houses, lawns, automo-
biles, vacations, security, the good life. It was no
mistake that Eisenhower clobbered Stevenson twice.
Eisenhower was a known quantity, a successful one.
Stevenson was yearning, theorizing, trying to articulate the contradictions and explore the paradoxes. It
wasn't a time to articulate; it was a time to consume.
The Son of Jesse wasn't in any of the Sunday supple-

ments with garden hoses, seeders, lawn mowers, and other outdoor specials designed to save you time and effort while improving the appearance and value of your property.

You might argue that for the Jews of Missouri, the State of Israel was also an unknown quantity, but it was far away and they tended to view it as left-over business from the Holocaust, a Marshall Plan for the Jews. They themselves were working hard to move, but not to Israel. They were killing themselves to get to the suburbs west of the city, the real promised land. Lightning out of Zion might have occupied a subtle recess of their consciousness, but it was horsepower out of Detroit that was in their eyes. In all our eyes. As kids we knew every model of every year. Roadmasters, Eighty-eights, and Chiefs. All of them, *oleihem hasholem*: the gracefully low-slung Hudson, the impressive boat-hulled Packard, and the slightly discombobulated Studebaker. And, yes, we too joined Henry Ford's grandson in sitting *shivah* for the Edsel with its weird, vertical grill.

If the establishment of Israel depended upon a Messiah, he was not featured as David, son of Jesse. The men and women who created the state did so precisely because they had given up on divine processes — if they had ever believed in them at all. They had had it with being a light among nations. They wanted to be a nation among nations. If American Jews were looking for cars, the Zionists were looking for a garage in which they could park their wandering nationalism. Who needed another Messiah as long as Ben-Gurion was on center stage? So it was all stacked against the Messiah. Nobody was advertising about him in the classifieds either way — Messiah Wanted or Messianic Position Desired, résumé supplied upon request. Given the times, my new situation came as a surprise. It was only the first.

I RETURNED to my roof and began awaiting the Messiah, a position for which I was not trained, but for which I did possess certain virtues. Some people go to pieces if they aren't busy; I'm not one of them. I just happen to like to paint. Everything I see possesses visual interest — a structure or design that can absorb my attention. To what extent the fruit of this aesthetic observation appears in my work has always been a question of interest to me. The connection is not obvious, if, indeed, it exists. It is as if I see with my eyes and paint with my gut or whatever viscera contain those deepest feelings and responses that are not developed but just are there. The artist and sports fan share this gut response that does not permit them to surrender to "obvious" facts and events. So it was I believed in the Messiah's imminent appearance; a people who refuse to surrender Messianic expectations after thousands of disappointing years can only survive on this deeper, gut level. Is it any wonder we make such loyal sports fans?

On my roof, I began to await the Messiah full time with a sense of vocation that had all but disappeared from my life since arriving in Jerusalem. And why not? Forget about your zone defenses and end-zone cameras. There is no instant replay for the great event and I have a seat on the fifty-yard line of the Temple Mount and Mount of Olives!

At half-time I left the roof and descended to the Wall to count the crowd and see whether the Messiah had wandered in without a ticket and was refraining from announcing himself for want of recognition. I would stroll among those present — some prayed, some stared, some just sat and basked in the Wall's presence like old men sitting on wooden benches across the street from the park. Close enough for "being at the park" with its sylvan aromas but far enough away to avoid ants and poison ivy. No Messiah in any of the groups.

I would finish my patrol by touching the Wall, my fingertips gently grazing the scoring of the stone — those random, patterned nicks from the stonemason's hammer. Each one was the work of a single man's single blow: personal and unique. Now the indentations were worn and smooth, but with my touch I felt the hammer's unyielding cacophonous assault when its head met the chisel's tail in screeching metal agony and the stone chips flew like crazed, driven snowflakes. The Creation Moment. It encouraged me; for beginnings imply ends: births, deaths, which are all part of the grand cycle of renewal that means time will have an end when the Messiah comes and everybody lives on the sunny side of the street with doves gently singing.

So I waited. I waited on the rooftop, and I waited by the Wall. I waited in the bus, and I waited in the grocery. I waited at my neighbor's during the week he sat *shivah*, and I waited at the cemetery again thirty days later when we dedicated the gravestone. He continued saying *kaddish* and I continued waiting. In the frenzy of this waiting, I didn't paint. How could I with the Redeemer coming at any moment? Just wait a minute, Mr. Messiah, until I get the green right, then I'll remove the paint from my hands with turpentine and welcome you properly.

Waiting as an act of faith demands expectancy. Expectancy demands attention because without attention, I would just be killing time, a low form of waiting, not the high pinnacle of expectation that places great prodding weights on the Messianic conscience to arrive already and get it over with. I tried to keep my mind on what I was doing. I waited so diligently that inadvertently I developed a new life style.

I realized that I no longer changed underwear very frequently. Only for the Sabbath. In this I was correct. According to the Talmud, the Messiah will not arrive on the eve of Sabbath or the eve of a holiday. When everyone is rushing around trying to get ready for the coming festivities, it would be terribly inconvenient for the Messiah to pop up. The Messiah might be slow, but he's thoughtful. So there was no problem changing underwear for the Sabbath since it was a day off for both of us.

Although I could have spared the time during the rest of the week, it would have been like purchasing a new calendar when the end is approaching. To order one both denies and reduces one's participation in the arrival. You might argue that it never hurts to take out a little insurance — straight-term B.V.D. — in case the Messiah doesn't make his move and it is time that marches on instead, accompanied by its human secretive essences and gatherings of lint.

The answer is simple. Faith is necessary to bring the Messiah, and faith, by definition, precludes looking before leaping, testing the water, and changing underwear. My underwear grew flat, tired, and gray. I itched because the body serves its earthly master as its Heavenly Master ordained. My underwear developed a palpable presence that was interesting, alarming, and unheard of in our family history. Well, not quite unheard of. To my surprise I did recall the odorific uniform. My Uncle Maxie hadn't always changed underwear either and it was to him, a man I had never considered seriously, that my thoughts were drawn as inexorably as an irrepressible itch. An itch of faith.

I don't want to exaggerate; there are differences. It took my uncle, actually my great-uncle, over ninety years to learn not to change his underwear, whereas I progressed to such a sublime spiritual state in approximately one-third the time. In all fairness, I had advantages that he never had: education, an affluent and stable youth, to name two. He, for his part, was rich in talents. He could sing, dance, and juggle with professional skill.

A short, bald man — in his younger years he was powerful, lithe, graceful, and dignified, but then, after seventy years, a rotund plumpness paraded above legs that bowed out under both the weight of the paunch and the weight of the years. He would carefully park a large two-door Plymouth in front of the house. It wasn't so much a parking as an august arrival, an aeronautic landing. If we called to him, interrupting his measured ritual, he would smile and throw us a wave while he finished putting the car in park, engaging the hand brake, turning off the engine, and removing the ignition key. He did this with concentration and concern, as if he were following a mental checklist, the way an astronaut must before emerging from his capsule.

When Uncle Maxie finally stepped out, you knew that Maxie was short for Maxwell. He had great bearing. Arrogant, but polite. A self-assurance and an ease that would have become a great aviator. He might have done better at Orly than Lindbergh. As it was, he had the airs without the achievement. When he entered a synagogue, the responsible dues-paying members detested him; for that little "fourflusher," as they called him, walked the way they only dared to in dreams

when the Dow went over a million. Uncle Maxie had at
best only an indirect relationship with the stock market
through his familial benefactors. Still, if we are all self-
appointed, Uncle Maxie had a better appointment, and
if we are not, then he was an impostor. Either way he
wasn't very popular with those who worked hard to earn
their place and expected others to waste away in envy.

To appreciate Uncle Maxie in those years (he changed
underwear then), it was best to be a kid because Uncle
Maxie could juggle eight eggs at once. Seeing is believing. Eight eggs, some white, some brown — count 'em
— never fell. For us, this Houdini was entitled to the
airs he possessed. And what did he look like while
juggling? Distracted merriment. Not the common touch
of a buffoon, but not arrogant either. Rather an artistic
dignity that is often appreciated in doctors. He enjoyed
it all right. What a shame the pillars of the community
couldn't have seen him then. It would have made
everything easier for everyone.

Well, not everyone. My mother was mildly frantic
during these performances, but Uncle Maxie was a
great charmer. What woman could get mad at him
without feeling that she was persecuting him? This
juggling exhibition took place in the living room on the
deep, plush gray carpet which we were constantly
admonished was not some oversized doormat. On that
score we could understand her hysteria. "Don't worry,
I won't drop one," he would assure his niece with
outrageous confidence.

"It's not you I'm worried about. It's the kids!" she
would respond in tones of monumental exasperation.
These were the principal, perhaps the only, tones the
female line used on Maxie. She probably appreciated
her uncle's feat better than we could, for she knew just
how old those hands were.

"What's wrong with the kids?" Uncle Maxie would ask, reflecting our feelings at the unjust accusation.

"They'll want to try it too!"

Of couse we would, although at the moment, we still tumbled through the air with Uncle Maxie's softly contoured floating eggs. All through the discussion the eggs were in the air. Tumbling, turning, soaring, floating, sailing, climbing, falling. Deftly controlled as if by suggestion from those small, well-proportioned hands. It was too much for the eye to follow. We saw only a pattern. One egg? Like trying to follow a falling leaf on a windy day when the trees seem to be raining them. His hands? Impossible without becoming hypnotized by their precise rhythmic prancings to and fro.

"Don't do it in the living room, kids," he would say by way of appeasement to his niece, but this perfunctory instruction lacked all conviction and interest. What he really meant was — kids, don't do it in the living room while I'm doing it. Uncle Maxie was not a rock-ribbed ally. In a pinch, he was not to be relied upon. We knew that he had deserted two wives, abandoning one with four little children. This predilection for hasty, unannounced departures distressed our parents and grandparents considerably more than it did us. We understood that that was part of the price one had to pay for greatness — the Benedict Arnold of Barnum and Bailey's. Now you see him; now you don't.

"For God's sakes, Maxie, use lemons!" she would implore.

After lunch, our appetites for juggling undiminished, we would be at it with the lemons in the kitchen. In open-mouthed despair we watched the dull, yellow fruit (how it had sparkled in his hands!) dodge and dart away from our fingers. It seemed an overwhelming task for a mortal with only two hands. In the midst of bruised lemons bonging off the radiator and clunking off the refrigerator, we were struck by the obvious and only reason for our failure: eggs were easier, lighter, more apt to float in minimal breezes, and less slippery than those slick lemons. My brother mustered the courage to open the refrigerator and wrest victory from the egg tray.

"They're lighter," he announced. Success was in his hands. He tossed the first into the air. The second followed, but not quite rapidly enough; for the third had to be launched with extraordinary speed if the first was not to fall onto the floor.

"What was that?" Mom called.

We glanced at the yellow splotch at our feet. The kitchen floor could be cleaned up easily. What fairly fascinated us, however, was the spreading, wretched yellow mass that was descending the wall, its rich, clinging nutrient glue conquering new areas without surrendering old ones. For an embryo it must be the perfect medium, but this golden, rich, nutritious mix was also spreading across our parrot.

This bird, rich in blue-green and red plumage, was really an astonishing creation. Regal, compact, and flamboyant, it cocked its beak in an egotistical smirk; there was no doubt that bird could talk and knew what to say. Most memorable, and fearful to a child, were its sharp grasping claws. If anything inspired me toward art, that bird played its part. Mom had painted it right before our eyes on demand. Although no juggler, she was not without her Uncle Maxian talents — talents that run rich and natural like great seams of high-assay ore that rarely reach the surface, but when they do break through on occasion, they dazzle the eye as only traces of great treasure can.

We never even knew where she kept the palette, oils,

and brushes, but once every few years she would bring
them out and execute whatever we asked for right on
the spot without so much as a preliminary sketch. At
first we leaned toward parrots, rabbits, ducks; later it
was trains, planes, and other wonders of technology.
No matter, she could do it all. Then she would step
back, admire it for a moment, and forget about it until
some years later some mysterious impulse sent her for
her oils again.

We were expecting some form of retribution to ex-
plode on our hindsides. To our surprise more than our
delight — unrealized expectations among primitives
always present a problem — we merely received a rep-
rimand or two. "God dammit, can't you kids ever listen?" A little "Why did God curse me with children
like you," but nothing with any emotion. She had
expected it. "Damnation," she muttered, angry and
sad, with the timeworn frustration of the sedentary
civilized against the destructive unrestrained joy of the
nomadic primitive. For all his genteel charm, Uncle
Maxie was a socioeconomic barbarian — a Hun of family life, an economic Vandal. She had known that once
the latter-day Visigoth had been permitted to perform
in Rome, it was only a matter of time until the Sistine
Chapel was sacked, if you will, for that parrot was a
very rich bird.

Then, too, Uncle Maxie was her uncle. Maybe she
remembered her childhood pleasure in having an uncle
who could juggle like that. Or again, maybe with her
palette and paints, she had some of the same chromo-
somal splendor and knew that it couldn't be totally
suppressed. Those Litvaks didn't worry so much about
skeletons in the closet; such calcareous residents
bespoke permanence and predictable behavior from
their dull, dark dwellings. What spooked Litvaks were

the mysterious twists of the essential, living genetic material. Tay-Sachs disease, Houdini juggling, and Raphael oils aren't in the blood; they're in the stuff that makes the blood and everything else. Little Litvak chromosomes that suddenly override the deep sustaining rhythms of life and break into a little tango all their own while the deep inner sustaining rhythms go to hell. Whatever else you say, it's worth the price of admission and it promises to be a show stopper.

There's some of the Litvak in me, too, although it's watered down by a Russian influence, less brilliant, more melancholy, but not without its own charm: deep obsessive perversions that alter the very basic rhythms. For the Russian, a minor fleeting theme lasts not seconds or minutes, but decades and in some cases generations. Potatoes versus daisies. Still, that Litvak chromosome or part of it is somewhere inside of me, undiscovered, but I fully expect it to burst forth some time. Whenever audience participation is called for, I cling to my seat for fear that some deep, mad force will propel me onto the stage where I shall perform a perfect *kazatzke*, skip marvelously along a tightrope, or recite from memory the epic poem of Peru. (Anything but juggle.) And I'm enough of a Litvak to feel disappointed in spite of all my Russian fears if it doesn't happen someday.

Being a bit of a Litvak doesn't mean I'm like my Uncle Maxie. No one was thought to be like Uncle Maxie. It was a great mystery and an even greater scandal that Uncle Maxie was like Uncle Maxie. His lack of apparent followers was cause for a collective familial sigh of relief. He was not the hero of the family, but rather the black sheep, although a very fair, blond, blue-eyed one. By the time he was my great-uncle, the hair had departed and the light complexion had garnered its fair share of those dark mottling marks which we called liver spots. But the eyes were something else — forever roving and forever blue — a rare, light, clear blue, the blue of a soft winter's afternoon sky when the cool light has just begun to recede. From appearance alone, one would hardly guess that we were relatives. Until I came to Jerusalem to await the Messiah, I was rather thankful for the lack of similarity. Now, however, I was here, and I found myself thinking about him with mixed emotions. And why not? Why should my emotions be any different from His mixed holy blessing of the Torah? After all, if pigeons and doves, why not a talking parrot with ruthless grasping toes? A kosher dove would never speak, but in America silence doesn't articulate and you need words for heaven's sake. Is it any wonder my emotions were mixed?

I found myself thinking that neither of us changed underwear toward the end. Whatever else you say about the rest of the family, they change their underwear daily, socks too. And there's a lot of toothbrushing as well. I used to change underwear religiously although the brushing of teeth was never my thing. Uncle Maxie, however, was a superclean man. I have no doubts that he brushed at least twice a day and showered at least once, probably twice. That whole family, my grandmother included, were hygiene nuts. The word "dirty" was pronounced with a grimace for fear that the powers of dirt might be so great as to permeate the word itself and contaminate the speaker. Even among the men in the family, the word "filthy" was used only in anger and wasn't even permitted in polite conversation. On this I differed from them. Insofar as they kept kosher, the motivation was cleanliness. On the Day of Judgment, none of them would have been surprised if the first thing the angels did was check behind their ears.

My Uncle Gabe, Uncle Maxie's younger brother, who had the honor of being Uncle Maxie's primary patron, warned me against all commercial hamburgers because he had been told that they were made from kangaroo meat and would give you a jumpy stomach. In addition, Uncle Gabe always demanded from hotels at least fifty extra towels to "sanitize" every exposed surface. His toothbrush lay above and below so many embossed, bleached white towels that the princess herself could have fallen asleep on the whole pile without so much as imagining a pea lay beneath, much less a bristly plastic toothbrush.

I tell all this for several reasons. For one, things that sound screwy — people, too — can often be on the level. The level, in a manner of speaking, has its ups and downs like everything else. Who knows for sure that there isn't a little frozen kangaroo meat in a Big Mac, and who knows for sure that the Messiah won't come today, or better yet, who knows for sure he isn't downstairs waiting for us now.

I have another reason, too — I wish to demonstrate that Uncle Maxie was a very clean person. As black a sheep as he was in a family that valued stability, loyalty, hard work, and decency, he could not violate the real taboo, cleanliness. Once when I pressed Uncle Gabe for any reason that could possibly justify Uncle Maxie's double desertions, he loyally defended his older brother: "His first wife was a very dirty person. After a day's work, he used to have to come home and clean the house. She once cooked a chicken without gutting it. Can you imagine that?"

Frankly, I could.

"What was wrong with the second one? The mother of his four kids?" I asked.

"She wasn't very clean either. Not like the first, but

she was dirty, too," he said sadly.

If Uncle Maxie stopped changing his underwear, there had to have been an unusual reason. He was still lucid and in good spirits, unless his sisters insisted that he change his underwear. Then a chase ensued around his small apartment. What the results of this steeplechase featuring two octogenarians and a nonagenarian were I never knew, although I do confess a great curiosity. For all of Maxie's former fleetness of foot, at that time I think my money would have been on my grandmother and great-aunt. My grandmother had great staying power. I do remember her distress. "It's so unlike Maxie; he was always such a clean person."

My mother claimed that his behavior was typical of old men. "They can't part with anything near them. It's related to impotence and death." I reject this analytic thesis for two reasons: Maxie was the least typical person I ever met, and his impotence was far from proven. A year later, in his final weeks, when he was well into his nineties, he was charming hospital nurses with all his old verve. "He's such a wonderful old man. We all love him," and it wasn't clear from what distance.

Uncle Maxie wasn't changing his underwear because he was waiting for something, something redemptive, and Uncle Maxie awaited it eagerly. His not changing underwear was an act of faith, an unarticulated faith that the Messiah would come. If there are closet homosexuals, perhaps my rascally old great-uncle was an underwear-drawer Messianist.

Uncle Maxie's juggling was intimately connected with his awaiting the Messiah. The Messiah will usher in a new era: strife will vanish, peace will reign. Historical time will be ruptured. Time will stop. We will be men but as in the Garden of Eden before sin. What a market there will be then for Messiah, Son of David's garden specials! It will be life of a very different consciousness. What in our world can now be glimpsed only in rare moments will in that world be the ongoing reality.

Uncle Maxie was a master of illusion, truly alive only in those moments when he directed the eight eggs into the air simultaneously. How tragic the world was for him when those eggs were not in the air. In those rapturous moments, however, when the tedious days, months, and years of clumsy gravity gave way to dexterity and flight, then Uncle Maxie knew there was hope. If the Holy Sabbath is said to be one-sixtieth of the World to Come, maybe a seventy-year-old's keeping all the potential chickens off the griddle is some small percentage of the Messianic Era.

I'm not claiming that he articulated all this. Let's face it, toward the end his memory was none too keen and the old man might have had moments when, if he weren't slipping toward senility, he wasn't keeping his distance all that well either. When his fingers lost dexterity, his eyes lost focus, and his body lost graceful coordination, and the day came when he spilled drinking water from his cup, he whose hands had once been so sure then strived to recover those days when he could juggle eight eggs while dancing a jig and singing Verdi. In those moments when he fought to recapture his past and focused on subjects swirling in memory, they did not have the scent of fresh eggs or the fragrance of Sunkist lemons, but they did have the whiff of redemption. He caught the scent of the Messiah or at least one-sixtieth of it.

Not that he was too good for this world. Quite the contrary. I suppose I shouldn't criticize someone whom

I am beginning to resemble, but I didn't come to
Jerusalem not to call them as I see them. Uncle Maxie
had marvelous God-given talents that couldn't buy
him a cup of coffee, be supportive of another human
being through love, or afford himself any measure of
stability. When it came to unrealized potential, Uncle
Maxie was a superstar. If he didn't need the Messiah, I
don't know who did, because what is the Messiah
going to do if not permit us to realize our divine potential?

In the world of Truth there must be a little book
where people are listed according to talent. Who knows
if Einstein, Moses, and Babe Ruth will lead the list? Or
if Maxwell Wein, Warren G. Harding, and Don Larsen
(the only perfect World Series game to his credit and
his career status shows more losses than wins) might
not be given a Messianic resurrectional instant replay
and rewrite the divine record books. When envy has
died, those eclipsed will cheer louder than the rest;
for they will be the most appreciative. Uncle Maxie
couldn't manage anything on his own. His brother
supported him, his sisters fed him, and the whole
family clothed him. He had more different initials on
shirt pockets than most commercial laundries ever
cleaned. And to top it off, he was a deserter. He left
those kids with his last name, I suppose, because he
couldn't take it with him.

Uncle Maxie was only for Uncle Maxie. The eternal
child. In some ways the perfect child: bright, beautiful,
talented, charming, and totally dependent. When his
parents died, his younger siblings assumed the nurturing role with generosity, love, and compassion. He
grew old, but he never grew up. His brother supported
him. His sisters changed his linen, did his wash, brought
him food, and, yes, they sprinted after him with clean

underwear. And in filial piety he promised never to reject their support nor to share the spotlight with anyone else. It was a great performance.

The whole world participated in his monumental commitments to self. Lyndon Johnson developed a Great Society just for him and his beautiful baritone. Or so it seemed when federal monies became available for the aged. Uncle Maxie rode the Golden Age Club boom the way IBM commandeered the space age. He joined and performed at every club for miles around.

Uncle Maxie was musical, but for him the bugle only blew retreat. Well, almost "only." He surrendered his children, his pride, his livelihood, any and all responsibilities (who said Americans don't surrender?) but he never surrendered center stage. That he wasn't about to surrender to anyone (who said Americans don't have principles?), including his great-niece who had been invited to perform Yiddish and Hebrew folk songs for the Jewish Golden Age Club. In the middle of "Aufn Pripatchik," as she strummed on her guitar, the attentive audience broke into raucous laughter. She looked up to discover her great-uncle had snuck up behind her and was making faces. Later, when the fourth generation of the female line that had indulged him shamelessly asked him to justify his behavior, he, not buying women's lib — or anyone's lib for that matter — answered, "We had 'em standing on their heads." Maxie was Shirley Temple's big brother, world's oldest performing child star. And it wasn't easy.

A child, his attitude towards death must have been a fear that fueled his rejection of anything so unpleasant. Young children believe that death is an exclusive province of the adult realm. At Uncle Maxie's advanced age, immortality must have been a difficult proposition to maintain. All his friends had died, and he could no longer juggle. Yet he himself wasn't prepared to give up his golden-age status, which represented such a rich investment in years.

What options were there? As things stand, there is no way to tell the Angel of Death to get lost, but there is the chance to change the rules. If you're losing in the fourth and final period, announce that the game has five periods. But games have rules. Only children don't understand that — and Maxie was the perfect child. He never accepted anyone else's rules his whole life. Maxie expected the Messiah to bail him out. Why should he have expected less? People had been bailing Maxie out for four generations. Let's be fair, the Messiah had been promised; it wasn't Maxie's idea. Why shouldn't the Messiah save him from dying? His ears were clean, weren't they?

If I sound too quick to judge, it is not without reason. To put it in perspective, the doves of the Wall are not the pigeons of Broadway. I don't care what the Litvak parrot says; birds of a feather flock together. The two of us don't molt our skivvies with the rest of the family. We let them wear out and leave them *in situ*. If I sound confused by all this, I am. When I came to Jerusalem, of all the people I expected to see balanced on top of the Western Wall, the last one was my Uncle Maxie — and juggling eggs in his underwear yet! And now I discover that I am scaling that holiest of walls to join him. I remember him not without affection. Without illusion, too. I remember him with fear. He deserted wives and children. This I didn't do yet, but I deserted everyone else by coming here to Jerusalem. We share a common economic attitude toward family and government called dependence. He was a superchild. And what artist isn't childish? Creation is an egocentric act. Every art-

ist knows full well that when the evil tongue is said to
kill, these words refer to criticism. No, if artists aren't
children, then politicians aren't liars, and lawyers aren't
thieves. In its proper context, each vice has its social
rewards.

Since arriving in Jerusalem, I've been in virtual
retirement. Uncle Maxie was one of the great retirees of
all time. When I look up there and see him sitting on
the Wall, I have reason to fear.

I have more than a sneaking suspicion who waits for
the Messiah. The Messiah is for losers. The big cop-
out. Yes, the Awaiters of the Messiah gridiron eleven
have perfected one play and one play only — punt
formation. Let's be honest, faith has its seamier side.
You can root for the right team for the wrong reason
and that team can still win, too.

I was frightened. I was frightened because I had
surrendered enough of myself already. The thought of
running around the rest of my life in shirts emblazoned
with everyone's initials except my own filled me with
dread. I was frightened because my brothers were too
far away. I was frightened because Maxie's life was so
unhappy when the eggs and lemons weren't in the air
and I didn't even know how to juggle. I was most
frightened to wait in a land where time was so strange. I
was so frightened that I went to work.

I took everything up to the roof. Without hesitating, I
cut the rope. Before I had everything set up, I had
already started blocking out the basic areas. Barely
looking up, because I knew what it looked like, I worked
with almost fevered swiftness. Possessed, I stayed with
it until the darkness descended. A contact drill Vince
Lombardi would have loved! Then, grabbing everything together at once like a mad refugee, I hauled it
downstairs into the house and continued until the

early morning. After a few hours' rest — I'm not sure that I slept — I returned to my painting. By midmorning, I had dragged everything up to the roof. I wouldn't answer the door. I told my wife not to call me to the phone. I didn't change any clothes at all, and I hardly ate. Finally, on Friday afternoon, an hour before the Sabbath, I finished. I brought the painting and all my equipment into the house and in continued frenzy I put everything away.

"I'm finished!" I yelled in triumph, seized with a great burning desire to prepare for the Sabbath.

"What can I do to help?" I asked my wife.

"Take a shower," she suggested.

"No, I must help," I said.

I collected the garbage from under the sink, the old newspapers, the bottles. I ran out the door, down the steps, and all the way to the garbage container. On the way back, I met my neighbor. It was the first time in three days I had left the house. He stared at me uneasily for he had not been permitted to visit while I was working.

"I'm finished," I said.

"You're not going to shower?" he asked.

"The picture," I explained. "I finished the painting. Please come and see it," I invited.

He looked at the pail of garbage in his hand.

"All right," he said, "when I'm finished with everything. Right before Sabbath," he added enthusiastically.

"Fine."

I ran upstairs to shower.


I was dressed except for my shoes when he knocked. He, too, was freshly scrubbed.

"I never had a private showing before," he said with a laugh. He entered with the sly, hampered step of the very curious and the very involved. He was my neighbor and he wanted my painting to be good so that he would mean all the kind things that he would want to say.

As I led him into the room that was my studio, my wife gathered the girls to light candles.

He looked at the painting once and his eyes widened. A man who is in very precise control of his emotions and his appearance, he quickly reined himself into a neutral mask of observation. Even then, his eyes moved too quickly, darting back and forth as if to confirm what he thought he had seen. Then he realized that he had to say something. In embarrassment, he looked down at his feet and hesitantly shifted his weight. He cleared his throat.

"It's late. We'd better go to pray. We can talk later," and then he quickly added, "It's very interesting, of course."

The poor man, his eyes always betrayed him. They were filled with disappointment and a twinge of disgust — for *this* you came to Jerusalem?

"It's based on the verse in Daniel," I explained. "The one about the Messiah: 'I saw in the night visions, and behold, one like the son of man came with clouds of heaven and he came even unto the ancient of days.'"

"Yes, I see," he said, seeing very little. "I'll be late," he added and he left.

I stayed and carefully examined my creation. It was the view from the roof: I had captured a beautiful Mount of Olives. The clarity, poetry, and decay of the cemetery. The tombstones of mere stone, but so deeply rooted in faith that from those roots amid the bodies returning to eternity they draw nurture that suggests that they themselves are the congregation of the faithful. And what faithful! Exuberant, boisterous, but disciplined — no straight lines, no right angles, but grouped together in a zone defense to block out every spirit and demon in creation. The mountain itself has the solidity of a mountain sitting on center stage of the earth and the soft, delicate magical potency and assurance of a hill as fragrant as an almond blossom. The cemetery, too, is part of this procreative paradox of passionately gentle deathly renewal.

And above the mountain, the cloud-acclaimed herald is arriving. Uncle Maxie sails in airy majesty. He is not alone. Blissfully silent and no longer grasping, the brilliantly plumed parrot sits on his shoulder like a dove, for this is the age of peace when silence articulates and beauty is shared. Uncle Maxie is not ascending as an El Greco would have him. Nor is he floating in aimless memory like some aged Chagall figure. Rather, Uncle Maxie is purposeful and masterful, a cross between Charles Lindbergh and Tom Corbett, space cadet. He is arrival. Arrogant — deservedly so, that's a good number flying along with the clouds — but polite. His jaw is set. His eye is firm. His stance is dramatic and aggressive, as well it should be. His flesh isn't youthful but it has good tone. This is the Uncle Maxie of seventy years. He has his bald head, his paunch, and his bandy legs, but he's a son of a gun, all right! There's life in those thighs. The lean pluck of an old rooster, flexing his comb before crowing the dawn of the new day, The Day. And you can see part of his thigh, too, because Uncle Maxie is wearing the purest ribbed white underwear you can imagine. But these are not modern B.V.D.'s. These are long, form-fitting underwear, appropriate for an elder, for a herald, and for the discretion of Jerusalem. The pants descend gracefully to mid-thigh the way they do in the old silent movies when disrobing did not imply indiscretion.

The T-shirt sleeves are halfway to his elbows. The flamboyant initials on his chest are at long last truly his: M.V.P. (When the dead live again, it goes without saying who gets that award!) His hands are held low in stately arrival. These are the hands that juggled eight eggs, but there are no eggs, nor lemons, for Uncle Maxie doesn't need them now. He himself is in the air. This is the age of the Messiah! All in the radiant stream of light.

I look up to find my wife by my side.

"For *this* I came to Jerusalem," I whisper.